The Amish Blacksmith

The Men of Lancaster County Series
By Mindy Starns Clark and Susan Meissner

The Amish Groom
http://bit.ly/AmishGroom

The Amish Blacksmith

The Women of Lancaster County Series
By Mindy Starns Clark and Leslie Gould

The Amish Midwife
http://bit.ly/AmishMidwife

The Amish Nanny
http://bit.ly/AmishNanny

The Amish Bride
http://bit.ly/AmishBride

The Amish Seamstress
http://bit.ly/AmishSeamstress

We have video clips showcasing our books.
Check them out at the web address above.

The Amish Blacksmith

MINDY STARNS CLARK
SUSAN MEISSNER

HARVEST HOUSE PUBLISHERS
EUGENE, OREGON

Scripture verses are from the King James Version of the Bible.

Cover by Garborg Design Works, Savage, Minnesota

Cover photos © Chris Garborg; Yanika / Bigstock

The authors are represented by MacGregor Literary, Inc.

This is a work of fiction. Names, characters, places, and incidents are products of the authors' imaginations or are used fictitiously. Any resemblance to actual persons, living or dead, is entirely coincidental.

THE AMISH BLACKSMITH
Copyright © 2014 by Mindy Starns Clark and Susan Meissner
Published by Harvest House Publishers
Eugene, Oregon 97402
www.harvesthousepublishers.com

Library of Congress Cataloging-in-Publication Data
Clark, Mindy Starns.
The Amish blacksmith / Mindy Starns Clark and Susan Meissner.
    pages cm.— (The men of Lancaster County ; book 2)
ISBN 978-0-7369-5736-6 (pbk.)
ISBN 978-0-7369-5737-3 (eBook)
1. Amish—Fiction. 2. Blacksmiths—Fiction. 3. Lancaster County (Pa.)—Fiction. I. Meissner,
Susan. II. Title.
PS3603.L366A76 2014
813'.6—dc23
                                                                2014007403

Printed in the United States of America

            14 15 16 17 18 19 20 21 22 / LB-JH / 10 9 8 7 6 5 4 3 2 1

In loving memory of
Robert Irwin Dickerson
1907–1977

Loving grandfather, amazing horseman,
wonderful man

ACKNOWLEDGMENTS

Many thanks to...

Everyone at Harvest House Publishers, in particular our lovely and gifted editor, Kim Moore.

Chip MacGregor, the literary agent who helped bring us together in the first place.

John Clark, for brainstorming, help with research, and so much more.

The Riehl and Fisher families of Lancaster County.

Elam Stoltzfus and Elias Stoltzfus, for sharing your Amish blacksmith shop and your friendship and patiently answering our many questions.

Meg Selway, for your insights into all things equine.

Emily Clark, Lauren Clark, Tara Kenny, Adam Sullivan, and Suzanne Scannell, for being so helpful throughout the process.

PART ONE

One

The muscles under the horse's chocolate-brown flank rippled as I pressed my hand against his warm side.

"Easy, boy," I said, my tone that of father to frightened child.

At my work station in the blacksmith shop, I shifted so the horse could better see me and continued running my hand across his body. Halfway down his left rear leg, I came to a stop when my fingers reached a puffy knob that shouldn't have been there. Bending closer, I gently palpated the hock. I'd already scraped out the dirt and turf imbedded around his shoes minutes before, but this swelling told me to take a second, closer look at the hoof.

I flipped on my headlamp and gave the horse's fetlock a tug. In response, he nervously shifted his weight but allowed me to hoist up his leg. Crouching, I studied the hoof's surface in the glow of the beam, noting how it was worn on the inside edge. I turned to Trudy, the young teen who stood nearby, her arms crossed as she watched.

"I think Patch's knees are swollen," she told me solemnly. "The back ones, at least."

"Actually, they're called 'knees' in the front but 'hocks' in the back. See how the joints bend differently? A hock is more an elbow than a knee. But you're right. There's some swelling here for sure."

She nodded, cupping a hand around her own elbow. Ordinarily, I wouldn't have corrected a customer, but Trudy was different. She wanted to know. She wanted to learn. Trudy's family lived in a neighboring Amish district in Gap, and they had been coming to this blacksmith shop—as had my family and I—for years.

"This looks worn and uneven," I continued. "I'd say he's been favoring the inside of his leg."

"He's been pulling to the right. Sometimes I think he's going to take us both straight into the ditch."

I lowered the horse's hoof to the concrete floor, and he tossed his head and nickered. I reached up a hand to remind him with a gentle touch that I was still there, that all was well. On the other side of the shop, my friend and coworker, Owen Kinsinger, was at the forge, pounding a flaming-red shoe against the rounded cone of an anvil. The horse rotated an ear toward the sound.

"Is there anything I can do for Patch?" Trudy asked. "He seems so sad."

I stifled a smile, thinking how much she reminded me of myself when I was her age. Like me, she had a fondness for horses and seemed to think of them as more than just a means of transportation. Also like me, she often lingered at the blacksmith shop, watching as the family horse was shod, rather than leaving the animal in the morning and returning for it later in the day the way most folks did.

The difference between us was that Trudy usually left once the work was done, while I'd always stuck around afterward for as long as I could, peppering Owen's dad, Amos Kinsinger, with a thousand questions about what he was doing and why. Growing up as a worker in my father's buggy shop, I had always gravitated toward the tasks that involved welding, learning so much over the years that eventually folks thought of me as the resident blacksmith. But there was one big element of the blacksmithing trade I'd never had the chance to learn: the task of being a farrier, or an official shoer of horses. Ironically, that was the only part of smithing that I really cared to do.

That's why Amos had always held such fascination for me. Though he, too, could weld with skill almost any item that came his way, what most impressed me were his skills as a farrier. Watching him, I'd always longed for that to be my job as well.

Now, at twenty-four, I'd finally achieved that goal, though it hadn't been easy—especially the part where I'd had to break the news to my *daed* about leaving the buggy trade. Once I managed to do that, I set about making it happen, first by spending four months at a farrier school out in Missouri and then returning home to step into this apprenticeship at Kinsinger Blacksmith and Welding. I had already been working here, mostly under Owen's guidance, for a year. That left one more year to go, at which point I should be experienced enough to take on pretty much anything that might come my way as a blacksmith or a farrier.

I shifted to the horse's other side. Funny how a person could put off doing something that really interested him, I thought as I ran my hand across Patch's flank, like how I delayed the switch from the job of building buggies to that of shoeing horses. But when you grow up in a family of buggy-makers, it's tough to be the first one to decide to do something different.

Once I did, though, I couldn't believe I'd waited so long. Sure, the work of shoeing was hard—and now and then my back ached something terrible at the end of the day—but I really enjoyed spending my hours working with horses. It also helped that my *daed*'s buggy business continued along fine without me, sparing me from feeling as if my departure had created a hardship for him or the family.

When I reached the horse's hip, I again ran my hand down his leg, only to find that this hock was swollen as well. A look at the hoof revealed that it was even worse than the other, and I pointed out the damaged, uneven area along the hoof's quarter to Trudy. No wonder the animal was having trouble. I couldn't imagine how long it had been since this horse was shod, surely a lot more time than the recommended eight weeks for a driving horse.

"Where did you say you got him?" I released the leg and stood up straight.

"He belonged to my uncle's neighbor, but then Patch started rearing up and not following commands, so the neighbor stopped driving him. He just put him out in the pasture and forgot all about him."

"When was that?"

"I don't know. Uncle Vernon didn't like how the man and his family were handling Patch, so he offered to buy him. He didn't ask a lot of questions."

"And how did the horse come to be yours?"

"He's calmer with me than he is with my uncle, so I asked if I could have him," she said. "I knew Patch might give me some trouble, but I had to do *something*. Like I told you before, he just seems so sad."

I gave the young teen a smile. "I think if I had hooves in as bad a shape as these are, I'd be sad too."

"So what happens next?"

"Well, now that his hooves are all cleaned out, we'll hot shoe him. That will give him a good fit and fix the problem of the uneven wear and tear."

"What about his not wanting to follow commands?" Trudy persisted. "What are we supposed to do? *Daed* knows you're good at helping horses with behavior problems. He told me to ask you about that."

I appreciated hearing those words of affirmation, especially considering I was still relatively new to the horseshoeing business. That I was known to have a way with horses—even before I went to farrier school—was what I hoped would allow me to establish my own shop someday. I liked the idea that people thought of me as somewhat of an expert on how to calm and coax an agitated or spooked horse. I wasn't sure why God had chosen to bless me with this particular kind of insight; I just knew that I had a lot of respect for horses and enjoyed helping them perform at the best of their ability.

"What kinds of behaviors are you seeing?"

"Well, for one thing, I'm amazed he's letting you stand there at his side. He usually hates that."

"Yeah, a horse will protect his flank when he thinks he's in danger. If he has a flaw or ache or whatever, he will hide it if he can. Horses don't want others to see their weaknesses." I turned to Trudy. "There are really just two kinds of animals, you know, prey and predator. Flight animals and fight animals."

Trudy's eyes narrowed. "Sure, maybe in the Wild West, but this is Lancaster County."

I smiled. "Horses understand which one they are, even in the domesticated world. They don't stop thinking like horses just because they start pulling buggies. Every horse knows he's prey, not predator, and that his flank is his most exposed vulnerability."

"You're saying Patch is scared he's in danger, and that's what makes him act the way he does?" Trudy looked from the horse to me, trying to understand.

I stroked the animal, caressing his long neck, hoping to draw out some of his anxiety through the gentlest of touches. "In the wild, a horse can never let on to the herd or a predator that he's easy to pick off or even wounded in some way. He has to hide all of that to survive."

Trudy moved forward to put her hand on the horse's neck near mine. Patch swung his head around and nodded, as if to say, "The man's right."

"How can I convince him I mean him no harm?" she asked.

This was always the part that intrigued me the most, figuring out how to get a horse to drop its defenses and learn to trust again. It usually took some time—and a little sleuthing. Some horses didn't like certain noises, some feared tall things or shiny things or painted stripes on the road or puddles or stop signs. Once I understood what the issue was, it all came down to trust. If I could get a horse to trust me, it was a lot easier to get it to trust its owner. And only when a horse trusted its owner would it obey despite its fear.

Back when I was still working at my father's buggy shop, friends and sometimes friends of friends would bring over their problem horses so I could work with them. It was no big deal, really, just an extra something we offered as part of the buggy trade. Usually, for a skittish driving horse, I would spend an hour or so with it a couple times a week, trying to figure out what it was afraid of and then helping it understand that the thing it feared was not going to cause it harm.

I would be happy to work with Patch as well, though not today. Amos and Roseanna—my boss and his wife—had instructed Owen and me to leave our afternoon clear. They had already left in a hired car for the Lancaster train station to pick up their niece, Priscilla, who was moving back here after having been away for six years. They wanted everyone to be available to welcome her home.

And it was to be a big welcome indeed. Much of the Kinsinger extended family was coming to greet Priscilla and share in a big celebratory meal. In fact, judging by the rattle of buggies out in the drive, it sounded as though some of them had already begun to arrive.

I'd been invited to eat with them, which ordinarily would have been a good thing. I bunked in a small structure here on the Kinsinger farm that had once served as a guest cottage, and though that cottage had a kitchen, there weren't many things I could make. I ate lunch with the Kinsingers almost every day, and I was always glad when they invited me to supper as well. Roseanna was a wonderful cook, not to mention that I would enjoy seeing Priscilla again after all these years.

The problem was that this was a Saturday, and I'd been planning to spend the whole evening with Amanda Shetler, the lovely young woman from the Kinsingers' district whom I'd been courting of late. For a while now, ever since my future as a blacksmith had begun to look more secure, I'd been thinking about marriage. After all, my nephew and best friend, Tyler, had gotten married last fall, and he seemed happier than ever. Wanting to settle down myself, a few months ago I'd started courting Amanda, who was as cute and easygoing and uncomplicated as they come. While I would have preferred spending the evening with her, I had felt obligated to accept the Kinsingers' invitation to help welcome their long-lost relative back into the fold. But that meant a lot less time with Amanda this evening—and no time to work with Patch this afternoon. Amos and Roseanna were due back with their niece within the hour, so I needed to wrap things up for now.

Turning to Trudy, I told her I was busy for the rest of the day, but that I should be able to follow up with her horse over the next few days. "If you can spare him, you should just leave him here," I added. "I'll work with him during my free time and see if I can't figure out what's bugging him."

Trudy crooked an eyebrow. "I don't...I don't have much saved up for this."

"That's okay. I have plenty of room in the barn for a guest, no extra charge, though I wouldn't mind your giving Amos a bale of hay or a small sack of grain once I'm done, if you want, since it's his barn and he covers the feed. Otherwise, we can just make it a part of the shoeing."

Trudy smiled. "*Ya?*"

"*Ya.* I'm happy to do it. I want to help him just like you do."

"Thank you, Jake," she gushed.

"No problem. Of course, now we have to figure out how to get you home. Want me to see if one of Owen's sisters can give you a ride?"

Trudy shook her head. "That's okay. I have a few stops to make along the way, so I'll just walk. It's only a mile or so."

She told Patch goodbye and as an afterthought asked me if she could leave her horse cart here too.

"No, sorry. You'll need to strap it on and lug it home with you."

She looked startled for a moment, but then her face broke into a grin when she realized I was kidding.

Together, Trudy and I moved the cart under the eaves of the machine shed. She set out on foot as I returned to the blacksmith shop. Owen had already started to hot shoe Patch, and the air inside was smoky and acrid. Hot shoeing smells terrible, but it makes for a nice indentation on the hoof for the shoe to occupy, not to mention there's less slipping, better fit, and a happier horse. Though some blacksmiths might try to get away with a cold shoeing now and then, we always hot shoed here. That was one reason Kinsinger's was known for quality.

Owen and I worked in tandem to finish Patch, with Owen shoeing and me tamping down the nails. We were both conscious of the time, but we wanted to finish this last job before calling it a day.

"We smell like something that crawled out of the burn pile," Owen said when we were done, four hooves and four hot shoes later.

"Nice way to welcome family, eh? Reeking of charred horse hoof."

Owen laughed. "Treva told me to make sure I came back to the house and got cleaned up before Priscilla's arrival, but that's clearly not going to happen. I hope my cousin remembers this is just the way it is. At least the stench should be familiar to her."

I had a feeling he was right about that. Priscilla was the daughter of Daniel Kinsinger, Owen's uncle, and she'd grown up on this farm. A frequent presence in the blacksmith shop her whole life, Priscilla had been an odd girl, rather distant and moody, almost seeming to prefer the company of farm animals to that of people. That said, she'd always liked me well enough, probably because I was the one person she knew who was as crazy about horses as she was.

Not that we spent all that much time together. She was four years younger than I, and since I lived a good eight miles away from here, I wasn't around all that often anyway. But whenever I was here with Owen or Amos, I always got such a kick out of her, the cute little black-haired tomboy who would rather muck out stalls and slop pigs and sit in the stench of a blacksmith shop than set one foot in a kitchen or a washroom—much to her mother's horror.

Priscilla's *daed* passed away when she was ten, but she and her *mamm* stayed on here after he died, living in the smaller house that now served as home to Owen, his wife Treva, and their new baby. The little guest cottage I lived in now had been a tourist rental back then, and from what I could recall, Priscilla's mother, Sharon, had been in charge of operating it.

The year I turned sixteen and got my own buggy, I started coming over more often, both to hang out with Owen and to observe Amos as he worked. Priscilla was twelve by then, and though she was still a total tomboy, I could tell she had a little crush on me. It didn't bother me. I felt sorry for her because I knew how smart and funny and likeable she was, but most people couldn't see it. They just thought she was odd.

Then came the year that Priscilla was fourteen, when her mother died in a tragic accident. I was eighteen by then and working full time in my family's buggy-making shop, so my trips to the Kinsinger farm had once again grown few and far between. But from what I'd been told, Priscilla had a terrible time coming to grips with her *mamm*'s death. Her aunts, uncles, and cousins did everything they could to help, surrounding her with love and care, but she was so traumatized that eventually she'd gone to Indiana to live with relatives there.

I was never completely sure why she left. For that matter, I didn't know why she was returning now. In a way, I felt bad that I'd never bothered to follow up or even ask Owen how his young cousin was doing. That's why I felt the least I could do tonight was pitch in and help make her feel welcome. I wondered if she was still as horse crazy as ever, or if that was something she'd outgrown since the last time I saw her. I also wondered if she still went around in stained skirts and skinned knees, or if she'd been "domesticated" in the past four years. Somehow, I doubted it.

As Owen and I put our tools away, I asked him about the reason for Priscilla's return.

He shrugged. "I guess she's ready to come home. It's been six years. She's not a kid anymore."

His use of the word "home" surprised me a little. Sure, this had been where Priscilla first grew up, but with both parents passed away—and after being gone for so long herself—I had to wonder if she still thought of this as home.

"If you don't mind my asking, why did she go away to Indiana in the first place?"

He seemed to consider my question as he hung his tongs in order of descending size along a row of hooks on the wall.

"Do you remember how overcome with grief Priscilla was when her mother died?"

I told him no, embarrassed to admit I hadn't even gone to the funeral. "I mean, I heard through the grapevine about how inconsolable she was, but I never saw for myself. I wasn't around here a lot during that period, if you recall. We were eighteen then, right? My days were busy, putting in overtime at the buggy shop."

Owen flashed me a grin. "Yeah, right. You were busy working days so you could pay for all those nights. Dating half the girls in the county isn't cheap."

I flashed him a smirk, ignoring his comment as I tried to remember more about that time. All I could recall was that Priscilla's father died of natural causes, but her mother's death had been sudden and tragic, the result of a bad fall.

"Sharon's death was a big shock, wasn't it? That would throw anybody."

Owen glanced my way. "Yeah. But Priscilla's behavior was over the top. It was…disturbing, to say the least."

I didn't know how to respond to that. I wasn't one for big emotions myself, but I'd seen the impact losing a parent could have on a child because of my nephew Tyler. He'd come to live with us after his mother—one of my older sisters—passed away when he was just six years old. He had grieved for her deeply, for a long time, and there had been nothing odd or disturbing about that. Death was always painful, even for those who held out the hope of heaven.

"But isn't that kind of understandable?" I pressed. "We are talking about the girl's mother, after all. And Priscilla was just a teenager at the time."

"Yes, of course, but…" Owen shot me another meaningful glance. "It's hard to explain, Jake. After Sharon died, Priscilla really fell apart, to the extreme. *Mamm* and *Daed* gave her room to work through things at first, but after a while they grew worried for her. She couldn't seem to accept what had happened. So finally *Daed* contacted his sister, my Aunt Lorraine in Indiana, to see if Priscilla could live with them for a while. Everyone was hoping a change of scenery might help, but I don't think anyone thought it would be permanent. To be honest, I'm surprised she stayed away from home as long as she did."

Before I could reply, we heard the sound of a car crunching up the gravel driveway.

"They're back," he murmured, putting away the last of his tools and heading out.

I considered Owen's words as I finished closing the shop. Then I took Patch's reins from the hitching rail and led him out the rear door and along the gravel walkway to the entrance for the smaller of the two horse barns. I stabled him next to my own mare, Willow, and forked some hay into the feeding troughs for both of them. Listening to the sound of voices on the breeze, I knew that the Kinsinger family members must have been watching for Priscilla's arrival from the house, because soon the volume and pitch of their chatter grew. By the time I finished with the horses and headed out to join the crowd, the driveway was filled with Kinsingers and the hired car was gone.

I stayed several yards back, letting the family welcome their niece and cousin home after six long years away. I couldn't see Priscilla at first, surrounded as she was by Owen's sisters and brothers and their children. But then the crowd parted somewhat, and I got my first glimpse.

Little Priscilla wasn't so little anymore. She had grown up in the years she'd been gone. Her hair was still nearly black under her *kapp*, but now she was tall and slender, bearing the womanly build of a twenty-year-old. I almost looked away for a moment, so surprised was I at how beautiful she had become. So much for stained skirts and skinned knees. This was no tomboy standing before me.

When she finally glanced my way, I was startled by the color of her eyes, which I'd forgotten were the deepest shade of violet. They were the same color the sky gets just before a drenching thunderstorm—the kind you want for the sake of the crops, but the kind you fear a little too.

She looked down to grab the handle of one of her bags, but then she raised her head toward me again—quickly, as if she had just figured out who I was—and met my eyes with her own.

Her face was expressionless, giving away nothing. I gave her a nod and a slight smile. In return, she just stood there for a long moment, holding our gaze.

Then she was again enveloped in a sea of cousins and ushered into the house.

Two

I managed to shower and dress in plenty of time for dinner, though as I took my seat at the Kinsingers' table that evening, I couldn't help but glance over at the clock on the wall. Perhaps I could still go over to Amanda's later, maybe take her for a starlit buggy ride—assuming this welcome home meal for Priscilla didn't stretch on for too long.

As everyone got settled, I leaned over to Amos and told him there was an extra horse in Willow's stable tonight, that Trudy Fisher's new Morgan had some anxiety issues and she was hoping I could help. Amos said that that was fine with him, as long as I did so on my own time and not when I was supposed to be working.

Finally, everyone was assembled and we bowed our heads in silent prayer. I ended my prayer by asking God to not only bless this meal and the ones who had prepared it, but also to help keep it brief so I wouldn't miss too much time with Amanda.

Or not, I quickly added to my prayer, feeling the heat of guilt surge in my face as Amos gave a somber "Amen."

The crowd at the table included everyone who resided on the Kinsinger farm: Amos and Roseanna, who lived here in the main house, their older son, Mahlon, and his family, who lived in a second house that was connected to this one via a breezeway, and their younger son, Owen, and his family, who lived in the smaller house that sat closest to the road. I lived here as well, in the run-down guest cottage that also sat out front, on the far side of the big garden. Rounding out the group tonight were Amos and Roseanna's three grown daughters—Lucinda, Grace, and Ruth, who all lived elsewhere—and their spouses and children.

It was a big, noisy bunch, though conversation seemed to flow along easily enough, and the food was amazing as usual. Feeling somewhat like an interloper, I mostly just listened and ate and tried to keep my discreet glances at the clock to a minimum.

Though Priscilla was definitely still the quiet type, I was able to pick up on a few things about her life these days just from what others said and asked. It seemed that her most recent employment out in Indiana had been as a companion to an elderly neighbor. Jobs were hard to come by in her area, and once the neighbor passed away, Priscilla had had trouble finding something else. Finally, she'd decided to come here instead—or, as she put it, she'd felt God's leading to return, and so she'd "had no choice but to obey." That wasn't exactly a rousing endorsement of life in Lancaster County, but no one seemed offended.

"You should be able to find something around here," said Treva, Owen's wife. "I could put the word out to see if any caregiver positions are available."

"Thanks, but no," Priscilla replied quickly. "I've had enough of that."

The conversation lagged for a moment, and I realized everyone else was probably thinking the same thing I was, that what she really meant was that she'd had enough of death.

"What kind of work will you be looking for?" Roseanna asked, pretending that the moment hadn't grown awkward.

Priscilla speared a pea with her fork. "I'm not sure," she answered softly. "Something temporary, I imagine."

That seemed to stop the group entirely—not just from speaking but from eating as well. When Priscilla looked around and realized the reaction her words had caused, her face turned a vivid red. "What I mean is," she ventured, her eyes back on the plate in front of her, "I don't plan on sticking around all that long. Maybe just for the summer."

Still no one spoke, so I decided to try to break the tension by dragging it out in the open. "Well," I said with a smile, leaning forward, my gaze on Priscilla. "This should make you feel good."

Her delicate cheeks still pink, she looked up at me, her eyebrows raised in question.

"To see how disappointed everyone is," I explained, gesturing around the table. "They were so excited to be getting you back that now they're sorry to hear they might not get to keep you for long."

I was afraid that was laying it on a little thick, but to my relief Mahlon's wife jumped in.

"Jake's right," Beth said, nodding vigorously. "We've really missed having you around."

That earned some "*yas*" from every side of the table, and though I wasn't sure if it was exactly true, I did know they all cared about this young woman and her welfare. And why not? About the only thing sadder than a girl losing both parents by the age of fourteen was a girl unable to recover from that loss and eventually having to be sent away to live with distant relatives. The Kinsingers were good people, and I had no doubt they had done everything they could to help Priscilla with her grief back then. I also knew the relief they had felt in realizing she had recovered enough from all of that to finally return.

"How about retail?" Roseanna asked, trying to steer the conversation back to the topic of employment. "I could see if there's anything available at the quilt shop."

I stifled a smile by shoving a big bite of chicken into my mouth. Shy Priscilla working with customers? I couldn't imagine a more uncomfortable position for her than that.

"Do you have any office skills?" Lucinda asked before Priscilla could reply. "I heard they might be looking for another secretary up at the hat factory."

Owen and Treva's baby, Josef, let out a sudden cry. As Treva placated him with a spoonful of mashed carrots, she added, "Or maybe you could find work as a mother's helper."

"Good idea," Owen echoed.

Lucinda seemed about to offer another suggestion when Amos held out a hand.

"Enough," he declared, his voice sounding stern, though there was a twinkle in his eye. "The girl has been here all of an hour, and already you folks are trying to send her off to a job. Leave her alone. For now, I would be happy just to see her pitching in around the house. Roseanna could use another pair of hands, especially on the days she works at the quilt shop." He turned to his wife and added, "In fact, instead of marching your niece down there for a job, you could ask for more hours for yourself. She could handle things here on the home front while you earn a little more pocket money."

Considering that Roseanna's paycheck helped put food on the table, I feared she might bristle at the term "pocket money." But she just smiled and nodded and said that was a *gut* idea. Priscilla seemed relieved as well, and soon the conversation had moved on to a completely different topic, something about new jars and canning fruit and the need to clean out the pantry before the peaches were ripe.

The meal continued, and the only other time the focus turned back to the guest of honor was at the very end, when one of Ruth's teenage sons asked Priscilla if she'd stayed in touch with any of her old friends here in Lancaster County. He'd been too young back then to realize that the girl hadn't had many—if any—friends when she'd lived here. To most folks, she'd always seemed the odd one out, the girl with the violet eyes who liked to talk to animals.

"I've been gone a little too long for that," she replied stiffly, and things grew silent around the table once more.

"I'm sure the horses will remember you," I offered, once again trying to ease an awkward moment. "I mean, the ones that were here back then."

In response, Priscilla gave me a look I could only describe as curious. "Think so?"

For a moment, it almost felt like the old Priscilla and the old Jake, just talking about horses as usual, as if not a day had passed.

"Of course. You spent enough time with them."

"*Ya*," she replied, her expression growing unreadable. "So did you."

I was trying to think of a response when Amos laughed and told her, "He still does. Jake's our newest blacksmith. He finally has a reason to be darkening my doorstep."

Priscilla again looked over at me, her eyes appraising but her lips silent.

"*Ya*," I said with a grin. "Owen and I give a very nice pedicure."

"*Very* nice," Owen added with a silly expression, and everyone laughed.

Finally, the meal was over and I could make my escape without seeming rude. With thanks to Roseanna for the delicious food and a last nod to Priscilla, I rose and excused myself for the night. Baby Josef smiled at me and gurgled a farewell, and I gave him a soft pat on the head as I walked past.

Stepping outside into the early summer evening, I decided that Priscilla

Kinsinger might be older and prettier now, but she still obviously struggled in social situations. I couldn't imagine why God had led her to come back to Lancaster County, as she'd said, unless it was to have her confront the last vestiges of grief over the loss of her mother. It would be perfectly normal for Priscilla to miss her late parents, but I hoped the past six years had allowed her to find at least some semblance of peace.

After a quick stop at the shed to roll out my courting buggy, I headed for the smaller barn to retrieve Willow. I'd just gotten her all hooked up when Amos appeared, startling me.

"Going out?"

"Nah. I just like to hitch and unhitch my horse to the buggy for fun."

I expected him to chuckle—he always seemed to enjoy my particular brand of humor—but instead he ignored my response and asked in a serious tone if I had a few minutes to talk. I gave him a nod, my heart sinking as I realized I must have done something he was unhappy about. Was I in for a lecture of some kind? I quickly went through a mental checklist of my evening chores, certain I had completed everything regarding the horses and the shop.

"Now that you've had a little time to catch up with Priscilla," he said in a soft voice, "I need to ask you a favor."

"Oh. Okay," I replied, relief flooding my veins. This wasn't work related after all.

"With her back here," he continued, removing his hat and running a finger along its brim, "Roseanna and I agree that the most important thing we need to do is to help her reconnect with other people her age. It's…it's urgent, actually."

"Urgent?" I understood how hard it must be for Priscilla to make friends with people who barely remembered her, but why on earth would something like that be urgent? When he didn't explain, I added, "You know as well as I do that establishing relationships takes time, Amos. Why the hurry?"

He looked down, and even in the gathering darkness I could see he was embarrassed to be talking about this.

"It's rather complicated, and I won't bother you with the details, but according to my sister Lorraine…" His voice trailed off as he reached up to pat my horse. "Priscilla has been seeing someone…out in Indiana…and he is, uh, eager for her return. Lorraine doesn't know the full situation, but she's afraid he's asked Priscilla to marry him."

"Why is that a problem?"

Amos sighed. "Well, Lorraine is glad that someone finally showed an interest, of course, and she said he's a good man. But she feels that this particular match might not be in our niece's best interest."

"Is he not Amish?" I asked, surprised at the thought of Priscilla dating outside of the faith.

"Oh, no, he's Amish," Amos said. But then he went on to explain that the man was much older and was a widower with eight children, several of whom were nearly as old as Priscilla herself. "I'm sure there are plenty of women who would recognize such an instant family for the blessing that it is," he added.

"But Priscilla probably isn't one of them," I finished.

"Priscilla probably isn't one of them," he echoed, shaking his head.

We shared a smile, both of us imagining the disaster that such a match would bring. Distracted, self-absorbed Priscilla didn't seem suited to the kind of selfless devotion and attention eight motherless kids would need—and deserved.

"In any event, my sister believes Priscilla has come back here in order to explore other options before she gives the fellow an answer. No one else in the family knows about any of this, but when Priscilla spoke at dinner tonight about only staying for the summer, I imagine that's about the longest her fellow was willing to wait for her to give him a yes or no."

"I see."

Willow, eager to be away, tossed her mane and nickered. I felt like doing the same. Though my sympathies were with Amos and his predicament, I couldn't imagine what any of this had to do with me. All I knew was that the clock was ticking, Amanda was waiting, and I was eager to be finished with this conversation and out of here.

"Regardless of how long Priscilla sticks around," Amos went on, "Lorraine, Roseanna, and I have high hopes that she'll meet someone closer to her own age here in Lancaster County, someone more suitable for marriage, a man she can have her own children with. We think she needs to create a new life for herself here."

"Makes sense," I told him, wishing he would get to the point. Again, what did any of this have to do with me? Surely Amos wasn't going to ask *me* to court his odd niece.

He cleared his throat. "Rumor has it that you've been seeing a certain young woman."

"Amanda Shetler," I replied with a nod. There was no reason not to confirm what Amos had already been told. In his day, most Amish courted with great discretion, even if word often spread along the grapevine about who was seeing whom. These days, however, couples were far more open about all of that, at least in the less conservative districts.

"Good," he replied, looking embarrassed for having had to ask. "In that case, what I'd like is for you and Amanda to take Priscilla under your wing."

I'd heard him, but I still couldn't help but respond as if I hadn't. "What was that?"

"Priscilla needs to get back into the circle of young people in our district. She won't do it on her own. She needs you and Amanda to help her remake those friendships. She won't meet anybody if she hides in the barn for the rest of her days, here or in Indiana. The best thing that can happen is that someone in our district or one of the neighboring districts will take an interest in her, court her, and marry her."

"But I don't know that I'm—"

"Just take her along with you to the singings and the games and get-togethers, Jake. Introduce her to people, and then watch out for her to make sure she doesn't just stand in a corner. You're welcome to use my spring wagon whenever you do since there'll be three of you."

I had no desire to do what Amos was asking of me. I wasn't in my *rumspringa* anymore. Mentally, I had moved beyond the youth group a few years ago when I took my vows of membership. These days, the only reason I attended events at all was for Amanda's sake, because she was still young enough to want to be a part of things. Now I was to bring Priscilla along with us as well? No thank you.

I wanted to tell Amos that he was asking too much of me, but the man had given me a job in his blacksmith shop and a place to live, and I ate with his family at their dinner table almost every day. He had been incredibly good to me. I couldn't say no.

But neither could I see Amanda and me insisting Priscilla come with us to these gatherings if she didn't want to come. And I was fairly certain she wouldn't. Actually, I realized, that might be my out.

"Is Priscilla open to this?"

Amos looked at me as if I were nuts. "Well, I'm not going to ask her if she'd like to tag along with you and Amanda. You must invite her. And be adamant about it. In a nice way, of course."

Great.

"Oh," I said.

"Talk to Amanda and have her help you with that. Roseanna and I would do it ourselves if we could, but we can't. The invitation has to come from people Priscilla's own age. I'm sure you can see that."

"Um…yeah."

Willow nosed me as if to say we'd been detained long enough, but I was still trying to figure out the ramifications of what was being asked of me—such as how Amanda was going to react and how long we would have to do this—when Amos clapped me on the back.

"We're all set, then. Thanks, Jake. We need to do what we can for Priscilla so that she can have a life of her own. One that's a better fit for…for someone like her."

"I'll do my best," I managed to reply.

Then I watched Amos amble back toward the house as if he hadn't just asked for the impossible.

THREE

One of the things I liked best about Amanda was that she didn't get all bent out of shape if I said I'd be over at six and it was closer to seven when I got there. She was laid-back and understanding and uncomplicated.

This time, however, was different. This time, I hadn't been held up for a short while by a belligerent horse or too many appointments packed into my schedule or a late-arriving customer. I'd been delayed extensively by a big celebration she'd known nothing about and to which she had not been invited. Sometimes I missed the convenience of having a cell phone, an indulgence I'd surrendered near the end of my *rumspringa*. Had I been able to pull it out and call her, I would have been able to give her a better idea of my timing.

As it was, when I finally got to her home, it was nearly dark outside and I was a good two and a half hours late. Usually, a quick rap at the door brought her right out, ready to go. But this time when I knocked, she simply appeared at the other side of the screen and stood there looking at me.

"Do you have a good reason?" she asked, her voice neutral.

"For being this late? Yes. Amos wanted me to—"

"I don't need to know the details," she said, cutting me off with a wave of her hand. "I just need to know if I should be mad or not."

I exhaled slowly. "No, you shouldn't be mad. But I feel bad about it just the same."

"That's enough for me," she said, and then she swung open the door.

As I stepped into the mudroom, she actually gave me a smile. I was surprised—and for a moment I assumed she was faking it—but then I recognized the warmth and welcome in her eyes. Her smile was genuine. Even though she required no explanation, I would fill her in later. For now, I was captivated by her demeanor.

"Do you know how rare and refreshing you are?" I whispered as I hung up my hat on a nearby peg.

"Do you know how disarming and charming *you* are?" she whispered in return, giving me a wink as she turned to go into the kitchen.

I followed her inside, where I was enveloped by the aroma of something fresh baked and delicious. Glancing around, I spotted Amanda's nine-year-old twin sisters, Nettie and Naomi, at the counter, grinning at me over several trays of what looked like chocolate chip cookies.

"Baking at this hour?" I asked, surprised not to find the kitchen tidied up and closed down for the night.

"I had to do something to pass the time." Amanda rejoined her sisters at the counter.

"Where's everyone else?" I asked, looking around at the otherwise empty space. At this time of night, her family was usually settled into the living room, reading or chatting or playing games.

"One of the horses is foaling," Nettie replied solemnly, "so they're all out in the barn."

"Ah, I see." Some things on a farm couldn't be set by a clock.

"Just let me finish here and then we can go," Amanda said, reaching for a spatula.

"It's okay, we can do it," Nettie told her.

"I don't mind," Amanda replied, giving her little sister a smile. "I appreciate you guys keeping me company. I'm sure things in the barn would have been a lot more exciting than hanging around in here and helping me bake."

With movements deft and efficient, she began to scoop up the cookies one by one from the tray and slide them onto a cooling rack nearby. The twins' eyes were on the cookies as she worked, but I couldn't see anything but Amanda. Under her black apron, tonight's dress was maroon, my favorite color on her and the perfect contrast to the curling wisps of her blond hair that had escaped the twisted locks framing her face. Beautiful.

"Do you like them with nuts or without?" Naomi asked, and I glanced her way when I realized she was speaking to me.

"Yes," I replied, giving her a wink, which made her giggle.

"Which is it?" Nettie, the more forceful of the two, insisted. "With or without?"

"Either way," I said, stepping closer. "What matters most is the chocolate. Everything else is secondary."

"Ah, then you want one of these," Amanda said, turning around and scooping up a cookie from a different cooling rack behind her, and then turning back to hold it out to me. "It's double-double chocolate."

Though I was nearly full to bursting from Roseanna's big supper, I tried to accept Amanda's offering with enthusiasm. I couldn't imagine eating another thing, but I brought it to my lips just the same and took a quick bite—and then immediately took another.

Watching me, the twins grinned.

"*Gut, ya?*" Naomi said. "Amanda makes the best cookies in the district."

"Naomi," Amanda scolded. "Hush. That's prideful."

"But it's true," the other twin piped in.

I couldn't agree more. Full or not, this was the best cookie I had ever tasted. Soon I had polished the whole thing off despite myself and was debating whether to have another.

I decided to test the different kinds, which I did while Amanda and her sisters made short work of cleaning the kitchen. Then she grabbed a light sweater, I retrieved my hat, and we all headed outside to the driveway. As the twins ran off to join their parents in the barn, Amanda and I veered toward the buggy. Even on a night like this when the two of us had nowhere to go, a ride would still be nice, simply because it gave us a chance to be alone. Of course, my courting buggy was an open-air vehicle, which didn't exactly afford us much privacy. But at least over the past few months of going out, we'd found some ways to steal a kiss now and then without being seen.

"How are you tonight?" I asked her once we were both settled in and ready to go. At my command, Willow pulled the buggy to the end of the driveway and out onto the road, where she began *clip-clopping* her way into a trot.

"I'm fine," Amanda replied, letting out a small sigh of satisfaction as our speed picked up and the wind played with the curls around her face.

After that, I was quiet for a moment as I contemplated how to launch into what I needed to say.

"So, apparently word has spread that we're a couple," I began.

"What do you mean?"

I shrugged, the reins loose in my hand as Willow led the way.

"Amos said something."

With a laugh, Amanda placed her sweater between us, and then she clasped my hand in hers underneath, where it wouldn't be seen. "It's been almost four months. Of course word has spread."

"I know. It just…I wasn't sure how you felt about that."

"About what? That people know we're courting?"

I nodded.

"Are you kidding? You're such a catch, Jake. I'd shout it from the rooftops if I could."

I laughed and gave her hand a squeeze. "Yeah? You really think I'm a catch?"

"I'm just glad you caught *me*," she whispered, and it took all the strength I had not to kiss her right there.

Back in my *rumspringa* days, I'd been much more cavalier about my dating habits, usually leaving it to the girl to set the limits of propriety. But once I became a church member, I took that sort of thing much more seriously, and I was always careful not to overstep the bounds of my commitment.

Because Amanda wasn't yet a church member, she lived by far fewer rules than I, and it had made for some awkward situations—like the time she wanted to go to a secret beer bash, or when she surprised me halfway through a dinner date by returning from the restroom wearing *Englisch* clothes. As she came to understand that I wasn't willing to compromise, we managed to work things out, and eventually she began to keep her more *rumspringa*-like activities to herself, for those times when she was with her girlfriends. I wasn't crazy about it, but I certainly understood. She was four years younger than I, after all, and she still had some growing up to do. I felt sure that the longer we courted, the greater an influence I would have over her behaviors. On the other hand, as a church member myself, I knew that our relationship could not advance beyond a certain point until she put all of these ways behind her, made a decision to join the church, and committed to the Amish faith for life.

I sure hoped that was how things would play out anyway, especially on nights like this, when the wind lifted the tendrils that hung loose from her *kapp* and her eyes sparkled brighter than the stars. There was a sense of freedom about Amanda, an ease I hadn't had with many girls in my life, and it wasn't hard to imagine her as a helpmate and a wife.

As we rode along, she shifted under the sweater so that she could lace our fingers together. I was immediately aware of how rough my hands were compared to hers. She spent her days as a nanny for a wealthy *Englisch* couple—both doctors—who lived in Strasburg. The dirtiest thing she had done that day was probably change a diaper. I, on the other hand, had been pretty much ankle deep in horse manure since morning.

I knew I needed to finish telling her about Priscilla's return—and about Amos's request—but I hesitated to break the spell of this night. It was just so beautiful out, the temperature perfect, the sky quickly becoming a starry delight, and our favorite road was just ahead on the right.

"Here we are," I said as we took the turn onto a dark and winding lane, and she squeezed my hand in response.

The street was Smuckers Lane, but we called it Smoochers Lane instead, thanks to a small stretch about halfway up that had thick trees lining both sides and no streetlights in sight. On quiet nights when traffic was light, Smoochers Lane gave us about a quarter mile's worth of total privacy, an opportunity we both appreciated.

Tonight was no exception. I couldn't get there quickly enough, and even Willow knew the drill. She picked up speed as we clattered along, but then as soon as we entered the canopy of trees, she slowed from a fast trot down to her most leisurely gait. I looked ahead and behind, and then I slipped an arm around my girlfriend, pulled her close, and lowered my mouth to hers to share a long, lingering kiss.

"Headlights," she whispered as we came up for air, so we pulled apart and faced forward again, staring straight ahead until the car had overtaken us and moved on past, out of sight.

Amanda leaned in for another kiss. "You taste like chocolate," she murmured as she teased my lips with hers.

"Mmm, you taste like…"

"Like what?"

I kissed her again, stalling as I tried to think of something special to say, something that a girl would find pleasing. "I don't know," I finally whispered. "Like rainbows? Sunshine?"

At that she burst out laughing—and couldn't stop until we were out from under the trees and back in the open again.

"Oh, come on, don't pout," she said once she'd calmed down, reaching out a finger and touching it to my lips. "It was funny, that's all."

I hefted the reins and chucked for Willow to pick up the speed. "I was trying to be romantic."

"Is that what that was?" she asked, bursting into new peals of laughter.

I wanted to be mad at her, but considering how much grace she had shown with my tardiness tonight, I didn't feel that I had the right. I decided to change the subject.

"Seriously," she interjected before I could do so, "I don't like hearts and flowers, and I don't need, um, sunshine and rainbows." Her voice nearly broke into another chuckle, but she managed to hold it in until the urge passed. Then she again took my hand and squeezed it tight. "What I need is a guy like you, Jake. Someone who's chill, you know?"

"Chill?"

She shrugged. "It's *Englisch* slang. Means easy to be with. Even-tempered. Uncomplicated."

I nodded, for those were the very things I liked best about her.

We rode along, chatting softly, enjoying the night and each other's company as we took our usual route, one that would make a big square and eventually bring us back to where we began. At first, we talked of nothing important, but by the time we made the final turn that would lead us to her house, I knew I had to get to the topic of Priscilla.

I started by explaining the reason for my delay tonight, the dinner for the returning Kinsinger cousin. I had thought Amanda would be surprised to learn that her old classmate had come back to Lancaster County at last, but as it turned out, she already knew. Of course she knew, I realized. The Amish grapevine prevailed.

"Has she come to stay?" Amanda asked, eager for details.

She's come to get married, have kids, and remake her life is what I wanted to say. According to Amos, that was the truth—even if Priscilla didn't know it yet.

"I'm not sure," I said instead. "It's complicated."

"She's been away a long time. Like, what? Five years? Six?"

"Six, according to Owen."

"I wonder if she wanted to come back or if they made her, for some reason."

"Made her? She's a grown woman, Amanda."

"She's a *strange* woman, Jake. Unless she's changed. Has she?"

I shrugged. "I wouldn't know. The only time I ever came in contact with her back then was when I was hanging out with Owen or pestering Amos."

"Well, trust me. She was a strange one."

Amanda's family lived in the same district as the Kinsingers, which meant she and Priscilla had attended the same school, the same worship gatherings, the same social events, and more. Considering they had practically grown up together, they would have known each other quite well back then.

"So what was she really like?" I asked. "I always just thought of her as Owen's odd little tomboy cousin."

Amanda let out a laugh. "What was she like?"

"Yeah. I'm curious."

Amanda thought for a moment. "Antisocial. Anti-*fun*."

"That bad?"

"Oh, yeah. You didn't live in this district, so you don't know. If a person wasn't a horse or a dog or some other kind of animal, they might as well have been invisible."

"So you two weren't close?"

"Are you kidding? Nobody was close to her—not before her *daed* died, not after her *daed* died, and certainly not after her *mamm* died. It was all so sad, of course. I'm not saying it wasn't. But she wouldn't let any of us get near her. She wouldn't connect, and she refused to accept our help."

A pang of empathy rose up within me. It was rare indeed for a member of an Amish community to be isolated, especially in times of grief. Even if it was by choice, I couldn't imagine what that must have been like for Priscilla.

"How old was she when her father died?"

"We were ten."

"Ten," I echoed, wondering why the other kids—Amanda included—hadn't worked harder to push through those walls.

"Honestly, Jake, I tried to be her friend." Amanda's voice was defensive, as if she'd read my mind. "She didn't seem to need friends before that, so I hadn't bothered. But once that happened, I really did make an effort to get close to her."

"Okay. I believe you."

She was quiet for a moment, the defensiveness gone when she finally spoke again. "It didn't work, though. After his death, all she wanted was to be with her horse. His horse, actually."

"His?"

Amanda looked off into the darkness, to a place in the past I couldn't see. "I'd sometimes spot her riding that horse after he died—and I don't mean with a cart. She'd ride it as though she were a cowboy or something, one leg over each side, with her dress hiked up past her knees. Her mother finally made her stop. I, for one, was glad. She was embarrassing herself, you know?"

I didn't remember this about Priscilla. I barely remembered anything very specific about her. Just that she was a cute but quiet little tomboy, hung around the blacksmith shop and the horses a lot, and had lost both her parents by the age of fourteen.

Up on the right loomed the entrance to Amanda's driveway, but I wasn't ready to end our conversation just yet. I asked her if she would mind my overshooting it a bit before I brought her home.

"Why?" she teased, squeezing my hand under the sweater. "So we can make another round on Smoochers Lane?"

The thought was tempting, but right now I was more focused on the issue at hand.

"No," I replied with a smile, squeezing her back. "So we can finish our conversation. It shouldn't take too much longer, and then we can make a U-turn."

Amanda didn't respond, so I kept going—past the driveway and past her silence—and on to my next questions.

"Can you tell me about her mother's death? What happened? Owen and I were talking about it earlier, but we were interrupted and never had a chance to get back to it."

Amanda exhaled loudly, letting go of my hand and crossing her arms in front of her chest. "I don't exactly mind, but why do you care?"

"Ha. I'll get to that in a minute."

"Mm-hmm."

"Really. This conversation does have a point. Trust me."

It didn't take long. Amanda wasn't the type to pitch fits or hold a grudge. With a final harrumph, she uncrossed her arms, retook my hand in hers again, and interlaced our fingers together.

"Fine. Whatever. If you say so."

"I say so," I replied, giving her a wink and leaning my shoulder into hers for a long moment.

Thus placated, she began her tale, some of which I already knew and some of which I didn't. I'd always heard that Sharon Kinsinger died by falling down a flight of stairs, but the full story was more complicated than that. Amanda said she'd share with me what she'd been told, but that no one had all of the details, because by the time Sharon was found, she was nearly unconscious, and then she died soon after.

Still, the events preceding her death hadn't been all that hard to piece together later by others. The best everyone could figure, Sharon had been alone in the kitchen late one afternoon, canning squash, when she accidentally cut herself with a knife. The injury was deep and angled across her hand and wrist in a way that caused it to bleed heavily. Unable to stop the flow of blood herself, Sharon went upstairs, probably to get help from Priscilla, whom she must have assumed was in her bedroom.

"What made them think that?" I asked, interrupting her.

"Can't you guess?" Amanda replied, eyeing me sadly. "Blood. The trail of blood. From the kitchen to Priscilla's bedroom door and then back again."

"Oh. Right." I swallowed hard. "Okay, keep going."

She went on to explain that Priscilla hadn't been in her bedroom after all, so at that point her mother headed back down the stairs, likely intending to run up to the main house and get help from Roseanna instead. Unfortunately, Sharon was already so weak from blood loss by then that she fell as she was coming down and ended up in a crumpled heap at the bottom of the stairs. No one knew exactly how long she laid there, but it had to have been at least an hour, maybe more, before she was finally discovered.

"Was Priscilla the one who found her?" I asked, disturbed at the thought.

"No. Priscilla was out in the barn, as usual, her head all wrapped up in her animals. Roseanna was the one who came."

According to Amanda, once darkness fell, Roseanna happened to notice that there weren't any lights on at Sharon and Priscilla's house. That seemed odd to her, so she went down the driveway to check on them and make sure everything was okay. Instead, when she got there, she discovered Sharon lying in a pool of her own blood at the bottom of the stairs, just barely conscious. Roseanna called for help immediately, of course, but Sharon died from a combination of blood loss and her other injuries not long after she got to the hospital.

"And Priscilla?" I asked, not wanting to hear any more of this sad, sad tale but needing to know.

"Priscilla heard all the ruckus and came running, but by then it was too late."

I closed my eyes, my mind conjuring the image of a fourteen-year-old Priscilla Kinsinger kneeling at her mother's crumpled form as her life slowly slipped away. No wonder she'd had trouble accepting it. Perhaps she even blamed herself. Opening my eyes, I peered out into the darkness ahead of us, fighting off a heaviness that was trying to settle around my heart.

"Of course, Priscilla was devastated," Amanda continued, her voice somber as well. "Who wouldn't be? But rumor had it she really went off the deep end."

"That's what Owen was telling me, that Priscilla had a hard time accepting her mother's death."

Amanda nodded. "You can say that again. Except for the funeral, I never saw her again. Rumor had it she never left the farm at all once her mother died, not even to go to worship meetings. A month or two later, she was sent off to live with relatives in Indiana."

It was hard not to imagine how horrible the entire experience must have been for poor Priscilla. No wonder Amos was eager for her to start a new chapter in her life now that she had grown up and finally returned.

"Did you ever try to contact her after she left?" I asked.

Amanda shot me a glance. "I told you, Jake. I attempted to befriend her when she lived here lots of times, but she didn't want my friendship, so once she was gone, there really didn't seem to be any point."

"How about the rest of your circle of friends? Did any of them write to her after she moved away?"

Amanda gave a grunt of frustration, clearly irritated at my line of questioning. "I doubt it. I mean, some of our parents probably did, simply as an encouragement, but we were just kids."

"You were teenagers."

"Yeah, *young* teenagers," she snapped, her tone even more defensive. "I was all of fourteen when this stuff happened. I get it now, sure. I probably should have bothered to pick up a pen and dash off a note or two. But at that age, why would I have taken the time to write to someone who clearly had no desire to hear from me?"

Understanding that Amanda's patience had reached its limit, I put on my left blinker, intending to make a U-turn in a parking lot on the other side of the street so I could get her home.

"Not a chance, buddy," she said, reaching across to flip the blinker back off again. "We're not finished talking yet."

"Okay, okay." I gave a shake to the reins and a cluck of the tongue to Willow, who pulled herself out of turn mode and continued on straight.

"Good." Amanda took in a deep breath and let it out. "Now. Tell me. Why are you asking me these things? What's all this about, Jake?"

Glad that she was once again calm, I launched in the only way I could think of, by telling her that it wasn't just Priscilla's party that had held me up this evening. "Amos stopped me as I was hitching up Willow, saying he needed a favor."

"Okay."

"He asked…" my voice trailed off as I sat up straight, trying to collect my thoughts. "Like I said earlier, he asked me if you and I really are seeing each other, as he'd heard, and when I said yes, he told me that he wants us—me and you, I mean—to help Priscilla get back into the swing of things here. I'm sorry, but Amos and Roseanna want us to bring her along to the young people's gatherings so that she can make friends here again. Meet people. Stuff like that."

Amanda's eyes widened. "Seriously? Why us?"

I shrugged. "I guess because the Kinsinger cousins are all married. Without any young singles in the family, I suppose I was the next logical choice. And you got roped into it because it wouldn't be appropriate for me to do this by myself. Amos needs a young couple to take Priscilla under their wing. He wants us to be that couple."

Amanda was quiet for a long moment. "So we're going to bring her with us on all of our outings?"

"Well, the singings and Sunday afternoon games for sure. Friday night barbeques. That kind of stuff." I flashed her grin. "Some outings, but not all."

"Not Smoochers Lane."

I laughed. "You got that right. Not on a night like this. With cookies. And moonlight. And the most beautiful girl in the world by my side."

Amanda poked me and laughed. Up ahead loomed the right turn that would take us to our private kissing spot one more time, but it was getting late. Reluctantly, I put on the left blinker instead and then crossed over into the dark, empty parking lot of a bank.

"Did you tell him that we'd do it?" Amanda asked as we pulled back onto the road in the direction we'd come.

"Yeah, I hope that's okay. Amos has done a lot for me, and I think I owe it to him. Besides, it's really sad what's happened to Priscilla. I figure we can do this for her."

Amanda nodded somberly. "I guess. But I can't imagine it's going to be easy unless she came back a different kind of girl."

I thought of Priscilla's demeanor when she first arrived and then at the dinner table. "Like I said, I didn't know her all that well before. She still seems a rather quiet person."

"What does she look like now?"

"Uh…well, I suppose she looks okay."

Amanda turned toward me with a smile. "Looks okay? Is that your way of saying she's pretty?"

I shrugged and laughed, eager to get the focus off of me and back on our project. "I suppose so. You can decide for yourself when you see her this weekend. We'll probably have to take her with us to the Chupps' for the volleyball game on Sunday."

"Ah," she said, leaning back and bracing her feet on the slope of the floorboard. "And how long will we have to have Priscilla tagging along with us everywhere?"

As long as it takes, was probably how Amos saw it.

"I guess we'll just have to see. It would definitely speed things up if someone took an interest in her and asked to court her."

"Priscilla? Married?"

"*Ya*." I didn't bring up the older man who was waiting for her back in Indiana, the widower who needed a mother for his eight children. Not only was that fact not relevant here, it wasn't anyone's business—not even mine. I wished Amos hadn't told me.

"Oh, my," Amanda said after a moment. "Can you imagine?"

I could imagine a lot of things. "Imagine what?"

"Priscilla being in love? Or someone falling in love with her?"

Sure I could imagine it. Anyone can love another person. Or be loved. It really wasn't that difficult. "Can't you?"

"It would have to be the right guy to pull her out of her shell, that's for certain. Let me think a minute."

"Think a minute about what?"

"Who we can set her up with, of course."

Whoa. That was not part of the assignment. I had no interest in involving myself in Priscilla's love life, or in anyone else's except my own. "Amos isn't asking us to do anything beyond bring her with us to the gatherings and make sure she mingles. The rest is out of our hands."

Amanda tossed her head. "Oh, come on. That will be the only fun thing about this situation. I might actually like it if I can set her up with someone. We can be matchmakers. This will be great, Jake!"

I didn't think so. No, definitely not.

I told Amanda as much, but it was obvious she wasn't really listening. Instead, she slipped her hand back in mine and scooted a little closer as the turn for her driveway came into view.

"So on Sunday, are you going to come get me first," she asked, her tone light, "and then go back home and get your second date for the evening? Or are you going to bring her with you when you come to get me?"

As I put on the blinker, I glanced at Amanda, who was clearly enjoying herself.

I decided I would enjoy myself as well. "Actually, I'll just send her over to fetch you. On a horse. Bareback. With her dress hiked up around her knees."

Amanda tossed her head and laughed heartily. I pulled into the driveway of her home, glad to end our time together on that happy note.

My smile didn't fade until I was driving back toward the Kinsinger farm and began to go over in my mind everything I'd learned tonight about Priscilla and her parents and her past. Thanks to Amanda, at least now I had a clearer picture of the challenge ahead of us in terms of helping the poor girl get reacquainted with the community.

The problem was, that picture seemed more daunting than ever.

Four

I awoke the next morning, a Saturday, to the sound of a gentle summer rain. Dawn was just beginning to turn the eastern sky a milky gray, edged with a slim line of pink that promised the rain would not last. The current cloud cover and hushed sounds of raindrops would have a calming effect on Trudy's horse; at least, I hoped it would. I wanted to begin working with him as soon as my morning chores were done.

As the sole apprentice at the Kinsinger homestead, it was my job to take care of all the family horses. Ten-year-old Stephen Kinsinger, Mahlon and Beth's oldest child, helped me in the afternoons, but the mornings were mine alone. I didn't mind the solo duty at dawn. I liked the solitude of being the only one in the horse barns in the morning.

I lit the bedside lamp and then peered up at the ceiling, pretty sure no leaks were in sight. Good. I had recently patched a new hole in the cottage's roof, but this was the first rain we'd had since then to test it out.

When I began my apprenticeship a year ago, Amos had offered me the cottage to live in in exchange for fixing it up in my spare time. After having sat empty for almost six years, the building needed a lot of repairs, so I was a little concerned at first, but the arrangement had ended up working out great for both of us. I had my own place, the rent was free, and I found myself really enjoying the renovations.

My bedroom was one of two in the former guest cottage and the only room I had completely finished in terms of repairs. I had fixed the holes in the roof, replaced a section of drywall that had rotted, and refinished the wood plank floor. The window trims had been repainted, and I'd fixed the drawer slides on the dresser that stood in the back corner. There was still much to do here, but so far the work had gone very well.

I got up and headed for the lavatory, which I had recently replumbed. Fifteen minutes later I was showered, shaved, and dressed in broadfall pants, a white shirt, and suspenders. I made my way to the combined kitchen and living area, which still needed much attention but at least was functional—not that I used it all that often. On workdays I went up to the main house after chores to have breakfast with the Kinsingers and joined them again for lunch as well. Suppers were a little more haphazard, though I would always go wherever invited, which meant that sometimes I ate with Amos and Roseanna, sometimes with Owen and Treva, and sometimes all the way over at Tyler and Rachel's.

On the weekends I either headed home and enjoyed my mother's wonderful cooking or, if I had customers coming in or other things going on around here, I would feed myself from my own limited repertoire of cereal, sandwiches, and scrambled eggs. Beyond that, I was helpless in the kitchen.

This morning, I didn't feel like making eggs, and I was all out of cereal, so I downed a quick cup of coffee with a French press Tyler had bought for me in Philadelphia, ate a banana, and then headed out in the drizzle. The rain made for a dreary morning, but that was okay because I knew it would please the local farmers. Early June rain on spring-planted fields was almost always a good thing.

As I crossed the long expanse of lawn, I passed Owen and Treva's darkened house on my right. Turning toward the main Kinsinger homestead, I could see lights on in the kitchen, and also in Mahlon and Beth's home, which was connected to the main house via a breezeway. A rooster off in the distance announced my arrival onto the gravel driveway that led to the blacksmith shop, the welding shop, and the barns and buggy sheds. I caught a faint whiff of cinnamon and nutmeg, which meant that one of the Kinsinger women was baking something wonderful. I hoped whoever it was would take pity on the bachelor in the guest cottage and offer me some. I entered the large area where the family buggies were kept, and my hat was so wet from the rain that

I took it off and tossed it on a hook by the door. I looked around for Comet, Stephen's dog, who usually accompanied me in the barn whether Stephen was with us or not. But he was nowhere to be found, probably thanks to the weather. When it was *suddlich* like this, Comet mostly lurked on Mahlon and Beth's front porch, staring out at the lawn and waiting for the sun to come out.

My thoughts were still on the weather as I headed for the smaller barn on the right that I used for Willow and any horses that stayed overnight with me. I was also thinking of breakfast and the anticipation of working with Patch when I stepped inside, but then I came to an abrupt stop. Farther in stood a figure. Once my eyes adjusted to the semidarkness, I realized that figure was Priscilla. She didn't seem to notice me. The pattering of rain on the roof must have masked the sound of my footfalls.

She was standing at the rails of Patch's stall. Patch was in front of her, his chocolate-brown head bent toward hers. Her hands were on his muscled jaw line, her face very close to his. I heard no sound from either one of them. It was almost as if she were about to whisper a thrilling secret, and he was intent on catching every word. Patch didn't seem to be aware I had entered the stable, either. Neither ear pivoted in my direction. His tail hung loose, as though he were asleep on his feet. Willow, in the stall next to Patch, raised her head at my silent approach, regarded me for a moment, and then turned her gaze to the spectacle of horse and young woman that was taking place next to her.

The sight was transfixing. I felt like an intruder in my own barn. Even Willow seemed to be saying to me, "You should probably go."

But I stood there, glued to the spot.

And then I heard Priscilla speak in the lowest of tones. I could not make out the words, but I could detect the lullaby timbre of her voice. Patch chuffed and nodded his head as if to say, "Yes, yes." She stroked his head, leaned even closer to him, and laid her cheek against his. Patch closed his eyes.

I had never seen anything like it.

Part of me wanted to ask her what in the world she was doing with my charge, and part of me wanted to stand there and be a silent witness to it. Instead of doing either, I forced myself to turn and leave as quietly as I had come. Something about the scene felt private and uninterruptable.

I turned soundlessly to enter the connecting buggy shed that was situated between the small barn and the larger one where the Kinsinger horses were stabled, careful to quietly close the wooden door behind me. In my effort to be silent, I almost ran right into Amos. He was bent over the back wheel of a buggy, tightening a nut.

"*Guder Mariye*, Jake," he said, crooking an eyebrow in surprise at my sudden appearance.

"Good morning, Amos."

He continued to look at me, and I suppose he thought I'd come to ask him a question, which he was politely waiting to hear.

"Um…" I began and paused. I pointed to the barn next door. "So…"

But I didn't need to find the words to tell him what I had just witnessed.

"*Ya*. I saw her in there. She was up before any of us. I think she came straight out to the barn. She's probably missing her horse from Indiana. Or maybe even her *daed*'s horse from when she lived here before. "

"Oh."

Amos stood and set his wrench down on the workbench next to him. "I sold Shiloh a few months after she moved away, once I realized she wouldn't be coming back any time soon. He'd been my brother's horse, but with him and Sharon both gone and then Priscilla off in Indiana for who knew how long, there was no reason to keep him around. We didn't need him anymore. At the time, Roseanna wanted me to keep him for Priscilla, but after a while we just couldn't justify the cost."

It struck me that Amos felt bad about that, almost guilty that he'd had to let the horse go. I tried to think of something to say that might make him feel better.

"Of course not, and Shiloh wouldn't have been very happy if you *had* kept him around," I said. "Nothing is sadder than horses with no job to do. They need to feel useful."

"True enough." Amos studied the wheel he had been working on as though it might speak advice to him. Then he turned to me. "Now that Priscilla is back, though, I'd like to get her a horse of her own. Lorraine and Otto had one she was very fond of, which she had to leave behind in Indiana. I think it would help her to feel more at home here if she had her own horse. She's always been so taken with them."

"Makes sense. But, uh, you heard what she said at dinner last night. Her stay here is only temporary."

Amos nodded, stroking his beard. "*Ya*, well, sometimes the right animal can help make a temporary situation permanent."

I smiled. "You're pretty sneaky for an old guy."

Amos flashed me a wink. "I think we can find her something quickly at auction. An easygoing Standardbred. Maybe a Dutch Harness. Young but well behaved."

"*Ya.* I'm sure you can," I answered. Every week, several popular auctions for buying and selling horses were held in Lancaster County.

"You don't have any customers this morning, right?"

For a second Amos had lost me. "Uh, no. No, I don't," I said, realizing too late that he was asking because he wanted to go to the auction today and wanted me to go with him. As different auctions were held on different days and this was a Saturday, that meant he had in mind the Stone Road Auction Ring in Ephrata, one of the largest in the region.

"You know more than I do about finding a healthy horse. I don't want to bring home an animal that has bad knees or rotting hooves or a sour disposition. I'd feel better about what I buy if you were there, Jake."

I really didn't have a good excuse for not going. Working with Patch that morning was the only thing on my agenda, and that could wait until the afternoon if need be.

"Okay," I said.

"Good, good. I'll go tell Priscilla." Then Amos lowered his voice and asked if I'd spoken to Amanda about the two of us showing his niece around and helping her get reacquainted with everyone. I assured him that I had and we were happy to do it. Not exactly a lie. I was happy enough to lend a hand. And it didn't seem to be a lie as far as Amanda was concerned. As long as she could play matchmaker, she was eager to help Priscilla get reacquainted with her old district.

"Very good. Why don't you start this morning's chores with my horses? I'll go talk to Priscilla now, and by the time you get to your animals, she'll be out of there and you can take care of Willow and the Fisher horse. Then come to the main house for breakfast. We'll leave for the auction as soon as the rain lets up. Or by eight at the latest, rain or not."

He left and I saw to the five Kinsinger horses. After sweeping the stalls, forking in clean straw, and filling troughs, I headed over to my stable to do the same for Patch and Willow, fully expecting to find only horses when I stepped inside.

It was after six thirty by then, but Priscilla was still there, this time standing right in front of the horses' stalls. Both animals were at the rails, leaning close to her, as though she were giving them instructions for the day and they were attentively making mental notes. Except that she wasn't talking, she was just standing, her arms crossed gently in front of her chest. I stepped further in and she turned. That's when I saw that she'd already done what I had come to do. The stalls were swept clean of manure, new straw had been laid, and the troughs were full. When Priscilla turned from them, they both bent their heads toward their troughs and began to munch on breakfast.

"Good…good morning," I muttered, stumbling over words everyone said every day of their life.

She just stared at me, and even from that distance I could see the deep lavender hue of her eyes.

"I'm sorry I messed up your schedule this morning," she said, though her tone wasn't exactly repentant. "Uncle Amos told me you usually start in here. I didn't mean to be in the way."

Though her words contained an apology, her voice sounded strangely accusatory. I believed her about being sorry for having messed up my routine—something I honestly couldn't have cared less about—but underneath the apology was a layer of near hostility. I didn't see how she could be mad at me. She hadn't been back long enough for me to do anything wrong. But anger was what I sensed under her confession.

"Uh, it's no trouble. And you didn't have to do what you did. Really. It's not a big deal."

She looked behind her to the cleaned-out stalls. Each horse lifted its head and glanced at her, munching as they did. She turned back to me.

"But I put you behind schedule. I'm sorry." Again, the tone was no match for the words.

I forced a smile regardless. "I am not that tied to a schedule. Honestly. It's no big deal. And even if I was, you wouldn't have set me that far back. There are only seven horses to care for here. It really doesn't matter in which order they are attended to."

Priscilla stood there for a minute, weighing my words, so it seemed. Testing them to see if I was being sincere, maybe? Or perhaps gauging them in light of her subtly discernible anger toward me.

I was annoyed that she was mad for no reason I could tell. I barely knew her.

My mind raced as I tried to figure this out. Clearly, her anger had something to do with the horses. Then it came to me. Perhaps the stalls where they now stood eating their breakfast were once the very same stalls used by her family when they lived here all those years ago. Maybe somehow it felt to her that I had taken over the place that should have belonged to her father's old horse.

"Look, if this is about Shiloh, I just want you to know…I mean, they didn't sell him because of me. He's been gone a long time. Years. Since a few months after you moved to Indiana."

Any veiled evidence of anger fell away and was instantly replaced with incredulity. She looked at me as though I were crazy.

"What are you talking about?"

A few moments of silence stretched between us.

"Uh. What are *you* talking about?" I asked.

"I wasn't talking about anything."

The next few seconds of silence were truly awkward.

"My mistake," I finally said. "I…I thought you were…you seemed upset, and I thought maybe my horse being in this particular stall was…" I let my words drift away because none of them seemed to be accomplishing anything.

She exhaled heavily and shook her head in what seemed like disbelief. In the mellow light of a cloud-covered daybreak, it was hard to discern which emotion she now wore. I had the feeling I'd disappointed her somehow. For some reason, I wanted to fix that, right then, at that very moment.

I took a deep breath and blew it out. "Amos told you that you'll be getting a new horse today, right?" I said, forcing my voice to take on a lighter tone. "There are always some good ones at Stone Road."

"So I hear."

"You've never been?"

She shook her head.

"How about the auction at New Holland?"

"Nope."

"Hoover's?"

"I've never been to a horse auction, Jake. Never had a reason to." She turned to Patch, who was still feeding. "Is this one yours?"

"No. He belongs to a customer. He's here for some therapy."

Priscilla whipped her head back around. "Therapy?"

"Sorry. That's what I call working with horses that need to be gentled. I—"

"'Gentled?' And what exactly do you mean by that?"

"You know. Taught to cooperate. To obey."

"I see," she replied, her tone clipped and tight.

"Anyway," I continued, "call it 'therapy' or 'gentling' or whatever, it's one of my specialties. I suppose I have a way with horses—at least, that's what other people say. And I really like doing it."

"Really." Her tone suggested I couldn't possibly know what I was talking about.

"Yes, really," I answered, and with enough emphasis to assure her I certainly did know what I was talking about.

"So he's not yours."

"No."

She placed a hand on her chest, her expression one of deep relief.

"Thank goodness," she said as we heard the bell calling us to breakfast from outside. "'Cause I was going to punch you if he was."

I laughed. "Punch me?"

Her face grew more serious again. "He's been abused, that horse," she said as she moved past me. "By a man. Don't wear your hat around him."

Priscilla stopped just inside the barn door and looked at me for a moment, perhaps making sure I understood. Then she turned and began running through the rain back to the house.

I remained where I was for several long seconds, watching her go, dumbfounded.

Then I grabbed my hat from the nearby hook, slapped it onto my head, and took off running as well.

FIVE

The rain tapered off during breakfast, giving way to the sun. Radiant beams spread over the wet landscape, turning every corn and alfalfa shoot visible from the kitchen windows a glistening green.

I left the table first, grabbing another slice of apricot coffee cake to eat as I set off toward my cottage. I changed out of my muddy shoes, grabbed my wallet, and then headed over to the barn, where I set about hooking up Amos's primary driving horse, Big Sam, to the family buggy.

Despite my odd interaction with Priscilla earlier, breakfast had been a pleasant enough affair. Roseanna had asked her how she slept—because mothers and aunts always ask that question of houseguests—and Priscilla answered that she slept better than she thought she would. It was an honest answer gently given, I thought. The only uncomfortable part of the meal was when my gaze kept settling on the striking young woman across from me. It happened more than once without my really being aware of it, which wouldn't have been bad except that she caught me. The only thing worse than being caught looking at someone is frantically darting your attention away from that person as soon as they do, which of course, he or she also sees.

The thing was, I just kept wondering what she had been doing with Patch earlier, when I'd first seen her at his stall. Not only was I intrigued, but I felt I deserved to know. Trudy had left Patch in my care. I had a right to ask Priscilla what she had been up to. I also very much wanted to know why she thought Patch had been abused, not by just anybody, but by a man specifically.

Those were the two reasons why my attention drifted toward her while we ate. But I hadn't felt right asking her with Roseanna and Amos there, because that would have revealed that not only had I seen Priscilla in the barn, but that I'd stayed and silently watched her for at least long enough to wonder what she'd been doing.

Awkward.

Instead, I'd just finished eating as quickly as I could and left. Now, as I was looping the last harness buckle in place, Amos and Priscilla emerged from the house.

"How about if you drive, Jake?" Amos said as they neared the buggy.

Without a word, Priscilla climbed into the backseat, and then Amos and I took our places up front. Though it was just a little after eight, now that the rain had stopped the morning was already growing warm. I signaled the horse to go and then opened my window as Amos rolled down his and Priscilla fiddled with the one in back. As the breeze swept through, we made our way onto the macadam, shiny from the rain. Our destination was about ten or eleven miles away, depending on the route we took. That was about as far as Amos liked to take Big Sam, who at twenty-two was getting on in years.

If we bought a horse for Priscilla today, I realized as we began to pick up speed, Amos would likely hire a delivery service to bring the animal home. That many miles on narrow two-lane streets populated not just by other buggies but cars and trucks as well was a long way to tow a horse you didn't know much about. Too bad Amos hadn't wanted to wait for the next auction at New Holland, because that would have been a lot closer and easier.

Regardless, we were on our way now. The drive would take about forty minutes, so I was glad when Amos found stuff to talk about. I didn't have to come up with anything and neither did Priscilla, who probably wouldn't have said a word anyway.

Amos mostly filled the time by updating Priscilla on the goings-on of every family from Ronks to New Holland and all places in between. He didn't talk about local life the way Roseanna would have, with news of weddings and births, but instead shared highlights of the good farm years and the not-so-good, new businesses and new schoolhouses, weather phenomena, who had been sick, and who had brought in interesting welding projects. By the time we reached the outskirts of Ephrata, Amos had covered nearly every month of the six years Priscilla had been away.

Once we arrived at the auction, I directed Big Sam past the cars, trucks, and trailers belonging to the *Englisch* and the Mennonites to a long rank of Amish buggies out back. We found an empty slot and pulled in. I climbed out first, and as I turned to help Priscilla down, I saw that her eyes were already busy scanning the horizon, which was bustling with activity.

"*Die Geil Vendyu,*" she whispered, more to herself than to me. *The horse auction.*

Amos and Priscilla stood nearby as I tied up Big Sam, gave him a couple carrots as a reward for the long trek, and then wiped down the lather on his body so he wouldn't draw flies while he was out here waiting for us. As I worked, I sensed Priscilla's focus on me, and I had the distinct impression she was making sure I was treating Big Sam well, especially after our earlier conversation regarding my skills as a horseman.

When I was finished, the three of us headed toward the auction grounds, which were already packed with people. Stone Road typically started off by auctioning tack at eight and then switched over to horses at ten. It was probably a little after nine right now, which meant we still had some time to check out the offerings before we would have to take our seats at the ring.

As we neared one of the holding pens, I gave Priscilla a glance, but I couldn't tell if she was excited or nervous or what. Mostly, she seemed distracted, which I supposed wasn't all that surprising. There was a lot to take in here, and for a first-timer it could be a bit overwhelming. She asked Amos about the general layout of the place and then said she would meet us in half an hour at the entrance to the stands.

"Don't you want to help pick out the ones we'll be bidding on for you?" her uncle asked, clearly startled.

She didn't answer. She had already wandered away.

Amos gave me a perplexed look, but I was as surprised as he. For a girl who was about to be given a new horse, she certainly didn't seem all that grateful.

Regardless, he grabbed a program and the two of us stepped up to the rails to get a look at the horses on the day's listing. We saw some Standardbreds that seemed healthy and weren't too young or too ancient. We decided on six good possibilities, and then we went inside the holding pen to give each of them a quick going-over. There wasn't the room or the time to do a full exam, but I was able to check their hooves, fetlocks, and knees while Amos looked at their teeth, ears, and eyes. Together, we narrowed our list down to four solid choices, and then we came back out and moved toward the bleachers.

The tack auction wasn't quite finished yet, so I offered to buy Amos some coffee while we waited to go in. He declined, turning and giving a hearty greeting of "*Hoe gaat het?*" to a familiar face, an Amish man I recognized as a welding customer. I headed off to get a cup for myself.

I wasn't sure whether Priscilla might want some too or not, so I scanned the crowd on my way to the food stands. I spotted her near a large cluster of men, most of whom were holding clipboards and chatting among themselves as they waited to go in. I'd expected to find her communing with the horses, so the sight of her standing there with actual people instead was odd, to say the least.

I was about to approach her when I heard the sound of my name from the other direction. I turned, surprised to see my friend Eric, a fellow student from my Missouri farrier school, weaving his way toward me through the crowd. Despite the fact that Eric was *Englisch* and I was Amish, he and I had become friends on the first day of class because we'd been the only two there from Eastern Pennsylvania.

Unlike me, he'd gone to the school not so he could become a farrier himself, but so that he could get a better understanding of what good horseshoeing involved. His family worked with show horses, so for him to learn the shoeing trade was, as he'd explained it, "kind of like a car dealer learning auto mechanics—it never hurts to understand how things happen under the hood."

We greeted each other now with a handshake and a quick one-armed hug, and then he asked me what I was doing. I told him I'd come to help my boss pick out a new horse for his niece.

"How about you?" I asked, trying to remember exactly where he lived. I knew it wasn't too far away, somewhere in Chester County, where the farms of the Amish gave way to the large estates of the *Englisch*. His family's business involved the transporting of show horses—not just on the ground but in the air as well.

"Same sort of thing. One of our clients needs a riding horse for her little girl, so I offered to come here with her to Stone Road. She's never been to a horse auction before."

"Yeah, neither has the niece." I glanced over to where Priscilla had been standing and was relieved to see that Amos had joined her. He seemed to be looking around for something, probably me, so I caught his eye with a wave and gestured toward the stands, indicating that they could go on in without me and I'd be along shortly. He gave me a wave and a nod.

"Find anything promising?" I asked, turning back to my friend.

"A couple possibilities. It helps that this woman's pockets are deep. She doesn't care what it costs. She just wants something with a good temperament." He went on to describe the horses they were interested in, but I couldn't weigh in because I hadn't paid attention to any of those. Amos and I had been looking solely at workhorses.

Eric went with me to the coffee stand, where we each bought a cup, and then we continued our conversation over by the baskets of sugar and creamer.

"So how goes the dream?" he asked, confusing me for a moment before it struck me what he meant.

Back in school, I had told him all about my hopes of one day combining a horseshoeing business with a horse-gentling business. I had no official training as a gentler. I just knew what I knew. And though I liked shoeing, I enjoyed even more the time I spent working with problem animals.

"It's going well," I said, adding that I was about halfway through my two-year blacksmith apprenticeship.

"And then what?" he prodded, so I went on to tell him about the plan, how in one more year Owen would be leaving the family business to take over his father-in-law's dairy farm, freeing me in turn to step into Owen's position at Kinsinger Blacksmith and Welding.

"What about working for yourself, man? You wanted your own business. That was the dream."

I shrugged, wondering how to explain the complexities of the situation to a guy like Eric. I still harbored hope that someday I might have my own blacksmith shop that offered both farrier work and horse gentling, but in the past year of working at Kinsingers, I had begun to realize that it wasn't going to come easily. There were a few big problems in the way. First was the simple matter of supply and demand—and noncompetition. A good blacksmith would always find work in Lancaster County, but Amos had hired me with the understanding that even if I didn't stay with him in the long run, I would never work in direct competition with him either. In the end, I'd had to agree to no blacksmithing within a ten-mile radius of the shop.

As for the horse-gentling side of things, I'd always assumed I'd have some *Englisch* patrons but that my primary customer base would be Amish. Lately, however, I'd begun to realize that it would probably have to be the opposite of that. The Amish were never fully going to embrace my techniques. There was too much resistance, with lots of scoffing or changing the subject whenever I tried to explain. It wasn't until they ended up with a problem horse themselves that they had any interest, but so far that hadn't happened enough for me to make much money at it.

I would always be there for my fellow Amish and their horse issues, of course, but for the gentling side of things, the *Englisch* were going to have to be my focus. They seemed far more amenable to "natural horsemanship," as it was sometimes called, and I felt that I could make a success of things with them eventually. But such an endeavor would take years of hard work—and contacts I didn't have. So for now, the dream was still just that—a dream. Not even close to being a reality.

Eric seemed to get what I was saying, but before he could reply, we both realized the crowd noises were dying down, signaling that the bidding was about to start.

"Let's get together sometime, Jake. Maybe I can come up with a few ideas for you."

"Sure. Thanks."

We tossed our empty coffee cups in the trash and then began weaving through the crowd, past the booths for pies, hot dogs, and root beer and toward the metal bleachers that looked out over the oval auction ring. We parted there with a shake, and he walked off to join his party as I scanned the crowd for mine. By the time I spotted Amos and Priscilla, the auction was already underway, but it didn't really matter. The horses we'd chosen wouldn't be up for a while yet.

Moving carefully, I worked my way to where Amos and Priscilla were sitting, but by the time I got there, I could tell something was wrong. Amos was going down the listing he held in his hand, describing the horses he and I had checked out and deemed acceptable, but Priscilla seemed to be ignoring his every word.

Granted, there was nothing amazing about those particular horses we'd picked, but they were fine equine specimens—certainly good enough for a young woman to have to drive a cart—so I didn't get her attitude. It was as if she couldn't care less. She kept looking down at each horse as it was paraded around the ring during the bidding, and then her eyes would dart to the people holding up their bid cards, or the children scampering around with bags of popcorn, or the distracted parents who were more focused on the auction than they were on their own kids. Several rows below us was that same cluster of *Englisch* men with clipboards Priscilla had been standing near earlier, and they were laughing and joking among themselves between bids. Even their mindless conversation seemed to be of more interest to Priscilla than whatever her uncle or I had to say.

I looked at Amos, and he shrugged helplessly. I could tell he needed me to jump in here. He'd thought having her own horse would cheer Priscilla, and he told me he'd even allotted a budget of up to six hundred dollars, plenty enough to get a decent animal. He was ready to plunk down that kind of money, and yet his reticent niece was more interested in her surroundings than in any of the horses he was offering to buy her.

I looked again at Priscilla, miffed at her lack of gratitude. When Amos turned away, I tried to get her attention so that I could somehow communicate with my eyes that she was being unkind to her uncle, especially considering his generosity. But she wouldn't look at me any more than she would look at him.

"Everything okay?" I asked her. Amos didn't deserve this.

She was slow to turn and face me. When she finally met my eyes, I saw that hers were filled with…what? Anger? No, *rage*. Not just rage, but something else too, something like dread.

Dread? Why?

None of us spoke for a few seconds.

"What is this place?" she finally said, the first words I heard her utter since she'd broken off from us earlier.

Amos shot me a worried glance before turning his attention back to his niece. "It's…it's a horse auction. Priscilla, are you all right? Are you sick?"

She didn't answer, and for a moment I thought maybe she was having a breakdown of some kind right here at the Stone Road Auction. She turned her gaze again to take in the whole of the ring and the bidders and the men with their clipboards. It took me a moment, but then I realized why she was so upset. She'd figured out how part of it worked. She'd seen the other buyers. Heard the conversations between those men.

Stone Road was not just a place to buy a nice horse. It was also a place where old horses were sold when they had outlived their usefulness, where troublesome horses were sold when they couldn't be tamed, and where unwanted horses were sold when their upkeep was more expensive than their overall value. Horses like these were bought for their meat. Stone Road was known as a "kill auction," a place where among the regular bidders were a number of "kill buyers," or those who purchased horses specifically for slaughter.

I supposed that could come as a bit of a shock to the uninitiated, and I tried to think of a way to explain it to Priscilla. We didn't eat horse meat in America, but people did in many other countries throughout Europe and Asia. From what I understood, in some places horse meat was as common as chicken and pork chops were here. It was just the way it was. Sadly, I didn't think too much about it anymore because that's how it had always been, but this was all new to Priscilla, a young woman who loved horses more than people and who had never been to any horse auctions when she was a child living in Lancaster County.

Getting her a horse at Stone Road had been a good idea. Bringing her here to pick it out was a bad one.

"We should go," I murmured to Amos.

"What?" he said, his brows furrowing into one long rut.

"Go?" Priscilla swiveled her head to face me, wide eyed. "You're telling me you want to just go?"

I blinked at her. "Uh. Yeah. Don't you want to?"

"You want to leave and not even save one of them? Not even one of these animals that those men down there are buying? Not one?"

She had obviously figured out who the kill buyers were, the ones who were here to fill their quotas for the international demand for horse meat by buying low-priced horses that still had muscle and life in them and then shipping them off to Canada for processing. I didn't like it either, but I didn't make the rules.

Below us, one of the men raised his card to bid on a dark bay Thorough-bred gelding that had attracted the attention of no one. The animal had no discernable flaws that I could see other than he was a Thoroughbred, not a workhorse, and thus was apt to have a bit of an attitude. The buyer was about to win him for a mere three hundred dollars when Priscilla grabbed Amos's card and shoved her hand into the air. The caller acknowledged her bid of three twenty-five with a tip of his head, and the kill buyer turned to see who had taken a sudden interest. He slowly lifted his card to raise the bid to three fifty.

"What are you doing, Priscilla?" Amos said, his voice incredulous.

"Bidding on that horse." She again thrust her hand in the air and raised the bid to three seventy-five.

"That isn't one of the horses we looked at!" Amos exclaimed.

"She's aware of that," I muttered.

"Priscilla, we don't know anything about that horse," Amos continued as the kill buyer raised his card.

"I know enough." She upped her bid to four twenty-five.

The kill buyer contemplated his bid for a moment and then shook his head, letting the auctioneer know he was going to let the fiery young Amish woman have the horse. There was no reason not to at that price. Sadly, there were plenty of other horses just like that one he would likely have to fight no one for.

The auctioneer declared Priscilla the winning bidder.

"You bought that horse!" Amos's eyes were wide.

"Actually, I think you did, Amos," I said.

"Priscilla, what is the meaning of this?" he demanded, ignoring me.

She turned to him. "He's the one I want, Uncle. You brought me here to get me a horse. He's the one I want."

"But he's not one of the ones we were looking at!"

Priscilla put her hand on her uncle's arm. "But he's the one I want. I will pay you back for him, I promise. It may take some time, but as soon as I get a job, we can figure out a payment schedule and—"

"What on earth are we going to do with him?" Amos interrupted. "He's not a workhorse."

She stood. "*We* won't have to do anything with him. He'll be mine. I'll handle everything."

She stepped past me to climb down the bleachers. She turned to Amos and me when we did not immediately follow. "Are we buying another? That's fine with me if we are." She nodded to the kill buyer, who was preparing to bid on a palomino mare.

"I guess we're done," Amos said.

He and I followed her down the steps.

It did not take long to pay for the gelding and arrange for his transport to the house later that afternoon. Then we headed over to the pen area to get a closer look at him. He was a handsome animal, a bit on the skittish side—a race horse who hadn't won enough competitions to earn his keep. He also had a name. Voyager.

"I doubt he'll want to pull a cart," Amos said, after I'd inspected his hooves and legs and determined he was in adequate health.

But Priscilla wasn't listening. She was at the horse's head, letting him nervously nuzzle her hand and familiarize himself with her voice and scent.

"Something tells me that's not going to be a problem," I said. Priscilla hadn't bought that horse to pull a cart.

She'd bought him to rescue him from the slaughterhouse.

Six

There was no reason to linger once the details for Voyager's transport were taken care of. I don't think I had ever been in and out of a horse auction so quickly before. We left the stables to head back toward the parking lot, but we hadn't gone more than a few yards when I heard someone calling out my name. I turned to see Eric, this time standing next to an *Englisch* woman and motioning me over to join them.

I asked Amos if he would mind waiting and then walked over to join Eric and the woman he was with.

She looked to be in her later thirties, and though she was attractive, her silky blouse and off-white pants were wholly out of place for the dust and dirt of a horse auction. Gold jewelry flashed at her neck and wrists, a gauzy scarf fluttered across her shoulders, and her shiny hair was a vibrant auburn. When I drew close to her, I could detect the fragrance of what had to be expensive perfume. The wedding ring she wore featured a sizeable diamond, bigger than any gem I had ever seen before.

Eric smiled at me. "This is the guy I was telling you about, Natasha. Jake Miller. The best student in our class at farrier school by far."

Before I could object to his praise, the woman stuck out her right hand. "Natasha Fremont."

We shook. Her skin was smooth and cool, her grip firm.

"Pleased to meet you."

Amos had a number of *Englisch* customers who trucked in their horses for shoeing every eight weeks or so, some from as far away as Baltimore, but none who seemed as fancy as this woman. I recalled what Eric had said about her deep pockets, which I supposed wasn't all that uncommon in her neck of the woods. Adjacent to Lancaster County, Chester was one of the most affluent counties in all of Pennsylvania and brimming with horse owners, trainers, and breeders, as it had been for centuries. No doubt, this woman was a part of that group, people who belonged to country clubs and lived on big estates and paid more for a single horse than I would earn in a year.

"Did you find a horse for your daughter?" I asked, wondering if they had called me over so that I could recommend a couple of healthy options for them. I had seen some excellent Saddlebreds in the stalls that morning, older animals that had grown into gentle, mature beasts perfect for giving lessons to young riders.

"Eric tells me you're not the average blacksmith," she replied, ignoring my question. "You're a horse whisperer."

That we were so very quickly not talking about riding horses or blacksmithing threw me for a second. "Uh…well, it's more that I have a way with horses," I managed to say. "I've been able to gentle a number of agitated ones, calm a few spooked ones, and soothe a few nervous ones. That kind of thing."

"But you're not licensed."

"No, I'm not. It's just something I've read up on and been interested in since I was little. I have a knack for it, I guess."

She regarded me a second, happy with my answer it seemed, but surely trying to decide if she wanted to continue talking with me.

"I have a three-year-old mare that I want very much to breed," she said. "I spent a lot of money for her, but something is bothering her. She spooks at just about everything. It's disturbing and disappointing. I can't even show her to prospective stallion owners right now because she comes across so poorly. I've been around horses all my life, and I can't figure out what's up with her."

"Have you checked with your—" I began, but she anticipated my question.

"I've had the vet out twice, and he's assured me that physically nothing is wrong, and that it's likely stress related. But for the life of me I can't figure out what this horse could possibly be stressed over. I was just telling Eric about her, and he said he'd run into a friend here who had some experience with this kind of problem. I'd like to know if you will look at her."

Ever since my apprenticeship had begun, I'd been hoping for this very thing, for someone in the world of the *Englisch* to approach me to ask about therapy for their horse so that I could begin to make inroads there. This was the moment I'd waited for, but now that I had a prospective *Englisch* customer standing in front of me who had actually sought me out, I was tongue-tied.

"Well, uh, I could…I could probably do that," I finally said, sounding like a five-year-old.

She didn't seem to notice or care. "When? Can you come today?"

"Today?" I echoed, now like a four-year-old.

"I live in East Fallowfield. It's about thirty miles from here, near Coatesville. You only need to look at her and tell me what you think. I'll pay whatever fee you charge."

The fact was, it was a good day for me. Weekdays were pretty much out of the question unless I asked Amos for the time off, and I really didn't want to do that. Tomorrow was Sunday, which belonged to God. So today would actually work.

The way she was standing there so expectantly, I had a feeling she wanted me to ride back with them now. But I had Amos and Priscilla to think about, both of whom were waiting patiently for me to take them home. Not only did I need to do that, but I still wanted to work with Patch a little as well. And it wouldn't hurt to give myself some time to collect my thoughts and mentally revisit everything I had learned in school and on my own. It also occurred to me that I would seem a bit more professional if I told this woman that the afternoon would be better.

"Mrs. Fremont, I—"

"Please call me Natasha."

"Okay. Natasha, I'm already lined up to treat a horse as soon as I get home, but perhaps if you would like to send a car over sometime this afternoon?"

"No problem. Where do you live?"

"We're in northeast Gordonville, sort of between Leola and new Holland."

"Oh, sure. That's even closer. What's the address?"

I pulled out my wallet and extracted one of my business cards, a bit worn at the edges from having spent several months smashed inside the billfold. Printed on my card along with my name and the silhouette of a horse in midtrot was my title—apprentice blacksmith—as well as the address of the blacksmith shop and the shop's phone number.

She looked at the card and then at me. "Apprentice?"

I wasn't sure how to reply without sounding defensive or immodest, but then Eric spoke.

"Jake went to school to learn the job in depth," he told her, "and not just to familiarize himself with the process like I did. Since then he's been working at it full time. He *is* a blacksmith already. The apprenticeship is just to learn each facet of the business for when he eventually goes out on his own."

"Oh?" She met my eyes.

I gave a half nod. That wasn't exactly it, but close enough.

Natasha studied my card again. "You've a phone?"

"It's in the shop. Yes."

"All right, then. Shall we say two? I'll send someone to fetch you." Natasha reached into her handbag and pulled out one of her cards, slick and glossy, and handed it to me. Printed on both sides in full color was an image of rolling pastureland and well-groomed horses grazing contentedly.

Natasha Fremont, Morningstar Stables. American Warmbloods. East Fallowfield, Chester County, Pennsylvania. Warmbloods were show horses. No wonder the card alone looked as though it cost ten bucks.

"Two o'clock," I said.

"Until then." She stepped away from me, taking big strides, as if she were off to acquire the next thing she wanted.

"I'll catch up," Eric called after her, and then he turned back toward me.

"Hey, thanks so much—" I started, but he cut me off.

"No problem." He leaned in close and lowered his voice. "So is that the niece you were talking about?"

He looked over at Priscilla, who was standing with Amos, still waiting, her attention on something far, far away.

I turned back toward Eric and gave him a nod.

Flashing a grin, he slugged me on the arm. "You bum. I heard 'niece' and I'm picturing another eight-year-old like the kid I'm here shopping for. You didn't tell me she was grown—and that she just happens to be super hot. Are you seeing her?"

"Eric—"

"Sorry, that's right. Courting. Are you courting her?"

I shook my head, trying to understand the emotion rising up inside of me in response to his questions. He wasn't being disrespectful, really, and it wasn't as though he was leering at her or anything, yet I found myself growing irritated just the same. More than irritated, I felt…what? Defensive? Protective? Whatever this thing was that was rising up in my chest, I swallowed it back as I did most strong feelings—especially those that were negative—and told him no, but that the girl I *was* courting was every bit as beautiful.

"I'll take your word for it," he said, giving me a grin and a clap on the back.

He told me he'd see me later at Natasha's, and then we parted ways, with him rushing off to catch up with her and me moving much more slowly as I returned to Amos and Priscilla. Maybe Priscilla was beautiful, but that beauty was marred by a difficult, emotionally charged personality. Our time here at the auction had only served to make that more clear.

"Trouble?" Amos asked when I reached him.

"No, not at all. My friend's associate raises warmbloods in Chester County. She has a horse with behavioral issues she wants me to take a look at. I'll be going over there this afternoon."

"I see." He gestured toward the parking area and the three of us turned and headed in that direction.

"Warmbloods? What's that? All horses are warm blooded." The question had come from Priscilla, and it was directed at me. She seemed calm now, almost repentant, which had to be why she was attempting to initiate a normal conversation.

I was still somewhat irritated at how ungrateful she had been to Amos, not to mention how she'd ignored the both of us for the past hour. When I didn't answer right away, Amos did, with a glance toward me.

"I think the term has to do with size and speed. Horses can be hotbloods, warmbloods, or coldbloods."

Priscilla turned her attention to him. "Huh. I thought I knew practically every horse breed there was."

"It's a classification, not a breed," I snapped. "Hotbloods have less muscle mass, which makes them small but fast, like racehorses."

"Jake's right," Amos added in a kinder tone. "Thoroughbreds, Arabians—both are considered hotbloods."

"Like Voyager," Priscilla said, under her breath. Then, to me, "Voyager is a hotblood, right? I mean, his *breed* is Thoroughbred but his *classification* is hotblood. *Ya?*"

"*Ya*," I said, trying not to sound as irritated this time. I had to admit that her persistence and humble demeanor were slowly bringing me back around. For a girl who always seemed to want to look as though she knew more about horses than anyone, it couldn't be easy to ask us—to ask me, in particular—such rudimentary questions.

"So what are coldbloods?"

"They're bigger but slower," I explained. "Like Percherons. Belgians."

"Draft horses," she replied, nodding.

"*Ya*," Amos said. "We Amish need our animals to be patient and calm, strong and durable, so we usually go with coldbloods. They don't spook easily, and they can be very powerful."

I knew what Amos was driving at, that Priscilla's purchase today of a hotblood had been utterly impractical. I glanced at her, but if she understood his insinuation, she didn't seem to care.

"So if hotbloods are small and fast and coldbloods are big and slow," Priscilla persisted as we reached the end of the cars and started along the row of buggies, "then warmbloods would be halfway between the two?"

Amos shrugged. "Suppose so. Jake?"

"Not really. The term 'warmblood' has to do with breeding. It takes something like five generations of equestrian sport bloodlines, chosen for excellence in dressage and jumping, to qualify as a warmblood."

Priscilla looked at me, eyebrows raised. "Okay. I get it. Warmbloods are for show. Except, what is dressage?"

"It's a type of competition that involves horse and rider working together to execute various moves, some of them fairly difficult."

"Have you ever seen it done?" she asked, sounding genuinely curious.

"No, but I can imagine it. Some people call dressage 'horse ballet.'"

"Horse ballet," Priscilla repeated, rolling the words around on her tongue. "Sounds beautiful."

"Sounds fancy," Amos scoffed. "Glad we don't have many dealings with show horses at the shop."

"You don't?" Priscilla glanced at me. "So how do you know this stuff?"

I shrugged. "I learned about it at farrier school. We were tested on the various breeds and classifications and types of competitions and things." I didn't add that I'd paid special attention to those particular lessons in the hopes that someday I could expand the farrier part of my own blacksmithing business to include non-Amish-owned horses as well.

Amos seemed intrigued by that, and as we finally reached our buggy and came to a stop, he asked if there was anything unique to shoeing a horse for dressage.

"The most important thing is that it be done very carefully and precisely," I said, moving to Big Sam and giving him a welcoming pat before untying him from the hitching rail. "Dressage horses need free and even movement, so you have to work with that in mind. As a farrier, you should compensate for asymmetrical pasterns and such. You also use a more squared off shape for the toe, and make sure the heels are fitted full. Otherwise, it's pretty much the same."

Our conversation drew to a close as they climbed into the buggy and I tended to the horse. We were quiet as we started off toward home, all three of us remaining silent throughout the ride, each ruminating on our own thoughts. My mind kept going back to my interaction with Natasha. I realized she hadn't asked me what I charged for my services. She'd just said that she would pay whatever that was. I supposed that meant that cost didn't matter to her, but I knew I needed to firm up an hourly rate of some kind. Or maybe a flat fee, depending on the health of the horse and how many sessions it might take to help her.

When we arrived at the Kinsinger farm, Amos told Priscilla she could have the last stall in the bigger of the two horse barns for Voyager, who would be delivered later today.

"Jake and Stephen usually muck out the—" Amos began, but Priscilla cut him off.

"It's okay. I mean, thanks, but I'll take care of everything myself." She shot me a pointed look, and I realized the comment had been directed primarily at me.

Amos started to walk away, but Priscilla reached out with her hand to stop him. "Thank you, Uncle Amos. Thank you for letting me get the one I wanted. I will pay you back for him."

"That's not necessary," he said, shaking his head. He seemed glad of Priscilla's gratitude but still a little flabbergasted at having bought a four-year-old former racehorse, a hotblood that had never done an Amish thing in his life.

Amos continued on into the house as she turned and headed for the building that was to be Voyager's new home. I trailed along behind her, leading Big Sam into the stable for a brush down after his long morning.

As I worked, Priscilla busily checked out the stall Amos had offered her. I decided now seemed as good a time as any to ask her about what I had seen earlier that morning, with her and Patch. The only trouble was, I didn't know how to start. No matter which way I phrased things, it would sound as if I'd been spying on her.

"Here goes," I muttered to myself, and then much louder, "Say, Priscilla?"

From three stalls away, she looked up at me.

"I couldn't help but notice, uh, what you were doing with Patch this morning."

She cocked her head and narrowed her eyes. "Patch?"

"The horse in the stable next door. The one in bad shape that you thought was mine."

Her narrowed eyes widened as she realized I had been observing her without her knowledge.

"I mean, you obviously weren't just hanging out with him," I stammered. "I could tell you were *doing* something. I didn't want to interrupt, so I left."

Priscilla pursed her lips and looked away.

"So what were you doing?" I prodded. I really did want to know.

"I wasn't 'doing' anything." She grabbed a pitchfork that was leaning against the wall and skewered a hay bale next to it.

"I don't mind that you were in there with him. I'm just curious."

She swung her head around. "Mind? Why on earth should you mind?" She tossed the hay bale into Voyager's empty stall—with some effort—and snapped a tie with one of the pitchfork's tines.

"I just said I didn't."

"And I just said why on earth should you."

"Because Patch is my business, not yours."

She didn't reply. Instead, she just jabbed even more furiously at the hay.

As much as I wanted to know what she had been doing and how she had figured out what she claimed was the root cause of Patch's problem, this was way too much drama for me. "All right. Fine. Don't tell me."

I turned from her and continued brushing Big Sam. I couldn't believe how prickly this woman had become in the years since I'd seen her last. Where was the cute little kid who used to follow me around babbling about horses? She'd been replaced by this snappish, sensitive person who was barely civil. I wasn't sure if she was that way with everyone or just with me, but if that's how it was going to be with Priscilla Kinsinger, then the best thing for me would be to just avoid her. Which wouldn't be too hard, considering she preferred to keep to herself anyway.

I no sooner had this thought than I remembered my promise to Amos, that I would befriend his niece and show her around. There wouldn't be an official youth gathering until next weekend's singing, but some of the young people were planning to get together for a volleyball game at the Chupp farm tomorrow evening. Amanda and I were going, and I knew Amos would want us to take along Priscilla as well. I sighed in exasperation, knowing I had to set things right with her now so I could extend that invitation to her later.

"Listen, Priscilla, I didn't mean—"

"To insinuate anything?"

"Huh?"

She grunted. "You said when you saw me earlier with Patch, you could tell I was doing something. Why not say what you really meant? You could tell I was doing something *weird*. Something nutty. Something a crazy person would do."

I gaped at her. "What?"

"That's what you were thinking, isn't it?"

"No. Of course not. That's not at all what I meant. I wasn't asking because it was weird. I was asking because I was curious."

"Oh, really?"

I stopped what I was doing, turned around, and looked her fully in the eye. "Yes, really. You obviously have a way with horses. As someone who also has a way with horses, I was just curious if that was a kind of technique or something."

For some reason, my words nearly brought tears to her eyes. She looked down, blinking furiously as she mumbled an apology.

"It's okay," I told her, wondering if she was always this way, if she felt every little thing in her life so deeply. She'd been here less than a day and had already experienced more ups and downs in that time than I usually did in a month—or maybe even a year.

When she didn't reply, I turned back toward Big Sam to finish my brushing.

"I just get so tired of it, you know?" she said finally, her voice so soft I could barely make out her words.

"Tired of what?" I asking, glancing at her over my shoulder.

Startled, she whipped her head up, and by the look in her eyes I had a feeling she hadn't meant to say that last part out loud.

"Tired of what?" I asked again, as gently as I could. I wanted her to know she had nothing to fear by being honest with me. I wasn't related to her, I wasn't part of the reason she left Lancaster County, and I wasn't part of the reason she came back.

She took a deep breath and let it out slowly. "Of people pointing their fingers at me and reminding me how peculiar I am. I'm tired of it."

It hadn't occurred to me that someone like Priscilla, who seemed so out of touch with those around her, would be fully aware of how she came across to others. I suddenly felt ashamed for how Amanda and I had spoken of her the night before. That's probably how everyone spoke of her.

And she knew it. No wonder she'd grown up to be so touchy. Just like a horse who was constantly in flight mode, Priscilla probably had to live her life always on the defensive.

"If I were you," I said, "I'd be tired of it too."

She stared at me, wordless, for a long moment. Given her surprise, I decided there probably hadn't been many in her life who had willingly validated such statements. After all, it was human nature to brush over those sorts of things and simply claim they weren't true. "Don't be silly," folks would say. "People don't think of you that way." But they did, and she knew they did. The fact that I'd been willing to acknowledge it, out loud, seemed to have a thawing effect. She visibly relaxed.

"I honestly can't remember a time when people didn't look at me as though I were from another planet," she said. "Just because I like to keep to myself, because I'm good with animals, especially horses, and then all the stuff with, well... I just... I just wish people would stop paying attention to me at all."

I had no idea how to respond to that raw and honest statement, but I did know that being good with horses was the one thing that had bonded us way back when, and it could be the common ground that drew us back together now. Once she was reminded of that long-ago connection and of how much I loved horses too, then maybe she'd let down her guard a bit and actually allow herself to befriend me again.

If that happened, then perhaps that would encourage her to relax a little bit with others as well and stop acting so aloof. Amanda and I would have an easier time getting her into the community of young adults in our district, Priscilla could finally make some friends, and my promise to Amos would be fulfilled.

"I think it's great that you have a way with horses, Priscilla. If you recall, I kind of do too, or at least that's what people say. Patch is here because he has some behavior issues, and his owner asked for my help. I know how *I* do it, but what's your technique?"

Again, I could sense her gauging whether or not to trust me.

"I don't have a technique," she said after a long pause. "I can just tell when they're upset or afraid or bored or confused. They have emotions just like we do. And their emotions are different, just like ours are. A scared horse is different than an angry horse, which is different than a sad horse."

That didn't sound so terribly odd to me. "So what were you doing with Patch when I saw you this morning? I really would like to know."

She hesitated a moment before going back to her work with the hay. "I was listening to him."

The hairs on the back of my neck stood at attention. This had become very weird. "Listening?"

Priscilla huffed as though I had understood nothing she had said so far. "I was paying attention to him, to his body, his unspoken language."

"Oh." That made at least partial sense to me. I had learned how to recognize stress in a horse by noting the physical cues, but nothing in farrier school or my own experience had instructed me on how to hear a horse tell me he'd been abused by a man.

Priscilla tipped her head. "What?" she said, in an annoyed tone.

"I'm just…I was just wondering how Patch told you he'd been…uh, abused by a man. That's all."

Priscilla shook her head and continued tossing forkfuls of hay into the open stall. Stubble flew everywhere. Was she not going to answer me?

"Can't I ask?" I said, laughing lightly.

"Can't you guess?"

I paused to sort through any possible ideas I might have as to how Patch communicated such a thing. I was stumped.

"No."

"You think he whispered it in my ear?" she said crossly.

I couldn't help but laugh again. "Did he?"

Priscilla stood erect and leaned the pitchfork against the stall's back wall. "According to Scripture, only two animals have ever spoken," she said, hands on hips. "The serpent, to Eve, and the donkey, to Balaam. Otherwise, it's not a part of God's plan for animals to talk to humans."

"Hey, you're the one who said you were listening to him."

"I wasn't implying actual speech!" She stared at me for a long moment, her eyes narrowing before she added, "And here I always thought you were different."

She started to come toward me and would have passed me and gone out of the barn had I not stepped in front of her.

"Wait! Come on. I thought you could take a joke."

She blinked at me. "Is that what we're doing here, Jake? Joking? Well, then in that case. Yes, Patch leaned in and whispered it in my ear. Ha-ha."

Again, she started to move past me. Before I could think it through, I reached out and stopped her. She looked down at my hand on her elbow, and I quickly dropped my arm.

"Priscilla, please. We used to be friends. Why are you acting like this?"

At least she had the decency to blush.

"Fine," she said. "It was clear to me just by interacting with Patch that he had been abused by someone. Then, when Uncle Amos came into the stable this morning to tell me about the auction, Patch reared up and became very upset. When you came in a little while later, Patch didn't react at all."

"So?"

"So the big difference between you and Uncle Amos was that he had his hat on when Patch saw him and you didn't. Patch was afraid of the person in the hat. Men wear hats. Thus, I concluded that he was abused by a man. Simple, see?"

She left me in the stable to think on this, which I did as I finished up with Big Sam and put the buggy away. While I appreciated Priscilla's interesting deductions, I doubted she was right. It couldn't be that easy.

Still, it wouldn't hurt to test out her theory. When I was done with Big Sam and finally free to work with Patch, I intentionally kept my hat on as I walked into his stall. My presence hadn't been all that disturbing to him before, but this time, to my surprise, the moment he saw me, he pawed the ground at his feet and whinnied as though he'd been poked with a hot iron.

I took off my hat.

Seven

Even hatless, the only way I could get Patch to calm down was to walk off and leave him alone for a while. My stomach was growling, so I decided to go back to the cottage, where I made myself a giant glass of iced tea and two ham sandwiches. As I sat at the table and ate every last crumb, I wrote out a fee schedule for my services and went over my notes from farrier school. Then I cleaned up my dishes, shoved four apples into a paper bag, and headed off. I still had nearly an hour before Natasha's driver would pick me up, which gave me enough time to work with Patch a little more, assuming he'd calmed down by now.

At the main barn, I hung my hat on a peg by the door, placed the bag of apples on the floor, and grabbed a handful of carrots from the bin. Then I moved on into the smaller stable, holding my breath as I stepped through the doorway. Just as I'd hoped, Patch's reaction to my appearance was completely different from before. I was the same guy, but with no hat on my head this time, the horse had no reason to fear. In fact, he barely gave me a glance as I walked toward him, only growing skittish once I got close, but for him that was normal. At least he let me feed him a carrot and pat him gently on the neck.

Incredible.

Now that I was pretty sure Priscilla had been right about the primary cause of Patch's problem, I could get down to the business of fixing things. Seemed to me, a phobia of hats had to be about one of the worst phobias a horse in Lancaster County could have, especially a horse owned by an Amish family. There would always be hats in Patch's life, which meant I would have to desensitize him to that particular fear while also training him to trust his handler whether he was frightened or not.

I took Patch, who seemed willing but wary, out to the smaller outdoor pen behind the welding shop, speaking in soft, comforting tones along the way. I set the carrots on the ground beside the fence and led the skittish horse to the center of the pen, pausing to latch the gate behind me. I waited until he was calm, and then I dropped the lead rope and took a step back. As soon as Patch realized he was free, he began to trot around inside the limited space, huffing and puffing and nervously trying to discern the limits of his boundaries. I left him alone for a few minutes, until he settled down again. When he finally came to a stop, I reached for a carrot and slowly began to approach the horse's flank.

I was about ten feet away when he spotted me and darted off, running frantically around the circle again in an attempt to escape. Classic flight or fight response. There wasn't really anywhere for him to go, however, so once he'd calmed down and come to another stop, I tried once more, moving with quiet determination toward his flank. It took several more tries, but finally I was able to get close enough to offer him the carrot. He took it from me, munching away greedily as I went to retrieve another and start over again.

The next time, though, I wouldn't let him have the carrot until he had calmed down a little more first. This became the routine, and after about fifteen more minutes of me approaching his flank and rewarding him with a carrot every time he stopped flinching, he began to visibly relax.

"See there, boy?" I told him, patting his neck as he chewed away. "I'm not going to hurt you. Nobody's ever going to hurt you again."

When our time was up, I led a far more compliant Patch back to his stall. We were done for now, but before I left, I retrieved the bag of apples, returned to the stall, and rewarded Patch's efforts by giving him one. He took the ripe fruit from my hand, emitting a grunt of pleasure as he did.

"Good session," I told him with a final pat. Then I headed back outside, snagging my hat and returning it to my head as I passed through the door.

By then it was nearly two o'clock, so I took a seat on a stump near the driveway and ate one of the apples myself as I waited for my ride. A sleek black pickup appeared just as I was finishing, and as it turned into the driveway and eased in my direction, I stood and slid the remaining two apples into my pockets for later.

I'd been in plenty of cars and trucks before, but never in one as classy and up-to-date as the vehicle Natasha Fremont had sent for me. The interior was all inlaid wood and leather, the dash looked like a small computer, and there was even a tiny fridge in the console. The driver, a twentysomething stable hand who introduced himself as Ryan Warner, offered me a beverage as soon as I'd climbed in and shut the door—at least I thought that's what he said, though he had the music cranked up so loud I wasn't sure.

"You like country?" he yelled over the din as he turned us around in the driveway.

"It's fine," I replied, because I didn't exactly hate it.

"What's that?" he asked, turning the volume down just a bit.

"I said it's fine." The twang of the tune that was playing was a different sound for me, and not exactly my favorite. I'd been a rock and roll kind of guy when I was younger and in my *rumspringa*. But I could deal with this for now.

"Go ahead," he urged, sensing my hesitation about his offer of a drink. "Help yourself."

As we headed off down the narrow road, I did just that, opening the console and viewing my options. Nothing looked familiar among the various bottles and cans. I chose something called Perrier, which sounded vaguely familiar. It turned out to be water with a fancy name.

"So you just graduated from farrier school?" he asked as he turned the music down a little more, much to my relief.

"Not exactly. I mean, yes and no. I graduated a year ago."

"Gotcha. How do you like it so far? Are you allowed to use modern conveniences back at your shop there?"

I had to think for a moment what he meant. Blacksmithing was an ancient art, so there weren't really any modern conveniences to speak of, except maybe the fact that we ordered our shoes from a catalog now, premade, as opposed to forging them ourselves. But those shoes were put on a horse the same way they were a century ago. An electric machine couldn't shoe a horse and probably never would.

"Well, our forge is propane powered, if that's what you mean," I said, taking a light tone.

"Oh, yeah. I guess there isn't much about shoeing that involves a computer, eh?" He laughed. I smiled with him.

"Have you been with the Fremonts long?"

"The last four summers. I'll be going back to Penn State in the fall."

He went on to tell me he was one of three students Natasha employed each summer. Apparently, they did a lot of the grunt work, such as cleaning out stalls, watering, grooming, repairing fences, and exercising a small contingent of horses she stabled for other owners, in addition to caring for their breeding mares and the foals.

"About the only horse over there we don't fool with is Duchess. She has her own stable, closer to the house, and Natasha prefers to handle that one herself."

"Duchess?" I asked, wondering if that was the horse I was being brought out to see.

"Long story," Ryan replied with a wave of his hand, as if to say he wasn't in the mood to tell it.

We were silent for a moment, and I tried to think of some other topic of conversation, lest my driver grow bored and decide to turn the music back up. "Natasha seems pretty nice," I finally managed to offer.

"Yeah, she's nice enough. Rich, but nice."

"Do you enjoy working with the horses?"

A new song came on, and Ryan began tapping out a rhythm on the steering wheel. "Sure, though warmbloods aren't my favorite. I like hotbloods. Arabians, actually. If I had my own horse, that's what I'd get. An Arabian."

"I hear you," I said, and I really did know what he meant. As Amos and I had explained to Priscilla earlier, hotbloods were fast and feisty, which made them much more exciting than the well-trained warmbloods of the horse show world. Definitely more interesting—at least to a guy like Ryan.

"You people probably don't have any show horses, though, right?" he asked. "I mean, what would an Amish man do with a warmblood?" He laughed again, clearly enjoying his own sense of humor.

"Yeah, that would make about as much sense as your taking a buggy with you back to college," I replied, and he howled with laughter.

We managed to converse easily enough the rest of the way to East Fallowfield, talking about horses and riding and all things equestrian. As we got closer, the subject came back around to Natasha, and from the way Ryan talked, it sounded as if she was more than just the money behind a successful horse breeding and boarding business. Apparently, she was also a top-level competitor in the sport of dressage.

"She made Grand Prix champion by the age of thirty," he said, as if I would know what that meant. "Can you believe it? The horse she won with is retired now, but she's working really hard to get there again, with Duchess this time."

I could act as though I knew what he was talking about, or I could just ask. I opted for the latter. "Grand Prix champion?"

"Sorry. Guess I forgot you're not part of the horse show world." He went on to explain that dressage had levels of achievement, with each horse-and-rider pair having to earn their way up the various levels at competitions until they reached the highest level, which was "Grand Prix."

"Right now, Natasha and Duchess are still three levels down from there, at the 'Prix St. George' level. But I have no doubt they'll make it eventually. The next qualifying event is in Devon this fall, and Natasha is determined to compete and earn up to the next level from there. If she can do that, they'll probably be able to make Grand Prix in another year or two."

"She must really be something," I said, my eyes on the gorgeous scenery that surrounded us. "But isn't she a little…" I stopped short, realizing such a question would be rude.

"A little what?" Ryan replied, crowing with laughter. "High strung? Intense?"

I shook my head, mad at myself and my big mouth. I wanted to drop it, but he wouldn't let it go.

"Fine," I said. "Old, okay? I'm guessing she's in her late thirties. I was going to say, isn't she a little old to still be competing in horse shows?"

"Oh." Ryan's laugh faded. "No, not at all. Gosh, Steffan Peters was almost fifty when he took gold at the Pan Am games a few years ago. And then there was that guy from Japan at the London Olympics—he was like seventy or something, wasn't he? Dressage isn't about age, it's about precision and training and having the ability to work with a horse in a really unique way."

He explained how, in dressage, the riders communicate with the animals physically, using arm and leg movements. They train their horses to understand all of their different, very specific physical cues, and the best horses will respond by doing exactly what's being asked of them.

"When it's done well," he said as he slowed and put on the blinker, "it's kind of amazing to watch, warmbloods or not."

Ryan turned off the road onto an expansive paved entrance. He came to a stop at an ornate wrought iron gate, reached up to the overhead visor, and pulled out a small device. A remote control.

"Welcome to Morningstar," he said as he pressed a button and the gate began to swing open. When it was wide enough, we pulled through to the other side, and he used the remote again, this time to close it behind us.

He continued on much more slowly, following a long driveway that stretched before us, surrounded on both sides by pristine pastureland. In the distance stood a massive stone-and-timber home surrounded by smaller buildings in the same graceful style.

I must have sucked in my breath because Ryan laughed.

"Told you they were rich. And established, if you know what I mean. That house has been in the Fremont family for a hundred years."

As we drew closer, I could tell that the entire place—house, stables, and grounds—wasn't just beautiful but perfectly manicured as well. I'd seen a lot of nicely maintained Amish yards where I came from, but none that was even close to being this perfect nor this big. We continued on past the house and down a ways, finally pulling to a stop in what looked like a small parking lot. As we got out of the vehicle, Ryan took a cell phone from his pocket, tapped the screen, and held it to his ear.

I assumed he would tell me where to go from here, so as I waited for him to get off the phone, I stood there trying to take it all in. The place was really something, even if it was over-the-top fancy.

"Not answering," he said, shoving the phone back in his pocket. "Come on, we can leave the car here and just walk if you want. You can see more that way."

We set out on a stone path which meandered past a covered patio, a gazebo, and a rose garden before rounding a hill. As we neared the top, I caught a glimpse of the stables on the other side.

They were huge, the biggest I had ever seen, stretching out like an elongated, one-story version of the house. On both sides were riding rings, one small and one big, though neither was in use at the moment.

We followed the path the rest of the way down to the stables, crossing another smaller parking area and going inside. As I stepped through the door, I was hit with a wall of cool air—a sensation so utterly out of context that it took me a moment to figure out what it was.

Air-conditioning, I realized, and then I had to stifle a laugh. I was plenty familiar with air-conditioning, of course, as was any Amish person who had been to stores or banks or other public places in the heat of the summer, but this was a new one on me. Air-conditioning in a stable? I couldn't imagine such a thing. I also couldn't wait to tell Amos, who would get a good kick out of it as well.

I followed Ryan farther inside, astounded at the beauty of the building's interior. Each stall was timbered in gleaming, treated pine. The painted, cement-floor alleyway in between the stalls was clean enough to eat off of, and there wasn't even a hint of the scent of manure. We passed four horses: a pair of warmblood mares, one obviously pregnant, and a couple geldings I assumed Natasha was boarding. Next came a foal and its mother, a russet beauty with a creamy star on its forehead. Nearby their stall sat a young stable hand on a bench, trying to untangle a rope.

"Natasha around?" Ryan asked her.

She tilted her head toward the nearest door. "Last I saw, she was heading out that way. But that was a while ago."

I followed Ryan back outside, where a pair of workers were putting in a row of fence posts.

"Have you guys seen Natasha?" he asked. The two men simply shook their heads.

"Sorry about this," Ryan told me as he turned to go back inside. "I know she's around here somewhere."

I was about to follow him to the door when movement in the nearby pasture caught my eye. Glancing over, I did a double take when I spotted the single most beautiful horse I'd ever seen. It was a mare, solid white, standing at the crest of a hill. She was staring off into the distance, her nose twitching in search of a scent, her ears pricked, and her white mane and tail lightly fluttering in the breeze. I stepped closer, placing my hands on the split rail fence as I gazed out at her.

"Told you she was something," Ryan said in a soft voice, coming to stand next to me.

"Huh?"

"That's Duchess."

Duchess. The one Natasha was pinning her hopes on to win the big dressage championship.

"Well, the name fits. That horse totally looks like royalty."

"Yeah. Too bad she—" He cut off his own thought midsentence, as if realizing almost too late that I was a consultant here, not an employee, and therefore it was none of my business. Instead, he just whipped out his phone again and pressed a button.

While he stepped away to talk, I returned my attention to the magnificent horse in the field. For some reason, part of a verse from Revelation popped into my head: *I saw heaven opened, and behold, a white horse; and he that sat upon him was called Faithful and True.* Surely, the horse I was gazing at now looked a lot like the one the verse described. I couldn't imagine a scene more glorious.

"Okay," Ryan told me, interrupting my thoughts. He put the phone away and gestured toward the stable door. "Natasha's coming. She'll be here in a sec. In the meantime, I'm supposed to show you January."

"January?"

He took off walking. "The horse you came here to work with."

It took me a moment, but then I caught up with him—literally and figuratively.

"I thought I was here to help Duchess," I said as we moved back inside.

He let out a laugh, as did the girl who was still on the bench with the rope.

"I told you, man," he said, shaking his head, "nobody fools with Duchess but the boss."

He led me toward the end of the building, coming to a stop at one of the last stalls. Inside stood a dark, caramel-hued mare with a honey-blond mane and tail, a beautiful palomino. I could tell she'd recently been bathed and brushed, as there wasn't a smudge of dirt or waste on her.

The horse looked up at our approach and immediately looked away, one ear swiveled in our direction. She shifted the weight on her back legs from a resting position to a poised one, as though she were preparing to dash off if need be. I slowly approached the railing so that she could smell me and look at me again if she wanted. She swung her head from side to side and chuffed.

"She has some issues," Ryan said.

"I can see that."

I was about to ask him for details when we both heard footsteps. I turned to see Natasha striding toward us, Eric on one side of her and an older gentleman on the other. She held a halter lead in her hand, and though she was now in jeans and boots—far more appropriate for her surroundings, I thought—gold and diamonds still flashed at her neck, wrists, and ears.

"Natasha," I said when she was closer.

"Jake," she replied with a nod. She turned to the gentleman beside her and introduced him as her stable master, Ted Wilding.

"Pleasure to meet you," I said, shaking the man's hand.

He seemed cordial but tentative, as if wondering what a mere blacksmith—and an apprentice at that—could do for this horse.

"And of course you know Eric," she added, gesturing toward my friend.

I was hoping Eric and I might have a chance to talk once I was done here, but he responded by saying he was just on his way out. "I only stuck around this long so I'd be here when you came," he added with a smile as he pulled a business card from his front pocket and held it toward me. I took it from him, a little puzzled until I saw that he had scribbled a number on the back.

"That's my cell," he said. "I know you're not exactly a phone guy, but call me sometime. We need to chat."

His words were accompanied by a meaningful look, which made me curious. Truth be told, I wanted to walk him out right now just to learn what it was he had to say. But I knew that wouldn't be appropriate, so I simply gave him a nod, pocketed the card, and assured him I'd be in touch.

Once he was gone, Natasha was all business again, stepping forward and lifting the latch on the horse's stall to open the door.

"Want me to bring her out?" she asked, glancing my way.

Before I could respond, the mare took a few steps backward, her eyes wide.

"Let's wait," I said. "I'd like her to get to know me a little bit first. How about if we just chat for a few minutes so she can acclimate to the sound of my voice?"

"All right," she said, though I could tell she was a woman who didn't like to be kept waiting.

"What's her name again?" Moving around Natasha, I took one step into the stall myself. "January?"

Natasha nodded. "The previous owner said she was born on New Year's Day. At first I thought the name was corny, but it's grown on me."

I turned my attention to the horse and spoke in a calm, gentle tone. "Well, that's a nice name. Hello, January." I took another step, but then so did Natasha—a little too quickly. In response, the horse lifted her head and seemed to zero in on the lead in Natasha's hand.

"How about you give the lead to Ryan? There's no need to use it right now. I'll just take a look at her here in the stall."

Natasha wordlessly passed the halter and lead to Ryan while I took another step inside.

"How long have you had her?" I asked.

"About five months. I bought her from a top stable in North Carolina."

I took another step and reached into my pocket for one of the apples I'd put in there earlier. "And when did the behavior start?"

"She arrived here a little skittish. I chalked it up to being in a new place. But if that's all it was, she should be getting better by now, not worse. The longer she's here, the more familiar this place should seem and the more comfortable she should be. But that's not what's happening. It's the opposite, in fact."

I asked Natasha about the horse's feeding habits and how often she was exercised. I took another step farther in so I was just a few feet away from January's head. I took a bite of the apple to draw attention to its scent and then placed it in an open palm and extended my arm. January hesitated only a second before stretching her neck and wrapping her lips around the fruit in my hand. The apple disappeared into her mouth. As she chewed I placed one hand on her jaw and the other in the nose hold.

"What kind of life did she have with her previous owner?" I asked as I gently swept my free hand up the horse's head.

"She was competing in dressage and won a couple regional competitions. But then her owner fell ill and had to pull out of all that. It's been a year since she's competed. But she was well cared for if that's what you mean. She comes from good stock. And her coloring is exceptional."

"She's a beautiful horse," I said, working my hand up to the area known as the poll, just past the ears. Having swallowed the apple, which had helped to distract her, January was now fully aware of my touch. She shook her head, and I waited until she stopped again before I continued. I laid my hand feather light on the atlas muscle near her neck, barely touching her at all. I wanted the mere warmth of my hand, not its pressure, to show her I meant no harm and that she had no reason not to trust me.

I could sense that the muscles in her neck were tense, and as I moved down her shoulder to the scapula, the tension increased. I slowly followed her spine down to her hind quarters, stopping every few seconds to let her respond to me if she wanted to. I had read that a shake of the head, a chew, a yawn, even a long blink were all signs that my light touch was encouraging her to relax. She barely allowed herself the luxury of a blink.

Something was causing January to be constantly vigilant. She was perpetually in preflight mode, even though she was clearly eating a healthy diet, was groomed regularly, and got plenty of exercise. It would take multiple sessions to get this horse to let down her guard and allow herself to trust me. I turned to Natasha and explained the situation.

"Are we talking every day, every other day, what?" she asked, nearly hoping, it seemed, that I could snap my fingers and make her horse better.

"Every day would probably be best," I said. "I'm thinking her relief would come in small increments. I can show you and Ted some of the techniques I know. They really aren't that hard. You don't have to be an exp—"

"Can't you come and do it?" Natasha said, frowning. "I'll send a driver over for you. And I'll pay for your time in transit. Both ways."

"Thank you, but I can't—"

"I want you to do it. I haven't seen her this calm in more than a month. Eric was right. You have already gotten further with her than any of us. Please?"

I wanted the work. I definitely wanted the work. I liked puzzles—and January's condition certainly puzzled me. Plus this was a great inroad into the *Englisch* horse world. The problem was that I didn't have two hours a day to spend treating this animal. There was just no way I could take that much time outside the shop.

"I'll pay you double your rate," Natasha said, thinking I was hesitating because of money. It really had nothing to do with that. And I didn't want word to get around that Jake Miller charged double to people who could well afford it.

"It's really more a matter of consistency," I said. "I think January would be best off with shorter stretches of treatment several times a day."

Natasha considered this for a moment. "How about if we brought her to your place? Eric told me you're working at a blacksmith shop on a big Amish farm. Surely there would be room to take her in there as a client."

I didn't remember having told Eric the "big Amish farm" part, but it was true. There would be room for January over at the Kinsingers', especially once Patch was gone. Then again, keeping Trudy's Morgan for a few days was one thing. Boarding this fancy horse for the duration of her treatment was another.

"How about it?" Natasha prodded. "Can she stay with you while you work with her? I'd pay her board and feed. And if you need to hire someone to exercise her, I'll pay for that too. I want her to have your treatment, Jake. I don't want anyone else doing it. And I don't care how long it takes."

Her solution left me speechless for a moment. All I could think was, what on earth had Eric told her to get her to trust me so completely, not to mention so quickly? The horse show crowd was usually disdainful of the Amish when it came to their animals, probably because the Amish were primarily farmers, and farmers as a whole treated their horses differently than those in the show horse world treated theirs. To farmers, horses were just one more kind of animal, albeit a useful one.

People like Natasha, however, saw horses as all kinds of things: friends, companions, loved ones, moneymakers, symbols of wealth and prestige, entertainment, and more. Natasha had to know we saw things differently. Yet here she was, ready to send this fancy show horse off to an Amish farm, sight unseen, and entrust her to a mere blacksmith—and an apprentice at that.

It sounded so odd, though I knew she could put her trust in me. On the how-I-saw-horses scale, I landed somewhere about halfway between the two positions. I did consider horses to be a step above other animals, yes, but not so many steps up as to be our equals. Overall, I guess I tended to think of them as *employees*, with a job to do, and I as their boss. The way I saw it, like any good manager my role was to facilitate their efforts in such a way that they could work to the best of their abilities.

That's why I knew I was up to the task with January, and in fact I didn't think she could be helped any other way. It was obvious Natasha didn't want to be trained on the technique and take a stab at it, nor that her stable master had time to fool with it either. I wanted the job, but I had to be realistic.

"I'm not a professional," I cautioned her. "I don't have a license or extra insurance or anything. If you bring her, I'm afraid it will have to be at your own risk."

"If you want me to sign something, I'll sign something. I don't worry about stuff like that. At least not with her."

"You're sure?"

Natasha gave me a nod. "She wasn't bargain basement by any means, but her price tag wasn't as high as some of the animals around here. If it makes you feel any better, let's just say I can afford this particular risk, relatively speaking."

"I guess it could work," I said slowly, which Natasha immediately took as a yes.

"Wonderful!" she exclaimed. "When can I bring her? Tomorrow?"

Sunday was not an option.

"How about Monday afternoon around four? My last customer is at three."

"Four o'clock it is." Natasha said happily. "Do you require a down payment? Can I write you a check? Can you take a check?"

I smiled. "I do take checks, but I do not require a down payment. If you've a special feed you have her on, bring that along, and her halter and lead."

"Will do. And how long do you think she will have to stay with you?"

I honestly didn't know. "Right now let's give it a week and see how she does. Then we can decide from there."

"A week," Natasha repeated, though I couldn't tell if she thought that sounded too long or too short or what.

"You can stop by and check in on her as often as you like," I offered.

Moving forward, Natasha reached out and patted January's nose. "Taking her to another strange place won't make it worse, will it?"

I had to tell her that it might. "Sometimes things get worse before they get better, but I'll do my best. I'm optimistic."

Natasha seemed to consider my words, and then with a nod and a handshake she left me to attend to the details with Ryan and Ted. Once we had everything worked out, Ted left as well. Before I was ready to go, however, I had one more thing to do. As Ryan waited patiently nearby, I went back inside January's stall and repeated the steps I had taken with her earlier, this time while standing on her left. I'd learned long ago that you had to work both sides of a skittish horse when you were with her, or you were only solving half the problem. By the time I was ready to go, January was more docile, and I had high hopes that she and I would get along just fine.

Ryan and I retraced our earlier steps back to the car. On the way, we again passed the riding rings, only this time one of them was in use. To my delight, the horse being ridden there was Duchess, and with a start I realized the rider sitting atop her was Natasha. Somehow, the woman looked completely different in the saddle, much more calm and relaxed yet also somehow intensely focused. I might not even have realized it was her if not for the telltale vivid auburn ponytail sticking out from the back of her riding helmet.

I paused to watch, fascinated by what I was seeing. They were in a canter, but then the animal slowed and began to do the strangest sort of step, an odd but rhythmic hopping-type action. Though the movement itself seemed completely unnatural for a horse, something about it was very compelling, perhaps because Duchess just looked so light on her feet, almost as if she were dancing. Horse ballet indeed.

"Incredible, aren't they?" Ryan said in a soft voice, from where he stood beside me, also watching.

"What is that, what they're doing? What's that called?"

"That's the piaffe. It's a dressage move. Didn't you ever see this on the Olympics?" Before I could reply, he chuckled, adding, "Oh. Right. Got it. No TV, no Olympics."

Finally, I tore my eyes away from the bizarre performance and we continued on toward the car. As we went, I just kept thinking two things.

First, that the show horse world was a bizarre place indeed.

Second, that thanks to Eric and Natasha, my dream of owning a blacksmith and horse-gentling business had been fully revived in the course of a single day.

EIGHT

When I arrived at home, a horse trailer was pulling out of the driveway, and I realized Voyager must have just been delivered from the
Stone Road Auction. Sure enough, as I climbed from Ryan's truck and
thanked him for the ride, I spotted Amos and Priscilla leading the animal
to the back paddock, probably to let him stretch his legs after his transport to the farm.

Though I would have liked to get a closer look, I figured Priscilla would
appreciate some time alone to get to know her new horse. So instead of following them, I headed for the main house. I needed Roseanna's help with an
idea for Patch I wanted to try. After that, my plan was to call Eric from the
phone in the shop to find out what it was he needed to tell me.

First things first. I found Roseanna in the kitchen, kneading a bowl of
bread dough, and I asked her if they had any old, used hats they could spare.

"What's wrong with the one you're wearing? It's in a lot better shape than
any I may find around here."

I explained I would be using them to help train a horse who had a fear
of hats, and thus old and bedraggled was fine. That seemed to be enough for
her. She finished up with the dough and covered it with a towel, and then
she asked me to set the bowl on the back of the stove while she washed her
hands. After drying them on a towel, she left me alone in the kitchen and

then returned a few minutes later with one very tattered black hat and three straw ones. I thanked her profusely, especially when she said she didn't need them back. Taking all four hats from her, I went back to the barn.

I rooted around in the storage closet until I came up with three garden stakes and a small tarp. Next came a quick detour to the tool bench, where I nailed each straw hat onto the end of each of the three stakes. Outside at the pen, I set the three hat-stake creations on the ground beside the fence, added to that the old black hat plus the hat from my own head, and then I covered everything up with the small tarp. I needed to keep it out of Patch's sight until I was ready for it.

Finally, it was time to get him. I went to his stall in the smaller barn, glad to find that he seemed to be in a docile mood. He didn't flinch as much at my approach as he had the last time I took him out, which told me we had made some progress already.

I grabbed some carrots on our way, and it almost seemed as if the horse knew exactly what we were about to do. I could feel him leading me to the pen, and once I latched the gate and led him to the center, he tossed his head as if to say, "Okay, I know the drill. Go ahead and drop the rope."

This I did, freeing him to trot around the circle and work off some nervous energy. When he finally came to a stop, I just let him stand there for a few minutes, catching his breath as I spoke in calm tones, showing him by my voice and body language that there was nothing to fear.

He seemed to relax—until I reached for a carrot, which he clearly took as a signal that I was about to approach his flank. Smart fellow, good memory.

I hesitated long enough for him to calm back down, and then I continued forward.

Walking toward him, I noticed several important cues that allowed me to gauge his fear level. Not surprisingly, his tail was down, his nostrils quivering, his eyes wide—all signs that he was preparing for flight—but beyond that he didn't skitter or jump or paw the ground as he had in our last session. It was as if he wanted to bolt but was willing to wait and see first whether that would be necessary or not.

I reached him without incident and he snatched the carrot from me, chomping away on it as I stood there at his side and slowly ran my hand from poll to dock.

"Good boy," I cooed. "Good, good boy." And I meant it. I was proud of him. We really had made progress.

Returning to the fence, I retrieved another carrot and tried again, and then again, both to reinforce the behavior and to convince myself that he was ready for the next step.

Once I was satisfied, I crossed over to the pile I'd left by the fence, reached under the tarp, and came out with the old black hat. So far, this animal had only been tested with straw hats, but that didn't mean he feared *all* hats. My first objective here was to see how he reacted to the black one instead.

I gave a cluck to catch Patch's eye and then held up the hat for him to see. So far so good; he didn't react to it at all. Next, I tried approaching him with the hat in one hand and a carrot in the other. That, too, was a success. It wasn't until I took that black hat and placed it on my head that he seemed to grow tense. Though his reaction was nothing like it had been with the straw hat that first day, a few signs of increased anxiety were there, most notably the dropping of his tail.

That was fine. I felt sure that his little black hat problem would go away if we managed to solve the much bigger straw hat one. I returned the black hat to the pile and pulled out one of the hat-stakes. Thanks to this morning's rain, the ground was soft, and I pushed the bottom of the stake down into the dirt as far as I could.

Patch didn't seem too happy about sharing his pen with a straw hat, even if it was on a stick and not on a man's head. His eyes showed white and his mouth took on a new tightness as he scampered toward the far side of the pen. Moving easily and speaking calmly, I retrieved another stake, walked a third of the way around the circle, and pushed it into place as well. Once I had the final stake in the ground—so that the three stakes with hats on them stood like points to a triangle—I grabbed a few carrots, broke them down into smaller pieces, and dropped those pieces at the base of each stake.

Patch didn't know what to make of my activities except that he wanted nothing to do with any of it. Finally, I removed myself from the pen, latched the gate, and simply stood and watched for a while.

Though he was free to move around the area as he wished, he remained frozen in place for a long time. Finally, he took first one tentative step and then another—ears pricked, nostrils sniffing—toward one of the staked hats, which told me he knew the carrots were there but that he was trying to weigh whether it was worth the risk of retrieving them or not.

Apparently not. To my disappointment, after just one step closer, he turned and darted away. Unfortunately for him, that move brought him over to a second hat, which startled him into another bolt. Fearing I had pushed him too far too fast, I was about to go back into the pen and remove all but one of the stakes when I heard Roseanna's voice behind me.

I turned to see her coming my way, a bucket in her hand.

"Maybe the old fellow just needs a better enticement," she said.

She presented me with the bucket, which contained a few bruised apples, a pear, some figs, chunks of rind from last night's watermelon, and a big spoon. Everything seemed to be covered in some sort of sticky glaze, and when I asked what it was, Roseanna explained that the entire mess had been drizzled with honey. "That's why the spoon's in there, so you won't have to touch it and get all sticky."

With a laugh and big thanks, I took the bucket from her, slipped back inside the pen, and made quick work of scooping the messy concoction onto the ground in front of two of the stakes. Just to make things a little easier for Patch, I removed the third stake, which gave him a larger hat-free zone to which he could retreat as needed. The whole time, the horse hovered at the far side, watching my every move. When I was finished, I used the toe of my work shoe to mush a bit of the fruit, releasing its smell, and he whinnied.

By the time I was out of the gate and standing next to Roseanna, Patch was already advancing toward the nearest pile. Together, she and I watched as he debated with himself for a few long, agonizing minutes and then finally, slowly gave in. Feet planted as far away as possible, he stretched out his long neck and head, nostrils still quivering as he leaned down and wrapped his big square teeth around a chunk of watermelon rind.

Roseanna and I cheered, though not so loudly as to disturb him.

"Looks like your special mixture saved the day," I told her, handing back the empty bucket and spoon. "You're a genius."

She let out a laugh. "Oh, it wasn't me. This was Priscilla's idea."

Priscilla. I turned my head toward the back pasture, expecting to spot her there with her own horse, observing us from a distance. But the field was empty.

"Is she in the house?"

"No, she's walking her new horse around, showing him the farm. They're probably up at the silo by now. She stopped by the kitchen for few minutes to put all of this together. Then she asked me if I'd mind bringing it out here to you."

"Thanks."

"You're welcome." Roseanna looked over at Patch and then back at me. "It was fun. Did you know horses shouldn't have tomatoes or broccoli or potatoes? While Priscilla was throwing this together, I was trying to help, but half the things I offered she didn't want. Said they could cause intestinal problems."

I knew about tomatoes and broccoli—and cauliflower and peppers and onions and a few other things, for that matter—but potatoes were a new one on me. Then again, when it came to horse treats, I rarely deviated beyond carrots, apples, or pumpkins anyway, so what did it matter?

Once Roseanna was gone, I decided to call it a day and put Patch back in his stall. But before I could even get the gate unlatched, I realized he was now standing right next to one of the staked hats, his body fully relaxed, chewing away contentedly on the grass underneath. The special mixture I'd put there was all gone, and at this point he was likely just trying to get every last drop of the honey that remained.

I took in a deep breath and held it for a long moment, watching him. Priscilla's gesture had been a kind and generous one, not to mention clever. More importantly, it had worked.

I decided the horse could use a little more time in the pen before being put away, so I left him there and headed for the blacksmith shop instead.

At nearly six p.m. on a Saturday, the place was empty and quiet. Moving through the shadowy room, I realized that with the forge off and not putting out any heat, it was a lot cooler than usual in here as well. I wasn't sure if this would be a good time for Eric to talk, but I would give it a try. The phone was over on the desk where Amos handled the paperwork side of the business, so I took a seat in the empty chair next to it, pulled Eric's card from my pocket, and dialed the number he'd written on the back.

He answered on the second ring, saying my name instead of hello. It startled me for a second until I remembered that with cell phones, you often knew who was calling. We chatted for a few minutes about the tennis game he'd just played and the dinner his girlfriend was cooking for him tonight, and then we got down to business.

"You must have done something right, buddy," he said, "because from what I hear, not only did Natasha hire you to unspook her horse, she's going to let you do it at your own farm."

I didn't clarify that it wasn't my farm. Instead, I told him I had a feeling that was thanks more to him than to anything I had done. "What did you tell her about me, anyway?"

Eric laughed. "Oh, I might have laid it on a little thick—made you sound like Robert Redford in that movie or whatever—but I wasn't lying. I remember how you interacted with the horses at farrier school. I'd never seen anything like it. Even the instructor recognized how good you were and said you had a special gift, remember? That's all I told Natasha, really, that you were gifted with horses. Oh, and that you were trustworthy and dependable. That sort of thing."

"Well, thanks. Thanks a lot," I said, uncomfortable with the high praise but deeply appreciative just the same. Eric was a good guy, the kind who was always doing for others.

"You're welcome, no biggie. It's just that our conversation this morning before the auction got me thinking. In my opinion, the best way to establish a reputation as a horse gentler is to succeed at it with somebody important."

"Important?"

"You know what I mean. Not merely rich but connected. Natasha Fremont is a real insider in the Chester County horse crowd. She's like the head cheerleader in high school, the one everybody's always flocking around and wanting to be with and talk to, you know?"

I hadn't had experience around cheerleaders, but I understood what he was saying.

"She's on boards and donates to all the right groups and attends all the functions and everything, sure, but what makes her stand out are her skills as a rider. There are plenty of women—and men—throwing their money around on horsey stuff and acting like big shots outside the ring, but they never get their hands dirty. Either they're mediocre riders, or they don't ride at all and just hire other people to do it for them." With another laugh, he added, "Most of them wouldn't know a caracole from a capriole."

I'd never heard of either, though I assumed they were terms related to the sport of dressage. I kept quiet as he continued.

"Anyway, unlike those kinds of people, Natasha is the real deal. She walks the walk, everyone knows it, and they all respect her for it. Do you understand what I'm getting at here, Jake? I'm telling you, if you can fix just one horse for her, you'll have twenty more people the very next day asking you to fix their horses too. If you really do want to expand the horse-gentling side of your business, she's the one to know."

I sat back in the chair, considering his words. Was it possible that one woman could have so much influence on others? Certainly, there were people in my world who folks tended to emulate, or from whom people sought opinions on various matters. An endorsement from a respected source was always a helpful and valuable thing. On the other hand, this tendency to follow in the wake of trendsetters seemed to be far more common among the *Englisch* than the Amish, perhaps because our lifestyle emphasized consistency rather than change—not to mention we weren't always searching for prestige or status or the next big thing. Quite the opposite, in fact. We placed our values on such principles as humility and community and simplicity.

Eric asked for my version of how things went at the stables today after he left, and I described my encounter with January. I also told him about seeing Duchess, and that she was the most beautiful horse I'd ever come across.

"Yeah, she's been Natasha's big ticket for a while now. She's the offspring of the horse Natasha took all the way to Grand Prix Champion thirteen years ago. Duchess has every bit of her father's talent, or at least everyone thought she did. But something's been off with her for a while, and Natasha's running out of time. Bottom line, if Duchess doesn't advance at least one level at this year's Dressage at Devon, then Natasha may have to get out of the horse business entirely."

"What? Why?"

"Long story. It's hard to explain, but bottom line, she's invested everything she has in this horse. If Duchess fails, her value as a show horse or even a breeding horse will plummet so far that Natasha may lose it all—not just the massive amounts of money she's put into things but also her time, energy, reputation, everything."

Though this was foreign to my own experience, business was business, whether showing horses or shoeing them. When an investment went south, sometimes you had no choice but to fold.

"So when is this big competition? I thought the Devon Horse Show was in the spring."

"The big one is. This is a more specialized show, solely dressage, held in September."

"Is the prize money big?" I asked, assuming that a win would not only increase Duchess's value but would also provide funds to infuse back into the business.

Eric snorted. "Nah. Winning at dressage is about the title, not the money. I mean, the highest purse there is only ten K or so. Natasha's attire alone costs more than that."

I blinked. "You're kidding, right?" I hated to sound naive, but I couldn't imagine such a thing. "A ten-thousand-dollar riding outfit? How is that even possible?"

"Well, boots are a thousand, coat's nine hundred, pants four hundred," he said, going down the list and adding in top hat, silk tie, and gloves until the total was closer to twelve thousand. "And that's just the rider. Then there's all the stuff the horse needs, starting with the saddle, which can run into the thousands as well. There's also training, upkeep, transportation, and on and on. It gets a little ridiculous."

I listened as Eric rattled off more types of expenses, more numbers, but I found that it all kind of blurred together—until he just happened to mention the cost of the horses themselves. Apparently, after her last win, Duchess had been valued at two hundred thousand dollars—and if she did indeed "rank up a level" at Devon in September as everyone hoped, that value would more than triple.

I let out a low whistle. "No wonder, then. It's all coming clearer now."

"I know, right? We're not talking chump change."

I thought about that, remembering what Natasha had said earlier about January, that she could afford the risk, relatively speaking, of sending her off with me. I shared her comment with Eric, adding, "Now that I know the kinds of numbers we were talking about, her words make a lot more sense. Of course January would seem cheap compared to Duchess. Most other horses would."

"Yeah, seriously. She paid twenty thousand for January, from what I recall. Compared to two hundred thousand, that is a big difference."

His tone was matter-of-fact, but I sucked in a breath, my heart giving a heavy thud in my chest. I was going to be taking delivery on a twenty-thousand-dollar horse? Unbelievable. If I'd had to guess, I would have put her price tag at a fourth of that at most. No wonder Natasha needed the animal gentled. Even if she did own other horses worth much more, twenty thousand dollars was nothing to sneeze at. It was time for January to start earning her keep.

Which meant it was time for my skills to be put to the test, now as never before.

Nine

I gotta be honest," I told Eric before we wrapped up our phone call, "I'm feeling kind of stupid right now. I had no idea this much money was involved."

"Oh, please," he said warmly. "Don't feel dumb. Why should you know? It's way outside your realm of experience. I mean, if an Amish farmer is going to plunk down big money on a horse, it'll be in the four figures, not five or six, and for a Percheron or a Belgian, not a warmblood. Am I right?"

"I guess. But it's not just the money. There's also all these terms and things I've never even heard of."

"Trust me, buddy, the world of show horses—especially in dressage—is so specialized, most people need a translator to keep up."

"You can say that again. It's like being in a foreign country."

"Uh-huh. And that's why it helps to have me advocating for you. I know these people. I've been moving around in their circles my whole life. Do you get what I'm saying?"

"Um...yeah?"

He chuckled. "I'm just trying to tell you, Jake, that if you're ready to grab the dream, keep me in the loop, okay? There's a lot I can do for you to help make that happen, especially if you can remedy this situation with January to Natasha's satisfaction. Like I said, do that and customers will be lined up at your gate."

"Thanks, Eric. I truly appreciate it."

"You're most welcome. And now I need to go. If I show up for dinner all sweaty from tennis, Vicki's going to kill me. It's time for me to get in the shower."

We both laughed and said our goodbyes, but after I hung up the phone, I sat for a long time in the quiet darkness of the blacksmith shop, thinking. There was a lightness to my heart, one likely due to the reawakening of my ultimate plan. Lately I'd been so caught up in the day-to-day around here that I'd forgotten to look beyond that, to what would eventually become my life, God willing. With Eric's help, maybe I really could make my dream happen after all.

I bowed my head to give a prayer of thanks for these blessings and ask for guidance. But after a moment I was interrupted by the distant sound of a familiar voice.

Rising, I said a quick "Amen" and then leaned forward to peek out the shop's front window. I was right. Amanda was here, standing in the driveway next to her cart and chatting with Roseanna.

Moving quickly, I walked out back to check on Patch, who was still doing fine in the pen. Then I crossed around the exterior wall of the welding shop to the driveway, coming to a stop at Amanda's horse.

"Hey, what are you doing here?" I said, forcing my voice to sound light as I reached out and took Pepper's lead rope from her.

"Gee, Jake. Try not to sound so excited, huh?" Amanda teased in return.

I smiled. "Sorry. You just surprised me, is all. What's up?"

"What's up," Roseanna answered pointedly, "is that I called on Amanda earlier today and invited her to supper tonight."

My eyes widened as I looked from one woman to the other. I was trying to think of a respectful way to say that I would handle the arrangements for my own dates, thank you very much, when she added, "For Priscilla. I invited Amanda over so she could visit with Priscilla. But of course you're welcome to join us too if you'd like."

"Ah, sure. Thanks," was all I could manage. I felt like an idiot, but fortunately the two of them jumped right back into their conversation, so I was able to cover my embarrassment by putting away her buggy and horse. I also took a few minutes to bring Patch back into the barn as well, praising him all the way and rewarding him with fresh water and a scoop of grain.

Roseanna and Amanda were still in the driveway when I made it back out, though they had managed to work their way up closer to the house. As I joined them, I found myself feeling like an interloper who had merely bumbled his way into a dinner invitation. For a moment, I considered backing out again, but then I decided to stick with it for Priscilla's sake. Amanda was a charming and friendly young woman, but I knew that to someone like Priscilla, she could come across as rather overwhelming. Obviously, Amos and Roseanna had gotten Amanda over here in order to hurry along the process of their niece's reintegration into local society. It was a good idea in theory, but there was such a thing as too far, too fast.

"So where is she?" Amanda asked both of us as she looked about.

"Who, Priscilla?"

"*Ya*, of course Priscilla! I want to see her."

Turning to Roseanna, I asked, "Does your niece even know she has company this evening?"

"No, she doesn't," the woman replied with a twinkle in her eye. "Why don't the two of you go tell her?"

With that, she turned on her heel and returned to the house to finish making supper.

"Isn't this fun?" Amanda whispered to me once Roseanna was out of earshot. "I really do want to see Priscilla again."

"Well, then let's go find her," I replied, hoping this scheme of Roseanna's didn't end up backfiring on all of us.

I suggested we check the horse barns, and sure enough that's where we found Priscilla, on the larger, Kinsinger side. She was attempting to lead Voyager into his stall, but the animal was tossing his head and prancing in place in resistance. The other horses were staring like a classroom of children watching a troublemaker give their teacher a hard time. As Priscilla strained to control him, her *kapp* popped off her head and fluttered to the ground.

"Stay here," I said to Amanda.

I closed the distance between myself and Priscilla, approaching Voyager from the side so that he could see me coming.

"Whoa, boy." I reached up to wrap my hand underneath the nose halter and gently grabbed hold.

Priscilla had not heard me approach. She startled and jerked her head to face me. Wisps of her dark brown hair had sprung free from the carefully twisted braid that framed her face. Her gaze on me was wide eyed.

"I have his head," I said. "Keep hold of the lead but don't tug on it. Let's get him to calm down first."

"I wasn't tugging on it," Priscilla muttered as she moved around from the front to Voyager's other side, the lead now loose in her hand.

"Easy, boy," I continued. Voyager grunted and tossed his head, making it clear he was not ready to go where he didn't want to go.

"There's a good lad," I soothed. On the other side I could hear Priscilla catching her breath.

A few seconds later, Voyager stopped stepping in place and reduced his head thrashing to a gentler nodding. He chuffed, turned to me, and chuffed again.

"Easy does it," I said, attempting to move forward with just slight persuasion on the nose halter. Voyager took one step with me and then stopped.

"How about you get inside the stall and toss around his feed some so he can catch a whiff?" I suggested.

Priscilla stared at me for a moment before dropping the lead and walking inside the stall. She headed for the trough, which was full of feed, and moved it around to release its scent into the air. Voyager's nostrils immediately took notice. I took another step and so did he. I waited until he took the next step forward and then joined him as he moved fully into the stall. He made for the trough, and Priscilla and I both reached up at the same time to unbuckle his halter.

"I have it," she snapped. Bits of hay had settled on her hair and were poking out like little windmill blades.

"Sure." I stepped back out of the stall, waiting for her to offer up a thank-you or otherwise acknowledge my assistance, but she removed the halter without saying a word—not even after she'd hung it on the hook, come out of the stall herself, and latched the door shut behind her.

Amanda chose that moment to step forward. In her hands she held Priscilla's *kapp*.

"*Guder Daag,* Priscilla. *Wie bischt du?*"

Priscilla pivoted at Amanda's greeting, surprise evident on her face. Obviously caught off guard, she did not reply. Amanda offered up her *kapp*, and after a moment's hesitation Priscilla took a step forward, reached for the head covering, and whispered a barely audible, "*Danke.*"

Amanda shot me an uncertain glance and then turned back toward Priscilla.

"Hey, I know it's been a while," Amanda said, obviously mistaking Priscilla's surprise for a lack of recognition. "But surely you remember me. I'm Amanda Shetler. We were in school together."

Still no reply, so Amanda added, "You and I were always the last ones standing in the spelling bees? We used to trade sandwiches at lunch sometimes? Our last year there, we worked together on that baby quilt for the Peruvian Indians? I can't believe you don't remember."

"Of course she remembers," I jumped in to say. "She's just surprised to see you here, is all." I turned toward Priscilla. "Right?"

She gave a vague nod, still looking like a deer caught in headlights.

"Roseanna thought you might like to have an old friend over for dinner," I explained to her. Unable to help myself, I added, "I didn't know anything about it until just a few minutes ago." For some reason, I wanted her to understand that Amanda's being here had nothing to do with me.

At least she managed to gather her composure. Replacing her look of surprise with one of timid acceptance, she finally spoke "*Ya*, of course I remember you, Amanda. I was just surprised."

Amanda broke into a wide grin. "Oh, I'm so glad. You had me worried for a minute."

Priscilla brushed a bit of dirt off her *kapp* but didn't put it back on.

"We're all so glad you've come back," Amanda added.

"We?"

"All of us. Me. Jake." Amanda flashed a smile in my direction. "Your old friends. All of us. The more word gets around, the more people are wondering when they'll get to see you themselves so they can say hello."

Frowning, I looked over at Amanda, skeptical that there was any truth in her words. In response her eyes widened innocently and she gave a subtle nod, as if to assure me that word really was spreading and people were indeed eager to see Priscilla again.

"Too bad tomorrow's not a worship Sunday," she added, again focusing on Priscilla. "Because if it were, you could get it all over with at once."

"Oh. *Ya. Danke*," Priscilla's cheeks flushed bright red as she looked down at the *kapp* in her hand and ran a finger along one of its dirtied ribbons.

"At least we have the Chupps tomorrow night," Amanda added. "I'm so excited you're coming. You'll see a lot of the old gang there. We'll have such a good time."

I hadn't had a chance to tell Priscilla about that. She whipped her head up. "What?"

"Didn't you mention that, Jake? Silly you," Amanda said, laughing. "We want you to come with us to the Chupps tomorrow night for volleyball. You remember Gabe Chupp, don't you? He's a year younger than us? Anyway, some of the group is getting together at his house tomorrow evening for some volleyball. It'll be fun. You'll love it."

"Oh. I don't—" Priscilla looked from me to Amanda, a curious dread in her eyes.

"Priscilla, you simply must come with us. Everyone is so anxious to see you. You have to be there. Please? Please say you will."

"I think I might be a little too old for—"

"No, you're not! You're the same age as me! Gosh, Jake's twenty-four and he still comes."

"*Ya*, but only because you make me," I replied, giving Amanda a smile. When I turned back to Priscilla, it struck me that she'd had no idea that Amanda and I were a couple until that moment. Watching her, I could see understanding dawn in her eyes, followed by a brief flash of what almost looked like…what? Disappointment?

Dismay?

Amanda was oblivious to all of it. "Please?" she urged. "Say you'll come."

Priscilla sighed heavily but quietly, the way I'd seen Amos sigh when something he was attempting to weld just wouldn't stick.

"We'd really like you to come with us," I added, meeting her gaze.

"I guess that would be all right."

"Oh, I'm so glad. We're going to have the best time," Amanda said.

The supper bell clanged then.

Amanda cocked her head toward the sound. "Oh, my. Here the meal is ready, and I didn't even offer to help get it on the table. How rude of me! I'd better get in there." She turned toward the door and began to walk purposely toward it, not bothering to wait for me or Priscilla to follow.

Priscilla made no move to leave the barn. I turned to her. A bit of straw that had been in her hair was now dangling just above her ear. She was watching Amanda as she strode out the double doors. It was difficult to read the look on her face, but if I had to guess I'd say she was thinking she wasn't ready to face all her old schoolmates again. Not just yet.

"The volleyball games are a lot more loosely organized than the singings," I told her gently, "but they really are fun."

She turned to me, a pensive look on her face. "What?"

"I think you'll have a good time at the Chupps'," I said, but with less enthusiasm. Maybe the look on her face had nothing to do with volleyball.

She turned toward the door again. The piece of straw in her hair swung like a pendulum.

"You have a bit of…" I reached for the straw and pulled it gently away. "There."

Priscilla looked at the tiny stick in my hand and said nothing.

"Coming?" I gestured toward the door.

She sighed again. "In a minute."

"Okay, then." I turned to leave.

"Wait."

I looked back.

"I need to ask you something. Can you please, um, can you please promise never to do that again?" Her voice was sincere, as if she hated to ask but simply had no choice.

I felt terrible.

"You mean put you on the spot like that? Yeah, sorry. I didn't realize Amanda was going to blurt it out that way. I should have told you sooner."

I really did feel bad for Priscilla. It must be awful to be so shy, to not have a gregarious bone in her body—especially being Amish because so much of our lifestyle involved community.

"Not that."

So what was it, then? I squinted, staring at her. Could she be this worked up over a bit of dried grass? "What, take straw out of your hair? We're going inside to eat. Most people—"

"I'm not talking about straw in my hair either, Jake. I'm talking about my horse. Please. Just don't get in between Voyager and me again unless I ask for your help, okay? I know it may sound dumb to you, but it's something I need you to do for me. I'd really appreciate it."

I stood there for a second, my brow furrowed. "Well, no offense, but if I hadn't stepped in to help, you'd still be yanking on that lead and Voyager would still be outside his stall." I felt a vague wave of irritation rise up inside of me and then fade back down again as she spoke.

"*Ya*, perhaps. But that's between him and me. Not you. Okay?"

I blinked, confused. "You really want me to have nothing whatsoever to do with your horse?"

She nodded, looking up at me, and I tried to decipher what I was seeing in her eyes. There was a sadness there, but also a sort of stubborn defiance.

"I guess I understand," I told her, my tone gentle. "Your horse is new. I can see that you need to establish that you're in charge. But—"

"In charge?" she interjected.

"*Ya*. I get that Voyager needs to learn you're the one he's supposed to obey. But—"

"Obey?" she said, her voice taking on a stronger tone. She shook her head. "Voyager needs to know I'm the one he can *trust*, Jake. That's what he needs to know."

Another wave of irritation rolled through me. The last thing I wanted was a lesson on equine behavior from her.

Then again, what did I care? I held up both hands, palms outward, as if in surrender.

"If you say so." I turned and headed for the door.

She dashed to my side and put her hand on my arm. We both stopped. "I…I didn't mean for it to come out like that. I know you were trying to help. It's just that…" Her voice died away.

I looked down at her hand, so petite for such a strong-willed young woman. I could feel the irritation draining out of me again. Priscilla was just a mixed-up soul trying to figure out why God sent her back here to Lancaster County when it was clear she hadn't wanted to come. What she needed here most was a friend.

"Don't worry about it." I said.

When she didn't respond, I met her eyes and repeated my words. "Really. Don't worry about it."

"I just need one thing here that is mine and only mine. That isn't…that someone else doesn't…"

She looked up at me, and all I could do in response was gaze into her eyes, her beautiful stormy eyes that were so full of questions. She couldn't finish her thought, but I didn't mind. She'd spent a lifetime having to justify herself to others. It didn't seem right to make her have to do that with me too.

Ten

It was just the five of us at dinner—Amos, Roseanna, Priscilla, Amanda, and I—and it went better than I thought it would, much to my relief. Things were uncomfortable at first, but Amanda was the perfect addition to the group. She was a natural conversationalist, talking and smiling and asking the right questions and making everyone feel more relaxed. By the time I was on my second helping of ham loaf, I realized I was actually enjoying myself.

Better yet, I was starting to glimpse a side of Priscilla I hadn't seen before. It started when Amanda said something about their school days together and how Priscilla had always been so quiet.

"You were smart, I remember that," Amanda told her. "But you should have talked more."

"Yeah," Priscilla replied. "You should have too."

We all fell silent for a moment, but when I looked over at Priscilla, who was contentedly buttering a role, I detected the slight, sly smile on her lips. She was teasing.

The moment Amanda caught on, she burst into a huge laugh. "Good one! You got me!" she exclaimed, and we all shared in the humor. Amanda Shetler was many things, but quiet had never been one of them.

As the meal continued on after that, it struck me that if anyone was going to be able to bring Priscilla out of her shell and get her to connect with others, it might be Amanda. She was definitely well suited to the task.

If only her plan didn't include matchmaking.

The next day was a nonchurch Sunday, which meant I'd be going over to my parents' house for a nice visit and an early lunch. I wasn't sure who else would be there, though I could probably count on seeing Tyler and Rachel. My older brothers and their families would sometimes come as well, as would my sister Sarah and her husband if they weren't busy with their own children and grandchildren. Everyone would bring something for the table, and we'd spend the morning or the afternoon enjoying each other's company, singing hymns together, sharing the news of the week with one another, playing board games—that kind of thing.

My parents lived eight miles southwest of the Kinsingers, on a hilly homestead near Strasburg that housed the family buggy shop. I set out early, Willow and I both enjoying the cool of the morning air before it evaporated into the heat of the day.

As it turned out, the only ones who were there for dinner were Tyler and Rachel, my parents, and me. Though I always enjoyed seeing everyone else, there was something nice and calm about so few of us being there.

We ate at eleven, a delicious spread of roast chicken, potato salad, and green bean casserole my mother had prepared the night before. Conversation around the table was light and easy, and I found myself telling them about Natasha and January and seeing Eric. I didn't bring up anything from my phone conversation with him later. I just said he and I ran into each other at the auction and he was the one who had made the connection. Thanks to him, I now had a little side job of horse-gentling for Natasha Fremont, which should be fun and rewarding.

Tyler was acting a little odd throughout the meal, stroking his less-than-substantial beard—the telltale mark of a married Amish man—as though he was contemplating a dozen perplexing thoughts. I was about to ask him if something was wrong when I figured out what it was that had him so distracted.

Rachel had made a big pan of monkey bread, but when she went to take it out of the oven, he suddenly jumped up and did it for her. She started to object, but he stopped her with a cluck of his tongue, as if to say she knew better. He set the pan on the stove, and then, as he handed her back the oven mitts, their eyes met and a look passed between them so sweet and joyful and intimate that it hit me like a bolt of lightning. Rachel was expecting. Tyler was going to be a father.

That wasn't something people talked about, but I found myself wondering if *Mamm* had figured it out yet. If not, she was going to be thrilled, as would *Daed*. We all knew the long road Tyler had been down in his life, and that if anyone deserved this kind of happiness, it was he.

Tyler's mother was my oldest sister, Sadie, the one sibling I'd never had the chance to meet. She left home when she was just eighteen, before I was even born. After breaking away from the Amish life and going to live in Philadelphia, she met a military man and married him not long after. By all accounts, their life together was a happy one, especially once Tyler was born. But then came the day, when Tyler was just six years old, that Sadie died unexpectedly of a brain aneurism. That left just Tyler and his dad, a reluctant single father who was about to ship off overseas at the time. That's why, after Sadie's funeral, he asked my parents—the Amish grandparents Tyler had never even met before—to take in their grandson temporarily, just until he completed his tour of duty.

That temporary arrangement ended up lasting for many years, and though it had taken Tyler a long time to decide which of the two worlds God wanted him to live in as an adult—this Plain one right here or the fancy one out there—he had chosen the Amish way in the end.

Now he was married to a sweet and lovely woman who adored him and who was having his baby. A part of me was so happy for them, but I had to admit that another part of me was a tad envious. By all rights, as Tyler's uncle and the older of us by several months, I should have been the first to marry and have a child. Instead, Tyler had outpaced me with both the wedding and fatherhood, moving along at full speed through the kind of life I wanted for myself but had yet to even begin.

That thought led me to think of Priscilla and the man out in Indiana who was hoping to marry her. Did he love her? For some reason, I doubted it. More than anything, he probably just needed her to be a mother to his children, cook his meals and clean his house and do all the things a good Amish wife would do. But I had to wonder, if they did end up together, was he the kind of guy who would understand her need for peace and quiet some-times, for being alone, for connecting with animals? Would he appreciate the violet of her eyes, the petiteness of her hands? The serene way she communi-cated with God's creatures?

"Penny for your thoughts," my mother said, and when I looked up I real-ized she was talking to me.

"Sorry, I was just thinking," I replied, spearing my last bite of chicken and popping it into my mouth.

"You looked like you were a million miles away," Rachel added, retaking her seat at the table as the monkey bread cooled on the stove.

"I was just…I was thinking about Priscilla Kinsinger, Amos's niece," I said. Then, turning to *Daed*, I added, "Remember the little girl who used to hang out at Amos's blacksmith shop when I was a kid?"

He shook his head.

"Sure you do. Daniel Kinsinger's daughter? Real quiet, kind of a tomboy?"

"Ah, yes," he said, nodding. "I remember. The girl whose mother died so tragically."

"Right, I remember that too," *Mamm* said. "We sent over a casserole and some pies. Her mother fell down the stairs or something, didn't she?"

"That's the one," I said. "Anyway, Priscilla has been living in Indiana for the past six years, but now she's back, at least temporarily. Amos and Roseanna are happy about it, and they're hoping she'll stick around. They want her to make a new life for herself here."

"I hope things work out well for her," my mother said. "And I'll certainly keep her in my prayers." She took a sip of her tea and then put down the glass and looked my way, her eyes twinkling. "Is she pretty?"

Oh, boy. I knew what she was insinuating, that this Priscilla person might be a good match for her youngest son. I answered her question with a shrug and tried to change the subject, but then Tyler had to open his big mouth.

"Jake's already seeing someone, *Mammi*," he told her, sounding like a much younger version of himself. *Jake ate the last slice of pie, Mammi; tracked mud in the house, Mammi; broke the flower vase, Mammi.* "At least that's what I hear."

I gave him my sternest glare even as everyone else at the table seemed delighted with the news.

"Is this true, Jake?" *Mamm* asked. "You may as well go ahead and tell us. Who is she?"

I couldn't believe my mother was asking me such a personal question, especially because she'd always been so good about respecting my privacy. Perhaps she, too, had been wondering when or if I was ever going to move into the next phase of my life with a wife and children.

I was trying to think how to respond, but when I didn't reply soon enough, Tyler spoke again.

"It's Amanda Shetler," he said, flashing me a victorious grin.

Mamm looked confused, so Rachel elaborated. "Her *daed* is a minister? Her *mamm* was Mary Ellen Fussner from Quarryville? They have those adorable twin girls?"

"Oh, yes," *Mamm* said finally, nodding. "Amanda is their oldest." Turning to me, she added, "I know her. My goodness, Jake. She's a lovely young woman. Just lovely."

"Just lovely," Tyler echoed, and I kicked him under the table.

"So?" *Mamm* asked, zeroing in on me. "Is Tyler correct? Are you really courting Amanda Shetler?"

"Seriously, *Mamm*?" I replied. "Why aren't you scolding Tyler right now? You've never abided tattling before."

She dabbed at her mouth daintily with a napkin and then returned it to her lap. "What can I say, son? That's when the two of you were still at home. Once a woman's children are grown and gone, she'll take information any way she can get it."

Everyone laughed, and Tyler gave a hearty, "Hear, hear!"

I gave up. "Fine. *Ya.* I'm courting Amanda Shetler. Have been for four months now."

"Four months," my mother said, glancing toward the calendar hanging on the wall in the kitchen. "*Gut.* Because it's already June."

They all chuckled again as they knew what she was implying. With our district's wedding season beginning in mid-to-late October, I would need to propose to Amanda by September at the latest if we wanted to marry this time around. If we didn't take that step then, it would be a whole year before we would have the opportunity again.

"Don't rush him," Tyler said, suddenly shifting to my side in the conversation. "You don't want to scare him off."

"Yes, dear," my mother replied sweetly, "but autumn will be here before you know it."

"And t'will be back again the following year," Tyler replied.

This time, I joined in the laughter. Tyler, more than anyone, knew what it meant to delay an engagement. After all, he'd known and loved Rachel since they were children together, but he hadn't asked her to marry him for years, not until he was almost twenty-four. Fortunately for him, she was a patient sort and had loved him enough to wait him out. Now they were blessed not just with a happy union but a new child on the way as well.

"My timeline with Amanda is on track whether we publish this season or next," I said, hoping to end the discussion there. They all knew it wasn't unusual for a couple to date for at least a year before taking that next step. They also knew that my relationship with Amanda was a private matter, not fodder for dinner table conversation. In fact, the only reason this discussion was happening at all was because there were only the five of us today. If my other siblings and their families had come too, the table talk would have remained at a far less intrusive level.

"You're not getting any younger, is all I'm saying," my mother told me in a singsongy voice.

"And she is a very special girl," Rachel chimed in.

"*Ya*, I know. I'm well aware that I'm no spring chicken, and that I would be blessed to have Amanda Shetler as a wife." Holding up both hands in mock surrender, I added, "Thank you all for your input. So, *Daed*, what do you think of the new polyurethane buggy grips for the four seventeen? Are they as solid as the steel ones on the two twelve?"

They chuckled, but they got the point. The subject was closed.

At last.

It wasn't until we were ready to leave that I had the chance to give Tyler a piece of my mind for being such a blabbermouth. I had already told my parents goodbye in the house, and the two of us were out front hitching our horses to our buggies.

"Pull that kind of tattletale stunt again," I told him, "and I'll…" My voice faded as I tried to think of a sufficient punishment.

"You'll what?" Tyler replied, struggling not to laugh.

"I'll tell them Rachel's expecting."

He stopped what he was doing and stood up straight, his eyes wide. "How'd you know?"

"So it's true?"

"*Ya*. About three and half months now."

He grinned, and seeing the joy on his face, I felt my earlier resentments slipping away. Tyler was my nephew and my best friend, and I loved Rachel like a sister. Truly, I couldn't have been happier for them both.

"Just bear this in mind," I said as I tugged on the cinch one last time before giving Willow a pat on her rump. "The fact that I didn't use that bit of information in there to divert the attention away from myself only proves that I'm the better man."

Tyler threw back his head and laughed.

"Always said you were, Jake," he told me, reaching out to give my shoulder a squeeze. "Always said you were."

Rachel emerged from the house and came our way, but instead of going straight to their buggy, she surprised me by walking over to me and taking one of my hands in hers.

"Before you go, may I be so bold as to give you a bit of advice?" she asked.

I cringed, knowing full well this was going to have something to do with my courting Amanda. Ever since Rachel and Tyler had gotten married, she'd begun to make a habit of doling out words of wisdom to me now and then whether I wanted to hear them or not. Usually I did, but this time, not so much.

"Sure," I groaned.

Smiling, she moved in even closer and spoke in a soft voice. "Now that you're in a relationship, you must keep your eye on the most important thing. Remember, the point of courting is not for you to decide if Amanda will become your wife."

My eyes widened. "It's not?"

"It's not?" Tyler echoed, also moving in close.

Rachel shook her head, her vivid blue eyes sparkling. "No. It's the time for seeking whether it is *God's will* that Amanda become your wife."

"Ah," I replied, nodding. Though I already knew what she was saying, it never hurt to be reminded of that. "*Ya.* Of course. Not my will, but His."

We said our goodbyes after that, and then Tyler helped Rachel into their buggy. Before he climbed in after her, I gave his shoulder a pat.

He flashed me a grin in return, seeming to know without words what I was trying to say, that the life God had willed for him was very blessed indeed.

ELEVEN

Rachel's parting advice had me so deep in thought that instead of return-ing directly to the Kinsingers', I detoured my buggy to the nearby Welsh Mountain Nature Preserve. After tying up Willow and giving her some water, I went for a long walk on the trails there and spent a good two hours in quiet prayer and reflection. Rachel was right. This was not about me choosing Amanda for myself. It was about God choosing her for me—or not.

I left in plenty of time for the volleyball game, stopping to pick up Amanda just before four with the intention of picking up Priscilla after that. Amanda had said she didn't care if I came for her with Priscilla already in my buggy, but I cared. In my youth, I had been known as something of a ladies' man, and even after I joined the church and changed my ways, it had taken a while for that reputation to fade. I had no intention of bringing it back now. People in our communities always tended to talk about whom and what they saw. Why feed the gossip mill for no reason? Besides, I was pretty sure Priscilla wouldn't have wanted to start any rumors either. No doubt, folks already talked about her enough as it was.

Amanda was her usual cheerful self, chatting easily as we made our way to the Kinsingers' farm. Under her black cape and apron she was in green today, which always looked so pretty with her emerald eyes and blond hair.

"So what about Matthew Zook?" she said out of nowhere as we were turning onto the last road before the Kinsinger place.

"What about him? Did something happen to him?"

She punched me playfully. "For Priscilla!"

I still didn't get it. "What?"

Amanda rolled her eyes and laughed. "For *Priscilla*. As in, let's introduce them to each other tonight. He's perfect for her."

It took me a minute to get into synch with Amanda's train of thought, which obviously had been chugging along at a brisk pace with regard to matchmaking.

"Matthew Zook?" I echoed, though I knew whom she meant. Matthew lived in Bird-in-Hand, worked alongside his parents and younger brother at their feed and tack shop, and was a couple of years younger than me. Tall, quiet, and curly haired, he had always reminded me of a scarecrow with too much hay posing as hair—though when I said that to Amanda now, she jabbed me with her elbow.

"Scarecrows are ugly. And trust me, Matthew is *definitely* not ugly."

I didn't respond, though I wasn't crazy about how emphatically she'd said that.

"He's perfect. He's shy and quiet just like she is, and he's never had a girlfriend."

I laughed. "How do you know he's never had a girlfriend?"

She frowned at me, a smile still hinting in her eyes. "Haven't you noticed? No matter how much the girls flock to him, he's too shy to ask any of them out. And it's a shame too because he's really cute. And nice."

I shook my head. "I agree that he's a nice guy, but how does the fact that he's never had a girlfriend make him perfect for Priscilla?"

"Think about it, Jake. He's as sweet as can be and hasn't shared any of that sweetness with anyone. He's never had his heart broken."

"Well, you can't know that. Quiet people don't broadcast when their heart's been broken."

"But he's never even dated anyone!"

"That doesn't mean he's never had his heart broken."

She harrumphed, crossing her arms.

"Or, maybe he *has* dated and just kept it quiet," I added.

Amanda clicked her tongue in disdain. "This isn't our parents' generation, Jake. People don't hide their dating relationships anymore."

"Some do. And if he's one of those, how would you even know? If they're hiding it well, you wouldn't." I wasn't sure why I was being so contrary, but this conversation was putting me in an irritable mood.

Still, I didn't need to take that out on Amanda. I was thinking I should probably apologize to her when she surprised me by saying, "Okay, maybe, you're right." She was quiet a moment longer before adding, "In fact, if he *has* loved someone secretly and it didn't work out, that would only make him even more perfect."

"*More* perfect? I didn't know there was anything that could be better than perfect."

"Oh, hush. You're just being difficult. Matthew is perfect because if he *has* been hurt, then he'll know how she feels. What it's like to be so disappointed."

"Disappointed? I would hardly call what Priscilla has been through mere disappointment. Tragedy is more like it."

Amanda's eyes narrowed as she finally reached her limit. "Why are you acting this way? You're so disagreeable today."

"I'm not—"

"Yes, you are. Matthew is perfect for Priscilla, so stop trying to tell me he's not. He's nice and polite, he has a good job, and his parents' *daadihaus* is empty, so there's room for him to take over the main house someday. He wouldn't hurt a fly. He's nice. He's perfect."

We were pulling into the Kinsingers' driveway. It was time to put some closure on this discussion. "Maybe tonight we should concentrate on just letting Priscilla make friends, *ya*?"

"Matthew Zook *is* someone she could be friends with," Amanda said easily, not the least bit dissuaded.

As I helped her out of the buggy, I decided there was a chance she was right. Maybe Matthew was just the guy to win over brooding Priscilla. I didn't know him well, but he seemed decent. He certainly deserved having someone to share his life with. As did Priscilla—especially if that someone was closer to her own age and didn't come with eight children.

"All right," I said.

Amanda looked at me quizzically. "All right, what?"

"You can introduce Priscilla to Matthew tonight."

She laughed sweetly and gave me a wink. "You're so funny. I wasn't asking permission. He's perfect for her."

Amanda strode for the main house to call for Priscilla, who I surely hoped was ready for what was about to befall her. While she was gone, I drove over to the buggy shed and switched out my two-seater courting buggy for one of Amos's four-seater spring wagons. Then I pulled it up to the front of the house, coming to a stop just as the two of them emerged.

Amanda had her arm on Priscilla's, and she was leading her along the flag-stone path to the hitching post as though they were strolling the downtown streets of Philadelphia, window-shopping.

Together, I had to admit, they made quite a striking pair—with Amanda the blond, breezy, cute one, and Priscilla the dark-haired, brooding, pretty one. Each was beautiful in her own way, but somehow the contrast of seeing them side by side made them both even lovelier.

As they drew closer, Priscilla flashed me a look that was difficult to read. It might have said something like "I've changed my mind. I don't want to go with you after all. I really don't. Please don't make me."

But I could also see Amos and Roseanna at the doorway, looking at their niece as she headed off to her first social event after her exile, for lack of a bet-ter word. In the face of their determination—and Amanda's—Priscilla didn't stand a chance of reneging on her agreement to come with us to the Chupps' field tonight. I felt sorry for her and annoyed with her at the same time. Part of me wanted to say to the whole of the Kinsinger compound "Enough already! Let her be!" and part of me wanted to look her in the eye and tell her she was an adult now and the time for hiding among the horses was over.

But I said nothing, of course. As Amanda and Priscilla climbed into the buggy, I merely acknowledged Priscilla's unspoken words with a slight nod of my head. I could tell in an instant she knew I had read her thoughts when no one else had. For a second she seemed relieved, and then the look was again replaced with apprehension.

Soon we were off. As I expected, Amanda chatted almost nonstop along the way, not because she was trying to monopolize things, I felt certain, but to save Priscilla from having to fill any of the silence herself. Mostly, Amanda focused on giving Priscilla the update Amos had not—a recap of all things social in the last six years. Priscilla listened politely and asked no clarifying questions. She either remembered everyone Amanda mentioned or didn't care that she didn't.

When we got to the Chupps' farm, many buggies were already lined up out back, so I let the girls off in the driveway and continued on, adding mine to the row and then putting Willow out to pasture with the other horses.

I usually avoided any "unofficial" events with the youth in our group, leaving Amanda free to attend or not as she wished. But tonight's game was a little different. Though it, too, was unofficial, Gabe's family would be there, providing refreshments and serving as chaperones. I was glad. For the most part, this group was pretty tame—especially compared to the one I'd run around with when I was in my teens—but there were a few who liked to push the limits of their *rumspringa*, and I had no desire to find myself out in a field at some wild party by mistake.

When I made it back to the gathering throng, I spotted Priscilla in the shade of a big maple tree in the front yard, pitching in with the food setup. The Chupps had created a nice long table by placing sheets of plywood over pairs of sawhorses and topping them off with green-checkered tablecloths. Priscilla was scooting things around, trying to make room as Gabe's sister Yvonne added even more platters and bowls to the mix. Thus far, the spread included all sorts of cookies and brownies and other sweets, along with chips and summer sausage and pickles and the like. It looked wonderful, but considering the rate at which the crowd was increasing, I had to wonder if there was enough. Even though the women were still just setting things up, I reached for a big, fat whoopie pie, as I knew those would be the first to go. Under the table were coolers filled with drinks, from which I took a bottle of water as well.

Amanda was nowhere to be found, so after greeting some of the others, I asked Priscilla where she'd gone.

"I don't know," she said, clearly preoccupied with her task. "She ran off somewhere with Katy Hinkel as soon as we got here."

A volleyball net had been set up out in the yard, and some of the guys were already dividing people into teams. Someone else asked if it was too early to light the fire pit. Again, I looked to Priscilla.

"You want to play volleyball?" I asked, taking a bite of the cakey, fluffy-centered whoopie pie.

She took her eyes from the food table to look out at the people who surrounded us and then shook her head. "You go ahead, though."

And I would have, were I not responsible for her. But with Amanda nowhere in sight, it would have been cruel to leave our charge all alone at a place she didn't want to be, with people she'd rather not have to see again or get to know.

I twisted the top off my water and took a long sip as I scanned the crowd, searching for my absentee girlfriend.

"Really, Jake. Go ahead if you want to. I'm fine."

"Nah, it's okay. I'm just checking things out, taking it all in."

"How long do you usually stay at these things?" she asked a second later.

I swiveled my head to look at her and laughed gently. "Are you telling me you want to go home already?"

She shrugged. "I don't know even half of these people. I didn't think it would be like…this. I was expecting something smaller. Not so noisy."

"I didn't realize there would be this many people here either, actually. This is the first big volleyball game of the summer. I guess word got around."

She pulled opened a bag of chips and dumped them into a big bowl, and then she twisted the lid off a jar of salsa and placed it beside the chips.

"To be honest," she murmured under her breath to me, "I think I'd prefer a singing to this. And that's not saying much."

I laughed. "Oh, come on. You're not a singing kind of gal?"

She paused in her food arranging again to shoot me a smirk. "What do you think?"

I finished off the whoopie pie with one last bite and then licked a smudge of the icing from my finger. "Frankly, I think you should belt out a hymn right now."

She actually cracked a smile, albeit a small one. "Why?"

"I don't know. Seems like a fun way to kick off a party."

Priscilla laughed lightly. Sarcastically. "Oh, yeah. Wouldn't that be something? Weird Priscilla makes her comeback in song."

My teasing smile faded. "Come on now. People don't think of you that way."

She shrugged. "I doubt much has changed in six years, Jake."

I looked at her, realizing she had a point. Once weird, always weird, the thinking might go.

Then again, I decided, there was no reason that history had to repeat itself. Things really could be different for her this time around. Suddenly, I felt a surge of protectiveness toward this fragile, difficult, socially awkward young woman. Considering all that had come before, this evening would be tough for anyone—but especially for someone like her.

"Come here," I told her, and when she didn't respond, I said it again. "I'm serious. Come with me."

With a word to Yvonne and a final shifting of platters, Priscilla stepped away from the table and did as I asked. Together, we walked to the far side of the lawn, and then I took her elbow and turned her so that we were looking back at the throng from a more removed perspective. Fortunately, no one else seemed to notice us or wonder what we were doing. There was too much chaos for that. People were swarming everywhere—around the food, along the driveway, and out in the yard at the net. They were chatting, laughing, eating, and gearing up to play ball. They were having fun.

"What do you see?" I asked her, gesturing broadly.

"What do you mean?"

"When you look around, what do you see here?

"Jake—"

"Humor me. Please. You said some of these faces are familiar to you, right? People you used to know, before you went away?"

"*Ya.* Some of them were in my district. We grew up together, went to school and worship and stuff."

"And do they look the same to you as they did the last time you saw them?"

"Of course not. It's been six years. They've grown up."

"Uh-huh." I released my hold on her elbow. "Imagine that. They've grown up and so have you."

Priscilla placed her hands on her hips. "Just get to the point."

"Look, I don't mean to be cruel, but it's not like anyone ever ostracized you. You chose to set yourself apart. Sure, you were an odd kid. I won't lie to you, but nothing says that you—the grown-up you, the one who's here now—nothing says you have to step right back into that old role. I know you're not a people person, Priscilla, and that's fine up to a point. But this is your community—"

"I'll only be—" she began to say, but I cut her off.

"I'm talking about for now, okay? Even if you do end up leaving at the end of the summer, this is your community while you're here."

"Fine."

"And because this is your community, and you are an adult, you have responsibilities. God made us to need each other. To support each other. To befriend each other."

"*Ya, ya,* the Amish refrain."

I chose to ignore her sarcasm as I continued. "But all that stuff is a two-way street, you know. What's the verse, 'Bear ye one another's burdens, and so fulfill the law of Christ'? Living in community isn't just a good idea; it's God's idea. I know you know that, even if it does go against your nature."

She was quiet for a long moment, and I could see her struggling internally with how she wanted to respond. Finally, she gave a sigh of resignation.

"Okay," she said softly. "I give up. You're right. I know it."

Before I could respond, she looked at me with a humorous glint in her eyes and added, "And thanks ever so much for invoking the Word of God to make your point."

I laughed. "Sorry. I'm not trying to bash you over the head with this stuff. I just had a feeling you might need a pep talk. Besides, I think if you give them a chance, you may be surprised. I didn't grow up with these people, and I've only been living in this neck of Lancaster County for a year, but I've come to know some of them, and they're really nice."

"That may be true for you, but I did grow up with these people. And I never made a close friend myself, not in fourteen years."

"Amanda wanted to be your friend," I replied. "She tried anyway. And she's trying again now."

Priscilla shot me a look, and I knew what she was thinking. *Friends don't abandon friends the minute they get to a party.* Amanda's disappearance was regrettable, but that was beside the point at the moment.

"Listen, all I'm saying is that it's not as though anyone actually disliked you back then. They just didn't know what to do with you. Maybe the reason God sent you here now was to give them—and you—another chance. Don't push them away, Priscilla. Let them befriend you if they want. You may even find that you like it."

She seemed to consider my words, and then she turned to me, her eyes radiant in the late afternoon sun.

"Okay. I'll try."

And to my surprise, she really did.

Her first opportunity came almost immediately, as we were strolling back toward the group and spotted Amanda. She was headed in our direction, flanked by her two best friends, Katy and Cheryl. Irritation needled me at the site of the three of them in their little clique—until Amanda came right over to Priscilla and pulled her in with them.

Though these girls and Priscilla already knew each other from when they were younger, Amanda introduced them all by name, as if this was the first time they'd ever met. To Priscilla's credit, she actually made eye contact in return. I hovered nearby, standing close enough to hear their conversation but not so close that I had to participate. If this went well, and Amanda really had things under control, then I'd be able to walk away and join the volleyball game.

Unfortunately, after that initial introduction, the four of them grew uncomfortably quiet. They all wore nervous smiles as they glanced around at each other, but apparently not one of them could think of a thing to say.

"Are you glad to be back?" Katy finally asked.

"Um. *Ya.* Good to be back," Priscilla replied.

"And where is it you've been living?" Cheryl asked. "Ohio? Iowa?"

"Indiana."

"With your aunt and uncle, right?" Amanda prodded.

"*Ya.*"

"On a farm?" Cheryl asked.

"*Ya.* Though I lived in town for a while, for a job as a caregiver."

"My cousin used to be a caregiver, but I couldn't do it. Too boring," Katy said. Then her hand flew to her mouth. "Sorry. No offense."

To my surprise, Priscilla laughed lightly. "I'm not offended. I agree. I nearly went stir-crazy in that job. I've never done anything so tedious in my life."

The other girls giggled, and for a moment it was as though they were the best of friends and Priscilla Kinsinger was not now, nor ever had been, the odd one out.

They began describing various jobs each of them had, or had had in the past, and once the conversation was really flowing, I leaned in toward Amanda and asked if I could speak with her for a moment.

"Sure," she said, telling the others she'd be right back.

The two of us strolled away from the crowd until we were mostly out of earshot. Then I asked her, as nicely as I could, if abandoning Priscilla the moment we got here was her idea of helping the girl make new friends.

Amanda's eyes widened. "It wasn't like that, Jake, not at all. There was something Katy and I needed to go and do, and we tried to get Priscilla to go with us, but she wasn't interested."

"Then maybe you shouldn't have gone right then. Couldn't you have waited for me first?"

She shook her head. "I didn't need to. I introduced Priscilla to Yvonne, who gave her a job helping with the table. I figured that would occupy her until we got back. You're making a big deal out of nothing."

When I didn't respond, she added, "Why? Did she seem upset when you got to her?"

I considered the question for a moment and then shook my head. Now that I thought about it, mostly she'd just seemed busy—until I stood there talking to her and got her all worked up.

For the millionth time, I was reminded that the word that most aptly fit my pretty, green-eyed, easy-going girlfriend was "uncomplicated." Amanda was the most even-tempered woman I'd ever known. That was one of the things I liked best about her, and here I was making a big deal out of something small. I knew I should apologize to her, but the truth was she didn't even seem offended. She almost never got offended.

I gave her an apologetic smile anyway, discreetly pressing my shoulder against hers. "So what was it that you and Katy had to go and do?"

"Can't you tell?" She leaned toward me, and I caught a whiff of fragrance, spicy-sweet. I could also see now that her eyelashes were darker, fuller, and curling delicately toward her eyebrows.

I blinked, startled. "Perfume? And mascara?"

She smiled as she blushed. "Keep your voice down! It's only a little. And it's just for fun. When I take my vows I won't be able to do stuff like this anymore."

This wasn't the first time Amanda had done something outside the *Ordnung* for enjoyment. After all, she was still in her *rumspringa*. But the fact that she sometimes did such things even now that we were courting surprised me. If she was serious about our relationship, her perfume and mascara days were going to have to come to an end soon.

I decided not to go into any of that for now, as this wasn't the time or place. I just told her she should probably get back over to the group before they ran out of things to talk about.

We walked there together, and as we got closer, I was surprised and pleased to see that it wasn't just Priscilla and Katy and Cheryl any more. Their little cluster of friends had now more than doubled in size—and Priscilla was right there in the thick of things.

Amanda flashed me a huge victory smile and then dashed ahead to join in the fun. I held back, standing and observing as the group continued to grow. Amanda once again took charge of the introductions, as more and more people began to realize that their old classmate was now in their midst.

Watching, I caught Priscilla's eye once, but then others got in the way so that I could no longer see her.

Good.

Great, actually.

Priscilla was making friends. Amanda was enjoying herself. The volleyball teams still needed people.

I headed for the nets.

TWELVE

By the time I had played a couple of matches—my team lost the first and won the second—I was hot and sweaty and ready for a break. Not only that, but other people wanted to play, and Amanda, who had come to cheer me on in the last half of the second match, was letting me know she was hungry. I retrieved my hat from her and then we headed for the refreshment table.

"How's Priscilla getting along?" I asked.

"I haven't seen her since I came to watch you play. But I'll have you know when I left her she was talking to Matthew Zook." Amanda flashed me a knowing look and a dazzling smile.

"Oh, really."

"Yes, really. I told you they were perfect for each other."

I laughed. "So you did."

We had reached the food table, which had been grazed over multiple times. There wasn't a whole lot left. I grabbed a couple brownies and a little paper bowl of caramel corn, and Amanda reached for two tall cups of lemonade. I was still heated up from the game, so I guided her away from the press of people to a more open spot. She handed me my cup, and I guzzled half of it in one swig.

"How did she seem when you left her?" I asked, picking up the conversation again.

Amanda took a sip from her cup and held out her hand for a brownie. "She seemed fine."

"And how exactly did you get her to go over and meet him?"

"Oh, that was easy. She wasn't real keen on the idea, so we just switched it around. I left Priscilla with Katy and Cheryl, and I went and got Matthew instead. I told him there was someone I wanted *him* to meet."

Leave it to Amanda to get her way somehow. "Clever. And he just came?"

"I had to talk him into it. At first when he realized I was trying to connect him with a girl, he just said no thanks in the most absolute cutest way ever. I've never seen a man blush so fast."

I laughed, imagining the tall, curly-headed scarecrow turning red down to his boots. "How did you convince him?"

"I told him he'd be glad he came, that his life was about to change, that kind of thing."

"His life was about to change?" I exclaimed, laughing louder.

"When you meet the person you're going to marry, your life changes," she said matter-of-factly.

"So he went with you."

"After a couple more tugs he did."

"And?"

She grinned at me. "Look how curious you are now."

"Okay, so I had my doubts. Tell me what happened."

Amanda took a sip of her lemonade. "He went with me to where I'd left Priscilla with Katy and Cheryl, I introduced them to each other, and then we three girls just kind of one-by-one edged away."

"And the two of them were talking to each other when the last of you left?" I was having a hard time picturing it.

"Yes, they were. She was telling him about some apple orchard in Indiana."

I offered popcorn to Amanda and started in on it myself. I was about to admit to her that she'd proven me wrong when I saw Matthew walk past us toward a group of Amish men standing by the bonfire, which was now fully ablaze even though the sun had not yet set.

"When was it that you left Priscilla and Matthew together?" I asked.

"Just before I came to watch you play," she answered, taking a bite of her brownie. "Twenty minutes ago or so. Why?"

I nodded toward Matthew's retreating form. "Because there he is and she's not with him."

Amanda whipped her head around, a look of surprise and disappointment on her face as she swallowed the bite in her mouth. "Oh, for heaven's sake! Do I have to do everything myself?" She thrust her half-drunk cup of lemonade toward me and then huffed off to catch him before he reached his male friends.

I didn't want to be any part of her relentless matchmaking. I finished off the last of the popcorn, tossed the empty bowl and the cups into a nearby trash can, and set off to look for Priscilla. I didn't see her at first, and for a brief moment I wondered if she had taken off on foot for the three-mile walk home. But then it struck me where she might be. I headed out back for the long line of Amish buggies and carts—and the pasture that stretched behind them. Sure enough, I found her there, at the fence, with Willow on the other side. Priscilla was feeding my horse tufts of grass as she talked to her in a soft voice.

"Of course," I called to her. "I should have known I would find you back here."

She didn't turn toward me, nor did she reply. Instead, she stayed exactly where she was, her posture unchanged, her attention focused solely on my horse.

I tried again as I got closer. "Hey, Priscilla. What's up?"

Again, she did not acknowledge me nor even seem to notice my presence, so I kept moving forward until I came to a stop just a few feet behind her.

"I know you can hear me, Kinsinger," I said, crossing my arms in front of my chest.

"Yes, but I'm choosing not to, Miller," she replied, holding out another tuft of grass to Willow.

I smiled, the desire to fuss at her for hiding back here by herself quickly fizzling out. Considering the effort she'd put forth earlier, how could I complain now just because she'd withdrawn from the crowd for a bit? Some people simply needed more alone time—or, in Priscilla's case, more alone-with-a-horse time—than others.

But I had to say something. Finally, my tone light, I asked if there was some reason she found it necessary to trade in all the other party guests for a rendezvous with a mare. "Why don't you come back with me? We'll rejoin everyone."

"No, thanks. I mean, I gave it a shot, Jake, I really did. But if I had to spend one more minute making nice with all of those people, I was going to scream."

"I guess I can understand," I said, wanting to add that I was proud of the effort she had made but not sure how she would take a comment like that. "It's a lot of people all at once. I think you're doing great."

She seemed to linger a second over my words, as though she wanted to hold onto them. "Well, I told you I would try," she said a moment later. "So I did."

We were both quiet, the sounds of the party muffled by the row of buggies behind us.

Leaning forward, I propped my elbows on the fence and placed one foot on the lower rail. "So how come I'm not allowed to go near your horse, but you can use mine as your own personal party date?"

She smiled, though I couldn't quite tell if it was meant for me or for Willow. "It's not my fault your horse is a far better conversationalist than anyone I've met at this party thus far."

"I thought you told me animals can't talk."

"Exactly."

I chuckled. It seemed to me that that little forced bit of interaction had actually been good for her. Her sense of humor was encouraging. But as the evening still had a ways to go, it was probably time for her to come back to the party.

"I hear what you're saying, Priscilla, and I don't doubt you needed a break. But people are asking for you, wondering where you are."

"No, they're not. Don't exaggerate."

"Yes, they are. Amanda has Matthew by the arm, and she's on an all-out hunt to track you down."

"Ha. Okay. So maybe one or two people at most." Reaching down for more grass, she added, "Thanks, but no thanks. I'm fine here."

I watched her for a long moment, thinking how much more relaxed her posture was now, alone, than it had been while amid the throng. Regardless, there was another reason she needed to force herself to mingle. After a moment's hesitation, I decided to spell it out for her, even though I knew it may end up sounding cruel.

"I'm just thinking," I said, clearing my throat before I continued, "after your efforts to be friendly and approachable earlier, do you really want to cancel all that out now by being the girl who slipped away from the people at the party to talk to the animals instead?"

As I feared, my question seemed to strike a nerve. She glanced at me, her body stiffening, the smile fading from her lips and her eyes.

"I am who I am, Jake. Don't try to change me."

"I'm not trying to change you."

"Then why would you say something like that?"

I felt bad for hurting her feelings, but I needed to be honest with her. "Because of what you told me yesterday evening in the barn. You said you were tired of people pointing their fingers at you and reminding you how peculiar you are. If you really meant that, then you would try to be a little more careful when you're out in public. That's all."

She didn't reply, so I kept going.

"You make it too easy, Priscilla. By hanging out back here—by gravitating to the animals rather than the people yet again—it's almost as though you're daring everyone to do just that, to call you peculiar. Point their fingers. Assume you haven't changed one bit and you're still that odd little girl who used to talk to horses. I just don't get why it's worth it to you."

As my voice fell silent, I realized I probably sounded as though I had all the answers. Plus, I wasn't sure why it mattered so much to me anyway. Why did I care what people thought about Priscilla Kinsinger?

Judging by Willow's behavior, she hadn't liked my over-the-top paternal tone with Priscilla either. Jerking her head back, she snorted as if to say, "Cool it."

"Why don't we just go back to the party?" I said.

"No, thanks." Priscilla reached up to pat Willow, and the horse nuzzled her neck.

"Really. Come on. I promise I won't abandon you for any more volleyball."

She turned toward me, her expression questioning. "Abandon me?"

I shrugged. "Yeah. Like earlier. I probably shouldn't have left you and gone off to play like that."

"Why shouldn't you have? You're not responsible for me. Do you think you are?"

"What? No. No!" I stammered. "I mean, I just wish I hadn't rushed off like that."

She turned back to Willow and stroked the mare's long head. "I'm capable of taking care of myself, Jake."

"And that's why you're hiding back here with the horses?" I said, trading her little jab for one of my own and regretting it instantly.

"I happen to like being with the horses," she said, unfazed. "They don't have expectations of me. No preconceived notions of who I am."

So it was back to the poor-me routine. "That's because they are *horses*."

Priscilla nodded toward the party taking place behind us. "Go on, Jake. I won't take my uncle's buggy and leave you stranded here if that's what you're worried about."

"That's not what I'm worried about. Just pull it together for a little bit longer. Come back to the party with me."

"No."

Amos was going to want to know how the evening went. I needed to have a better story to tell him than this.

"Come on, Priscilla. Please?"

"I'm fine where I am. And why do you care so much whether I come back to the party or not? You barely know me."

Her words were another jab to my gut. Sure, we weren't exactly lifelong chums, but we'd been buddies, in a sense, way back when. If not buddies, kindred spirits at least. We'd also interacted a fair amount since she'd arrived Friday afternoon. What else had that been about except getting reacquainted?

"Fair enough," I said finally, trying to keep my voice light. "Maybe I don't know you, but in a way it feels like I do, I guess because of when you lived here before. I mean, I always enjoyed talking to you, even if you were younger. I thought you were a neat kid."

"Neat," she echoed.

"*Ya*. Smart. Funny. Quirky. Really in tune with the animals. I got a kick out of you. Now that you're back, I've been hoping we could become friends again."

Her eyes met mine and she held my gaze. "Why?"

"Because…" I did not want to lie to her. I did not want to lie to myself. It wasn't just because Amos asked me to help her out.

The truth was, I wanted to be her friend because I knew she was a person worth getting to know.

And there was more to it than that. It saddened me so much to see the way she was letting her life slip by her. Hiding from others. Isolating herself. More than likely still clinging to her grief.

"I just hate to see you so burdened," I said finally.

That caught her attention. "Burdened? By what?"

"You tell me. Grief? Loss? Guilt? I know what you went through…back then…was horrific, more than a lot of people could bear. I can't even imagine the depths of your pain. But God didn't design us to be tied to those kinds of feelings forever. If we are living in His will, then we surrender the right to wallow in our misery or blame ourselves or refuse to move on. That's all I'm saying."

She stared at me for a long moment. "You know what, Jake? You don't want to befriend me. You want to *fix* me. Just like you fix horses."

I shrugged. "Maybe I want both. Is that so bad? I have a lot to offer, and you could use a friend—especially one like me, who could help you learn not to get so worked up about everything."

She locked her gaze on mine, and I could see a flash of anger in her eyes.

"You know what I'm trying to say," I added, hoping to smooth things over. Why did my conversations with her always turn out like this? "You just get so, uh, emotional sometimes."

She barked out a laugh. "At least I feel something. I'm beginning to wonder if you, on the other hand, ever let yourself feel anything truly deep."

A moment of stunned silence passed before I spoke. "Pardon me?"

"You're one of those people with just one long, even keel, sailing through life down the middle in the shallowest water possible, where nothing ever really gets to them at all. I'm right, aren't I?"

I was dumbfounded, both at what she was saying and the fact that she was saying it. The fact that I was an easy-going guy was what people always said they liked best about me.

"At least I feel *something*," she continued. "And I'd rather feel too much than nothing at all."

She brushed past me and headed for the sea of young people out in the field.

"Hey!" I took off after her. "You can't just say that and then walk off."

"Why not? Nothing bothers you anyway."

She was talking in riddles. "Priscilla, you're not making any sense."

She said nothing as she lengthened her strides to get back to the crowd of people congregating at the bonfire.

"So *now* you want to go back to the party?" I said, matching her pace.

"Isn't that what you want me to do?"

Could she be any more incomprehensible? "What I want is for you to tell me what in the world you meant about me being a...what? A boat? A keel? That I don't care about anything?"

"Why? Because I hurt your feelings? Because you're angry with me?" She stopped and looked at me, her eyes narrowing. "Or because you're afraid I might be right?"

I shook my head, completely at a loss. When had this suddenly become about me? "No, I just—"

She turned away and resumed walking toward the happy sounds ahead of us.

"Yeah," she said. "That's what I thought."

Thirteen

Priscilla found a way to quietly blend in with the crowd when she and I returned from our strange conversation at the pasture rail, planting herself within a clutch of younger teens who welcomed her into their conversation. I rejoined Amanda and her little gang, which at the moment included Matthew. I had no doubt that in Amanda's mind tonight had not been a matchmaking failure so much as step one in a multiphase matchmaking plan. When she set her sights on something, she could be incredibly tenacious. From what I could tell, she'd decided to throw in the towel for now, but that didn't mean her little scheme was over. Far from it. In fact, I had a feeling it had barely begun.

That's why I decided it might be a good idea for me to try and get to know Matthew a little bit better myself. Amanda was a good judge of character, but it never hurt to get another perspective. Besides, it was going to take a very special sort of person to break through the walls Priscilla had erected. I might as well see if Matthew had what it took—or if I should advise my girlfriend to throw this particular fish back into the pond and rebait the hook.

Unfortunately, I didn't make much progress in my quest. Being rather shy, Matthew wasn't the easiest guy to get to know even under the best of circumstances. But tonight was noisy and chaotic with numerous interruptions, so after a few minutes of asking about his family's feed and tack store, and talking about the weather, I finally gave up. I was feeling too distracted now anyway.

I spent the rest of the evening hovering near Amanda but thinking about Priscilla. I just couldn't understand how she had come to such an odd conclusion about me, that I didn't allow myself to feel things very deeply.

Where had that come from?

Had she not noticed I was courting a girl I was nuts about? That I had the job of my dreams and a promising future as a blacksmith in my own right? That word was spreading about my services as a gentler of troubled horses? That I had a loving and supportive family who had always been there for me? Wasn't it obvious God had given me a wonderful life and I had much to thank Him for?

Clearly, she didn't know me at all.

When it was time to go, I looked for Priscilla among the group of girls with whom I had last seen her talking, but I found her instead back at the pasture rail with the horses, waiting for Amanda and me. Big surprise there.

While I hitched Willow to the wagon, I heard Amanda making small talk with Priscilla, asking if she'd had a good time and other similar questions. Priscilla's answers were polite and to the point. Yes, she had had a good time. It was nice to see everyone again. Yes, she was glad she came.

Talk of the event continued in the buggy at first, but the day had been long, and soon the conversation became Amanda's comments alone. Seeing how tired I was, she insisted I take her home first, even though my intention had been for the two of us to deliver Priscilla to the Kinsingers' and then loop all the way back to here. Though ordinarily I would have enjoyed some alone time with my girlfriend, especially after being surrounded by other people all night, I really was exhausted. It had been a long day, and I was counting the minutes to my pillow.

When I dropped Amanda off, I was glad to see that my date and perhaps future wife had washed off the mascara she'd been wearing earlier.

"Oh, good," I said, feigning great relief a moment later as I walked Amanda to her door. "You're back to being you again." We stopped at the steps to her porch. I touched the soft corner of her eye to clue her in as to what I was talking about.

She laughed. "It was just for fun. We wanted to feel...pretty."

I touched her chin with my finger tip. "You already are pretty. You don't need all that."

She beamed. "Good night, Jake."

"See you."

I climbed back in the wagon, turned around in the Shetlers' driveway, and headed for the road as I prepared myself for whatever might come next. Priscilla ran so hot and cold that I didn't know if she was going to stay silent the rest of the way home or if she would be lighting into me again, recounting even more of my supposed faults. I decided not to say a thing, hoping that would encourage her to keep quiet as well.

As it turned out, however, once we were on the road again, Priscilla broke our silence with an apology. Actually, she started with a cookie.

"*Pfeffernusse?*"

"Excuse me?"

"Would you like a *pfeffernusse?* I tucked some in my pocket at the party and forgot all about them until just now."

I glanced over to see that she held a paper napkin cupped in her hand, inside of which were nestled three of the tiny white powdery delights. With her delicate fingers, she lifted one of the cookies from the pile and held it toward me. I hesitated, wondering if this were some kind of peace offering. Finally, after a brief hesitation, I gave in and accepted the confection from her. Popping it into my mouth, I had to close my eyes for a second, it was that good. A few more of those might make me forget every cruel word she'd uttered.

"I shouldn't have said what I did earlier, Jake," she told me as she looked down at her hands in her lap. "It was mean and uncalled for."

For the second time that night she had completely surprised me with just a handful of words. "It's all right," I said quickly. "No harm done."

"No, it's not all right. You have been nothing but nice to me since I got here." She glanced up at me and then looked away again. "I am so sorry."

She fell silent with only the *clip-clop* of the horse's gait sounding between us. I was tempted to hold my tongue the rest of the ride and let her apology be the end of it. But the truth was, I wanted her to know she had not only been wrong to say what she'd said about me, she'd been wrong even to think it. Just because I didn't make a big show of emotions didn't mean I was a lightweight when it came to things that mattered. But how to explain that?

My first thought went to Tyler and Rachel and today's realization that they were expecting a baby. That moment had held both positive and negative feelings for me, both envy and happiness. Sure, my envy had not been the roiling, gut-wrenching type. It was more like a typical, mild, sort of sibling-related type. Neither had my happiness been the ecstatic, jump up and down over-the-moon type. It had been the normal, everyday I'm-really-happy-for-you-guys type.

So maybe that wasn't the best example.

I needed something else, but the longer I scrambled around for proof of my emotional depth, the more I came up empty. Staring out at the road ahead, I tried to picture the last time I had been thoroughly angry or sad or happy or excited about anything. But the truth was, I simply wasn't a man of extremes. I never had been.

"Look, I do feel things. I get angry when I see a horse that's been mistreated. And I truly love my parents, who are wise and godly and more wonderful than a kid could ever hope for. I almost punched a man once when I saw him get fresh with a girl in town. I nearly cried the day my nephew Tyler joined the church." I glanced at Priscilla and then back at the road again. "If I have an even keel, it's because that's how I am. It's just my personality."

She said nothing in return at first, and when I looked over at her I saw that she was wiping a tear from her eye.

"You don't owe me any explanations, Jake. I'm the one in the wrong. I really am sorry."

The tenderness of her tone struck me for some reason. I wanted to reach across, squeeze her hand and tell her I very much wanted her to understand who I was. Inside.

"Please don't feel so bad about it, Priscilla," I said instead. "Truly no harm done."

I figured we were finished talking about it after that, which is why I was surprised to find myself wanting to say more. I didn't know if it was the events from this evening or the lull of Willow's steps against the hard pavement or the door this conversation had opened in my heart, but I soon found myself telling Priscilla about the closest I'd come to feeling anything deeply in a while, when I went to the park earlier today and prayed that God would make His will for me known.

"The other night, at the big family dinner, you told us that the reason you were back here in Pennsylvania was because God made you come."

She cracked a smile. "I don't think I said it exactly that way."

"You know what I mean. You talked about God's will for you as if He had dialed you up and left a message in the phone shanty saying the bus leaves at four. You seemed so sure."

"I'm anything but sure, Jake. I don't know yet why He wanted me here. I thought I had an idea at first, but..." her voice trailed off for a second. "But that didn't pan out. At this point, your guess is as good as mine."

"I'm not talking about the why; I'm talking about the what. You may not know why He wants you here, but you do know that He does want you here. Right? Does that make sense?"

"*Ya.* I see what you mean."

"So how did you know? How could you be so certain you were supposed to come here, especially when you didn't even want to?"

She shrugged. "You are a man of faith. Are you telling me you've never been able to discern the will of God?"

"No, of course I have. I was absolutely certain of His will when I joined the church. When I went to farrier school too, for that matter. Even when I took the job with your uncle, God's will was very clear for me."

"So what is it you're asking, then? Obviously, you know how to discern the Lord's leading."

I sighed, wondering how to explain. "Yes, but those things—joining the church and going to school and getting a job—that was all stuff *I* wanted too. Trust me, it's not hard to find the will of God when it turns out you're both on the same page."

We shared a smile.

"But you came here against your own will. You didn't want to come, and yet you did anyhow—solely because God told you to. I just want to know, how could you be that definite? Do you hear the voice of God in the same, inexplicable way you say you hear horses?"

"I don't know how to explain it," she said thoughtfully. "I've always had the feeling that I would have to come back here eventually. But somehow, in the past few months, the weight of that feeling began to grow more heavily on me. In my prayer time, in my Bible readings, in my quiet moments. I don't know how I knew. I just knew. And for that reason I couldn't say no, even though I very much wanted to."

I nodded, considering her words. I wanted to bring up the part about the marriage proposal from the man with the eight kids, but I didn't. How that fit into this picture along with everything else was Priscilla's business, not mine.

"So you still haven't figured out yet why God wanted you to come?"

She shrugged. "Everything was such a mess back when I left six years ago—*I* was such a mess—so I've always expected that at some point I would need to return here and finish whatever it was I had left undone by going away in the first place. That's my best guess at this point, anyway. That there's something here left undone that I still need to do."

I let her words sit there between us for a long moment.

"Undone?" I said gently. "Like what?"

She sighed, clasping her hands in her lap. "I'm not sure. There are just so many 'if only's, you know? Maybe they need to be revisited from a more mature perspective."

I held my tongue, not quite certain what she meant but willing her to continue.

"And there are other things too. I've never seen my mother's grave. Never gone to the cemetery, never brought flowers. Never really said goodbye to her."

"Except for the funeral."

She gazed straight ahead, though whatever she was seeing was far in the past. "No, not even then. I couldn't go to the cemetery that day. Amos and Roseanna forced me to be there for the part that was done at the house. I had no choice. But when it was time to leave and head over to the graveyard, I simply couldn't do it. I got all worked up, screaming and crying and everything, so they finally gave in and let me be. They left without me. It never came up again."

As she said this, the Kinsinger drive came into view. Almost reluctantly, I turned onto the gravel.

"I could take you there sometime," I said as we came alongside the barn and I pulled Willow to a stop.

"Excuse me?" She paused with one hand on the dash rail.

"To the cemetery. Where your mother is buried. I could take you if you want."

She seemed to consider my words for a second and then turned her gaze toward me, the violet of her eyes reflecting the moon above like gems sparkling in the night.

"*Ich eschtimere sell,*" she said softly. *I'd appreciate that.*

Fourteen

The next morning I was up before the sun so I could prepare the second stall on my side of the barn for Natasha's horse. Owen and I had a full day ahead in the blacksmith shop; Mondays were usually that way. I wouldn't have another long stretch of minutes except for these before dawn.

After getting dressed and downing a quick cup of coffee from my French press, I went out into the damp, dewy darkness to the horse barns. Once inside, I remembered to take off my hat, and then I turned on the battery-powered shop light and greeted Willow with a scratch behind her ears. I gave breakfast and fresh water to her and to Patch, and then I mucked out both stalls and replaced the soiled straw with fresh while they were eating. With both of them taken care of, I set to work on the third, empty stall, the one where I would be putting January. I replaced the straw bedding, filled the trough with water, and even swept away the webs from the eaves. Patch was busy munching fresh hay, but Willow watched me with casual interest.

"I'm bringing in a new girl," I said to her, "and I want you to be nice to her, okay?"

She chuffed a response that sounded a lot as though she thought I was joking.

"I'm serious now. I want you on your best behavior. You too, Patch. Don't you be a bad influence on her."

Hearing the sound of my own voice in my ears, it suddenly struck me that I was no better than Priscilla. Talk about being an influence—that girl had me talking to animals the way she did.

When I was finished, I stood back to make sure the stall for January looked as nice as I could make it, considering the standards Natasha was used to. The result wasn't close to mirroring the Morningstar stables, but it was the best I could do. My stalls were small and rustic, but at least they were clean.

After that, I headed over to the Kinsinger side to take care of the other horses. When I got there and switched on the shop light, my breath stilled for a second. Voyager's stall was empty. My first thought was that he'd busted the hinges off his gate while we all slept and had run away. I quickened my steps to check that out and was reassured to see that nothing was amiss. That's when I realized his halter and lead rope were gone. The gate had been unlatched, not busted apart. Voyager had been led out.

I spun around, as if I expected the horse and whoever had taken him to be standing behind me. But, of course, except for the other animals, I was alone.

My mind raced. Had Priscilla run off in the middle of the night? It sounded silly, especially at her age, but why else would someone take out a horse under cover of darkness?

I strode from the stables, pausing in the driveway to look up at the main house. There was a single light on in Amos and Roseanna's upstairs bedroom, so I headed that way, intending to alert them to the situation. I was nearly to the flagstone path that led to the porch steps when I saw movement out of the corner of my eye. Turning that way, I spotted two figures far off to my left, slowly headed in my general direction. One was a horse, the other a woman, and they were luminescent in the fading, silvery moonlight.

Voyager and Priscilla, no doubt.

They walked at a lullaby speed as though they hadn't a care in the world. As their slow pace brought them closer, I confirmed that it was indeed Priscilla—and that she wore nothing but a nightgown with a light sweater over it. Voyager's lead, dangling from his halter, was dragging on the ground. Priscilla stopped for a moment and Voyager, after taking a few forward steps, stopped as well to look back at her. Priscilla stepped up to where the horse was, and the two of them just stood there. As she stroked his long neck, I could see that her hair was down and braided loose along her left shoulder. She pulled something from the pocket of her sweater and offered it to her horse. Voyager took it and chewed as Priscilla leaned into his neck.

She was clearly not expecting anyone to see her out here, not with her hair down like that and in her nightclothes. I was suddenly wishing I had stayed in the barn and not gone marching off to talk to Amos. It seemed a private moment between Priscilla and her horse—one that quickly grew even more private when she lifted her head toward the house that was now Owen and Treva's place, the very house she used to live in with her parents.

The house where both of her parents had died.

As I waited for the chance to sneak back to the barn unnoticed, Priscilla folded her arms across her chest and just stayed there, staring at the house. Voyager, availing himself of the pause in their walking, dropped his head to the grass and began to munch. They remained like that for a long time, silhouettes in the predawn glow, and I had no choice but to stay where I was too, watching them. This was starting to become a habit, Priscilla communing with horses and me ending up witness to it through no fault of my own.

The last time it happened, she'd been with Patch in the small stable and I had simply ducked back out unseen. This time, however, it wouldn't be nearly so easy to disappear unobserved. We were both outside, the morning light slowly starting to dawn. She hadn't noticed me yet, but I knew if I moved at all, she surely would.

Of course, I could have pretended not to see her, turned around, and walked back to the barn. Then, at least, she wouldn't have to be embarrassed because she would assume I was oblivious to her presence. But I didn't want to do that. It was almost as if I owed her this moment. If she was in prayer—and I had a feeling that maybe she was—the prayer would end the second I took a step, her quiet reverie broken.

So I stood there and attempted a prayer of my own, which was pretty much just a repeated plea for God to arrange it so that I could get back to the stalls unnoticed.

I don't know how long she stood staring at the house where her mother had died, but at some point, lights came on inside it. Both of us startled at the silent but noticeable intrusion, and then we startled again when lights came on in the kitchen of the big house as well. Priscilla snapped her head my direction. That was when she saw me, and it was as if I could read her thoughts.

Time had gotten away from her. She hadn't meant to stay out that long with her hair down and wearing nothing but a nightgown and sweater. And now Amos and Roseanna were up and in the kitchen, and Owen and Treva were up in their house, and I was standing between her and the horse barn. I saw her glance from the main house to the smaller house and then back to me. She was stuck. Amos and Roseanna would question her about why she had been out, before dawn, in her nightgown. And if Owen and Treva stepped out their kitchen door and saw Priscilla standing there in the grass in her bed-clothes, staring at their house, that would be even worse. And then there was the matter of Voyager, who needed to be taken back to his stall.

I knew what I could do to help her. I started for her, taking long strides. She turned her head this way and that, looking for an escape, but there was none to be found. I was close enough now to see the frustration in her eyes. When she opened her mouth to speak, I quickly laid a finger to my lips. As I neared her, Voyager lifted his head and whinnied, whether in greeting or warning, I couldn't tell. Priscilla reached back for his lead. When I drew close enough to them to speak to her in a hushed tone, I held out my hand for the rope.

"I'll take him back. Go in through the breezeway that leads to Mahlon's house. That side door is always open. You can head up the stairs in the main house through the laundry room. No one will ever know."

When she didn't answer, I simply took the lead and clicked for Voyager to follow me, which thankfully he did. I didn't wait for Priscilla to say a word. I just started walking away with her horse. I had taken only a few steps, and I sensed she had not yet moved.

I turned around. Sure enough, she was still where I had left her, the end of her long loose braid gently lifting on a tiny breeze. "Go on," I said softly to her. "I have Voyager."

This time, after I started walking, I could hear her moving across the grass behind me. When I turned a second time, I saw her, barefoot, hurrying to make her way toward the vegetable gardens and up the stone steps that led to the breezeway, which connected the main house to Mahlon and Beth's. I turned back and increased our speed, thankful that it had been a cool night and everyone's windows were closed. I was thankful as well for the strip of grass that ran along the gravel driveway, which deadened the sound of Voyager's footfalls.

I had just hung up his lead and halter when Amos stepped into the barn. He seemed surprised to find me in that particular horse's stall.

"Jake, I know you probably mean well, but I don't think Priscilla would appreciate you looking after her horse like that," he said warily. "You know how she feels. She doesn't want you or Stephen or me or anyone else dealing with him at all. Only her."

"*Ya*. I know. I just…just wanted to make sure he had fresh water. That's all." I walked out of the stall, closed the gate, and let the latch fall into place. Then I turned to Amos to engage him in a conversation so he wouldn't notice that Voyager's hooves and ankles were wet from dew.

"I have that *Englisch* woman coming today. She's bringing her horse here," I said, even though I knew Amos would not have forgotten.

"*Ya*. I remember. As long as it doesn't interfere with your other work I don't mind."

I moved to the first stall, as far from Voyager as I could get, to where Big Sam was stabled, and opened the gate. Amos followed me.

"How did it go for Priscilla at the young people's gathering last night? Roseanna and I were already in bed by the time she got home."

He waited for my answer with worry in his eyes.

"I think she had as good a time as anyone should expect of her, Amos. She just got back. She hasn't seen any of her old friends in six years. I'd say she did pretty well, considering. At least she made an effort."

He nodded, taking that in, but concern was still etched in the lines on his face.

I started in on the first stall, a bit taken aback when he jumped in to help. He usually had his own set of tasks to get to in the mornings before we opened the shops, so his actions surprised me at first. Then I realized he was hovering because he wanted to hear more. There wasn't much else about last night that I wanted to share with him though, so instead I asked him the question that had been in the back of my mind for a while now, ever since my conversation with Priscilla about God's will and why He had brought her here. She had made reference to the fact that there were "just so many if only's," which I hadn't really understood at the time. But later it struck me that she must have been talking about guilt. *If only I hadn't done this. If only I hadn't done that.* I felt bad that I hadn't recognized it before.

"Amos, do you think Priscilla blames herself for her mother's death? Sometimes I get that impression."

He faltered for a moment, nearly dropping the pitchfork. I was beginning to wish I hadn't asked the question, especially when he didn't say anything at first, but then he finally spoke.

"Why? What did she say?" He looked almost stricken.

"Um. Well, nothing actually. I just wondered if maybe she does."

"She didn't say anything?"

I stopped what I was doing and looked at him. "Say anything about what?"

"About…about what really happened back then?"

What really happened? Sharon fell down the stairs and died. "I'm not following you."

He sighed and leaned on his pitchfork. "I wasn't going to mention it because I don't know what the six years away have done for Priscilla. But the fact is, when she left here it was worse than her just blaming herself for her mother's death. She was saying that she *killed* her mother."

My mouth fell open. That was a little different than feeling responsible. "Really?"

"*Ya.* She said it to me and Roseanna right after it happened, so we brought in the bishop, and she said the same thing to him. She said she was the one who killed her mother."

"But Sharon fell down a flight of stairs, and Priscilla wasn't even in the house when it happened, right?"

Amos nodded. "She was in the barn. That's why we couldn't make any sense of what she was saying. The more we told her it wasn't her fault, the more upset she would get. It was terrible."

"Could no one help her see that because she couldn't hear her mother's cries for help, that didn't make her responsible for the woman's death?"

I paused in my duties to go to the open doorway and look outside. The night sky had peeled back and a tangerine glow was embracing the horizon. From where I stood, it was easy to see that the house that had been Priscilla's back then sat closer to where I was standing than any of the others. But "close" was relatively speaking, as it was still a good fifty yards away. How could anyone expect to hear someone calling for them from that great a distance? Moving back inside, I asked that of Amos, who was bent over a tack box, rummaging inside it.

"You can't make people see what they don't want to see, Jake. We tried. She just wouldn't listen."

I remembered the sight of Priscilla in the predawn moonlight this morning, her black hair against her nightgown as she stared at her old home. What had she been thinking about? Did she still see things that way, that she killed her mother? Or had time and maturity taught her that what happened that tragic day had ultimately been the will of God and not due to some action—or inaction—of her own?

I moved to the first stall and started back in with my work where I'd left off.

"Look, Amos. I want to help Priscilla find her place back here, and not just because you asked me to. But I really don't know what I am dealing with. What else ought I to know?"

He sighed heavily, as if just the thought of such a conversation was weighing him down. But then, as together he and I fed and watered the rest of the horses, cleaned out their stalls, and tidied up the barn, Amos told me everything he knew.

FIFTEEN

F or Priscilla, it all really started the day her father died of a heart defect
no one was even aware he had," Amos began. "She had always been so
close to him, much more so than with her mother."

He went on to say that Daniel seemed to understand Priscilla's quiet,
reserved nature in a way few others did, and that he often tried to help her
feel better about herself. He had a beautiful, ebony-hued Saddlebred named
Shiloh who was kind of a loner—Shiloh didn't care to be around other
horses, and the only human company he seemed to welcome were Daniel and Priscilla—and Daniel used to say that Shiloh and Priscilla were a lot
alike that way.

"He told her that particular quality was neither good nor bad," Amos said,
"it was just the way God made them. I knew she appreciated hearing that. It
made her feel a little less odd, you know?"

As a child, Amos continued, Priscilla preferred to spend her time outside
and in the welding shop with her father and uncle rather than in the house
with her mother or with friends. She could play by herself for hours on end,
lost in her own imagination. Sadly, though Sharon and Daniel had wanted
a large family, they were not blessed with any other children. Though they
struggled to accept this as God's will, it was especially hard for Sharon, who'd

had to deal a number of times with the physical and emotional pain of what Amos called "a very special kind of loss," by which he meant miscarriage.

Sharon had always dreamed of having a house full of children, and the fact that Priscilla was the only surviving child made her overly protective. She kept her daughter close to the house when she could, fretted over letting her do things that she thought were too dangerous, and didn't want her spending time with the horses, not even Shiloh, because of the threat of injury. Daniel served as a buffer between them, balancing his wife's excessively cautious nature with his daughter's need for freedom. It wasn't ideal, but they managed to make it work, at least while he was alive.

Daniel was a devoted husband and caring father, but because of a weak heart valve that none of them knew about, he tired easily and was never a man of great physical strength. He did have an eye for the artistic, however, so he ended up specializing in ornamental welding. That left the heavier and more functional jobs—including the farrier work—to Amos and his growing sons, Mahlon and Owen.

When Priscilla was ten, Daniel had a massive heart attack one night at the dinner table. There were no warning signs, and there had been no way of saving him. He was dead before help could arrive. Sharon and Priscilla took his death hard, as each lost the one person who seemed to understand her. After her father's death, Priscilla retreated further into her shell, distancing herself from every other girl her age and preferring to spend all her time with Shiloh. Sharon seemed adrift on a sea with no purpose other than raising Priscilla. Amos and Roseanna could see that Daniel had been the cushion between Priscilla and Sharon. With him gone, Sharon's hypervigilance was exasperating to Priscilla, just as much as Priscilla's moodiness was frustrating to Sharon.

In the middle of this tough time of transition, Amos's father died. He and his wife had been living in the *daadihaus* at the time, but after he passed away, his mother didn't want to live there alone. Her younger, widowed sister had a home in Gap, so she moved there instead, leaving the *daadihaus* empty.

Meanwhile, Amos knew that it was up to him to see that Sharon and Priscilla were taken care of in the wake of his brother's death. They would still need some kind of income, however, so once the *daadihaus* was empty, Amos proposed that they turn it into a guest cottage instead, one Sharon could manage. Amish bed-and-breakfast-type establishments were slowly becoming sought-after accommodations as tourists began to grow more and more interested in the Amish lifestyle. All the proceeds would be hers, Amos said, and she could run it however she wished. Sharon slowly warmed up to the idea, though she took several months to think about it before she agreed.

Finally, a year after Daniel's death, the guest cottage was ready for its first paying customers. Fliers were put up in visitors' centers. Colorful postcards were displayed at various retailers, including the quilt shop where Roseanna worked. Friends at the tourist bureau helped get it listed on the Internet and in several reliable guidebooks. As Sharon was an excellent cook and competent housekeeper, word got around—both locally and through online reviews—that the guest cottage at the Kinsinger place was a great option for tourists looking to stay at an authentic Amish homestead in Lancaster County. Noting Priscilla's keen interest in animals, Roseanna had suggested that she put together a petting zoo for the children of the families that stayed at the cottage. According to Amos, a smaller barn used to sit between Sharon's house and the guest cottage, so that's where they ended up putting the little zoo.

Priscilla, usually not one to show much outward emotion, had been exuberant about the idea. In short order two goats, a miniature pony, a yearling lamb, several chickens, and two rabbits had been installed in the part of the barn that Shiloh didn't occupy. Priscilla was in charge of keeping the animals and showing them to guests who wanted to see them.

For the first time in a year, it seemed that both Priscilla and Sharon had a measure of happiness. The guest cottage was booked nearly every weekend, even in the colder months, and there was a waiting list for the warmer months both weekends and weekdays, as well as during fall foliage. Amos and Roseanna hadn't minded too much the intrusion of tourists onto the homestead. For the most part, visitors respected the family's privacy and stayed near the cottage and barn. And it was clear that Sharon was enjoying making her own income and having something to occupy her day. Priscilla didn't cease to be a reserved person with the running of the petting zoo, but she seemed to miss her father less and didn't butt heads with her mother nearly as much.

At the end of the summer of Priscilla's fourteenth year, however, a crushing end came to this newfound and hard-won contentment.

It was early September, and Sharon had just picked a batch of acorn squash she was preparing to roast for canning. She also had guests in the cottage, a college professor and her teenage son who were spending the last four weeks of the summer before heading back to Long Island and school. The cottage guests, however, were not on the premises that autumn afternoon when Sharon, struggling to cut open an obstinate squash, accidentally slit her hand and wrist, slicing through a major artery. I couldn't imagine how someone could end up with an injury that bad just from a slip of the knife, but Amos reminded me how solid and hard acorn squash can be, not to mention how sharp the knives are an Amish woman uses when preparing vegetables for canning.

He continued on with his tale from there, and though I had already heard much of this part from Amanda, his version filled in some blanks. I asked about the actual cause of death, technically speaking, and he said that from the amount of contusions on Sharon's head and back, the county coroner determined that she died from multiple injuries, including blood loss and trauma to the head after striking it repeatedly as she fell the length of the stairs. How long she lay at the bottom of the staircase, or if she was conscious the entire time, or even if she cried out, was anyone's guess.

When he got to the part where Roseanna first discovered what had happened, Amos choked up for a moment. I wasn't sure if his tears were for the needless pain and suffering of his sister-in-law or for the shock and grief such a grisly sight had caused his wife. Probably both.

Amos said that as soon as the discovery was made, Roseanna dashed out of the house, screaming for help. Priscilla, who had been in the barn with Shiloh, was the first to come running. When she got there, Roseanna sent her on to the welding shop to get Amos and have someone call 911. By the time Priscilla returned to her mother, Sharon had already lost consciousness. She never regained it again.

Her breathing was ragged and shallow, and her skin deathly pale, when the ambulance whisked her away to the hospital in Lancaster, Priscilla riding along up front. Amos and Roseanna got there by hired car an hour later, but by then Sharon had already been pronounced dead.

Priscilla was inconsolable. Back at home later that night, they moved her from the smaller house up to a spare bedroom in the main house. There she cried and slept to the exclusion of everything else for the next twenty-four hours. A day later, when Sharon's embalmed body was delivered to the house by the mortician, Priscilla refused to see it or even go anywhere near it, even after Roseanna and some of the other women had finished dressing Sharon in her burial clothes.

As always following a death in the Amish community, the casket was placed in the main room, and Amos and Roseanna's home soon filled with people, not just the friends and relatives who had come to pay their respects, but also those who were there to take over the Kinsingers' housework and farmwork so that they would be unencumbered by the daily routine during this period of visitation and mourning. And though Priscilla had gone by then from a state of near hysteria to one of numbed shock, no one could convince her to come downstairs to view her mother's body one last time.

At the end of the second day, they knew something had to be done. So the next morning, before the house began to fill up with people again, Amos and Roseanna rounded up several close relatives and friends to talk to her, hoping one of them might make more headway than they had.

It didn't work. In the end, Priscilla simply lay in bed in the main house until it came time for the funeral. That was when Amos finally put his foot down, insisting that she rise from her grief and attend.

"I wasn't trying to be cruel," he told me now, as if he still felt bad about it, "but I knew she needed to do this. Funerals serve a purpose, you know? They remind us that it is God who holds life and death in His hands. They allow us to say goodbye."

According to Amos, Priscilla managed to make it through the hour-and-a-half service in a daze, but when it came time to head to the cemetery, she completely fell apart. There would only be a brief word said graveside, but she refused to go. At that point, the Kinsingers simply allowed her to stay home.

When they returned, they found her not back in bed in the main house as expected, but instead on her knees in front of her own home, her hair unbound and no *kapp* on her head. Amos stopped the buggy and they both climbed down. As he stood respectfully a few steps away, Roseanna knelt beside her niece and put an arm around her.

"That's when Priscilla said it the first time," Amos told me. We had finished with the animals and were standing just inside the barn, our gaze on what was now Owen and Treva's house but had once been the home of Daniel, Sharon, and Priscilla.

"Said it?" I echoed.

Amos shook his head. "That she killed her mother."

We both fell silent for a few moments. From where I was standing, I could see the place where Priscilla must have knelt and spoken those words.

"Roseanna told her not to think that way. It wasn't her fault. She told her that we live in a world where accidents happen. God called her mother home. But Priscilla wouldn't hear her. She just kept saying it was her fault, over and over. Roseanna told Priscilla she couldn't blame herself for being in the barn when her mother fell, no more than Roseanna could blame herself for being upstairs in the bedroom and not outside where she might have heard Sharon calling for help. But everything Roseanna said seemed to fall on deaf ears."

Amos exhaled heavily. "Then I stepped in, asking Priscilla why she insisted on blaming herself, but she would only shake her head and say that she should have been up in her room when her mother came for her, or she should have heard her calling for her from the barn. And that was that."

I nodded, trying to follow the logic of her claims. If Priscilla had been in her room, as her mother obviously thought she had, then the chain of events would have played out differently. Priscilla would have simply come down with Sharon, helped her bind the wound, and then gotten her to the hospital in Lancaster.

Barring that, had Priscilla been elsewhere but heard her mother's cries for help, she could have come running sooner, helped her bind the wound, and then gotten her to the hospital in Lancaster. Either way, the worst that would have happened was that Sharon would have had some stitches and a scar.

Instead, Sharon's cries—if there had even been any, which no one could ever know for sure—went unheeded. And without anyone aware of what was happening, she had lain at the bottom of the stairs and slowly bled to death.

"What happened after all that?" I asked, needing to know but not wanting to hear.

Amos slid his hands in his pockets as his shoulders drooped. "We had a rough couple of months of it, with Priscilla withdrawing into herself and her grief and her guilt more and more. We tried to love her and reassure her and pray for her and talk with her, but nothing seemed to make any difference. At fourteen, she should have been spiritually mature enough to understand that such a stance went against everything we know to be true about God. Sharon's death was His will, and Priscilla's refusal to accept that was an affront to His plan and a rejection of His sovereignty."

"How long before you sent her away?" I asked. I felt bad for putting it like that, but I couldn't figure out how else to say it.

"About three months. Lorraine and I had been corresponding back and forth, and we finally decided that if Priscilla was not getting any better here, perhaps she needed a change of scenery. The bishop and the ministers agreed, so we sent her off to my sister's with the hope that somehow she might find healing there. Heaven knows, she hadn't been able to find it here."

Amos and I gazed out at the scene that had been the site of such tragedy as we pondered the frailty of life and the fact that none of us could see the future or change the number of our days.

"So when you asked me if she still blames herself," he added, looking my way, "I wasn't sure how to answer you. I hope and pray she doesn't, but to be honest, Jake, I simply don't know."

He turned then and stepped back inside the barn to extinguish the lamps. I remained in the doorway, watching the last of the morning mist disappear.

Such a sad, tragic tale all the way around. I could only hope that even if Priscilla did still blame herself, she might be willing to take a fresh look at the circumstances from back then and recognize all the errors in her thinking.

If she'd let me help, I realized, I would probably start right here. I would get Priscilla to stand in this doorway and look out across the grounds at the house where her mother died and ask how her fourteen-year-old self could possibly have heard her mother's cries from that far away.

When Amos again rejoined me at the door, I said as much to him, but he turned his gaze from the scene in front of us to face me.

"Priscilla wasn't in *this* barn, Jake. I'm talking about the other barn, the one that used to be down there."

"Down there?"

"*Ya.* Between Sharon's house and the guest cottage, where Owen and Treva's vegetable garden is now. You don't remember it?"

I squinted, trying to think. "Vaguely."

"It was Daniel and Sharon's barn, so I guess you wouldn't have spent any time in there. I took it down a few years ago after a wind storm damaged it. But that's where Shiloh and the petting zoo animals used to stay. That's the barn Priscilla was in when her mother fell down the stairs."

I felt a tiny chill sweep through me at his words. Even in the dim light, I could see how close the buildings would have stood to each other. I felt certain that, had Sharon called out for help that day, her cries would have reached the barn.

I thought of last night, at the party over at the Chupps' farm, out back, when I called to Priscilla and she pretended not to notice.

I know you can hear me, Kinsinger.
Yes, but I'm choosing not to, Miller.

Maybe that was something Priscilla often did. Maybe it wasn't unusual for her to tune out people when she didn't want to hear what they were saying. Maybe she really had heard her mother's calls that day and simply chose to ignore them.

If so, then no wonder she blamed herself.

Sixteen

I didn't see Priscilla at breakfast.

Truthfully, I was okay with that. I couldn't mentally get past the sad notion that perhaps she *had* heard her mother calling her that day, hadn't realized the gravity of the situation, decided to ignore the summons, and learned too late at what cost. Her motivation would not have been malicious. Probably, she'd just wanted to be alone.

My prayer was that she would release any lingering guilt about what had happened that day, that she would come to accept that her mother's death had not been her fault, and that she would finally move past her grief, guilt, and pain, perhaps even to find happiness in the arms of a nice guy like Matthew—or maybe even the widower who was waiting for her back home. If Priscilla was anything like the horses I worked with and was harboring anxiety within the physical tissues of her being, then she needed to know it was okay to let go of what happened back then and move on. Perhaps at some point I might find a way to convince her of that.

Owen and I typically had a full day on Mondays, especially after all the spring plantings were in and people were back in maintenance mode, and today was no exception. Normally, from the moment he and I saw our first client at seven until we stopped for lunch at a little after noon, we were shoeing nonstop. Then, after the midday meal, we would be back at it until four or so. We had developed a routine on our busiest days. One of us would remove the old shoes, clean out the hooves, file them smooth, and essentially get them ready for either new shoes or the same ones, depending on their condition. A good set of shoes for driving horses, with normal wear and tear, could last up to a year. The other of us would heat the shoes in the propane-powered furnace, pound out imperfections, and then nail the hot shoe in place. The nails were driven into the hoof at an angle so that the pointed ends would emerge through the hoof and then were tamped down so as not to snag on anything. The process typically took about forty-five minutes per horse, and we usually had three horses in the shop at a time; two being shod and one ready for his or her turn. Sometimes the owner would tie up his or her horse outside at our hitching post and come back for it later. Sometimes they waited and watched while seated in wooden chairs by our appointment desk. Most didn't particularly care for the aroma of burned hoof and the accompanying smoke from the hot shoeing process, and we'd see them duck out. No one complained, though, because hot shoes meant the hoof wall was the exact image of the shoe.

Owen and I also made sure that every horseshoe we nailed was properly clipped—meaning we hammered an upward turn at certain places on the shoe while the metal was red-hot, so that the shoe could clip on the hoof. A well-positioned clip helped to hold the shoe in place and allowed for greater stability on multiple kinds of surfaces.

Shoes were attached on the palmar area of the horse's hooves, which were very much like the human toenail, anatomically speaking, though obviously larger and thicker. Getting shod didn't hurt a horse any more than trimming toenails hurt a person.

It could be stressful for them the first time or two, though. That's why we always told our customers to prepare for their young horse's initial set of shoes by gently tapping on the hooves with a hammer to get the animal used to the feel and sound of the shoeing process. Some horse owners didn't shoe their animals at all, which was called letting a horse "go barefoot." But even barefoot hooves still needed to be trimmed, just the way human toenails needed to be trimmed, especially if the horse wasn't active enough for normal wear to take place.

Among the Amish I knew, there were few horses left to lead a barefoot life. It didn't make sense not to shoe them, considering the role they played for a typical Amish family. Shoes for a horse meant protection, just as with humans. Considering how much time our horses spent on blacktop, to not shoe them would have been an act of cruelty.

I learned in farrier school that no one is completely sure as to who invented the horseshoe—a very important device considering that a horse's massive body rests on hooves collectively weighing less than eight pounds. A thousand years after the birth of Jesus, bronze horseshoes had become fairly common in Europe, followed by the manufacturing of iron horseshoes by the thirteenth century. It was an old trade, which was perhaps one of the reasons I was drawn to it. It was a changeless art, done by hand, and unaffected—as near as I could tell—by the technology age.

When I was in the shop, even awkwardly bent over with the bottom half of a horse leg sandwiched between my knees, I felt that I was participating in something that never lent itself to the unknown or the frustration of thorny matters. It was simple. Constant. Blissfully uncomplicated for the most part. It fit my life.

I never wanted to be one to lie awake at night wondering how to undo the knotted threads of a problematic existence. It seemed such a sad expense of time. If someone like Priscilla took that as a sign that I lacked the ability to feel…well, at least I was happy, which was more than I could say for her.

Our last horse for the day was shod by three thirty. I was grateful for a few spare minutes before Natasha arrived with January. While Owen settled with the owner, I headed back to my cottage to wash up and change into a clean shirt. As I walked back, I was at once mindful of the space in between Owen and Treva's house and my cottage, where there was now a wide vegetable garden, potato patch, and raspberry bushes. I mentally took in the proximity of their house to the garden's edges. The barn Amos had told me about had to have been a small one, with just enough room for one driving horse and smaller stalls for the petting animals. Perhaps Sharon had moved their driving buggy and cart to the main barns to give Priscilla room to have her petting zoo here.

I heard baby Josef crying from upstairs as I moved past, and that sudden sound drove home the fact that if the windows had been open the afternoon Sharon died, as they were now, and if she really had called out for help, anyone in the barn would have heard her. There wasn't that much space between the house and the far edge of the garden. So either the windows hadn't been open or Sharon had been too badly injured from the fall to cry out for help. Or Priscilla had heard her mother but pretended she hadn't.

I feared the third option was the real truth of the matter.

As I was making my way across the gravel, I saw Priscilla walking up the driveway from the road. She'd been out. She saw me about the same time. Our paths would intersect; there was no way they wouldn't unless she decided to turn back. Her speed faltered just for a second as she also realized this. But then she continued toward me with even more directness, as though she was composing her thoughts. This would be the first time we'd seen each other since this morning's incident on the front lawn in her nightgown, so even though I was fine, she was probably embarrassed.

"*Guder Nummidaag*, Priscilla," I said, when I reached her. She stopped and so did I.

"*Ya*. Good afternoon." Her brow was slightly furrowed, as though she had a buffet of choices of what she wanted to say to me and wasn't sure which sentences to pick.

"Been out?" I said, trying to act as though I didn't know this was uncomfortable for her.

"Uh, *ya*. I...Treva told me about a family in Paradise looking for a nanny three days a week. I went to meet with them."

"Oh. That's what Amanda does. For a family in Strasburg. She likes it very much."

"*Ya*...I know." She bit her lip.

"Did it go well?"

My question seemed to startle her. "What?"

"Your interview. Did it go well?"

"I guess. It's hard to tell. They said they have other people they still need to talk to."

"Ah. Well, if the Lord wants you to have the job, you will."

Priscilla nodded absently. "*Ya*."

"In the meantime, I need your help with something, if you don't mind. Any chance you might be free tomorrow afternoon around three or four? I have to get Patch back to Trudy, and I need someone to follow me over to the Fishers' in my wagon so I'll have a way to get home once I'm finished there. I was thinking if you do it, then maybe on the return trip we could stop by the cemetery. If you still want to, that is."

I expected her to look grateful, but instead she just nodded and said, "Okay. Listen, about this morning. I..." Her voice trailed off. She looked pained. I felt bad for her.

"You don't have to explain anything."

At this her creased brow arched slowly upward. "Excuse me? You think I owe you an explanation? About…about what you saw this morning?"

"No, I said you *don't* have to explain."

"I know. But by freeing me from having to give an explanation, you're implying I owe you one in the first place."

I frowned, trying to follow her crazy logic. Why did every conversation with Priscilla have to be so difficult?

"*Is* there something you want to explain to me?" I asked.

"No. I'm saying the opposite, that I don't owe you an explanation."

Was she nuts? "That's what *I* just said. *You don't have to explain.*"

"Which means, essentially, that I *should* but that I don't *have to*. There's a difference, Jake."

I simply stared at her. I'd never met a person who could complicate a matter as quickly as she could. Being around her was mentally exhausting.

"You know what? Never mind." I started to walk away.

She was quiet for a moment but then called after me. When I heard my name, I stopped but kept my back to her, the sound of footsteps crunching in gravel as she ran forward.

"I'm sorry," she said, coming to a stop behind me and lowering her voice as she continued. "I do owe you something. My thanks. I just…I want to thank you for helping me out this morning. For…for taking Voyager back to his stall. I'm grateful. Really, I am."

I could hear a tenderness just under the surface of her resolve to be stoic—a desire to be understood and to have my friendship without conditions. Turning toward her, I could almost see this softer side shimmering there. It suddenly occurred to me that few people had done for Priscilla what I had this morning. I had helped her—truly helped her—without a word, because I had known instinctively what she needed. And now she felt I was retreating back to the place most people took when they were around her because she was so hard to get close to—the place of not trying hard enough to understand her, the place of wanting information from her.

Explain yourself, Priscilla, is what she heard from everyone, even though none said it exactly that way. *We don't get you at all.*

"I want to be your friend," I said, as gently as I could. "But I'm not perfect. I honestly didn't mean to suggest I was owed an explanation for what I saw this morning. But as a friend I will say that it's time to decide whether you want to live like this the rest of your life."

"Like what?"

I sighed heavily, realizing there was just no getting around my suspicions, that she *had* heard her mother that day but had simply chosen not to respond. Though I didn't put it in those words, I blurted out more than I'd intended to say. "You don't trust anybody with the truth. You don't even trust yourself with it."

Her mouth dropped open, but she said nothing.

"Here's the truth as I see it," I went on, knowing I had no choice but to continue. "You don't want to face what really happened six years ago, and you don't think you deserve to be happy. You hang on to the events of the past— which I'm sure are just a little bit different than what everyone else believes them to be—and you've guilted yourself into thinking you're not worthy of a life with any kind of happiness in it."

She stared at me.

"Tell me I'm wrong," I challenged, softly, and with as kind a tone as I could muster.

She was still staring at me, wide eyed, when a truck and horse trailer pulled off the road onto the gravel driveway.

January was here.

Priscilla brushed past me and started for the house, the question between us unanswered.

Seventeen

Natasha stepped out of the driver's side of the same truck that had brought me to her stables two days before. In the cab was a pair of little girls. After they climbed out, she introduced them as Hope and Samantha.

"Samantha's eight and Hope is six," Natasha said, looking down at her golden-haired daughters. They had surely seen plenty of Amish men before, living as close as they did to Lancaster County, but I had the impression that they had perhaps not had the opportunity to meet and talk with one up close before. They stared at me with smiling eyes and shy grins. I had asked Stephen to help me once they got here, so as he emerged from the barn, I waved him over and introduced him to them as well.

"Stephen is ten," I added with a nod.

They both gave him shy smiles in return, but then his dog, Comet, an eight-month-old Labrador mix, appeared too. The girls instantly left us and gravitated to the dog, who began to furiously wag his tail.

"Don't let him jump on them," I cautioned.

"I won't," Stephen replied, seeming offended that I'd even said it.

"Mommy, look how cute!" Samantha cried.

Both girls oohed and aahed at the excited pup as Natasha turned back to me. "I admit I was starting to have second thoughts about bringing January here. I hope this is a good idea, you know, putting her in a strange place when she's already so anxious."

I could tell she wanted me to set her mind to rest, but I knew I couldn't guarantee anything.

"I hope it's a good idea too."

Thankfully, Natasha got my sense of humor and gave a laugh.

"Seriously, though," I continued, "if I can convince January that she's safe with me and can let down her guard, she'll allow her pent-up tension to release and then she can move past it. I really do think this stay will help far more than it could ever hurt."

Natasha exhaled heavily. "Well, I guess it's worth a try, right? Nothing else has been effective."

One of the girls squealed in delight as Comet licked her face.

"Mommy!" Samantha called out. "We want a dog like this one! Please?"

"Please?" chimed in Hope, the two sisters jumping up and down as if that might help convince their mother.

"Girls. Quiet. Come on. I'm too busy with the horses. I don't have time for a dog too."

They tried to object, promising to care for it entirely themselves, but she cut them off with a soft but firm, "That's enough. Case closed."

The two little blondes looked like a pair of deflated balloons. But then Stephen asked if they would like to see his dog do a trick, and they were happy and giggly again.

"Stephen, why don't you and Comet take the girls over by the house a ways while we get the mare unloaded from the trailer?" I said. I didn't think all this extra noise would be helpful.

He nodded, whistled for his dog, and then the three of them plus the bounding Lab headed for the lawn in front of the house, away from the trailer and perhaps an agitated horse.

"Shall we get her out?" I asked.

"Sure."

Natasha and I walked to the back of the trailer, a glistening, white contraption with the stable's logo painted on both sides.

"We'll just take it slow and easy," I said.

"Sounds good to me."

Natasha lifted the pin on the latch of the trailer door and raised the lever.

She swung the door open slowly. January was parallel to the trailer entrance, but with the chest-high triangle-shaped gate in place, all I could see of her was her back end. She grumbled, moving in place. I could see the muscles on her flank tightening.

"Want me to unlatch the gate or unload?" I asked.

"I think I got her," Natasha said as she stepped in with a lead rope in her hand.

"You sure?"

"She went in okay. Sort of." Natasha bent over and maneuvered herself under the triangle-gate. I heard her speaking in gentle tones to her horse as I stepped inside as well.

"You all set?" I said, with my hand on the latch.

"We're ready."

I lifted the latch and slowly fanned the gate to the side. January swiveled her head wide eyed and yanked on her lead.

"Whoa. There's my good girl," Natasha said softly, but January wasn't interested in tender words. She yanked her head again and took a step backward. Her rear end touched the trailer's side.

"Get her out," I said, jumping away myself.

Natasha swung the lead to the right and moved out of the way as January quickly jerked herself toward the open door. The horse took the step down too fast and hit the ground with a clatter that set her off. She reared up and the lead came loose from Natasha's outstretched hand. I dashed forward to grab it, along with the nose ring on January's halter.

"Whoa. It's all right, girl," I said gently. "Nothing to worry about. You're fine. You're fine."

I let January walk a couple circles in the gravel as she tossed her head and grunted her disapproval at how her afternoon had turned out. Natasha stood watching, doing shoulder circles with her right arm.

"Are you okay?"

"It's not the first time I've had a horse try to pull my arm out of its socket. I'll be fine."

For the next few minutes I just let January walk and stop when she wanted. Several times she seemed as if she might bolt, but then she'd look at me almost as if she needed instructions on what she should do instead. From the lawn, I could see that Stephen, the girls, and even the dog were watching

January. Just as I was about to turn the animal and attempt a slow walk to the barn, I caught a glimpse of Priscilla in an upstairs bedroom window. She backed away a step as soon as our eyes met but did not leave.

She was watching too.

I took a few steps toward the barn. January took only one and then stopped.

"How about if you walk in front of us," I said to Natasha.

Natasha did as I suggested and clicked to her horse. "Come on, girl."

Again I took a few steps toward the barn, but January took only one and stopped.

"Got anything from home with you?" I asked Natasha. "Something that smells like her own stable?"

"Just some tack supplies and her feed."

I thought for a moment. "Maybe a horse blanket?"

She frowned. "I didn't think to bring one. That was dumb."

"How about the girls? Would seeing them make her think she's at home?"

Natasha cocked her head. "I don't know. Maybe. The girls aren't in the barn all that often."

"We could try it."

"All right." Natasha turned to the girls on the lawn. "How about it, girls? Can you come show January how easy and fun it is to walk into the barn? Stay at a distance, though. She's nervous and that makes her unpredictable."

The girls sprang to their feet and Stephen joined them. Soon all three kids and the puppy were standing at the entrance to the barn. They were close enough for January to see them but not so close that she could hurt them.

Samantha clicked like her mother had. "Come on, January! Come on!" She clicked again.

And then to our surprise, January moved forward without a trace of dread.

"She's coming!" the girls squealed.

They dashed inside, with Stephen and the dog following.

"Get all the way to the back there and stand by the gate to the empty stall, *ya*?" I said. The kids dutifully obeyed. January willingly walked the rest of the way, the children easing backward as directed. We drew closer, her gaze roving between the girls and where I was leading her. I got her inside the stall, complimenting her the whole time, telling her what an amazing horse she was.

I backed out and closed the door.

"Let's let her get used to the feel and smell of the place." I said as I latched the door. The five of us stood and watched her.

"I've never seen a horse with an imagination like this one," Natasha said as she leaned against a rail. "It's as though she thinks there's danger lurking everywhere. And the more she thinks about it, the more she convinces herself all is lost."

"But she wasn't this way when you bought her, right?" I asked, trying to remember the details of what Natasha had told me when I was out at her place on Saturday.

"I sure didn't see it. And I've talked to the owner since then. He said she was fine when she was showing. But he admitted he didn't spend much time with her. He had professional trainers and groomers taking care of her. He checked all her medical and training records. Nobody noticed a behavior change before she left."

"And her transportation to you from her old home? That went well? No accidents or near misses or squealing brakes or anything?"

Natasha shook her head. "No. Eric drove her for me himself. It was a long trip, but an uneventful one."

"Maybe she misses being in the shows!" Samantha said.

Natasha smiled down at her daughter. "Maybe she does, sweetheart."

As if she knew we were talking about her, January swiveled her head around to look at the five sets of eyes trained on her.

Then the kids ran over to Willow's stall next and began trying to pat her on the head. From his pocket Stephen produced sugar cubes, and soon the girls were squealing and laughing at the feel of Willow's velvety lips on the palms of their open, sugar-cube-bearing hands.

"I hope I didn't make a mistake buying January," Natasha said as we watched them play. "I paid a lot for her, maybe more than she was worth considering her number of wins and her early retirement."

"Why did she retire early?"

"Her scores started to taper off, and her owner felt it best to quit before the drop in her standings became noticeable to everybody. It happens all the time. She's still a beautiful horse."

"That she is," I replied, taking in the graceful line of her crest and withers.

"And it's not as though I plan to show her or anything. I bought her for breeding purposes."

"Right."

"Anyway," Natasha said, suddenly all business again. "How long are you thinking this might take?"

I shook my head. "As I said the other day, let's start by giving it a week and then we'll see. What I can tell you is that if I've made absolutely no progress at all in that time, I may not be the one to help her."

"But you think you will, don't you? Make progress, I mean?"

I smiled. "I'm optimistic. I've seen this kind of behavior in a lot of horses."

She turned her gaze to January again. "She's such a lovely animal. And from good lineage. I just know she'd have beautiful foals."

We stood there a moment longer, but the girls became bored once they had used up all the sugar cubes. They scampered out of the barn, the dog happily barking at their heels, with Stephen following them. Natasha and I made our way back to the trailer, and together we unloaded the feed she had brought for January, as well as the tack supplies she had tucked inside a gray Rubbermaid tub.

"Well, I guess that's it then." She cast a glance toward the barn where her troubled horse now stood out of her line of sight.

"For what it's worth, I haven't met a horse yet I haven't been able to help," I assured her. "And I don't mean to sound prideful. Horses will let down their guard when they trust the person in charge to be their protection."

Natasha brushed a strand of hair from her face and furrowed an eyebrow. "Not *all* horses, though."

I shrugged. I had meant what I said. "I'd say all horses."

She cocked her head and laughed, but there was no amusement behind it. "Clearly you haven't met Duchess," she muttered, almost under her breath.

I was instantly curious to know more about the beautiful white horse that Eric wouldn't elaborate about over the phone and that Ryan had said had issues. Whatever those issues were, my desire to fix was instantly on supercharge.

"May I ask what's wrong with her?"

Natasha turned her head toward me. "She's fine. She's perfect—at home. It's when I take her to competitions that she goes nuts. The crowds make her crazy. She's a show horse, so that's a huge problem. Huge."

I wanted to know more, but my follow-up questions stuck in my throat when I saw the look on Natasha's face. Clearly, this was a topic not open for discussion.

"Well, I would help you with her if I could," I said, knowing full well she would never bring a horse worth more than two hundred thousand dollars to this place—nor that I would want her to.

She cast another glance toward the open barn doors. "Tell you what, Jake. You figure out what's bugging January, and I just may take you up on that."

I quickly replied that I was only kidding, but she swung her head around to face me. "Well, I'm not. I have to find a solution by the time the horse show rolls around in September or everything's going to fall apart. And I mean everything."

Before I could respond, the girls came running toward us with Comet happily chasing after them. Stephen was not far behind.

"All right, girls. Time to head home," Natasha said brightly, as though we had just finished up a conversation about equine hoof health.

The girls both frowned.

"We want to stay and play with Comet!" Samantha whined.

"You've been playing with the dog since the moment we got here. We need to get home, and these people need to get on with their day. Come on. In the truck."

Natasha's daughters grudgingly obeyed.

I suddenly remembered I had made an estimate of what I was planning to charge Natasha for January's stay. I had settled on a hundred and fifty dollars for the week. That seemed like a fair price considering January had her own food and I wasn't a professional. I was planning on giving Amos a third of that. I felt fifty dollars was fair compensation for the use of his stable and pastures.

"Oh," I said, pulling the sheet of paper from my pocket. "Here's what I am suggesting as a fee for January's stay here. I probably should have shown that to you first."

Natasha took the piece of paper and barely glanced at it. "That's fine." She shoved it in her pants pocket and then gazed back toward the barn, a slightly concerned look on her face.

"I will do my best to help your horse, Natasha," I said. When that didn't seem to reassure her, I asked, "Would you like to see her one more time before you go?"

She shook her head. "No. I don't want to mess anything up. She was okay when we left."

"You can call anytime. We're not always in the shop, but when we are, someone usually answers the phone. Or just leave a message if they don't."

"Thanks. I appreciate that. Okay, then."

"I'll secure the trailer door."

As she got inside her truck, I closed the door, lowered the latch, and set the pin. I stepped away so she could see I was finished.

"You have plenty of room to turn around," I called. I moved to the edge of the barn to help her with clearance, and a few moments later the truck was making its way down the gravel drive to the street.

Natasha honked once, and then they turned onto the road.

Eighteen

It seemed best to let January have some time to recover from her trip from Chester County, so I didn't attempt to work with her after Natasha and the girls left. The horse seemed a bit uneasy when I brought in her feed and tack, and she kept an ear trained toward the open barn door as though she expected something or someone to come running through it. I distracted her by offering her a few carrots, and then I took Patch out to the round pen for what I hoped would be my final session with him.

This time instead of hats on stakes, I held one in my hand, waited for Patch to stretch out his neck to smell it, and then touched Patch lightly with its brim. I started with his neck, then moved down to his midsection, touching and releasing and waiting for Patch to stand perfectly still as I moved about him with the hat. When my hat-touching elicited a calm response, I rewarded him with a carrot chunk. When he startled, I waited and tried again. After an hour of this, he was allowing me to touch my hat to his face and neck with only a slight swish of his tail—a huge improvement and proof to me he was ready to go home. It would be easy to show Trudy how to do the same pressure-and-release technique with her father's hat so that Patch's "trust conditioning" could continue.

I was getting set to lead him out of the round pen when Roseanna showed up at the rail. Judging by the basket of carrots on her arm, she'd been pulling up the vegetable component for tonight's supper and had decided to check on our progress on her way back to the kitchen.

"Looks like you won't need another bucket of goodies for that horse," she said, smiling at me.

"You were watching, eh?"

"It's pretty amazing how you did that. I once saw Mahlon try to calm a horse spooked by its own blanket—but with completely different results." Roseanna laughed. "He was running around behind that mare, trying to get close enough for her to see it was nothing to be afraid of. The horse wanted nothing to do with that blanket. It was pretty funny to watch."

I laughed too as I walked Patch toward the pen gate. "I can imagine. Guess Mahlon didn't know that horses are more inclined to go toward something that's moving away from them rather than coming at them, especially something they would prefer to avoid."

Roseanna swung the gate door open for me. "Funny what horses will fear, isn't it? Like this horse here. Imagine an Amish driving horse being afraid of a hat."

I patted Patch's neck as we moved past Roseanna. I reached for my own hat waiting for me on the fence post and slowly put it on my head. Patch faltered for only a moment.

"Actually, it wasn't about a hat. It was about what the hat represented. Same with the blanket and Mahlon's horse, I'm thinking."

"Interesting," she said, closing the gate behind me. "I have never really thought much about why horses spook so easily."

We started for the barn, and I liked it that Roseanna fell in step with me, obviously wanting to learn more.

"Horses tend to react to whatever is happening around them or to them with an eye to flight mode. When they see or hear or feel something, that stimulus becomes information that they must naturally react to. They're wired to react. We humans do the same thing, except that we have a capacity for reason a horse does not. A horse will see a dark spot on the road and think it is a hole he could fall into, break his leg, and then be unable to flee from danger. The dark spot might be just a puddle of water or a patched piece of tarmac that's a different color than the rest of the asphalt, but to the horse it looks like a hole, so it's a hole."

"How do you tell a horse that a patched piece of tarmac isn't a hole?" she asked as we neared the barn door, where she would likely leave me.

"A horse must learn to put his confidence in his owner or handler in such a way that he will respond in obedience rather than react in irrational fear. It's a matter of patience and consistency. And a little ingenuity, I guess."

"You make it sound simple, Jake, but I'm sure it's not," Roseanna said, smiling. She patted Patch's neck, a silent gesture I found very affirming. "If only people were that easy to train."

I smiled ruefully. "Funny, I was just thinking that same thing earlier." With a glance toward Roseanna, I lowered my voiced and added, "About Priscilla."

I didn't want to overstep my bounds here, but Roseanna looked curious, not offended, so I kept going.

"The more I get to know her again, the more it seems to me that she has the same problem many of these horses have, that she's mentally stuck on something and can't move past it. I'm trying to coax her into trusting me to be her friend in the hope I can help her move past what she fears. Like I did for Patch, but in a different way, of course."

"Do you think fear is the real problem here, not just grief?"

I shrugged. "At least part of it. Fear of trusting others. Fear of letting go of the past. Fear of believing she's not entitled to happiness."

Roseanna's eyes took on a deep sadness as she nodded. "I see your point."

"To be honest, to me Priscilla just seems kind of locked up inside, you know? As though she's chained to the past and can't find a way to forgive herself and move on. It's so sad. I wish I could help somehow."

Our eyes met, and Roseanna gave me a look of gratitude as she reached out with her free hand and patted my arm.

"I think you already have, Jake. You've helped her more than you know."

"It's not enough, though. I just keep remembering her as a little girl before either of her parents died. She was such a unique child, and I mean that in a good way. The first time I ever met her was inside the blacksmith shop, where she was lining up her dad's welding tools and naming each one. Smart as a whip, that kid, and not one ounce of fear around horses that were ten times her size."

I glanced at Roseanna, who was smiling now despite the tears that had pooled in her eyes.

"That's the girl I want to help," I added, "the one who knew what an angle grinder was by the time she was seven."

Roseanna nodded and took her hand from my arm. "Then in my prayers, I will ask God to give you insight and wisdom for how you can continue to help." With that she turned and headed for the house, where her chores awaited.

Feeling thoughtful and subdued, I led Patch to the barn, and Stephen soon joined me. We started on our afternoon tasks, mucking out the stalls, bringing in Mahlon's and Owen's horses—Stephen had taken them out to the back paddock earlier for air and exercise—and doling out the second feeding of grains for the day. We also raked the beds down, prepared the feed for the morning, gave everyone a quick brush, and checked all the water troughs. January seemed to grow more relaxed as we worked, which relieved me greatly.

Over on the Kinsinger side, we purposely left Voyager alone so as not to get ourselves into trouble with Priscilla, though he watched us with interest, snorting a time or two to let us know he was there in case we'd forgotten.

When we were about done, Amos arrived from an errand in town, and I took Big Sam from him while he put the buggy away. By five thirty we were all finished in the barn, Stephen and Comet heading home as Roseanna rang the bell for Amos's supper. As I stepped out into the late afternoon sunshine, she called out to me from the porch on the big house.

"You can come too, Jake."

I hadn't made other plans, and all I had at the cottage in the way of supper options were a few cans of beans and some soup. It wasn't hard to accept her offer.

In the excitement of getting January situated and then having the evening chores to do, I had forgotten about my last encounter with Priscilla, earlier, just before Natasha came. She hadn't been very happy with me then, and I was reminded of that now when I saw the look she gave me. After washing up in the mudroom, Amos and I stepped into the kitchen, where Priscilla was just putting a bowl of peas on the table. She stopped midstep to flash me a frown of displeasure.

At least that's what it looked like to me. She quickly turned away so I didn't have time to study it.

After our silent prayer, Amos wanted to hear all about the new four-legged client I had in the barn. I explained the situation with January and what I hoped to be able to do for her. At first, he just listened with polite interest, but then Roseanna jumped in, telling him with enthusiasm about our earlier encounter and what I had taught her about calming an agitated horse. He listened without comment, but I felt that his respect for my little side business definitely got a lift.

As we were finishing up the meal, we heard a buggy outside, making its way across the gravel.

Roseanna peered out the window. "It's Amanda," she said, and she then turned to me. "Think she'll want a plate?"

"She's probably eaten already," I said. I rose, intending to secure Amanda's horse and cart to the hitching rail out front, but she was already looping her reins when I stepped out. She smiled and waved me over.

"This is a nice treat," I said, to which she smilingly replied that she wasn't here for me. She'd come for Priscilla.

"I have a surprise for her," she added, eyes bright with anticipation. "Just the best idea ever."

"Oh? Best idea ever, huh? Then somehow it must involve double chocolate chip cookies."

She grinned. "I could arrange that, I suppose."

"Yeah?"

She nodded. "A welcome home party for Priscilla!" she whispered with delight as she eyed the windows of the house.

"Oh." That would be a great idea if Priscilla were the type to like parties, which I knew she was not.

"Here's the best part. Guess at whose house!"

"Uh...yours?"

She slapped my chest. "Of course not. The Zooks'!"

"Where?" I was sure I hadn't heard her right.

"Matthew Zook's house!"

I tried not to grimace. Amanda had to have been working overtime to make this happen. Talk about matchmaking. I feared this was pushing things too far, too fast.

"What's wrong with that?" she pouted.

"Um...well, isn't it a little soon? They barely spent half an hour together at the volleyball game. Besides, he's a guy. I doubt he's ever thrown a party before."

"Very funny, Jake. Katy, Cheryl, and I are the ones really throwing it.

Matthew's just providing the house where it will happen. It wasn't that hard to talk him into it. I think that must mean he really likes Priscilla and wants to get to know her better."

"Okay. Maybe," I said, with plenty of doubt in my voice.

"Matthew's mom thinks it's a great idea, and she's even letting me be in charge of organizing it. It's perfect. We'll have the party there, and Matthew and Priscilla will have to spend time together. It will be at *his* house. And she will have to stay for the whole thing because she's the guest of honor. See?"

I wanted to tell Amanda that this was probably a bad idea. Almost certainly a bad idea. But when I looked into her pretty green eyes and saw the delight that radiated there, I didn't want to be the one to extinguish it.

"Come on! Let's go tell Priscilla," she said, and I had no choice but to follow, like a tail on a kite.

When we got inside, Priscilla was at the sink scraping plates, Roseanna was gathering dishes from the table, and Amos was finishing up his last bite of meat loaf. Priscilla turned slowly, a forced half smile on her lips when she saw Amanda.

"Oh, Priscilla!" Amanda rushed to her. "I have the best news! We're throwing you a welcome home party on Friday night."

"Pardon?" Priscilla said, a sheen of dread appearing in her eyes in an instant.

"At the Zooks' house. It's going to be so much fun. You'll be able to reconnect with even more people than you did at the volleyball game."

"That's wonderful," Roseanna said from the table. "Isn't it, Amos?"

He nodded in happy agreement and nearly winked at me.

"What can I contribute?" Roseanna asked.

Amanda turned to face her. "Thanks for offering. I'm in charge of the food. How about you bring your seven layer bars, the ones you made for the Christmas pageant last year? Everyone loves those."

"Be happy to," Roseanna replied, smiling wide.

"And if you don't mind, pass the invitation along to any other family members you think might like to come, would you? Beth could do her artichoke dip, and maybe Treva could bring a vegetable dish."

As the two of them talked recipes and who was bringing what, my attention was on Priscilla, standing at the sink, dripping water on the tops of her bare feet without even realizing it. I could see the wheels in her mind turning, trying to figure out what to make of this new circumstance. She looked my way and our eyes met.

I smiled wanly and shrugged, wanting her to know I understood her reluctance. She turned back to the sink as if to say I understood nothing.

Amanda stayed for another hour or so, first for some of Roseanna's triple berry Bundt cake, and then she and I sat outside on the porch for a little while until I convinced her to head back home before darkness fell.

As I walked her to her horse and cart, she leaned into me. "Matthew is such a nice guy," she said softly, as though Priscilla were right behind us, intent on hearing our every word. "I was over there today talking with him and his mother, and he was so kind and polite."

"Wouldn't it be easier to have this party at your house, though?" I asked, hoping to lessen the impending awkwardness for Priscilla.

"Can't. My *daed* found some dry rot in the floorboards. He'll be tearing out part of the living room floor in the next few days. And don't even suggest that we have it here, where Priscilla can disappear to her room if she gets the notion. It's best to have it at Matthew's so she can meet his parents. They are so nice. And Matthew's *mamm* wants to have the party there. So stop over-thinking it."

"I'm not overthinking. It just seems to me that for Matthew's sake too you might want to slow down a little and—"

"Yes, you are overthinking it. Matthew and I talked and talked. I know he seems shy, but it's more that he's kind of quiet at first until he gets to know you a little bit. He's exactly the sort of person to bring Priscilla out of her shell, and it won't be because he's trying to. You see what I mean? That's just how he is. So that makes me the best matchmaker ever!"

"No doubt," I said, hoping she would be proven right in the end. "Just make sure you give Priscilla lots of time to warm up to him, okay? She might need more than one party to, well, you know, fall in love with the guy."

"Fine. But don't be surprised if it happens sooner than you think."

I decided not to argue the point. I unwound the reins on Amanda's horse as she stepped into her cart. The sun was just starting to dip into the horizon.

"You be careful on the roads. The *Englisch* drive at their worst at sunset." I rubbed some mud off one of the cart's side reflectors.

"I will. And don't let Priscilla find a reason not to come on Friday. You have to bring her."

"*I* have to bring her?"

"Yes. Well, you and Amos and Roseanna and whoever," Amanda said, gesturing toward the various houses that surrounded us on the Kinsingers' farm.

"I'll already be there helping to set up everything. Come a few minutes after seven, not before. I want everybody to be inside when she arrives. And don't let Roseanna forget her bars."

It was already sounding like a huge production, and all I could think of was poor Priscilla.

"Amanda, I don't know—"

"Hey. This is exactly the kind of thing Amos asked us to do for Priscilla. And we already said we would. I don't go back on my word, and I know you don't either. Come on. It'll be fun."

Her confidence and the ease with which she envisioned this party were difficult to ignore. "I hope you're right," I said, captivated again by her easy smile.

"Of course I am!" She blew me a kiss and then slapped the reins. She waved to me as she turned onto the road.

When she was gone, I started for the barn to check on January, glancing back toward the house as I went. When I did, I was shocked to see Priscilla standing just off to the side of the porch, maybe thirty feet away, pouring birdseed into the feeder.

I felt the color drain from my face, remembering Amanda's words.

This is exactly the kind of thing Amos asked us to do for Priscilla.

Surely Priscilla hadn't overheard us, had she?

No, impossible. Because if she had, she wouldn't be calmly filling the birdfeeder now.

Not a chance.

Nineteen

The next morning, I got up an hour earlier than usual so I could get some time in with January before work. Step one was to begin establishing mutual trust between us, and to do that I had to present opportunities for January to *need* to trust me, which meant introducing the tiniest bit of fear and then quickly showing the horse that she had nothing to worry about. Though over the coming days I would likely try a variety of triggers, such as a crinkly plastic bag or a shiny aluminum pan, this morning I brought in a big red rubber ball I'd borrowed from Stephen last night. All I did was hold the ball near January, which she did not like at all, and then I waited until she settled down and rewarded her with a carrot. After that, I moved the ball closer to her, waited, rewarded, then put it on her back, waited, rewarded, and so on. After twenty minutes, she was okay, to a point, with the giant ball. Really, it was more that she was okay with *me* in spite of there being a rubber ball between us, which was exactly the response I wanted. She had decided to put her confidence in me even though there was a giant red round thing in the stall. I would likely have to repeat the process the following day. My goal was to have her not react to the stimuli but respond to me.

Our morning session had been a success, and though I was a few minutes late getting to work, nobody else was around to notice. Owen and I shared the farrier shop, and he wasn't even there yet. When he showed up a few minutes later, I learned he'd been at the main house getting some filters from his *mamm* to use with our coffeemaker down here.

Amos and Mahlon worked in the welding shop, which sat farther down the row, on the other side of the barn. Though they sometimes forged new products in the shop, more often they were doing repair work on existing items, such as buggy wheels, axels, farm implements, and swing sets. I had put in a little time there myself when my apprenticeship first began, but thanks to my years of welding experience in *Daed*'s buggy shop, it had become obvious early on that those particular skills weren't the ones I needed to practice. That's how I'd ended up apprenticing almost exclusively on the farrier side of things, which was more than fine with me.

Today I had a steady stream of horses to shoe, but the work went fast, and my last client was gone by three. After that, I put my tools away, did a quick cleanup with Owen in the shop, and then I was finished for the day. Though I was eager to work again with January, there were two other tasks I needed to do first. One was to return Patch to Trudy Fisher. The other was to take Priscilla to the cemetery to see her mother's grave.

Trudy's cart was still in the buggy shed where she and I had stashed it, so I retrieved Patch and hooked him up to it, and then I hooked Willow to my own courting buggy. Priscilla came out, ready to go, just as I was finishing. I still didn't know if she'd overheard my conversation with Amanda the night before, but judging by her calm and friendly demeanor now, she had not. Feeling relieved, I gave Willow a final pat and we set off, with me leading the way in the cart and Priscilla following behind in my buggy.

We arrived at the Fishers about four thirty. As I handed Patch over, I told Trudy and her uncle all about what we'd discovered and worked on over the past few days. They both seemed quite impressed, and when I brought Trudy and Patch out to their pen to show her the exercises she would need to do, she took to them right away. Within half an hour, I was confident that girl and horse would be fine together from here on out.

Trudy's Uncle Vernon was so impressed with what I'd managed to accomplish that he tried to pay me extra for it after all. I refused—a deal was a deal—but somehow by the time Priscilla and I were ready to go, the back storage rack of my buggy was weighed down with an entire flat of fresh-picked strawberries, five big jars of pickles and preserves, two loaves of bread, and a shoofly pie.

Priscilla had been quiet during much of the stopover, but as we drove away, I detected a sly smile on her lips.

"What?"

"Nothing."

"No, really. What?" I pressed. She looked like the cat that ate the canary.

"It's just…well, I think Trudy has a little crush on you."

"No, she doesn't."

"*Ya*, she does. And trust me, I would know."

"Oh, yeah?" I asked with a laugh. "I assume you're speaking from personal experience?" I expected her to laugh in return at my mention of her long-ago attraction to me, but she didn't.

"Don't make fun," she said instead. "It's not a joke when a young girl has her first crush. And yes, I do mean from personal experience."

My laugh sputtered away. Had her little crush on me back then been more than just a girlish passing fancy?

"Oh. I didn't mean…that is, I…I wasn't making fun of you," I sputtered. "That was such a long time ago, and I…" My voice fell away. I was just making things worse.

She turned from me, sighing gently. "It's all right, Jake. I know you thought I was just a rough-and-tumble tomboy who hung around the blacksmith shop because I liked the horses."

"But you *were* a rough-and-tumble tomboy who hung around the blacksmith shop because you liked the horses."

"Yes, but that's not the only reason I lingered in the shop." She swung her head slowly back to face me. "I hung around because of you."

And there it was. Though she'd been just a child back then, her feelings for me really had run deep—or at least as deep as they could have at that age. I felt terrible for having ridiculed her now.

"That's so sweet," I said by way of apology. "I shouldn't have laughed."

"It's okay," she replied, and then she grew silent.

My mind, however, was now racing with questions.

"So what was it that you…that attracted you to me?" I asked, unable to stop myself. I wasn't fishing for compliments. I really just wanted to know.

To my relief, Priscilla smiled. Then she shrugged.

"You saw me," she said.

"I saw you?"

"*Ya*. I was practically invisible to everyone, but not to you. You always said hello to me. Always. Sometimes it was all you said, but you said it. You *saw* me."

For some reason, her words saddened me. Had she really grown up feeling invisible? "Of course I did. Like I told you the other night, you were a neat kid."

She took that in and then continued. "As a little girl, I thought you were so nice. I guess as I grew older, it just kind of struck me one day that you had even more going for you than that. Like…" Her voice trailed off, and with a glance I could see that her cheeks were flushed a pretty pink.

"Like what?" I prodded, trying to keep my tone light but really wanting her to keep talking. "Go on. Don't stop."

She smiled, waving away her embarrassment. "Like, I don't know…" Again, her voice trailed off as she seemed to dig around in her memory for an example. "There was this one time you came over to help Owen fix a busted axle on the family wagon. I was about twelve then, which would have made you sixteen. I remember I was sitting on an old tire swing in the front yard, just watching, and you had to pick up a big heavy pile of iron rods all by yourself. I'd already thought of you for years as Owen's nice friend who always talked to me about horses. But that day, I don't know." She shook her head, a slight smile coming to her lips. "You were just so strong. And handsome. And kind. I'd never really looked at you that way before, but that day…I guess you could say you came to change an axle and ended up stealing my heart."

She grew quiet after that, and after a long moment, I thanked her for telling me. I didn't remember that particular event myself, but I did recall the time period, and how it seemed that little Priscilla had begun looking at me in a not-so-little-girl way. Somehow, I had never imagined that the tomboy could fall for anyone—at least not very deeply, especially given her young age. Clearly, I had underestimated her feelings for me back then.

Curious, I was about to ask at what point her love had finally begun to wane when I remembered the tragedy of her young life. That adoring little girl had been forced to grow up very fast, no doubt leaving things like childish crushes far behind.

I changed the subject instead, and to my relief, conversation flowed easily as we drove. Priscilla seemed more talkative than usual, and I wondered if that was because she was nervous about our destination. This wasn't going to be easy for her, to see her mother's grave. But until we got there, I intended to seize the opportunity and keep her talking. After all, just like with horses, the more I could learn about her, the better able I would be to help her.

In answer to my questions, she began to tell me about her life in Indiana and some of her relatives there. I could see she was fond of the aunt and uncle in LaGrange who had taken her in six years ago, but her eyes really sparkled when describing a beloved great-aunt who lived next door to her maternal grandparents, on a small apple orchard in Elkhart. Priscilla did not bring up the widower who was also in Indiana, waiting for her answer on a marriage proposal. I really wanted to know more about him, but I couldn't figure out a way to broach such a personal topic, so I had to leave it alone for now.

Instead, I asked her if she'd made any decisions about staying in Pennsylvania beyond the end of the summer, and she replied that that was presently on hold, that she was still waiting for God's guidance regarding why He had wanted her here in the first place.

"Any word on the nanny job?" I asked, thinking of our chance encounter yesterday afternoon when she'd been on her way back from the interview.

"*Ya,* they left a message this morning. They went with someone else."

"Oh, I'm sorry."

"It's just as well." She shrugged. "I didn't really want it anyway."

I reminded her of what Amos had said that first night at dinner, about how instead of getting an outside job, maybe she could take over more of the duties at home, freeing Roseanna to put in extra hours at the quilt shop.

"*Ya,* I was thinking about that too. I'd be happy to do it as long as it's something Roseanna wants as well. I know money's tight for them right now, and they could use the extra cash."

It was an odd statement for her to make, and I was quiet for a moment as I considered her words. From my perspective, I couldn't imagine anything to be less true. How could money be tight for the Kinsingers when Owen and I had a steady stream of customers in the farrier shop from morning to afternoon?

I said as much to her now, and her response surprised me. Though work was steady on the horseshoeing side of the business, she said, things weren't going nearly as well over in the welding shop.

Kinsinger Blacksmith and Welding had always had more farrier customers than anything else, but I hadn't realized quite how unbalanced the situation had become until Priscilla said that as far as she could tell, there was barely enough work on the welding side for two people. Considering how skilled both Amos and Mahlon were at what they did, that was a real shame.

She and I both grew silent after that as my mind was busy going over this new information. There had been a lot of times lately when Mahlon wasn't even around, but I'd just thought he was off doing deliveries or something. Now I felt kind of dumb for not seeing this before. More than likely, he'd either been out trying to drum up more business or looking for a side job that might carry him through this current financial crunch. These thoughts concerned me, but I decided to put them out of my mind for now, as we were nearing our destination.

Once we crested the hill and the cemetery came into view, I could sense Priscilla's body stiffening next to me. This couldn't have been easy for her, and I half expected her to tell me to turn the buggy around and take her home. She didn't say a word, however, and soon we were pulling to a stop over on the grass alongside the fence.

We climbed out of the buggy and then just stood there for a moment, staring at the rows of headstones. It occurred to me that she wouldn't know where to begin to look for her mother's headstone because she hadn't visited the grave before. To look upon the long field of the departed and not know where to start would surely be daunting.

"I can help you find her marker," I said gently.

She took a step away from me and moved toward the rows. "I know where she is."

I stared after her a moment before suddenly realizing that of course Priscilla would know where her mother was buried. Sharon would be right next to Daniel. Priscilla had no doubt been to her father's grave, perhaps many times.

I didn't sense that she wanted me to accompany her, so I looped Willow's reins around a fence post and leaned against it as my horse bent her neck to nibble weeds.

Priscilla stopped about thirty yards away at a section of the cemetery that enjoyed a bit of shade from a towering oak. I watched as she knelt on the grass in between two small, raised rectangles of carved stone. A gentle breeze toyed with the strings of her *kapp*, but she didn't seem to notice. She was lost in the moment, her body perfectly still. She wasn't close enough for me to see the features on her face, so I couldn't tell what effect being at her *mamm*'s grave was having on her. I just hoped it wasn't serving to feed any guilt she still had about how her mother died.

I wanted to give Priscilla enough time here, but as the sun sank lower in the sky, I began to wonder if we were lingering a bit too long. Visiting the grave of a loved one could be a good thing, a healthy way to find closure and be reminded of faith and our belief in eternity. But it could be a bad thing as well, an opportunity to wallow in sorrow and grief, nursing the ache of loss.

After waiting as long as I thought I should, I finally strode with quiet purpose to where Priscilla knelt, coming to a stop behind her. Looking down, I read the two stones, each of which held exactly four lines of information: name, date of birth, date of death, and age at death. I was aware of the fancy-type headstones that *Englischers* often used, but our cemeteries were always like this. Identical stones, identical listings, and nothing else. It was our final act of humility and community, to be buried in such a way that no headstone was ever more elaborate than any other.

"Are you okay?"

She nodded without looking up. "We can go," she said, but she made no move to rise to her feet. Instead, she reached toward the stone bearing her mother's name and touched her fingers to the etched words there, almost as though she were laying her hand on her *mamm*'s fevered brow. Then she got to her feet and, without turning to me, began to walk back to the buggy.

It wasn't until we were pulling out onto the road that she spoke again.

"*Danke*, Jake. I know you had a lot to do today. It was kind of you to bring me here."

"You're welcome. Did you find what you were looking for?"

She hesitated a moment, causing me to glance over at her. She was staring out at the passing fields of green all around us. "I guess you could say that." When she looked back at me, I could tell she had indeed found some sort of answer at her mother's grave, but I had no idea what it was.

Twenty

There was still about an hour of sunlight left when we got home, so I unloaded the pile of goodies the Fishers had given me, stopped at the main house to give Roseanna first pickings, and then headed to my cottage to put away the rest. I moved quickly, eager to get in some time with January before dark.

I worked with her again the next morning, making some headway but not nearly as quickly as I had with Patch. There was something different about January's case, though I hadn't yet figured out what it was.

On Wednesday afternoon, right after the shop closed for the day, I headed over to the back paddock where January and Willow had been sunning themselves since lunch. Rainstorms were in the forecast for early evening, so I needed to take advantage of the time I had until then. The paddock, which was really just an elongated oval, was bigger than the round pen near the barn that I usually used. My intention was to work with January there, watching her, walking the oval with her, and bonding.

Once I rounded Mahlon and Beth's house and the back paddock came fully into view, I saw that Priscilla was standing just outside the oval, her arms bent at the elbows as she rested them on the rail. Voyager was at the water trough drinking, Willow was standing nonchalantly in the center, and January, a few feet from Priscilla, watched her from the corner of her eye.

January was the first to sense my movement. The horse raised her head, looked at me, and then turned away. As I came closer, Voyager noticed me as well, but only Willow came over to greet me when I reached the fence.

Priscilla and I hadn't interacted at all since our time at the cemetery, mostly because she'd seemed in a bit of a funk since then. I was figuring out that was her way, to draw up inside of herself when faced with difficult situations, but it bothered me to see her dark and distracted frame of mind drag on like this.

I nodded her way as I let myself in through the gate, but she barely acknowledged me in return, so I decided to leave her alone for now. Turning my attention to Willow, I gave her a good scratch under her jaw. Just to be polite, I would have done the same with Voyager as well, but I didn't dare bring on the disapproval of his owner. Instead, I continued on past him to January, who seemed skittish at my approach, but at least she let me close enough to grasp her halter and hook on the lead rope.

I began our session by spending several minutes there at her side, gently working my hands across the planes of her sleek body, from the front of her muzzle to the back of her cannon. As I did, I kept my breathing even and deep, my demeanor calm and relaxed but in charge. January seemed to respond somewhat positively, especially once I moved to her other side and repeated my actions again.

By the time I was finished and ready to take her for a walk around the ring, I glanced toward the fence line and was surprised to see Priscilla still standing there. What was she doing? Did she intend to stay the whole time?

Then again, I realized, it wasn't exactly as if she were watching me. She was more just sort of staring off into the distance, her eyes empty and unfocused. Sad.

With a tug of the lead and a click of my tongue, I started around the ring with January, allowing the rope to loosen in my grip as she began moving along steadily at my side. I was glad to see that for the first time all week, the horse never once paused or jerked or showed other such blatant signs of fear. I could tell by her eyes and tail that she was still on alert, attentive to her surroundings, and scanning for any and all possible threats, but at least at this point she seemed to trust that I would deliver her safely around the ring.

After our second loop, it struck me that it might be helpful to see her from a slightly more removed perspective. Priscilla was still over at the fence, though no longer gazing off into the distance. Instead, Voyager was there with her, and she was doing that thing she did with her head, leaning in close to his. I hated to interrupt their little moment, but I decided to request her assistance. Not only would it help me in my work with January, but my hope was that it might help Priscilla too, by pulling her out of this incessant fog.

She didn't seem to mind when I asked, and soon we had traded places, with her slowly walking January around the elongated oval track and me sitting on the fence, observing. She led the horse with less authority than I would have liked—pace uneven, path less exact—but at least it allowed me to observe the horse from afar. I focused in on January, looking for signs of anxiety or mistrust—from the way she held her eyes, nose, and jaw to the tension in her shoulders and hips to the posture of her tail. By the time they had made it three-quarters of the way around the ring, I was pleased to see that my efforts with the warmblood this week had netted at least some results. Her problem wasn't solved yet by any means, but at least her progress was sufficient enough that I felt we could move on to the next step.

When Priscilla drew closer, I took back the lead rope from her and thanked her for her help. I assumed that at that point she would call to her own horse and they would leave, but instead she surprised me by returning to the fence and leaning against it again, clearly intending to stay and watch some more.

"I'm not sure if you want Voyager in here for this part," I told her as I led January out to the center of the pen. "I'm going to do some pressure-release exercises with her, and they may spook him."

Priscilla stared at me for a long moment, her mouth growing tight, her eyes narrowing. "Voyager is free to run to the other end of the paddock to get away from you if he needs to."

Whatever that was about, I pretended not to notice the attitude. Instead, I just tuned her out entirely and got to work.

I started by pulling from my pocket a plastic grocery store bag I'd brought for just this purpose. Turning toward January, I kept my hold on the lead rope with one hand while I held up the bag with the other and began squeezing and shaking it to make it crinkle.

The skittish animal didn't like that one bit, but I kept at it just as I had with the big rubber ball the other morning, moving patiently through the process of challenge, wait, and reward. This we did over and over until she finally began to accept the fact that she could trust me to protect her despite this crinkly thing between us.

Finally ready to up the ante, I gave her an extra carrot for good measure, retrieved my training stick, and hooked the plastic bag onto the end of it. Holding out the stick in front of her, I gave it a few shakes as the wind caught the bag and made it rustle even more.

January reacted by jerking herself backward and letting out a whinny, just as I'd expected her to. In response, I simply pulled back the bag a bit and waited, murmuring to her calmly until she settled down. Once she was finally calmer, I rewarded her with a carrot.

I was about to repeat the same cycle again when Priscilla called out to me.

"What do you think you're doing?"

Startled, I whipped my head around to see her leaning forward over the fence, her hands flat on the rail and her eyes narrowed in displeasure.

"Excuse me?"

"What do you think you're doing?"

Glancing to my right, I saw that Voyager was now down at the other end of the long pen, hovering near the placid Willow. I looked again to Priscilla and let out a sigh.

"I told you to get him out of here."

"I'm not talking about Voyager. What are you doing to January? Why are you treating her this way?"

For a long moment I stood there gaping at her, wondering what on earth she was so worked up about. Did she not understand the first thing about how to gentle a horse? More importantly, did she not get that I was busy right now and we could talk about this later?

I didn't feel like launching into a lesson on technique, but by the set of Priscilla's jaw I could see she wasn't going to let this drop. So I gave her the short version, hoping that would be enough to shut her up and let me get back to my job.

"My goal is to help January move past her fear," I said evenly, trying to sound informative rather than defensive. "I'm trying to teach her blind trust."

"Blind trust?" Priscilla laughed, but not in happy way. Definitely not in a happy way. "What is that?"

Good grief. "That's having trust in her owner in the moment, regardless of whatever dangers may be present. She needs to be able to move past the thing that is bothering her and respond by blindly trusting the humans who care for her. Okay?"

To my surprise, Priscilla's anger began to fade into something more like disappointment.

"No, that's not okay," she said in a more subdued voice. "That's not okay at all."

I took in a deep breath and said a quick prayer for wisdom. Debating with Priscilla wasn't my favorite activity, but at least I could deal with it elsewhere. Right now, I hadn't the time or the attention or the energy to get into this with her.

Still, I told myself as I reached out a hand to give January a pat, Priscilla clearly wasn't going to leave me alone until she had her say.

"Fine," I said to no one. I dropped the lead rope and the stick, and walked over to the fence. I came to a stop directly in front of Priscilla. "What is it you want to tell me?"

"What you're doing—" she began, and then she stopped midthought. "Horses aren't mindless machines, Jake. They should never be scared into submission. They need—"

"Whoa, wait a minute," I said, holding out a hand to stop her right there. "*Scared* into *submission*? Mindless machines? You think I'm mistreating this horse? Breaking her will until she has no choice but to obey?" My voice began to grow louder, but I didn't care. "I'm not scaring her into submission, Priscilla. I am teaching her that she can trust me. I am teaching her to react not to some frightening stimuli but instead to the protection of my presence. I'm not scaring this animal for the sake of oppression. I'm using tools like that plastic bag to teach her that she's safe with me no matter what."

"Really."

"Yes, really. She needs to know her handler can be trusted, even if there's a bag coming at her. Even if there's a big red rubber ball beside her. Even if someday she's on a trail and runs into a snake, or in her stall and hears a loud noise, or near a crowd and a child comes running at her. The ultimate lesson this horse needs to learn is that no matter how she is being threatened, the person who's there with her can be trusted to protect her."

My little lecture complete, I stared at the woman on the other side of the fence.

She peered at me in return and then slowly began to shake her head.

"Don't you understand? Figuring out *why* they are afraid is every bit as important as knowing *what* they fear."

"I know why January is afraid right now, Priscilla. Because there's a crinkly plastic thing waving in front of her face! What else do I need to know?"

"You just don't get it," she said, shaking her head sadly, as if she pitied me in my ignorance. "Horses are emotional creatures, Jake."

"I never said they weren't."

"But until you connect with their emotions, you haven't helped them at all. And you don't deserve their trust. You're not *listening* to them!"

I couldn't help but laugh. It just sounded so silly. Connecting with a horse's emotion. Listening to them. So it was back to that again.

Her expression soared right back to anger. I had laughed at her, and now she was mad at me again.

"Look, I think maybe you should go and let me get back to work," I said, weary of it all.

Priscilla stared at me for a long moment. Then, without a word, she let herself in through the gate, strode over her to horse, and led him back out. "You can be as heartless as you want to me, Jake. I don't care. But there's one thing you need to know about that horse you're working with before you go on tormenting her this way."

Had this woman not heard a word that I'd said about what I was doing for January? "Priscilla, I'm not—"

"January's problem is not that she's scared." She looked past my shoulder to gaze at the animal behind me.

"Oh? And did she tell you this herself?"

"Not in so many words," she replied, ignoring the sting of my barb.

"Okay, then. If she isn't scared, what is she?"

Priscilla continued to look at January a moment longer and then turned her eyes back to me.

"She's sad."

"Sad."

Priscilla nodded. "I don't know why or what it's about or where it came from, but I do know this. January may seem scared to you, but there's another emotion behind all her fear, and it's sadness. Do with that what you will."

Twenty-One

Sadness.

In the broad range of possible responses to a situation, sadness had always seemed to me a waste of time. Not only was it draining, it was fruitless. It accomplished nothing, gave nothing, fixed nothing, changed nothing. Anger or frustration I could understand, or at least tolerate because action usually followed. But sadness was one of those feelings I just didn't see a purpose for. The best way to handle sadness, in my opinion, was to move past it and make room for something more useful.

These were the thoughts rolling around in my head after Priscilla and Voyager walked away. Returning to January and again taking her lead, I tried to pick up where we left off. As we worked, though, my heart was no longer in it. I should have been angry at Priscilla for ruining what had started out to be a very promising session, but the most I could summon now that she was gone was a vague, unsettled irritation—along with the needling notion that what had happened here today between us had to do with far more than just horses.

I could tell January was picking up on my mood, so finally I decided to call it a day before I made things not better but worse. The gathering clouds were also an indication that it was time to wrap it up. I pulled the bag loose from the stick, which I tossed to the side, and then I crushed the crinkly plastic back into my pocket. I decided we would end today's session with a final lap or two around the ring. We started off, her lead rope in my hand, walking at a regular, steady pace.

As the horse and I moved along side by side, I prayed for insight, after which I began to sense that I should go back over Priscilla's words, hoping to look beyond my own aggravation to the core of what she'd been trying to say. She had been right about Patch. Was there at least a kernel of truth in what she was saying about January too?

The problem was, even if I gave her the benefit of the doubt, her theory made no sense. What on earth would a horse—especially this well-cared-for, physically-healthy horse—have to feel sad about?

In my mind, I went over what I knew of January's life, but there just wasn't much to work with. Sure, her problems had begun once she moved to a new home, but why should that have made any difference? It wasn't as though horses became homesick, was it? The fact that I was even asking myself that question made me groan aloud.

So what else could it be?

One of Natasha's kids had suggested that maybe January missed competing, and perhaps somewhere inside her tiny apple-sized brain she did. But I refused to believe that something as basic as that could cause a horse to be sad. Horses retired all the time and probably enjoyed their life of leisure far more than they ever had their time in the ring.

As horses did not mate for life, I doubted she was missing an old boyfriend.

I supposed some horses developed deep bonds with their humans and would feel sad if those bonds were broken, but January hadn't been the beloved pet of some little girl whose whole life revolved around her pony. January had been a show horse, which meant that even if she'd only had one previous owner, she'd probably lived through a series of handlers and trainers and riders, with none of them around her long enough to ever form that kind of bond. Natasha had specifically said that January's owner wasn't involved in her day-to-day care at all.

As my mind pondered these thoughts, I noticed movement off to my left and turned to see Stephen heading my way. Glancing at the diminishing sun, which was now low in the sky, I realized it was time for our chores in the barn. January and I finished out our loop, and I rewarded her with one final carrot. Then I led her from the paddock, waited as Stephen took Willow, and we started across the grass together.

When we reached our destination, we put the horses away and got busy, starting in on the Kinsinger side of the barn and methodically working our way across, cleaning the stalls while Comet played nearby with a cricket he'd discovered among the hay. I could hear thunder off in the distance and knew the rain was finally rolling in. Natasha had told me that bad storms were one of January's triggers, so a part of me was glad. I'd been working with the animal for less than a week, but if we really had made some progress, as it seemed, then this coming storm might provide the perfect proving ground. Better yet, Priscilla couldn't accuse God, as she had me, of heartlessly sending a trigger January's way just to scare the animal into submission.

As Stephen finished with the last of the Kinsinger stalls, I moved to my side of the barn. The storm was growing ever closer, and it sounded as if we were in for a drenching tonight. January was already acting anxious, hoofing the ground and shaking her head, sure signs that she wasn't too happy. Now that I was here, however, if my presence served to calm her, then that would be a good indication of her newly blossoming trust.

Even Willow was a little bit antsy, though, so I went to her and gave her some long, soothing pats down the line of her neck. Then, after a carrot and a "Good girl," I returned my attention to January. As the first of the rain began to fall, I positioned myself just outside the closed door of her stall. Resting my hands casually across the top rail, I spoke in low soothing tones to the frightened animal, assuring her it would be all right, that I wouldn't let anything hurt her.

She didn't seem to get the message at first, especially once the steady patter of rain was followed by a solid boom of thunder. In response, she tossed back her head, her eyes wide with fear. Though I would have preferred being in the stall with her, where I could better provide the soothing comfort of touch, I knew that wouldn't be safe. A frightened horse can be a dangerous horse, so the best I could do was to remain just outside her reach and try to get her through this ordeal with only the sound of my voice and the assurance of my presence as protection.

It didn't seem to work at first. The louder the storm grew, the more frantic her behavior became. By the time Stephen had finished with Big Sam's stall and come over to my side to join me, January was so agitated that I feared for her safety. What a disappointment. Apparently, we hadn't made any progress yet after all.

Then again, I told myself as I looked out through the open door at the rain, this was a doozy of a summer storm, made worse by the fact that it was passing directly overhead. Maybe I was being too impatient, and if I just stuck it out a little longer, I would see some results after all.

I heard a whimper nearby and looked over to see that even Comet was a bit rattled. He had come in from the other side of the barn and was now standing at Stephen's feet, looking up at him with sad eyes. Obviously, Comet didn't like this weather any more than the horses did.

"Hey there, fella," Stephen said, pausing in his work and setting the pitchfork aside. Then he bent down and put his arms around the dog who was almost instantly comforted in the safety of his master's embrace.

"If only I could get my arms around you," I cooed to the large, frightened horse in front of me. In a way though, I told myself, I *was* holding her, by staying close until the worst of the storm had passed.

Ultimately, my plan seemed to be working. When the next loud clap of thunder came, I braced myself for January's reaction. And though the whites of her eyes still showed from nervousness, her muscles were no longer trembling and her feet remained firmly on the ground.

Could it be possible? Had she really been taking something from our lessons after all? I nearly held my breath until another clap of thunder came, so eager was I to prove our success. This time, when she barely reacted, I felt like jumping for joy.

We had done it! Though January still had a ways to go, it was clear now that she felt safe with me, at least to an extent. Eventually I hoped we would reach the point where she was secure and confident in every case, no matter the threat, whether man-made or flashed across the sky by God.

Now that she was calm, I turned my attention to the work that still awaited me in the barn. The good news was that even when I had to move farther away from her and my attention was distracted by other things, she still remained reasonably at peace. Every time I glanced back at her, a part of me wanted to point all of this out to Stephen and share with him about my success, but I knew I wouldn't be able to resist gloating, so in an attempt to stay humble, I kept quiet and just smiled to myself, the proof of my technique standing quietly in her stall nearby, munching on hay.

Eventually, the worst of the storm had passed, though the rain lingered and we could still hear distant rumblings in the sky. Once the dog stopped whimpering, Stephen got back to work, too, but soon all that remained was to clean out the stall I'd been using to house Patch. As that arrangement had had nothing to do with the Kinsingers, I told Stephen I would handle it myself and sent him on home.

That ended up being easier said than done. In fact, Stephen had such a hard time coaxing the rain-shy Comet to leave the dry safety of the barn that I was nearly done cleaning the empty stall by the time they finally left.

In the quiet, I exhaled slowly, allowing myself the smile I'd been stifling since January first calmed down. Feeling deeply pleased, I reached for the fattest, juiciest carrot in the box, a reward for my star pupil: January the palomino, picture of peace.

Except that she wasn't acting so peaceful anymore. The last time I had looked over at her, minutes before, she had simply been standing there, chomping at the fresh hay, the whites of her eyes no longer even visible. Now for some reason, though the worst of the storm had passed, she seemed nervous again, her nose twitching, and her muscles tense. Another low murmur of thunder sounded in the distance, the storm's rumbling farewell. In response, January tossed her head and suddenly began pawing the ground.

I was confounded. For a guy who claimed to read horses pretty well, I hadn't figured this one out at all. Calm one minute and terrorized the next, January was challenging everything I thought I understood about the gentling of horses. As I stood there, hands on hips, surveying the situation, I began to wonder if perhaps she had some sort of physical issue, something that wasn't behaviorally related after all. Then again, Natasha had talked about how thoroughly she had been checked out by experts, so I doubted that was it.

Closing my eyes, I asked myself the only question I could come up with in this moment. What had changed? Other than the fact that the storm was still moving farther and farther away, what else was different between the point when January was calm and now? Had my movements spooked her as I was cleaning? Did she have a fear of pitchforks like the one I was holding in my hand?

Finally, I opened my eyes, feeling like an idiot for not catching on before. The difference between when January was calm and now was Stephen.

The key here was Stephen.

My mind raced. Was it possible there was something about the boy that had a calming effect on the horse? If so, I couldn't imagine what, until I remembered my earlier theory. Priscilla's insistence that January was sad had led me to question whether the horse was missing someone or something from her life with her previous owner. As a show horse, yes, she had probably been exposed to a never-ending series of trainers and riders and such, but who's to say there hadn't been a certain constant in this mare's life? The constant of a young boy. Perhaps the owner or the stable master had a son, one who spent enough time with the horses that he and January had managed to form a special bond.

That had to be it.

Pulse surging, I knew I had to test this theory—and right away, before she grew even more distressed. Leaving her alone in the stable, I grabbed my hat and ran out into the rain to Mahlon's house.

I got there just as the family was sitting down to supper, and though Beth invited me to stay, I said thanks but no thanks, that what I really needed was to borrow their son for just a few minutes. They didn't seem to mind. As Stephen and I dashed back through the rain together, I realized he thought he was in trouble, that perhaps he had done something wrong with one of his chores. I assured him that wasn't it at all, and then I explained the situation as simply as I could. When I was finished, I could tell he seemed pleased at the thought of a horse being calmed simply by his presence.

Once we were back to the stable, however, we could both see that my theory was wrong. Even when Stephen stood close to January's stall door and spoke to her in calming tones, she was still in an agitated state. We gave it a good five minutes, thinking maybe she just needed time to calm back down, but if anything she only seemed to grow worse. Finally, I thanked him for coming and told him we were done here.

My shoulders heavy, I put out the lights and Stephen and I headed back into what was now just a drizzle. We walked together part of the way, and then with a solemn good night the boy veered right to go to his house and I headed left toward my cottage. I had only gone a few steps, however, when I froze and turned around.

There on the porch, Stephen had paused to greet his excited dog before going back inside. Comet had been with us in the barn when the storm first started, and January had calmed down about the same time he showed up near her stall. Then, once he and Stephen left, January had grown agitated again. Just now when I came back to get Stephen, it had still been drizzling and Comet had chosen not to come along. Wherever Stephen went, Comet always went too—except when it was raining.

"Hey, Stephen!" I called, just as he was about to head inside. "Mind if I borrow Comet?"

Understanding slowly dawned in the boy's eyes as I approached, and with a big grin he whistled for his dog and the three of us raced back to the barn. As we stepped inside, we could already hear January's agitated huffing and snorting, but the moment Stephen led the dog over near her stall, it was as if someone had flipped a switch.

Suddenly, the body of the anxious, twitching, pawing horse grew still. She gave us a look as if to say, "It's about time you figured it out," and then she took a big bite of hay and stood there calmly chewing it, as if all was right with the world.

"Well, would you look at that," Stephen said, turning to flash me a wide grin.

The horse had been missing a dog.

Twenty-Two

When I awoke the next morning, I wondered for a long moment if it had been a dream. Somewhere in the night, had my imagination conjured up a horse who was so desperate for some canine companion that she grew agitated and easily spooked in its absence? As I climbed from bed and slowly came more awake in the predawn darkness, that sense of unreality faded, and I knew it had actually happened. I had solved the mystery of January.

Of course, I couldn't wait to test it out again, just to make sure I'd been right, so over the next hour, not only would I confirm the theory, but I had managed to test January with the ball, the plastic bag, some clanging pots, and more. Each of those items caused her some level of distress when exposed to them alone, but as soon as I brought the dog into the mix, there was almost nothing I could do to disturb her. The horse I'd spent so much time with that first morning, desensitizing her to a rubber ball, was now allowing me to bounce the ball on the ground around her feet and even throw it into the air not far from her head—as long as Comet was in sight.

I'd never seen anything like it, but when I told Amos the story over breakfast, he didn't seem all that surprised. In fact, he said he'd known of similar pairings—not just horses with dogs but one with a rabbit and another with a turtle.

I couldn't wait to tell Natasha. My first client at the farrier shop was sched-uled for seven, too early to squeeze in a call beforehand. But after that client left, another came, and then another, keeping me so busy that I never got a chance to take a break until lunch.

Natasha sounded skeptical over the phone, but I assured her I knew what I was talking about. We set it up for her to come with the horse trailer on Sat-urday, and though she still seemed hesitant, she said she would be "googling" this in the meantime.

When I hung up the shop phone, I realized there was someone else I needed to share the news with. And apologize to.

I found Priscilla on the side of the big house, bringing in the family laundry.

"Hey."

Even though I lived on the premises, I had not talked to her since our argument in the paddock the day before and had barely seen her on the prop-erty. When she turned to face me, I wondered if she was still mad at me.

But I saw no traces of lingering indignation, just a quiet melancholy.

"What is it, Jake?" she said, glancing at me once as she turned the crank on the pulley.

"I owe you an apology."

She paused for a second, midcrank, but then she was back at her task. "An apology? For laughing at me?" She turned the wheel and the next set of work shirts floated her way.

"Yes."

Priscilla swung around, the laundry line temporarily forgotten.

"You were right about January," I blurted. "She is sad. She's missing a dog back at her old place."

"A dog? How did you figure that out?"

I told Priscilla what had happened in the barn during the previous night's storm. She listened with growing interest, her blue mood slowly being replaced with delight.

"That's...that's great, Jake. I'm really happy for you. And for January."

She was about to turn back to the laundry line when I took a step closer. "Priscilla, I'm really sorry about what I said at the paddock yesterday. For-give me?"

She looked down at the clean clothes in the basket at her feet. "I'm the one who should be apologizing. As you have already seen, I say too much when I get mad. And in the wrong way."

"But you were correct about January."

"That didn't give me any right to talk to you that way. I'm sorry too." She looked up at me, and I could see that her joy at my figuring out January's dilemma was only matched by her disappointment in herself.

"How about we put the whole thing behind us?" I offered, anxious to get back to the normal routine.

She smiled, and though it wasn't a wide and easy grin, I could see she agreed.

"Okay, then," I said as I turned to go. "See you around?"

"Sure, Jake."

It was a relief to have that whole business taken care of. I looked back once as I made my way to the cottage. She was again at the laundry line, pulling off clothes and folding them into the basket, a clear sign that all was well between us. And a good thing too. The following evening would be the party, and I knew Amanda expected Priscilla to be in an amiable mood by the time I got her there.

On Friday night at twenty minutes to seven, I left my cottage, freshly showered after working with horses all day long, and headed for the buggy barn. I couldn't say I was especially looking forward to the party itself, although I was a bit curious to see what chemistry there might be between Priscilla and Matthew. I hadn't even spoken to Amanda for a few days because she was busy with preparations for the event, and I'd had a full week myself, but I was pretty sure she was still singing Matthew's praises as the perfect man for Priscilla. I wondered as I hitched Willow to my buggy how hard it was going to be for Matthew to work up the courage to ask Priscilla if he could court her. Just picturing it made me laugh and then frown.

No self-respecting guy—especially someone as shy as Matthew—would ever ask such a risky question in a house full of people. The party was just a means to an end. I was already eager for this event to be history so that Amanda could let the courtship take its course, so that she could focus her attention back on me, and so that Amos would be satisfied that Priscilla had been successfully reintegrated back into the community.

Because Mahlon and Beth already had plans for the evening with her family, they wouldn't be making it to the party, but Beth sent along her artichoke dip, as well as a box of wheat crackers and instructions on heating the dip once we got there.

That left Amos, Roseanna, Priscilla, Owen, Treva, baby Josef, and me. There was no reason to take three buggies, so we decided that Priscilla could ride with me in my two-seater and Amos would bring everyone else in the family wagon.

Because Amanda wanted Priscilla to be the last to arrive, the others set off to the Zooks' house around six thirty, bringing all of the food with them.

I had told Priscilla we'd leave at a quarter to seven. I was glad that at exactly six forty-three she appeared on the porch and then walked to the gravel where the buggy waited.

"Are you sure you're ready for this?" I said lightly, wanting her know I was aware this was not how she would have liked to spend her Friday night.

She shrugged, politely declined my offer to help her step up into the buggy, and climbed in.

"Looks like it's going to be a quiet ride," I murmured to Willow as I strode to the driver's side and climbed in myself.

We started out on the macadam. Because I was certain Priscilla was no longer mad at me about our argument at the paddock, I decided that maybe she just needed some quiet to prepare herself for an evening of noise and frivolity. I sat back and had just decided I liked the peaceful ride myself when she spoke.

"I've been wanting to ask you something."

"Oh?" I replied, thinking she wanted to know more about the revelation regarding January.

"What did Amanda mean the other night when she said you and she were doing just what Amos asked you to?"

The calm in the cab and in my chest disappeared in an instant. "What was that?" I asked, more to buy myself a second or two of time. I had heard what she said. I was just wholly unprepared for it.

"The other night when Amanda came to tell me about the party. You were saying goodbye to her, and I had come out to fill the bird feeder. I heard what she said about Uncle Amos."

"Look, Priscilla. We were just trying to help," I said, hoping against hope this unplanned-for conversation wasn't going to ruin the party after all Amanda had done to prepare for it.

"I just want to know what she meant."

Priscilla didn't seem angry. Or hurt. Or disappointed. I couldn't put my finger on how she sounded. And that worried me a little.

"I think I have a right to know," she added when I said nothing.

I sighed heavily. "He asked us to help you reconnect with the young people in the area. That's all," I said, still trying to come up with the best answer. "Your aunt and uncle are hoping you will stay here." I thought hearing that would make her feel good, make her feel that she was wanted. Because it was the truth. Amos and Roseanna did want Priscilla to stay in Lancaster County. "They think if you make some friends, maybe even find a husband..." My voice trailed off as I looked toward her.

She didn't respond, so I added, "I don't know if what they did was right, but I do know they did it out of love. For you."

She nodded, taking that in. "So that's why you've been nice to me?" she said, looking out at the passing landscape, not at me. "Because Uncle Amos asked you to?"

"What? No! I wanted...Amanda and I both want very much to help make your transition back to Lancaster County as welcoming as we can."

She laughed lightly. "You and she both very much want it," she echoed, looking chagrined.

"Yes," I assured her, hoping I sounded sincere. Because I was. "Very much."

She glanced over at me, her gaze just visible past the pearly white edge of her *kapp*. A veiled admission—or accusation—was in her eyes, I couldn't quite tell which. Finally, she turned away again.

"Priscilla—" I began, wanting to make sure she knew Amos and Amanda and I had only her best interests at heart.

"It's all right, Jake. I'm not angry."

"Okay, but you don't seem too happy about it, either." I looked over at her. Her expression was impossible to read in the fading light.

She said nothing for a moment. "I guess I'm glad you told me the truth."

"So we're okay?" I said, still trying to get a read on her mood. We were just a half mile away from the party and all of Amanda's many preparations.

She cracked a smile. "Don't worry. I won't spoil the party. I will try to have a good time. I will try to be nice to Matthew."

"Amanda thinks you and he would make a great couple," I ventured, glad we were getting back to casual conversation.

"So I've gathered."

I wanted to add that he was quite a bit better husband material than a man twice her age with eight kids, but I didn't want to mess with the sense of calmness Priscilla had created for herself and tonight's big event.

A few minutes later we arrived at the Zook place, and I was happy to see so many buggies and carts already there. The same sight, however, seemed to ruffle Priscilla a little bit.

I held my tongue, allowing her a few minutes of silence to process everything as we pulled to a stop and climbed down from the buggy. I unhitched Willow and led her through the gate to the pasture, where she gladly joined the other horses.

"Don't worry," I said as I hooked the latch and Priscilla and I set off toward the house. "It's a Friday night and there's a party. You don't have to try to impress anybody."

"Except Matthew."

I smiled. "Not even him. Just be yourself, Priscilla."

She smiled in return. "Surely you're not serious, Jake. If I did that, I would be out in the pasture with all the horses in ten seconds flat."

It was good to be laughing about this as we made our way into the house. Amanda was on us in a second, taking Priscilla's arm and flashing me a grateful grin. I'd somehow managed to bring in a laughing Priscilla to the party. I was Amanda's hero. Priscilla was now instantly the center of attention, which I knew had to be hard for her.

There was nothing for me to do then except fade to the background, eat cake and little ham sandwiches, and let Amanda and her cohorts execute their plan. I watched from a corner as a while later Amanda sidled up to Matthew with Priscilla in tow. I continued to watch as tall, shy Matthew attempted to make small talk with Priscilla. Amanda stayed with them and kept interjecting to keep the conversation going. Several times he looked over to Amanda in obvious gratitude for not leaving him to his own meager devices.

As I watched without trying to be obvious about it, I was happy to see that Amanda was not wearing even a hint of mascara—though I knew that could have been because this was a multigenerational gathering. Either way, something about her seemed different tonight. More *Amish*, for lack of a better word.

Her selfless attentiveness to Matthew and Priscilla was also endearing. I had never seen her quite so…compassionately involved with anyone before. It was a pleasant surprise.

What I liked best about the party was that it wasn't yet another youth event. I was so tired of those gatherings that it was a relief to be with other people my own age and older. Occasionally, Amanda would come my way to tell me how wonderful everything was going, but otherwise I spent time tossing horseshoes in the backyard with a group of older men, talking horses with a family that was expanding their stables, and eating some of the most delicious food I'd had in ages, going back for seconds and thirds.

As far as I was concerned, the party was a success. Everyone seemed to be having a good time. Even Priscilla, who wasn't a fan of crowds, seemed to find little pockets of people throughout the evening where she could have conversations that were more intimate and more to her liking. I caught her looking for assurance from me a couple times, and I was happy to give it. The only drawback was that she didn't spend as much time with Matthew as Amanda had hoped for. I was glad I had told Amanda a few days ago to let those two take it slow.

When the party ended, I was more than ready to head for home. And I could tell Priscilla was too. I knew Amanda had driven here in her own cart and wouldn't need a ride home, but she didn't seem close to leaving when we were. I offered to stick around, but she wouldn't hear of Priscilla and me hanging back to help clean up when the party had been in Priscilla's honor.

"Besides," she whispered to me, "I need to see how things went."

"How things went?"

"With Matthew and Priscilla. You do the same." And then with a wink she was off to her post-party activities.

But Priscilla wasn't talkative on the way home. The evening had exhausted her the way crowds will do to folks like her. When I asked her if she had a good time, she merely said that she was grateful for all the effort Amanda went to putting the party on for her.

"Does that mean you *did* have a good time?" I asked with a laugh.

"It means I'm grateful," she said tiredly.

Despite Amanda's orders, Priscilla and I would not be talking about how things went with Matthew, which was totally fine with me.

TWENTY-THREE

Natasha arrived in the morning, her truck and trailer crunching on gravel as she pulled up the drive. I was expecting to greet the same skeptical woman I'd spoken to on the phone the day before, but the Natasha who jumped out of this vehicle seemed like what might be called, for lack of a better word, a true convert. Smiling ear to ear, eyes aglow, she barely said hello before launching in about all the reading she'd done online.

"I had no idea separation anxiety was such a common problem for horses," she enthused. "Usually, it's because they miss other horses, but it can also be for humans and other kinds of animals too."

"This was a new one for me as well. In fact, I might not even have figured it out if not for someone else." Gesturing toward the house, I explained that the Kinsingers' niece was visiting from Indiana for the summer, and that she was the one who first suggested that January was more sad rather than scared. "Once she told me that, I was able to think things through from a different perspective. It took a while, but thanks to Stephen and his dog and Wednesday night's storm, it all came together in the end. I can't wait to show you the difference in your horse."

Because it was a Saturday, Stephen would be around. I'd asked him to listen for Natasha's arrival because I would need him—and Comet—once she arrived. Now, as she and I walked toward the stable, boy and dog emerged from the side of the house and headed our way.

Natasha gave him a warm hello. "I understand you were a big help to my horse."

He smiled shyly, otherwise ignoring the compliment. "Where are Hope and Samantha?"

As the three of us plus the dog continued on toward the barn, Natasha explained that Hope was at her gymnastics class and Samantha at her first riding lesson. "Hope loves gymnastics, and Samantha was thrilled to start her lessons, but when they found out where I was going this morning, they both wanted to ditch all that and come here instead." She laughed. "I don't know who they wanted to see more, Stephen. You or your dog."

I smiled. "Speaking of dogs—"

"Yes, I spoke to January's previous owner, and he confirmed that his stable master, who lives on-site, does have a dog. After we talked, he checked with the guy and then called me back again to give me a little more info, which I thought was nice of him."

We entered the barn and crossed to the smaller stable area where January was housed.

"Apparently, the dog has been a constant figure around the stable for a long time, and she was especially fond of January. The man described her as a medium-to-large-sized mutt with long, brownish-gold fur, so I already have my people on the hunt for a nice golden retriever, or maybe a collie, that we can buy. In the meantime, a friend is loaning us her Irish setter, who will be there waiting for us when we get home."

I had groomed January just a short while before Natasha arrived, so the beautiful animal looked sleek and shiny and majestic when we came to her stall. Making sure that Comet was clearly visible to the horse, I unlatched the door, attached her lead, and walked her out. Handing over the rope to Natasha, I grabbed the big rubber ball and we all returned to the driveway.

Natasha led January out to the middle of the gravel, and then I told Stephen to position himself on the other side of the horse.

"Check this out," I said to Natasha with a smile. Then, checking to see that the dog was still nearby, I dribbled the ball a few times, raised it up, and tossed it in an arc over January to Stephen, who caught it. The horse didn't bat an eye.

Stephen tossed the ball back to me, and I tucked it under my arm as I pulled a plastic bag from my right pocket. Moving closer, I crinkled the bag not a foot from January's head. Again, she seemed not to notice one bit.

"I can keep on demonstrating as long as you want," I said, turning to Natasha, "but I think you can see this problem has been solved."

I expected a grateful smile in return, but Natasha's eyes were on her horse. As she reached forward to place her hand on January's neck, I could see the relief and joy on her face.

"Good girl, such a good girl," she cooed to the animal. "I think it's going to be smooth sailing for you from now on."

I spent the afternoon over at Amanda's. It wasn't our usual routine, but she was still flying high from last night's party and wanted to go over everything. The fact that I couldn't care less—and told her so—didn't seem to matter. Undaunted, she replied that she had to talk about it with somebody, and because Priscilla was my responsibility too, it was my place to sit and listen.

We ended up at the kitchen table, the plans and lists and charts that Amanda had used for the party spread out in front of us as she went through and recounted even the tiniest detail. I would have been bored out of my mind after the first five minutes had it not been for the presence of her mother and her twin sisters, Naomi and Nettie, who were over at the counters working together to can what looked like about four bushels of peaches. Not only did they let me hop up and pitch in whenever they needed something heavy lifted or a jar twisted open, but they all talked and laughed a lot as they chopped and sliced and boiled and stirred and poured, making a difficult job quite fun. They also kept up a running banter about the over-the-top event Amanda had pulled together, forcing me to stifle a smile several times.

They were just teasing, but I knew there was a little truth behind their words. Amanda's mother, in particular, seemed rather put out with her daughter, and I didn't blame her. The Amish had things like parties and gatherings and food and games down to a science. There was a way you went about this stuff that followed a fairly standard formula. That made it easier for everyone, and it lessened the possibility of pride because no one party was ever more outstanding than another.

Amanda, on the other hand, had been determined to put on something truly unique and special, qualities not valued among our people. The longer

I sat listening to her, the more I had to wonder whom she had been trying to impress. Not until I was leaving did it strike me that perhaps she'd seen it as an opportunity to show off to me the kinds of skills one might look for in a wife. My only wish was that her gifts with planning and cooking and entertaining were equaled by a gift of humility.

As I drove home late in the afternoon, pondering these things, my mind went to the party's guest of honor, the one who had been the beneficiary of Amanda's efforts. With a laugh to myself, I realized that, in a sense, Priscilla was the un-Amanda. For her, just the thought of being unique and special and impressive and noticeable would send her running in the opposite direction.

Priscilla was still on my mind as I neared the Kinsinger farm and turned into the driveway. The first house on the left was Owen and Treva's, the same house where Priscilla had once lived—and where her mother had died.

As I reached the barn and pulled to a stop, I sat there for a long moment, thinking again of that tragic accident, a fatal slice of the knife while canning acorn squash. That, in turn, led me to think of Naomi and Nettie at the Shetlers' today, working with their mother to put up the peaches. Then it struck me.

Canning was hard work that required many hands. Any other 14-year-old Amish girl would have been in the kitchen with her mother at canning time, not out in the barn nor up in her bedroom.

This thought led me to a new theory, that on the day Sharon Kinsinger died, mother and daughter had had an argument, one that ended with Priscilla being sent to her room. Later, when Sharon accidentally cut herself, she had gone up there for help, expecting Priscilla to be inside. But she hadn't been. Instead, she must have slipped out when her *mamm* wasn't looking, leaving the room empty. No wonder Priscilla felt responsible.

By sneaking away from the house, she'd essentially sealed her mother's fate.

Twenty-Four

Amanda's vision of romantic bliss between Priscilla and Matthew did not materialize. Over the course of the next week, Amanda popped in to see Priscilla a few times, chatting up all of Matthew's qualities and his general wonderfulness, but it seemed to make no difference. Priscilla wasn't interested. Realizing that for himself, Matthew had already politely declined to pursue things with her on his end. Or, as Amanda put it, he was going to back off, despite how much he liked her, because he wasn't a pushy kind of guy.

I wasn't all that sure, however, whether his interest in Priscilla was genuine or just a figment of Amanda's imagination. From what I had seen at the party, at least, Matthew hadn't exactly been falling all over himself to get to know the guest of honor. Instead, he had been shy and stiff and his usual scarecrow self, treating her like one guest among many.

And yet Amanda persisted. After her third "girl chat" with Priscilla of the week, I felt just bad enough about her intrusiveness on the matter that I decided to apologize on my girlfriend's behalf.

Here at the end of June, the days were growing longer and sunnier, and a brief cool snap had been making the weather just about perfect. It was nearing sunset on the last Saturday in June when I finished up some chores and went looking for Priscilla. I checked all the obvious places and finally found her down in Treva's vegetable garden, alone, carefully thinning out some cabbage plants on her left and replanting them in an empty row on her right.

I asked if I could help, and though her expression made it clear she wished I wouldn't, she said I could if I wanted to. I jumped right in, glad to have something to do with my hands as we talked. That always made for easier conversation, just two people chatting as they worked on something together.

"If you're the second wave sent in to extol Matthew's virtues, don't bother," she said.

In return, I couldn't help but laugh. Loudly. "Quite the opposite, in fact," I assured her. "Mostly I just wanted to, um, apologize for what has turned into a one-woman crusade that is probably driving you crazy. I don't know why Amanda is so determined to see you and Matthew together, but the next time I talk to her, I'm going to request she back off."

Priscilla continued with her digging without a reply.

"If you don't feel like dating anyone, then you shouldn't have to date anyone," I added diplomatically.

Her head jerked up. "You don't think I should be dating?"

"Of course not. I—"

"That there's not a man alive who could possibly be interested in poor, weird Priscilla?"

And there it was. The side of this woman that was as prickly as a pinecone. The side that drove me crazy.

I couldn't even think how to reply, and I didn't want my tone to sound as irritated as I felt, so I kept silent for a while, doing my part with the digging. In the quiet, she must have realized she'd overreacted, because after a while she glanced over at me again and spoke in a much softer, almost repentant tone.

"There is someone, a man back home," she said, her face blushing a pretty pink. "He's older than I am but quite kind. And he doesn't think I'm weird at all."

My first thought was a snarky one. *Even if he did, he wouldn't say so because he needs a mother for his eight children.* Of course I couldn't blurt that out loud. I dug at the ground with vigor as I replied.

"I never said men wouldn't want to date you, Priscilla. I was just saying don't feel bad if you don't feel like dating Matthew—or any other guy around here, for that matter—if you don't want to."

I looked up to see that she was staring at me with an odd expression, one I couldn't read. Then she returned her attention to the earth in front of her and said, simply, "I'm here only temporarily, remember."

Again, for some reason I couldn't explain, I found myself digging with intensity, my jaw set. Finally, I could hold my tongue no longer. Sitting back on my heels, I stabbed the spade into the dirt and crossed my arms over my chest.

"Seriously? You're seriously considering that guy's offer?"

Priscilla also sat back, her eyes narrowing as she looked back at me. "Offer?"

With a flush of heat, I realized I had no business sharing with her something Amos had told me in confidence. Backpedaling just a little, I muttered, "You just said there's a guy back home. I assume he wants to court you?"

"Not that it's any of your business, Jake, but Noah and I have already been courting. He's asked me to marry him."

"What did you tell him?"

"Again, not your business, but I said I would have to think about it first." Waving away a persistent bumblebee, she added, "When I felt God leading me to come back here to Lancaster County, I broke things off with him—temporarily, at least. I didn't know how long I would be gone, and I felt he should be free to date others in my absence."

"Sounds like true love to me," I quipped.

She ignored my sarcasm. "Like I said, I told him I would have to think about it first. So that's what I've been doing. Thinking about it."

"Thinking about it."

"*Ya*. Would you have me say yes—or no—in an instant? Without genuine consideration? Without certainly of God's will?"

"It seems to me that you either know or you don't."

"It seems to me that I already told you this was none of your business," she said. Then she put aside her tools, stood, and marched off toward the house.

I didn't see Priscilla again until the next morning, as we all gathered in the driveway, ready to go to church. I'd had all night to think about our conversation, and I felt terrible about it. Even though apologies never came easily to me, I didn't hesitate now to pull her aside to tell her how sorry I was for butting into her private affairs.

"I was way out of line. I don't know what got into me."

She seemed to consider my words thoughtfully and then responded with a nod. "*Danke*, Jake. I forgive you."

She turned to move away, but I reached out and caught her elbow.

"One more thing."

I dropped my hand as she paused to look back at me.

"Next Friday is the Fourth of July, which, you know, is big with *Englischers*. Natasha is having a barbecue at her estate, and she's hired me to be there for the fireworks part, just to stay in the stables and help keep an eye on any of the horses that might get spooked by the noise. I told her how you helped with January, and she suggested I bring you along too." When Priscilla didn't respond right away, I added, "She'll pay by the hour, in cash, at the end of the night."

Looking into Priscilla's face, I could almost see the battle raging. After our conversation in the garden, I was most likely the last person she wanted to spend time with. On the other hand, not only was this a paying job—albeit a brief one—but it would mean spending time with horses.

"*Ya*. I could do that."

I thanked her and turned away before she could see the relief in my smile.

Because I had the Fourth of July off, as did everyone at my *daed*'s buggy shop, my parents decided to have a big family picnic at their place. Priscilla and I didn't have to be at Natasha's until the evening, so I decided to come for the day—and to bring Amanda with me. *Mamm* said that would be fine as it would provide a nice opportunity for the whole family to get to know her.

Amanda was nervous about coming, but any anxiety was quickly eclipsed by her love for parties, get-togethers, and games. I thought she would fit in just fine with all the members of my family, but as the afternoon wore on, I found myself wondering if everyone else was as relaxed and comfortable around Amanda as she seemed to be with them. *Mamm*, who I thought would be the most excited about my courting a beautiful girl, seemed to be contemplative throughout the afternoon. Tyler and Rachel also weren't nearly as enthusiastic about Amanda as I thought they would be, which I found perplexing. Amanda was as easy-going as they come. She laughed at everyone's jokes, was kind and helpful, cooed at the babies, and seemed for all the world as though her mascara days were long behind her.

I had to leave by five, and the opportunity to ask Tyler or my mother what was up never came. As a happy and chatty Amanda and I drove back home, I wondered if perhaps I had only imagined these things.

I certainly hoped so, anyway.

After all the stress of the day and the long ride to Amanda's and then home, I was tired by the time I had to go to Natasha's. Back at the cottage, I changed into a fresh set of clothes, and then I wearily headed out to the driveway, wishing we could have done this on a different night. But then Priscilla came out of the house to join me, and as soon as I saw the anticipation in her eyes, I could feel myself begin to perk up as well.

I didn't bother kidding myself that her excitement had anything to do with me. She was about to be paid to spend an evening with a bunch of beautiful horses, helping to get them through a difficult situation. That was her idea of bliss. Everything and everyone else was far, far secondary to that.

Ryan showed up right on time, and though I hadn't thought to prepare Priscilla for our driver's eccentricities, he seemed to dial things back a bit once she and I were both inside the truck, much to my relief. He offered us something to drink, so before she could reply, I reached into the console with absolute nonchalance, pulled out a bottle of water, and held it toward her. "Perrier?"

The look she flashed me from the backseat was a mixture of amusement and astonishment. Had we been alone, I would have warned her that it was only to get more bizarre from here.

Once we arrived at Natasha's, I couldn't help but see the place through Priscilla's eyes. Like me the first time I had come here, she seemed to find it beautiful and impressive, but also like me, she did not seem covetous of it. "This world is not my home," was something Christians often said, but being in a place like this, it felt more like, "And *this* world is *really* not my home."

I thought we would be ushered right to the stables, but Ryan said Natasha had insisted we come to the party to say hello and hit the buffet first.

"You have about an hour before the fireworks start," he told us, peering toward the darkening horizon, "so you guys can just fill up a plate and then head on down to the stables yourselves. That should give you enough time before all the noise to walk around and let the horses hear your voices and get used your scents. You know the drill. You can eat as you work."

"Sounds good," I said, but I could see Priscilla instantly stiffening beside me.

"I've already eaten," she said quickly to Ryan, "so maybe I'll just go on straight to the stables."

He shook his head. "Sorry, but you and Jake and your success with January are all anyone's talking about. Natasha is eager to meet you in person, Priscilla."

I shot my companion a consoling glance, but she seemed okay. This was a paying gig, after all, and I guess the worker in her accepted her fate, knowing it was just part of the job.

What was not part of the job, I realized a few minutes later as we were greeted by Natasha and introduced to her guests, was being someone's token Amish, as if we were party favors that could be shown off and passed around. More than once she laughingly referred to us as her "little pair of Amish horse whisperers," which felt rather offensive to me. At least when I glanced Priscilla's way, I was glad to see that her expression was more bemused than anything else.

Once we were freed to get our food and go, we did so quickly, moving down the line of the buffet, scooping this and that onto our plates without even taking the time to see what it was, and then laying across the top of each a second plate, upside down, just to keep the food warm and debris-free as we walked.

We headed for the stable, waiting until we were inside and alone before we burst out laughing. I apologized to Priscilla for dragging her into this, but she just grinned and said not to worry, that the horses made it all worthwhile.

She was eager to see them, so we set our plates aside and went on a tour. Over the next half hour, she and I slowly moved from stall to stall, greeting each animal, allowing them to get comfortable with us, and familiarizing ourselves with their personalities as much as we could, watching for signs of the more anxious ones. As we neared the end of the long building, we were both especially glad to see January, who seemed happy as a clam, thanks to the beautiful dog lying on the ground asleep, nearby.

I wasn't sure what we'd be in for once the fireworks started, so as the time approached, I suggested we close all the doors and windows to block out as much of the sound from outside as possible. Ordinarily, they would have all been closed anyway, just to keep in the air-conditioning, but this was a cool night, so apparently the breezes had been enough.

In any event, after we were all sealed in, we returned to our party food and began to eat as we waited. I'd never seen Priscilla in such a good mood, and she was even a little silly as we tasted the various items on our plates and ventured guesses as to what they were.

"Pickled Kiwi eggs imported from Australia," she said in a snobby British accent as she held up a deviled egg before popping it into her mouth.

"Sea squid from the depths of the Indian Ocean," I replied, biting into a curvy French fry-type item. I'd just been kidding, but I realized too late that whatever it was actually did taste like seafood, so for all I knew, I'd been right.

As we were finishing our meals, I heard a soft sort of booming sound in the distance and realized that the fireworks had begun. Jumping into action, we tossed our paper plates into the trash. Much to our relief, there was hardly a reaction at all. One Appaloosa got a little bit spooky, but we figured that was because she was closest to the door and could hear the noise a little too well. Once we relocated her to a stall farther back in the building and on the other side, she calmed right down.

"Easy-peasy," I said to Priscilla, holding out both hands, palms upward, with a grin.

The smile she gave me in return rivaled the beauty of all the fireworks in the sky.

Clearing my throat, I turned and began to make another stroll up and down the aisle. Behind me, I could hear Priscilla moving in the opposite direction, toward January. Once I pivoted and headed down that way myself, I was surprised to find her comforting not the horse but the horse's dog. Kneeling on the floor, she had her arms around the beautiful retriever and was cooing softly as she stroked the animal's fur.

"The poor thing was shaking," she said, glancing up at me with a smile

I just smiled at her in return, but then an image popped into my head: Priscilla as mother, cradling a baby, and cooing just this way. Maybe a house full of instant children would end up being a perfect fit for her. Everyone was always underestimating her, and I decided I would not do the same.

On the other hand, something about the image of her with some other man's children depressed me, so I moved over to the far side of January's stall and busied myself by looking out of the window. Instantly, a burst of red and yellow light exploded in the sky in front of me.

"Come look. You can see them from here."

Priscilla came toward me, the dog at her heels. She joined me at the window and we stood there, side by side, both of us ooing and aahing at the beauty of the display. From time to time, I tore away my attention from the drama outside to make sure all was well in here. The horses seemed fine. As I turned back to look out of the window again, my chin brushed across the starchy white fabric of Priscilla's *kapp*. Suddenly, I was all too aware—of her proximity, of her beauty, of the very *femaleness* of her. Closing my eyes, I breathed in slowly, taking in the scents of cinnamon and lavender that wafted from her hair.

When I opened my eyes, I realized she had turned toward me, looking as if she, too, had become aware of some hidden longing in this very moment. Our mouths were mere inches apart. She took in a small, quick breath. My heart began to pound.

I don't know who leaned in first. All I know is that as the fireworks lit up the sky just outside, we somehow began to move together inside, slowly closing that small distance between us. It wasn't until our lips were millimeters apart that I managed to come to my senses.

"I'm sorry," I whispered, jerking my head back, my mind suddenly filled with images of Amanda and some guy named Noah and Indiana and Pennsylvania and all the many, many reasons why this could never ever happen.

"I'd better check on the Appaloosa," I said, turning and quickly striding away.

Priscilla did not reply at all.

In fact, we barely said two words to each other the rest of the night—not in the stable, not in the pickup, and not even when we got home and climbed out onto the driveway.

Mostly I felt guilty.

Mostly she looked embarrassed.

As Ryan gave a final wave and drove off, I knew I ought to say something, anything—an apology? An explanation?—but as soon as I opened my mouth to speak, she shook her head and turned toward the house. I decided to hold my tongue, because, really, what was there to say? I didn't understand what had happened.

All I knew was that it couldn't ever happen again.

Twenty-Five

The next day was a quiet one, with work to keep me busy and not a single glimpse of Priscilla anywhere. That afternoon, I went looking for Amos up at the house and found Roseanna sitting at the kitchen table, her hands wrapped around a mug of coffee. The sun cast a mellow, almost sympathetic hue around her. A crumpled tissue rested near her elbow, and her eyes were rimmed with glassy, ready-to-fall tears. My first thought was that someone close to the Kinsingers had died. My real reason for coming inside the big house skittered away.

"What is it, Roseanna? What's the matter?"

She startled, picked up the tissue, and dabbed at her nose. "Oh, Jake. I didn't hear you."

"What happened? Are you okay?"

"I'm fine." Roseanna smiled sadly. "She's leaving."

"What? Who's leaving?" But I knew in an instant whom she meant.

"Priscilla. She decided to go back to Indiana."

The air in the room seemed to shift. I couldn't quite wrap my head around Roseanna's words. Priscilla's leaving would certainly mean that her social life was no longer my responsibility. But instead of feeling relieved, my initial sensation was a wave of disappointment.

"What do you mean, she's leaving? It's only the fifth of July."

Before Roseanna could answer me, the truth filled my mind. She was leaving because of what happened between us last night.

A surge of guilt swept over me. My careless behavior the evening before was certainly the reason she was deciding to leave now, well before the end of the summer. The accompanying thought that she was returning for a secondary reason, to accept a marriage proposal from a man I just knew she did not love, sent me to the chair next to Roseanna.

"Please, please tell me she's not going back to marry that guy."

Relief swelled inside me when Roseanna shook her head. "No. She said she's still holding to the end of September before making a decision on that."

So it was just me she was running from, I thought to myself. It had to be me who was driving her away.

"She's not going back to Otto and Lorraine's, though," Roseanna continued when I said nothing. "She's going to live with her Great-Aunt Cora and serve as her caregiver. At least for a while. Cora's been under the weather."

"Priscilla told us she was done with caregiving. She's going to be miserable there."

Roseanna dabbed at her nose. "I know. That's exactly what I said to her. But she thinks it'll be different with Cora. The woman lives next door to Priscilla's grandparents on a small apple orchard near Elkhart. Part of the job involves working the orchard, which means Priscilla will be outside a lot. Plus she gets along well with her grandparents—and she's especially fond of Cora."

An unwelcome ache was forming in my chest at the thought of Priscilla packing her bags. It bothered me, and the fact that it did also bothered me.

"So she's leaving? Just like that?"

Roseanna traced the handle of her mug with a finger. "I wish we had been able to make her happy here. This will weigh on Amos. He felt he owed it to his brother to do right by Priscilla. And yet I suppose I can understand why she wants to go back. I think she tried to make it work with us. She tried hard to find her place here—"

"No, she didn't."

Roseanna looked up at me. "What?"

"I don't think she tried very hard. It's only been a month. I don't call that trying very hard."

"Yes, but you're...you're a man, Jake. I don't think you feel as deeply about things as she does. I don't think even *I* do. It's different for her. She's always been such a sensitive girl. I know people think she's aloof and indifferent, but that's not what she is. She just takes everything to heart."

That didn't seem like an excuse for running away. Not to me, it didn't. "That doesn't mean she should."

"You can't help being the kind of person you are."

I wanted to say, "Of course you can." When I said nothing, she went on.

"Amos and I are very grateful for all that you and Amanda did for Priscilla. You both went out of your way to include her and make her feel a part of things here. We can't thank you enough."

But I didn't want Roseanna's gratitude. I wanted to talk some sense into one Priscilla Kinsinger.

I stood and pushed in my chair. "Where is she?"

"Her mind's made up, Jake. Don't feel bad. You and Amanda did your best."

"*Ya.* Sure. But where is she?"

"In the barn with her horse." Roseanna brought the coffee cup to her lips. "Amos told her she could leave Voyager in Stephen's care for the time being."

As I strode across the gravel drive, I kept thinking that the last thing Priscilla should do was leave Lancaster County the same broken girl she was when she'd left it before. Somehow, I would have to convince her to stay. I didn't know exactly why it mattered so much to me, but I wasn't going to take the time to analyze that now.

I walked into the barn. Priscilla and Stephen were at the back, inside Voyager's stall. They were talking in gentle tones, and Stephen was brushing Voyager with the purple curry brush that was Priscilla's. Comet, curled up just outside the stall, was gnawing on a plastic milk jug. He thumped his tail when he saw me coming. When I reached Priscilla and Stephen, they both looked up.

"Hello, Jake," she said, her tone affirming that she knew I'd been informed of what she had decided to do.

"Priscilla's going to Indiana to live with her great-aunt," Stephen volunteered, his voice sad and enthusiastic at the same time. "She's letting me take care of Voyager for her."

"So I heard," I said, my eyes never leaving Priscilla's.

She looked away first.

"Stephen, would you mind giving me a moment with Priscilla? I need to tell her something."

After a beat, he seemed to realize I was asking him to leave us. "Oh. Okay." He handed the brush to Priscilla, reached up to pat the horse, and then walked past me. He turned to her as he went. "*Danke*, Priscilla. I will take good care of him."

"*Ya*. I know you will," she said as she resumed brushing where Stephen had left off.

He whistled for Comet, and the dog trotted happily after him. Once the boy was no longer in hearing range, she looked at me with pleading in her eyes.

"Don't let them take Voyager back to the auction ring," she said softly. "He really can learn to be useful here. Don't let them, okay?"

"He's not my horse, Priscilla. Not my choice."

"You know what I mean. Uncle Amos promised me he wouldn't. Just make sure he keeps that promise, okay? It may take a while, but I'm going to save up enough money to pay for Voyager's transport out to Indiana."

I couldn't imagine going to all that trouble—for a mere Thoroughbred, no less—but I knew Amos was a man of his word. I was trying to decide whether to remind her of that or try to talk her out of the idea entirely when I saw the look on her face. She was so earnest that in the end I simply replied, "Okay. I'll make sure."

"Thank you."

I took a step closer to her. "Don't do this."

She turned her head to me as she brushed. I couldn't read her expression. "Do what?"

I felt heat rush into my face. "Don't use what happened…with us, last night, as your excuse for leaving. That's not the real reason you've decided to go."

She stared at me for a long moment and then turned away again, intent on her brushing. "It's not?" she asked, her voice strangely calm. "Then what is?"

I sucked in a deep breath, willing her to understand. "You're leaving because of your mother."

Her brush strokes paused only a second. "My mother."

"Yes. Because of what really happened the day she died."

Priscilla again froze for a brief moment, and then she shifted farther along the horse and launched back into her brushing with vigor.

"What do you think happened, Jake? Go ahead, tell me. Clearly, you've uncovered some big secret."

"It's just a theory," I said, watching her work. "I mean, how could I really know for sure? You hide everything from me."

She raised one eyebrow, so I added, "From everybody."

"If I hide everything, then what makes you so certain my leaving has to do with my mother?"

"Because it's so obvious—to everyone."

"Everyone?"

I shrugged. "Well, to Roseanna and me. But I know Amos will see it too once he finds out you're going. As will Amanda."

Priscilla's hand stilled for a second. Then she continued brushing. Instinctively, I reached out and placed my hand on top of hers. A tingling sensation seemed to course through me. She must have sensed it. She turned her head quickly to face me as though my hand had trapped hers.

"Priscilla, please. Don't run away from what happened here back then. You can't live your life regretting things this way."

She pulled her hand out slowly from underneath mine. "You know nothing about the past or what I would do differently if I could go back."

"I know that even now you still blame yourself for your mother's death. When all is said and done, you still believe that you killed her, don't you?" There seemed to be no way of avoiding the question anymore. The time for polite pretense was over.

Priscilla's eyes widened for just a moment and then grew narrow as her gaze locked on mine. "Is that what you think?"

"Do you?"

She turned back to her horse and stroked his head. "It's pretty simple, Jake. If I had made different choices that day, she wouldn't have died."

"Our days are numbered by God."

"That doesn't mean the choices we make are without consequences."

"So that's it, then? You're leaving here with a buggy load of unfinished business you'll carry with you until the day you die? That's the kind of life you want?"

She closed her eyes and seemed to draw strength from the warmth of Voyager's body under her hands. "I'm doing the best I can," she said a moment later.

But I sensed hesitation in every word. She was escaping to Indiana, not returning. She was running away, very much like the last time when she had been sent away. She and I both knew it.

"Why did you even come back? If all this was for nothing, why did you even come?"

She placed the brush inside the bucket hanging on the rail post. "You and I have discussed this before. You know full well that I came here because I believed that's what God was telling me He wanted me to do."

"Exactly. Don't you think it was for a reason? And now you're leaving before you've even managed to figure out why."

She seemed to think on this for a moment. "Maybe I was wrong about that. Maybe I only thought this is what the Lord wanted me to do." She frowned as though she didn't even believe it herself. "Look. I retraced my steps and revisited every moment. I don't know...there isn't...I think it's time I moved on."

Her cheeks had blossomed crimson as she struggled to complete her thoughts. She would not make eye contact with me.

"Is this about last night?" I said, heat rising to my cheeks a little too. "I promise you, that won't happen again."

Priscilla winced when I said this, as though I had burned her with a hot iron. "It's just time for me to go."

"Because I almost kissed you?"

"Because of a lot of things."

"But you've fixed nothing!" I exclaimed. "Surely God brought you back here to put to rest once and for all that it was just an accident that your mother fell. Do you really think she'd want you to be hanging on to this, unable to envision a life of happiness for yourself?"

"Hanging on to what?" Priscilla asked, her tone heavy with disappointment and uncertainty. As I'd said earlier, she was using my mistake the day before as a cover-up for the real reason she was going back to Indiana, I was sure of it. She couldn't live with the daily reminders of what she had done, so she was heading back to a place where there weren't any.

"Come on, Priscilla. Don't pretend you don't know what I'm talking about."

She took a step toward me and looked me straight in the eyes. "You're the one who doesn't know what you're talking about."

"Oh, really?"

"Yes. Really."

"All right. How about this then? How about I tell you what I've figured out and you tell me how far off the mark I am? How about that?"

I expected her eyes to fill with dread at the idea that I'd put the puzzle together, but she just crossed her arms in front of her chest. "Fine. Tell me."

The few times I had envisioned having this needed conversation with Priscilla, I had imagined it being a little less fractious. A lot less fractious. I had pictured my gently telling her what I'd come to surmise about the day her mother died, and her crying softly as the weight of six years of holding it in fell off all around her. I never guessed we'd be standing in a horse barn with arms crossed, voices raised, and tempers flared.

Nonetheless, I prayed a silent prayer for favor and hoped God would grant it. In that second of prayer, I sensed my anger subside a bit, thankfully.

"I am not trying to make this worse for you. I'm really not. I just think you need to face the truth of what happened here and move past it."

"Tell me," she repeated, with only slightly less rancor.

I hesitated. "Your family thinks you couldn't hear your mother calling for you and that you'd slipped out to the barn but forgot to tell her. That's why they think you've no reason to believe it was your fault. But I think maybe you *did* hear her calling for you. I think maybe you and your *mamm* had an argument that afternoon. That's why you were supposed to be up in your room, right? Any other fourteen-year-old girl would have been in the kitchen with her mother while she was canning, but the argument ended with you being sent to your room, and you were angry, so you snuck out to the barn. And you *did* hear her calling for you, but you didn't answer because you were still angry and didn't want to talk to her then. You didn't know the reason she was calling for you was because she'd cut herself and needed help. So you didn't go in. She stopped calling for you, and you just stayed in the barn, didn't you? You didn't know she'd fallen down the stairs until you heard Roseanna. That's why you think it's your fault."

While I spoke, Priscilla's facial expression did not change. I saw her eyes widen only slightly when I said I believed she and her mother had argued.

After I was finished, I waited for her to respond. I expected either outright denial or tearful confession. I was confident I had hit the nail on the head.

She didn't respond, so I spoke again, my tone as gentle as I could make it. "I'm right, aren't I?"

She looked away for just a second, as though to gather her thoughts.

When she turned back to me, her words were even and low and without a trace of anger or anguish. "Not exactly, no," she said, but then her face took on an oddly determined expression, her eyes hard, her chin firm. "You want to know what really happened that day?"

I nodded once.

She grabbed Voyager's halter and began to maneuver him out of the stall.

"When was the last time you rode Willow?"

"What?"

"Can you ride Willow? Can you ride her bareback?"

I hadn't ridden Willow since I was a teenager. It just wasn't something Amish men did. "I suppose so."

"Then come with me and I will show you."

Twenty-Six

When we were outside on the gravel, Priscilla led Voyager toward the back paddock. I followed with Willow, who naturally gravitated toward the railing the closer we got to it, thinking she was being led there for a late afternoon stretch. I eased her away, only to have her nose me toward the gate when we were about to pass it.

"Hang tight, girl. We're not going into the paddock today."

Willow nickered a response that was hard for me to read. She was either excited to be doing something unexpected or wary of a bend in routine.

When we passed the paddock fencing and she could no longer see it, Willow settled back into an easy walk again. I could tell we were headed toward a dirt trail that ran through the Kinsingers' back cornfields. Amos, Mahlon, and Owen grew these acres for silage only, thank goodness. Picking season wouldn't kick in for a few more weeks, which meant there probably wasn't anyone out here right now to observe what we were doing.

"Have you ridden Willow before?" Priscilla said, as the Kinsinger houses and buildings fell away behind us.

"It's been a while."

"She won't throw you?"

I honestly didn't know what Willow would do if I attempted to ride her. I sure hoped she would remember the last time we had done it, and that it had been fun. But that was back in my *rumspringa* days, when some buddies and I had started riding our horses into the back country using a couple of old saddles we'd bought at a mud sale. We just did it for sport and to sample one of those friend's uneducated attempts at brewing his own beer. It was stupid, riding off as though we were cowboys out West, drinking beer and pretending we liked to smoke cigarettes. Whenever I thought of the last time I rode Willow, I thought of how foolish we had been.

"I don't think she will. The last time was with a saddle, though."

"You don't need a saddle," Priscilla responded quickly. "You just need to know how to sit. Do you?"

"Sure."

The Kinsinger farm buildings were no longer in view, but farm buildings belonging to other people—albeit from a distance—were. When we got on our horses, anybody out in their garden or field who had good vision would be able to see two riders on horseback. Two Amish riders on horseback. Nervousness began to creep over me at the thought of someone recognizing me with an Amish young woman, on our way to apparently nowhere civilized. What was I doing?

The Amish frowned on riding horses for several reasons, beyond the fact that buggies were more practical for families and for toting things around. Horseback riding was also considered by some to be a worldly form of sport, not to mention an area for pride and—for Priscilla at least—immodesty. Bottom line, as a church member, I shouldn't have been out here.

And yet, given the extenuating circumstances, this could be considered a sort of gray area—or at least that's what I was telling myself now. As Christians, we were to love one another and bear one other's burdens. If this was what it was going to take to get Priscilla to share her particular burden with me, then maybe it was a risk worth taking. At least my bishop was a good and reasonable man, the kind who listened to every side and took in all the facts before acting on accusations.

But that didn't mean Priscilla and I shouldn't be careful.

I considered suggesting that she and I wait a few hours, when we could do this under cover of darkness. I held my tongue, though, fearing that any delay might cause her to have second thoughts about sharing the truth with me. Better to risk being seen on horseback than to lose out on this opportunity entirely.

A bend in the farm trail led us to a grove of ancient sycamore trees, mostly living, though a few had succumbed to lightning or wind storms. Several limbs lay strewn about, and sawn off trunks revealed that someone had harvested the fallen trees for firewood. Priscilla stopped at a sizeable stump. She led Voyager alongside it. Then she kicked off her shoes, stood barefoot on the stump, and hiked up her dress past her knees. I started to turn away but then realized she was wearing cut-off trousers under her skirt. She saw me looking at her.

"Owen gave them to me." She lifted herself easily onto Voyager's bare back, swinging her right leg over as though she had done it a hundred times before. She probably had. Maybe not on Voyager, but on other horses. He tossed up his head and pawed the dirt a few strokes.

"Easy, boy," Priscilla said gently as she leaned her head toward the horse's long neck and stroked him. "Let's wait for Jake."

"Does Owen know you made riding britches out of his old trousers?" I asked with a nervous laugh, not sure if that solved the modesty issue or not.

"Owen doesn't ask such personal questions." She lifted the reins into her lap, pressed her legs gently to Voyager's side, and eased him away. "Use the stump if you think Willow's going to balk at your climbing onto her back."

Without stirrups or a recent experience of me hoisting myself onto Willow, I decided that was probably a good idea. I led her to the stump, breathed a prayer for protection, told Willow what an amazing gal she was, and heaved myself on her back. She immediately swung her head up in surprise and danced a few steps toward Voyager and Priscilla. I cinched the reins to gain more control.

"Whoa, there, Willow. Whoa. Whoa," I said as she pranced about in a circle, obviously needing a moment to familiarize herself with the feeling of having a man on her back.

"Don't press your legs to her side to stay on. She'll think you're telling her to go," Priscilla said as she and Voyager calmly watched Willow and me. "Feel her beneath you. Let her feel you. When we start to canter, rock your hips forward toward her ears to absorb the bounce of her trot. If you squeeze your legs, she'll take off."

"I *know* how to ride a horse," I said, more defensively than I wanted to.

"Okay, but right at this moment you look as if you don't trust her. You need to relax, Jake. She can tell you're wondering what she's going to do. If I can see from ten feet away that you're uptight about her, then you can be sure she senses it too."

"I'm not uptight!" I shot back.

"Right."

I hated to admit that she was correct, but it had been too long since I had ridden Willow. I had lost my confidence, not just in myself to ride, but in her to carry me.

"Okay, you win," I sighed as I attempted to loosen my grip, my legs, my sit, my control.

"It's not a competition," Priscilla responded. "Feel Willow beneath you. You will sense when she believes you are ready."

"When *I'm* ready?" I retorted and Willow yanked on the reins in my hands. It took a stretch of seconds, but I finally realized what Priscilla meant. As I allowed myself to think of Willow as my partner and not my vehicle, I also began to sense she was starting to treat me as less her rider and more her companion. I had never really considered Willow as an equal when it came to riding. She had been my chauffeur too long. My employee. But now, sitting atop her bare back, I could feel my horse's strength and power. I also sensed her vulnerability, her desire to be safe.

In that sense, she was no different than any of us. No different than me.

"Good girl," I said, as the connection between us strengthened and Willow settled into her reins.

I turned to Priscilla. "I think we're ready."

"Do you remember what I said about sitting the canter without a saddle?"

I didn't.

"When Willow starts to canter, rock your hips forward toward her ears to absorb the bounce. You'll hurt her if you don't. And don't squeeze your legs to keep your balance. She won't know what you want, especially if you pull back on the reins at the same time."

"Okay," I said, hoping I could keep my balance after so long a gap between rides.

"Do you know where Blue Rock Creek is?"

I looked up and toward the rolling landscape in front of us. Owen had taken me there to hunt crawdads when we were kids. It was a good two miles away and nestled in between farm holdings. The good news was that it hadn't been hard to get to if you stuck to the trail, sight unseen. I hoped it was still that way now.

I nodded.

"Can you find it if we get separated?"

"Separated? It's not that far."

"*Ya*," she said, grabbing the strings of her *kapp* and tying them in a quick bow under her chin. "But Voyager's going to gallop there."

I laughed. "Can't control your horse?"

"He knows I like it. And I know he does too."

And with that, Priscilla clicked her cheek and pressed her legs to Voyager's side. He took off without so much as a whinny. In seconds they were a hundred yards away.

"Great. All right, Willow. Let's see what you've got."

I tapped her side with the heels of my boots, and she reared up a bit and then cantered off, like a little steam locomotive puffing out of a train station. At first I had my rhythm all wrong. I was sitting her too tight and our bodies weren't in sync. She was hurting me and I had to be hurting her. I made a concerted effort to do what Priscilla said and timed my upward hip movement to coincide with Willow's. A few strides later, we seemed to find each other. She increased her speed, and at once I could tell that she longed to run. What horse didn't if given the freedom to? I could see Priscilla on the trail ahead, her *kapp* flopping at the back of her neck by its ties, her bare feet comfortably at Voyager's sides. The two of them looked like one seamless creature. They would soon be a speck if I didn't let Willow gallop to keep up.

I pressed my legs to her flanks and said the words she was probably itching to hear. "Giddy up!"

My horse joyfully obeyed, and though it took me a second to recalibrate my hip movements with hers, soon we were flying down the trail in pursuit of our companions. I felt my hat lift off my head and dance away, but I didn't look back to see where it landed. My lungs filled with the sweetness of the rushing air around me as Willow ran, her neck stretched out in front, the dirt at her pounding feet flying up like powdered snow in winter.

I couldn't remember ever having felt so invigorated and alive. It was as if everything around me and within me was suddenly charged with energy and clarity. It almost took my breath away, and I wondered as we flew down the path if it was wrong somehow to feel so refreshed to the depths of my being. In truth, it was nearly intoxicating.

Yet all Willow was doing was what she'd been enabled by her Creator to do. Run. And I sat a willing passenger, in awe of this animal's speed and power, both of which had been given to her by God. It felt like praise, rushing down the path like that. There really weren't adequate words to describe it any other way.

In far too quick a span of time, we were descending the trail to a little valley and Blue Rock Creek. Ahead of me, Priscilla slowed Voyager to a canter and then a trot. I grudgingly followed suit. She looked behind and seemed pleased I had been able to keep up.

The creek meandered across the county, branching off here and there and changing names from mile to mile. Here, where the water was at its widest, was known as Blue Rock Creek.

As we slowed our horses to a walk, we led them closer to the banks. The creek below us was a good thirty feet across and deep enough to go wading, although I was glad no one was enjoying the cool of the day here. Trees of various types lined either side of the creek, and reeds and cattails had sprung up in the marshy patches where the water was the stillest. Dragonflies darted about, and a pair of wood ducks quacked their annoyance at our intrusion. The sun behind us had dipped low in the sky, casting golden light on the pastoral scene. The trail was just barely wide enough for me to bring Willow alongside Voyager.

"You lost your hat," Priscilla said, turning her head to look at me.

The pins in her hair had loosened, and her *kapp* straggled across her back like a downed sail.

"You barely held onto yours," I returned.

I expected her to realize then that her hair had practically fallen around her shoulders and to reach back for her *kapp* and hastily replace it on her head, but that's not what she did. She just let it continue to hang by its strings, which remained tied at her neck. And as for her hair, she merely swept away a dark long lock that framed her face.

"You can probably find it on the way back," she said.

We continued to walk our horses at a gentle pace along the top of the bank so they could cool down.

"There's a place up ahead in the birch grove where they can drink," Priscilla offered.

"You've been here before," I said, partly in jest. It was obvious she had been here before. Lots of times.

"I used to come here with my *daed*. We'd ride here on Shiloh. He'd put me in front and hang on to me with one arm and guide his horse with the other. *Mamm* never knew *Daed* let Shiloh gallop here. She thought we walked him."

I looked at her face, wrapped in the memory of a wonderful time in her life. She seemed serene, though, not pained. I said nothing. I just wanted her to continue.

"And I came here a lot after he died, which unfortunately *Mamm* did know about. She didn't like it. She was sure I would get hurt, that Shiloh would throw me or I'd fall off or I'd drown in the creek or I'd get struck by lightning or the earth would simply open up and swallow me whole."

I waited.

"And she was pressured by other people to tell me it wasn't right that I was riding a horse like that, like a boy, like a rebel. A respectable Amish girl didn't ride a horse. Certainly not like that. And not bareback."

She looked out over the landscape and was quiet for a moment. The creek here had become more of a brook. It moved below us and past us with speed, bubbling over boulders and stones as though there was somewhere it needed to be.

"I was forbidden to come here, at least by horse," she said, and she turned away from the water to stare at the trail ahead and the copse of trees we walked toward. "I tried to obey, but sometimes I just couldn't. On full moons, when there was light enough to see, I would come here. I knew it wasn't right, but I thought I'd go mad if I didn't. *Mamm* was so protective of me all the time. I was suffocating in that house. I didn't have friends to talk to, and I felt so alone."

"Amanda tried to be your friend then," I said gently, after a moment's pause.

Priscilla shook her head. "You've told me that before."

"Are you saying she didn't?"

"I don't mean to insult your girlfriend or anything, but she and the other girls thought I was weird. I know they did. And they were right. I wasn't like them. And I guess if that's what weird is, that's what I was. I didn't like their gossip and their little games and the way they talked about boys—and yes, Jake, they started noticing boys at ten—or the way they thought of everything as a game. They seemed so superficial."

She turned to face me. "I'm sorry to say that. I am. But it was how they seemed to me. They…they still seem that way."

Words to defend Amanda were about to fall off my tongue, but Priscilla filled in the momentary silence before I could say it wasn't true.

"I shouldn't have said that. I'm sorry. I am the weird one. Forget I said that. Please?"

I could only nod my head as it dawned on me that maybe she was right about Amanda. About a lot of things.

"I didn't bring you here to talk about that," she said.

At that moment I suddenly realized Priscilla had every right to go back to Indiana. There was only lingering nothingness here for her.

"You don't have to tell me anything."

"No. I want to. I think maybe…I'm supposed to."

We entered the copse of trees. She slid off her horse and so did I. The bank of the creek was level here and a perfect little jetty had formed for an animal to get a drink. We led Voyager and Willow to the water's edge and they lowered their heads. We looped their leads onto a low-lying branch.

Priscilla pointed to a log a few feet away that had been rolled into place by long-ago hands. Her father's perhaps. Or maybe hers.

We sat down on it.

"You think you've figured out what happened to my *mamm* the day she died, and you're right about one thing. There had been an argument. She sent me to my room, and I snuck out without her knowing it. But I didn't ignore her calls for me because I wasn't in the barn when she fell. I was nowhere near the barn."

Clarity fell across me like a spill of light into a dark room. "You came here that afternoon. To be alone? And maybe away from her?"

Priscilla looked down at her hands and shook her head. "Yes. I did come here. But no. It wasn't about me and her. I came here to meet up with the boy I thought was in love with me."

PART TWO

Twenty-Seven

In the days, weeks, and even months that would follow our conversation in the birch trees, I would look back on the stretch of time when Priscilla shared her story as though it existed outside the span of our appointed days. As she talked, time seemed to stop, and I was ushered into the quiet, private folds of her memories as a rare guest. The only guest. Her words would stretch across my mind and stitch themselves into the fabric of my own needy soul.

She had crept out of her room the afternoon her mother died to meet a boy. His name was Connor, and he was a guest at the cottage. He was sixteen, *Englisch*, and the first boy to ever show even the slightest interest in Priscilla.

The summer she was fourteen, Connor Knight and his divorced mother, Elaine, were guests at the cottage. They came at the beginning of August, Elaine to work on her dissertation on how historical cultures struggle to survive despite modernity, and Connor because she wouldn't let him stay home alone for a month at their house on Long Island. Connor had made some poor choices earlier that summer and during the school year, so this was her form of discipline. He was cut off from his rowdy friends, the drinking parties, his Xbox, and the video games she didn't approve of. She took away his cell phone, and he was stuck in Lancaster County with a case of books she required him to read—old classics, mostly—and running shoes she insisted he use. Apparently, he had been on the track team that spring until he was put on academic suspension for failing grades.

It was obvious to Priscilla that Connor wasn't happy about being there, but she could also tell within a few days after meeting him that he didn't really want to wreck his life. He felt bad about the mistakes he had made and the peer pressure he'd caved in to. He didn't want to be at the cottage with his mother, but he also didn't want to go back to New York and be the same guy he was when he left. He found Priscilla easy to talk to because she was so quiet. She just sat and listened. Priscilla would bring the Knights their breakfast in the mornings, and many times Elaine would be holed up in her room tapping away at her laptop when Priscilla came back for the dishes. Connor would be sitting on the steps with one of the books his mother had instructed him to read, but he'd just be staring off toward the grain fields that stretched beyond the Kinsinger dwellings. Before she knew it, she'd be sitting next to him, listening to him talk about his friends back in New York and how hard it was to figure out life.

Priscilla wasn't attracted to him at first. She felt sorry for him. And when he asked her if she had ever done something with a friend she'd never do if she were alone, just because the friend did it, she was completely honest with him. Because she wasn't trying to impress him, she plainly told him that was a dumb reason to do anything. Any friend who would like a person less because he made his own choices was no friend worth sacrificing his convictions for.

Connor had laughed and said convictions were for criminals. Priscilla told him he might want to try having some before brushing them off completely, as it was obvious he didn't really know what they were. And he told her he had never met anyone like her before. But she could tell he meant it in an admirable way—Connor didn't think she was weird.

One evening, he came into the petting barn as Priscilla was taking care of the animals and asked her what was the use of having ironclad convictions if it meant you were alone. Priscilla said she'd rather be alone and make her own decisions about the person she wanted to be than to be surrounded by people she was so desperate to please that she copied their every stupid move.

Connor began to seek her out after that. He'd come back from a run, and Priscilla would be weeding the vegetable garden or hanging laundry, and he'd stand there and talk to her, sometimes for an hour. In these talks, Priscilla learned that Connor's parents had divorced when he was eight and his dad now lived in Florida. He saw him two weeks in June and at Thanksgiving. She told him about her *daed* and how she missed him. Even though they were worlds apart, Connor and Priscilla had two huge things in common. They missed their fathers, and they both felt trapped by their current situations. He felt trapped in friendships that were bringing him down and by the strict rules his mother had laid out for the summer, and she felt trapped by her mother's constant protective hand on her.

One day they were in the petting barn, and Connor was helping Priscilla feed and water all the animals. They were talking about what they would change about their lives if they could. She told him she sometimes snuck away to a lovely birch grove on moonlit nights, that she rode her father's horse there, bareback, and it was in those moments that she felt she wasn't trapped after all. She felt free. Those secret midnight rides made all the other days of her life possible. He asked her when the next full moon was and if she would bring him there. Priscilla thought maybe he was joking, but he took her hand and said he really wanted to see the creek—and her—by moonlight.

He was still holding her hand when Sharon stepped into the barn to tell Priscilla something; she didn't even know what because Sharon never actually got to it. The look she gave Priscilla was one she'd never forget. Connor let go of her hand and said hello to Sharon, but she didn't acknowledge him. She just said Priscilla was to come to the house. Priscilla told her she'd be there in a minute, that she was almost finished, and her mother said, "No. Now."

Priscilla, embarrassed and angry, followed her mother into the house. Inside, Sharon told Priscilla that she was not to be alone with 'that *Englisch* boy,' as she called him, for the remainder of the Knights' time at the cottage. She was to have no contact with the Knights at all. Sharon would bring their breakfast to them for the last week of their stay. And she would have Owen take care of the barn animals if Priscilla could not see to it that she did it without that *Englisch* boy's company.

Priscilla told her *mamm* that neither Connor nor she had done anything wrong, that she had only been encouraging him to make better decisions with his life. But Sharon didn't want to hear it. She told Priscilla she'd seen the way Connor was looking at her just then, when her hand was in his.

It didn't matter how much Priscilla tried to tell her mother she was wrong, she wouldn't listen. And the more she tried to tell her, the more Priscilla became aware of how devastated she was that her time with Connor was over. She hadn't realized how attached she'd grown to him in the three weeks she had known him. He was her only friend, and now she was forbidden to see him. When Priscilla begged her *mamm* to reconsider letting her see Connor, Sharon told Priscilla she had to trust her on this. Nothing good could come from her continuing to see that boy.

Priscilla told her *mamm* his name was Connor and she moved past her, went upstairs to her room, and shut the door.

That night, the moon wasn't full, but it was bright and the sky was awash with stars. When Priscilla got into bed she heard a tapping at her window. She moved the curtains and saw Connor standing below. Priscilla raised the window and asked him what he was doing. He said he was waiting for her to take him on that ride she had told him about. That was the first time Priscilla snuck out of the house to be with Connor. It wasn't so hard. Her *mamm* was already asleep in her room. Priscilla knew which stairs creaked, and she knew how to open the front door without making a sound. She haltered Shiloh, and together they walked him slowly across the gravel so that his hooves didn't make a racket. As soon as they were past the back paddock, she got on him and Connor climbed up behind her. Shiloh was a big horse, and Connor was slim and not much taller than Priscilla. The horse did not seem to mind the extra weight. Connor put his arms around Priscilla's middle and in doing so, pulled her close to him. Priscilla's heart fluttered at his touch and his nearness.

"Do you know how to ride?" Priscilla asked Connor, as she attempted to gain control of her pounding heart.

He had replied with, "How hard can it be?" and tightened his hold on her.

Priscilla told him that when she went up, he had to go up. And he said all right. Priscilla didn't let Shiloh canter until they were well away from the farm. And then, when they were on the farm trail where the stump was, she let Shiloh take them away. After a few strides Connor fell into an easy rhythm with her. Their bodies moved as one with Shiloh. The moon was pearl-white and brilliant and the stars sparkled. It was a beautiful night. It didn't occur to Priscilla that she was disobeying her mother. It was as if she were numb to everything she had been taught about honoring her parents. All she sensed was wonder and delight. They arrived at the copse of birch trees and got off Shiloh to let him rest and drink at the creek. Connor told her that was the most thrilling thing he had ever experienced and he put his arms around Priscilla's waist and pulled her to him. He told her he wished he could take her back to New York with him, that he felt as though he was a stronger person when he was around her, and that she was the best thing that had happened to him in a long time. And then Connor's lips were on hers. She had never been kissed before. She had no idea how scary and amazing and breathless a kiss could be. Priscilla said she could have drowned in that kiss. Would have drowned if Shiloh had not whinnied then and she broke away.

As she told me this, Priscilla stopped, and a faraway look seemed to overtake her gaze, even though we were in the exact spot she'd been in when Connor kissed her. I felt as though I were an intruder on that memory, and yet I was also inexplicably jealous.

A few moments passed before she continued.

Connor started to kiss Priscilla again, but she told him they needed to get back before her *mamm* realized she was gone. He reluctantly agreed. On the way back they took a slower pace, and Priscilla told him her mother would be bringing his and his mother's breakfasts for their last week at the cottage and that she had been forbidden to see him. He said, "Just because she saw us holding hands?" and he pulled Priscilla closer to him. He laughed, as though it was the silliest thing he'd ever heard. She told him it would be hard for her to find ways to be with him, and he said he would find a way to steal kisses from her. He wasn't bothered by any of it. Not even her *mamm*'s outrageous edict that she not go near him.

At this moment in her telling me this story, Priscilla seemed at last to realize her hair was loose and falling around her shoulders. It was as if the memory of this episode with Connor Knight reminded her of how close she had been to laying aside her Amish upbringing to be with this *Englisch* boy. She reached for the loose strands and tucked them back into the bun in a haphazard way. Several seconds passed before she continued.

"I should have realized then, when nothing about that day fazed him, that I was far more invested in him than he was in me," she said as she slowly pulled her *kapp* back on her head. "But I didn't. I had completely fallen for him. He had held my hand, held me close, and kissed me. He told me he wanted to bring me back to New York with him. I wasn't thinking with my head anymore, Jake. I wasn't even thinking with my heart. I just wasn't thinking. I was lost in the fog of desire and delight."

She paused, waiting for me to respond to her honest and transparent confession. I suppose she thought I would say I knew what it was like to feel that way, especially when you're young.

But the blistering truth was that I didn't know what it was like to feel that way about someone. I didn't think Amanda felt that way about me. I never sensed her getting lost in any of my kisses.

And I had never felt myself lost in one of hers.

Our kisses were sweet and playful and preliminary. They hinted at what we would share as husband and wife. I looked forward to the marriage bed like any other man my age, but those longings seemed purely physical, unifying, and necessary in comparison. I wanted to be with Amanda because I had been created to be with a woman. God had not designed man to be alone.

But I had never been in the kind of fog Priscilla described.

I didn't even know it existed.

Twenty-Eight

Sharon had watched Priscilla like a hawk after finding her and Connor holding hands in the barn, but she couldn't trail after her daughter every single second. Connor and Priscilla found ways to see each other on the farmstead. It had been almost like a game. Priscilla would come around the corner of one of the outbuildings, and Connor would pop out from behind a wagon or a grain bin or doorway and pull her into his arms and kiss her deep and quick. Then he'd walk away as if nothing had happened. He'd look back at Priscilla and wink as if he couldn't wait for the next time he could catch her alone and kiss her again. Elaine always stopped writing and researching by six, and she and Connor would go into town to eat or shop or see a movie. Priscilla would hear them coming back each night through her open bedroom window. That last week she was especially tuned in to the sound of their car returning.

Two days after the first ride to the trees, Connor hid a note in the petting barn telling Priscilla he wanted to go on another moonlit ride before he left. The previous night had been cloudy and too dark to risk another trip. Priscilla was just starting to write a note in return that she very much wanted to do that, but that they needed a sky without clouds. It was as she was writing her answer that Connor snuck into the barn from behind and swept her into his arms. She nearly fell over in shock. Priscilla tried to tell him her *mamm* might see them and he just laughed and kissed her neck. Priscilla staggered back against the wall of the pen she was standing in, breathless with surprise and dread and desire. She told Connor he had to stop, he had to leave. But his kisses were so wonderful and sweet. She might not have gotten away from him had his cell phone not trilled in his pocket. She had not seen him with a cell phone up to that point because his mother had taken it from him when they got to Lancaster County. But he had it that day.

He frowned at the interruption but yanked the phone out of his pocket and looked at the screen. She was afraid he would get into trouble, and she asked him if his mother knew he had his phone. Connor smiled and said that Priscilla had been such a good influence on him that Elaine had given it back to him a week early. He told Priscilla he was pretty happy that decent coverage was in that part of the county because he had a lot of catching up to do. She didn't know what he meant by "coverage," so she asked. "Bars," he replied, but she still didn't know what he meant. He leaned into her again, kissed her forehead, and said she was adorable.

The phone made another noise. Connor looked at it again, tapped the little keyboard, laughed, and typed some more. Priscilla said he should probably go as her mother was liable to come into the barn any minute to check up on her. He smiled wide and said he had looked on the Internet and saw that there would be a full moon the next night, and that they should meet out at the back paddock at nine o'clock for another ride, clouds or no clouds. She told him ten so that she could be sure her *mamm* was in bed and asleep. He kissed her again and then they heard Sharon's voice nearby. He scooted out the back door.

The next evening, Sharon was up later than usual, and Priscilla kept waiting for her to go into her room, shut her door, and turn out her light. It had been tense in the house between the two of them, and Priscilla could tell the situation between them weighed on her mother. They had barely spoken at supper. Sharon had tried to engage her daughter in conversation, but Priscilla was nervous about meeting Connor. She just wanted the clock to hurry up and get to ten o'clock, and for her mother to hurry up and go to sleep. She needed a few minutes to get to the barn, get Shiloh out of his stall, and then get out to the paddock without being noticed. Rushing him would make him noisy. Priscilla had hoped to be tiptoeing out to the barn a few minutes before ten. But at five minutes before the hour, Sharon was still moving about in her room and Priscilla could see a thin line of light under her door. Priscilla had long since turned out her light so Sharon would think she was already asleep. She would have to just be extremely quiet and leave.

It was a humid night, clear and warm, and she hoped the sounds of crickets outside the house's open windows would mask her footfalls as she passed her mother's room and headed for the stairs. She opened the front door as quietly as she could and stepped out into the moonlit night. There were no lights on in the big house, or in the new house Mahlon was building. A lamp shone out of the window of the guest cottage, but she didn't know if that meant Connor's mom was still up or that Connor had left a light on to return to. She ran across the wet grass to the barn. Priscilla had purposely left Shiloh's halter on him from earlier in the day so that she could just lead him out. She stepped inside to get him and spoke softly so that he wouldn't nicker or whinny. She had just started to lead him out when Sharon appeared in the doorway.

Priscilla stopped. She hadn't heard or seen her coming. All of the sudden she was just there, demanding to know what Priscilla was doing with Shiloh at that time of night. Priscilla tried telling her that she was just taking him for a walk because she couldn't sleep, but Sharon didn't believe her. She kept asking Priscilla where she was going. Priscilla repeatedly told her nowhere. And then the very thing she didn't want to have happen next, happened. Connor, who had probably begun to wonder what had become of her, walked back to the barn from where he had been waiting. He stopped just at the entrance when he heard Sharon's voice and saw that she was in the barn with Priscilla. And then Sharon saw him as well, and she put two and two together. She asked them both what was going on, and Priscilla's eyes grew wide with feigned innocence. Nothing. She said nothing was going on.

Connor thought up a quick lie and asked if everything was okay. He said he had heard voices in the barn, and he'd come out to see if someone needed help or something. But Sharon didn't believe him. She knew the two of them had planned to meet up and have Shiloh take them somewhere.

Sharon turned to Connor and thanked him for his concern, but in the most ungracious tone ever. Then she told him he'd best get back to the guest cottage before his mother worried where he was. She said it as if she was two seconds from going to his mother herself and telling her, paying guest or not, that Connor was to stay away from her daughter. Priscilla could tell Connor wanted to say something in her defense, but she pleaded with her eyes in the dusky moonlight spilling into the barn to say nothing. Then Sharon took Shiloh's lead out of her hands, walked the horse back to his stall, and slammed the stall closed. She grabbed Priscilla's arm and steered her back to the house, all while Connor stood there and watched.

When they were inside, Sharon sent Priscilla to her room because she said she was too angry to speak to her then, and she needed to think and pray and that Priscilla needed to do the same. Back in her room, Priscilla tried to obey, but she couldn't pray for anything except for more time with Connor. She only had a few days left with him. Sleep didn't come for a long time. In the morning, a Thursday, Sharon took Connor and his mother their breakfast, leaving it just outside their door in a covered basket. When she came back inside, she told Priscilla she was not to go out of the house for the next three days. Not until after Connor and his mother left to return to New York on Sunday morning. She said she and Owen would take care of the animals. Priscilla was to spend her time doing household chores and thinking about what it meant to honor those in authority over her. If she so much as set a foot outside, Sharon would tell Uncle Amos, who just might decide to sell Shiloh because of it.

"But why?" Priscilla had yelled. "What did I do that was so wrong?"

Sharon didn't answer her exactly, she just said nothing good would come from Priscilla seeing that boy at the guest cottage. Only sadness. He was *Englisch*, Priscilla was Amish. He lived in New York, she lived here. He was leaving, she was staying. Priscilla began to cry then because she was already missing Connor so much. She was already missing his touch, his kisses, his hand on hers, his embrace. She told her *mamm* she was ruining her life and a few other things she still wished she hadn't said.

For the rest of that day and the next, Priscilla moped around the house and in her room, sitting by the window, looking for Connor, wanting to catch a glimpse of him. She saw him return from a couple of runs, and from trips into town with his mother. Sometimes he would be looking at his phone when he passed underneath her window, sometimes he would be looking up and he'd wink and blow her a kiss.

On Saturday, his last full day there, Connor waited until Sharon went out to the petting barn for morning chores before coming to the mudroom door, opening it and calling for Priscilla in a strained whisper. She was in the kitchen and she came running to him, at once both elated and terrified. He said he and his mom were leaving the next morning, which Priscilla already knew. "Want to go to the grove tonight?"

She shook her head, her heart nearly breaking, and told him her mother wouldn't let her leave the house. He just crinkled his brows as if to ask what did that have to do with anything. She said he didn't understand, that her *mamm* was so suspicious she was even peeking in on Priscilla late at night, long after she'd gone to bed, just to make she was still there.

"So do it earlier, then," he replied. "I can go for a sunset run. I'll take a roundabout way and meet you there at the birch grove. No one will see us together."

"I'd still have to sneak out though," she said, and he just shrugged and replied, "So sneak out." And with that he spun away back toward the guest cottage.

As an afterthought, he turned and held up his phone toward her. He mouthed the word "smile," but Priscilla could barely give him more than a Mona Lisa grin. He snapped the photo and seemed quite pleased with it.

Priscilla was a nervous wreck the rest of the day which, she realized, she could use to her favor. When Sharon picked up on her daughter's uneasiness, Priscilla told her she didn't feel well. At three, Sharon decided to pick the first of her acorn squash. She brought a basket of them into the kitchen to roast and can that afternoon. And of course she expected Priscilla to help. Priscilla told her she needed to go lie down because she was feeling worse and had a terrible headache, but Sharon said Priscilla was just pretending to be in pain because she was still mad and didn't want to help her. Priscilla was still mad— and the more Sharon insisted that Priscilla help her, the madder she got. When Priscilla's words and tone finally grew too disrespectful to bear, Sharon did what Priscilla had wanted all along: She sent her daughter to her room.

Priscilla knew she could probably get out of the house undetected, but she would have a harder time sneaking Shiloh out of his stall without being spotted or heard. The sun had dropped low in the sky, but it was still light enough to see. Amos and the boys were gone that afternoon, but if Roseanna happened to be looking out her bedroom window, she would notice the girl walking toward the back paddock. Priscilla had to hope that Roseanna wouldn't. But even if she did, and if she called out her name, Priscilla decided she wasn't going to stop. She didn't care at that point. If she got in trouble, then so be it. It would be worth it. Connor was leaving the next day, and she didn't know how long it would be before she would see him again. Surely he would make arrangements of some kind. Surely he would visit again, especially because he'd told her he was going to get his driver's license when he got back to New York. Surely he would come see her somehow. Priscilla never stopped to consider that Long Island was almost two hundred miles away.

At fifteen minutes to six, she tiptoed down the stairs. Sharon was at the sink washing the dirt off her squash. The force of the water out of the tap and splashing against the gourds was the perfect sound cover. As soon as Priscilla was out the front door, she ran for the back door to the barn, tossed the halter onto Shiloh, and led him out onto the grass behind the guest cottage so that his hooves would make less noise. Then she and the horse were out onto the last bit of gravel, and past the back paddock. She looked back only once to see if anyone was watching her. But she saw no one, heard no one. She pulled herself onto Shiloh's back well before the little sycamore stump, pressed her heels into his side, and they flew down the path.

Priscilla was the first to arrive at the grove of birch trees. She slid off of Shiloh and led him to the place where he could drink and then she waited. She didn't know how long she stood there; it seemed like quite a while, at least an hour or more. She could only gauge the time by the diminishing light. The longer she waited, the more she worried that something had happened to Connor, or maybe he'd gotten lost trying to find his way from another direction. She was about to climb back onto Shiloh to look for him before the sun disappeared completely when he came jogging into the grove, one hand on his throat as though he were making sure he still had a pulse and with the other he thumbed the screen of his phone. Priscilla ran to him, asking if he was okay. He looked up, smiled in surprise, and said of course and why was she asking. And Priscilla said, "Because you're late." How could he not know how late he was? He replied he had a phone call just before he left the cottage and that put him behind. Connor leaned forward, sweaty and grinning, and kissed her forehead. "Sorry," he said. His phone made a noise and he looked at it before slipping it into the pocket of his running shorts.

He put his arms around her waist and said that she had made bearable what would have been a terrible end to his summer vacation. He said it with such finality, as though he were telling her goodbye for forever. For a second or two she could say nothing, and he took her silence as shock at his tender goodbye. "I hope you don't mind that I said that," he told her. Priscilla finally found her voice, but all she could say was "Mind?" and her eyes filled with tears. He pulled her to his chest and said she was the sweetest, kindest girl he had ever met, and he was so glad they had the chance to get to know each other and that he would never forget her. Priscilla didn't know how to say she didn't want what they had to end. She couldn't believe he didn't see anything in the future for them. So she just said, "Don't go." Connor laughed, not in a mean way, but as if he was flattered and maybe a little apprehensive. He was perhaps just starting to get how hard Priscilla had fallen for him. He tried to make light of it. He said he wasn't good enough for her, and he was jealous of the guy who was. She told him he was wrong. She wasn't any worse or better than he was. She was just a girl in love, and that's when she said, "I love you, Connor."

When Priscilla said this, she stopped, flicked away a falling tear, and exhaled heavily, her breath broken and bumpy. She glanced at me and then laughed lightly, shaking her head.

"I won't embarrass myself further by telling you exactly what he said after that." She sighed again, heavily, using her exhale to draw strength. "I don't think he meant to hurt me. He never meant for anything truly deep and meaningful to happen between us, neither love nor hurt. He kissed me because he had kissed a lot of girls he liked. He thought I was pretty and fun, and he liked that I wasn't afraid to say what I was thinking. And that I wasn't a drama queen, whatever that is. I had helped him figure things out, and he was grateful for that. But there was a girlfriend back home, someone who had broken up with him at the end of the school year and who wanted to get back together now that he had his life straightened out. He was going home to this girl. He had called me out to the birch trees to thank me for the great talks, the good advice, the moonlit ride, the kisses, and to say goodbye."

Priscilla said she couldn't get onto Shiloh fast enough. She was embarrassed and hurt. Connor kept apologizing and wanting to hold her and make sure she was all right, but Priscilla didn't want his touch. She didn't want anything from him. She took off, letting Shiloh carry her away as fast as he wanted to. The sun was gone now, and the twilight sky was just starting to throw everything around her into shadow. She heard Connor calling her name once, but Shiloh loved to run. She only heard it the one time.

Priscilla knew her face was streaked with tears, and she also knew getting back inside the house would prove to be more difficult than it had been sneaking out of it. As she neared the farm, she climbed off of Shiloh and walked him back, cutting through the pasture and the far side of the guest cottage in case her *mamm* was looking out the living room window, which she didn't think she would be. If Sharon was still tending the squash, she'd be in the kitchen. If she'd realized Priscilla had snuck out, she'd be standing on the porch watching for her or even inside the barn, waiting to catch her as she came in.

But Sharon wasn't in either place, so Priscilla assumed she hadn't been found out after all. She took Shiloh into the barn, brushed him down, gave him food and water, and then just stayed there as the dusky interior grew darker and darker. She heard Connor return to the cottage. She heard him go inside, and then a few minutes later she heard the front door to the cottage open again. Priscilla was afraid he was coming in to the barn to look for her, but then she heard two voices, Connor's and his mother's. Two car doors opened and shut. She heard the motor start and the tires crunch on the gravel as the Knights drove away, probably out to have dinner on their last evening in Lancaster County.

After the car left, the darkness in the barn was complete. A bit of the moon was spilling in around the seam of the closed door, but it was nothing more than a thin ribbon, like a *kapp* string. Priscilla sat there in the straw with Shiloh nosing her now and then, wishing her *mamm* would come looking for her. She wanted to fall in her arms and tell her she was right. Nothing good had come from loving that *Englisch* boy. Her *mamm* had tried to protect Priscilla from what she was feeling at that very moment, and Priscilla had shoved her away.

She didn't know how long it was before she heard Roseanna's shouts. Her aunt was yelling for help. Priscilla got to her feet and opened the barn door. Roseanna was running toward her, figuring that's where she was. She didn't tell Priscilla what was wrong other than her *mamm* was hurt and needed to go to the hospital.

She told Priscilla to run to the welding shop. Amos and the boys had just returned from a neighboring farm and were putting the buggy away. "Tell your uncle to call 911. Tell him your mother's fallen down the stars. Then make sure he waits for the ambulance by the road so that they come to the right house," Roseanna had said. And she told Priscilla to hurry.

Several seconds passed before Priscilla continued her tale. A breeze, as if in consolation, rustled its way through the birch leaves all around us. I found myself in no rush to hear the rest. I already knew what happened next.

"But help came too late," Priscilla finally said, with a shrug, her voice breaking over the words as if they were made of splintered glass.

Another stretch of seconds went by. I instinctively reached for Priscilla's hands, folded on top of her bent knees, and covered them. I felt her fingers tremble under mine.

"By the time the ambulance arrived, *Mamm* was nearly gone. The paramedics worked so fast, I could tell they were worried we were losing her. When they had her ready and on the stretcher, the one EMT named Brad said I could ride up front with the driver as he'd be in the back of the ambulance with *Mamm*. He told Roseanna which hospital they would be going to. As they were loading *Mamm* inside the back of the ambulance, I told her I loved her and that I was coming with her. But I don't think she heard me. She was already unconscious by then."

Tears were now falling freely down Priscilla's face. She palmed them away and gathered her composure. "She went into cardiac arrest as we drove, though, and nothing Brad did made any difference. She was gone when we got to the hospital. They let me sit with her while everyone involved did their paperwork. It was busy in the emergency room. Everyone was rushing around *Mamm* and me. So many other lives were at stake. But our little story was over. *Mamm* was gone. And I was still there. I stayed with her until Aunt Roseanna and Uncle Amos came in a hired car."

Neither one of us had words for the next span of minutes. I wondered if Priscilla had ever shared with anyone else all she had just shared with me. I was pretty sure she hadn't.

When she turned to me, her face was serene despite the story she had told me and the tear tracks on her cheeks. "Now what do you say, Jake? Am I at fault for what happened to my mother? No. But do I wish I had made different choices? Yes. Every day. I don't want to ever forget that when you choose the way of self over others, terrible things can happen."

For a moment her words, reverberating in my head, silenced me. "Is that why you think God guided you back here?" I finally asked. "To make sure you *wouldn't* forget?"

She shook her head. "I didn't need to come back here for that." She looked away, as if needing to search the horizon for the reason she had returned to Lancaster County. We were silent for a few seconds as she contemplated what had brought her back. I knew if it were me, I wouldn't have returned. Then she swung her head slowly back around my direction, a very different expression on her face than she had worn seconds earlier. Something had suddenly dawned on her, as defining and obvious as the breaking of a new day.

"I see it now," she said, almost in a whisper.

"See what?"

Her eyes filled with the look of amazement. "I think the Lord brought me back for a reason that hasn't much to do with me at all. Oh, I *see* that now!"

I didn't follow. "See what?" I pulled my hand away from hers.

"Of course. It all makes sense!" She was nearly breathless.

"What? What makes sense?"

"It's you. You are the reason."

Twenty-Nine

For several seconds I could only stare at Priscilla. How could I have had anything to do with her coming back to Lancaster County? I had barely known her before she left.

"What are you talking about?" I finally sputtered.

She rose to her feet, and in seconds she was at Voyager's side. She placed her hands on his back, as if to draw warmth and energy from him. He turned his head toward her and nodded, his bit jangling. "I just couldn't see it before."

I rose to my feet too and walked over to where she stood. "See what?"

"I'm not the horse," she said, stroking Voyager. Then she turned to me. "You are."

I suddenly wanted to get back on our mounts and return to the real world. We'd been down memory lane a little too long, obviously. Priscilla was freaking me out. "What was that?" I said, though I had most definitely heard her.

"You're the horse, Jake. I'm not the one locked up inside. It's you."

I could only stare at her, dumbfounded. I was no horse.

The look of clarity on her face was again intensifying. It was as if she had struck gold. "All along, since the first day I got here and saw you in the driveway, I had a feeling my coming had something to do with you. But the longer I stayed, the more I told myself it couldn't possibly have anything to do with you, so I thought maybe instead God wanted to assure me I'd finally come to terms with what happened here, even though I was pretty sure I had. But I finally get it now. It was never about me. It *was* for you that I came back, Jake. Not for me. For you. To help you see this very thing."

"See *what* very thing? You're not making any sense."

Priscilla looked into my eyes. "First, you need to understand something." She took a deep breath as she seemed to be sorting her thoughts. "You already know about the feelings I had for you when I was young, long before I left Lancaster County, long before I met Connor."

I nodded. We'd talked about her girlhood crush the day we went to the cemetery.

"Anyway, you were older and so handsome and popular, and deep down I knew you would never be interested in me. But I hung onto the dream of you regardless, because it was the one good thing I could think about. At that time in my life, I had only a few possessions that seemed truly mine. I had my father's horse, the birch grove, moonlight, and my imagination. And I guess I decided those few things were enough. Until I met Connor the summer my mother died. He was actually a welcome distraction from my attraction to you. I can see now how my heart was looking for a way out of being in love with a dream."

"I'm so sorry," I said, feeling guilty for having underestimated the depth of her feelings for me all those years ago. What I had called a crush was actually a very young but very real kind of love.

"Don't be sorry. I'm not bringing this up now to make you feel bad. I bring it up because I need you to understand that I've been studying you for a long time, Jake. I know you."

"Um, well, not exactly, Priscilla," I said, not so eager to switch the focus of the conversation to me. "You've been gone for six years."

"But that's just it," she said, reaching out to touch my arm. "I *have* been gone six years. I've changed. Yet you're exactly the same. You still won't let anyone into the deep places in your heart. You won't even let yourself in. You don't drop your guard for anyone."

I laughed nervously, wanting very much now to be heading back. She truly was making no sense. "We should probably get going." I started to move past her to get Willow's reins, and she reached out her arm to stop me.

"You see? Even now you won't allow yourself to consider that I might be right. You run away from anything that goes too deep. You want to run away right now."

I eased my arm out of her grasp. "What I want is to get back home. It's late."

Priscilla shook her head. "It's not even dark yet. You just want to go back because you don't want to talk about this."

"Talk about what, Priscilla? I have no idea what you mean!"

She nodded, her eyes tight on mine. "I know you don't."

A few seconds of tense silence passed between us. She was waiting for me to ask her. "All right," I sighed. "What are you getting at? How am I a horse?"

"Not *a* horse, Jake. *The* horse. You told Aunt Roseanna I was like one of those horses that you try to coax into trusting you so that they will mentally move past whatever they're afraid of. You told her I was all locked up inside, chained to the past and unable to forgive myself and move on. That I was *that* kind of horse."

I felt heat rise to my cheeks. I had not known Priscilla had heard what I'd said to Roseanna the last day I'd been working with Patch. "I hadn't meant for you to hear that," I murmured.

"I know you didn't. But I'm glad I did, so that I can tell you this. *You're* the one locked up inside, Jake. It's you, not me."

I laughed, but I was starting to get perturbed. "Right. And how do you figure?"

"I've already told you. You refuse to listen."

"Told me what?" I said, sensing anger in my voice.

"You run away from anything truly deep and meaningful and powerful. You don't have lingering regrets or achingly beautiful memories because you don't want to hold on to anything that cuts you to the heart, good or bad. You work with these horses to get them to move past their fears and hang-ups, but you never stop to consider *why* they are afraid or sad or angry. You only want them to stop feeling anything at all so that they'll simply eat, sleep, and pull a buggy."

"That's not true," I began, but she cut me off.

"It is true. You didn't care what had happened to January to upset her; you just wanted that horse to forget it. Forget it all. That's why you flashed bags at her and made noises and all that other nonsense. You told me yourself that the horse needed to learn to ignore all external stimuli in order to behave. The reason why she was afraid didn't matter to you, only that it cease to matter. You want to be numb to everything that the heart might hold dear so that you won't be hurt when you suddenly find yourself without it."

"That's enough."

But she wasn't finished.

"You're very fond of Amanda, but you don't love her with your entire soul and being and you don't want to. You don't want to feel that strongly about anything."

"Oh, yeah? You think it was easy to pull back from you last night? To keep from kissing you when every fiber in my being wanted that more than anything?"

"I—"

"What do you think made me stop, Priscilla? It was the thought of Amanda, my feelings for her. I couldn't do that to her."

Priscilla sat back for a moment, regarding me. "I doubt it. Don't you see? I think your pulling away from me last night had a lot less to do with your feelings for Amanda and a lot more to do with your own fears. You pulled away because you couldn't bear to consider what a kiss like that would really mean. You don't love her, Jake. Not the way you should."

Priscilla had stepped over the line. "And what would you know about loving someone?" I shot back. "You call what you had with that New York boy love? That's what you call deep and ardent love? That's the kind of miserable longing you want to hang on to and protect at all costs?"

I expected her to lash out at me, even storm off perhaps. But she just stood there, absorbing my cutting words like a sponge taking on water. "That is *not* what I call love," she answered. "I was infatuated with Connor. It was all about me and what I wanted from him. Deep and abiding love is never like that. I have not thought about Connor in a long time."

"You expect me to believe *that* after that story you just told? Come on, Priscilla. I am not that stupid. We've been out here an hour."

She grinned slightly, a pitying smile. "Yes, you are that stupid. You think this last hour was so that I could tell you how much I loved Connor and how deeply he hurt me? This wasn't a story about Connor or even me. Or you. It's a story about the love my *mamm* had for me. That I had for my *daed*. That they had for each other. *Mamm's* love for me was sometimes hard because she didn't want to lose me. *Mamm* would have laid down her life for me in a heartbeat. *Daed*, the same. And lest you think I am only speaking of the love parents have for their children, my *daed* and *mamm* would have walked through flames to save each other. That is how much they loved each other, even though she lost her soul mate when *Daed* died, and she missed him with a sorrow that some criticized. I don't want to feel anything less for the person I marry. You shouldn't want to, either. Christ loved the church with ardor and an aching longing to see her redeemed. You are to have that same love for your beloved. You must have it, Jake, and not just for her, but for every other person and virtue that truly matters to you. Live your life insulated from passion, and you will have lived a life of pretense and shallowness."

Words failed me. From somewhere deep inside, a wall I didn't even know existed seemed to shudder as if the earth beneath my feet was trembling.

"I keep feeling as though something must have happened to you, Jake, something that made you afraid to give your heart fully to anything. Something happened to you that makes you think marrying Amanda is safe, and easy. Something makes you think that when you feel worry or fear or fervor or even anger, the best thing is to just brush it off or push it away. If so, then you have to figure out what that was."

"Nothing happened," I said, practically tripping over the words in my anxiousness to get them out. I'd had a happy childhood. Great parents. Good friends. A job I loved. Dreams for the future that made a lot of sense. I had no wounds, and I said as much to her.

"You sound awfully sure. But how do you know?"

"Because I know!" I exclaimed. "I may not be emotional like you, but that doesn't mean I have wreckage somewhere inside me I've buried."

She studied my face, looking for a chink in my armor, or so it seemed to me. "I told you once before that horses were emotional beings, and you laughed at me."

I laughed again now, lightly though, because as much as I wanted to ignore it, the shuddering barrier inside of me was still rumbling. "Horses are easily frightened by what they don't understand, Priscilla. They have a heightened sense of their need to survive. That's all it is."

She cocked her head. "My point exactly."

"What? What's your point?"

"You, too, are easily frightened by what you don't understand. And you've a heightened sense of *your* need to survive. You just want to eat, sleep, and pull a buggy. Because that kind of life seems easy and you won't get hurt. But what kind of life is that, Jake? It's an empty one. You were created in the image of God Almighty. You were never meant to live a safe and easy life. You were meant to exhaust yourself in loving and serving people with everything you have."

The crumbling inside threatened to topple me, split me in two. I willed the shuddering to stop. This was nonsense.

"You're wrong, Priscilla," I said, a second later. "I'm happy with my life, right now and in the past. Nothing *happened*. And I have no desire to eat, sleep, and just pull a buggy. I have plenty of goals for my life. Being happy doesn't have to be that complicated. I like where I am headed, how I plan to get there, and who I want to spend it with. I'm sorry, but you're wrong."

Priscilla stared at me for several seconds, and then I saw her eyes fill with tears. She reached up a hand to wipe the shimmering wetness away. "Maybe. Maybe not."

She pulled herself up onto Voyager. "I have to go home and pack," she said as she looked down on me, fresh tears rimming her storm-colored eyes.

Voyager eased past me, and Priscilla tapped her bare feet against him. She leaned forward and the horse took off in a gentle gallop away from the creek, the birch trees, and me.

This time, her *kapp* stayed put.

Priscilla didn't want the same attention at her farewell that she'd had when she'd arrived a month before. She asked Roseanna not to trouble all the immediate family to come say goodbye, but her aunt wouldn't have it any other way. All the Kinsinger brothers and sisters, spouses, and children came for breakfast the next day to see her off in the hired car that would take her to the train station in Lancaster. I stayed in the background when everyone came outside to wait for the car. I wasn't a member of the family and not expected to be in the mix of those hugging her goodbye and wishing her well in Indiana.

I hung back by the barn, fiddling with tack that didn't need fiddling with, watching and waiting to see if she would look for me in the huddle of cousins, second cousins, and aunt and uncle. I wanted to assure her that she needn't worry, that she was wrong about me, but I had slept poorly the night before, and her words to me at the birch trees were still echoing in my head. I doubted I could say I was fine and sound believable.

My desire to make sure she knew she was mistaken about me was as much for me as it was for her. There was no terrible thing in my past that made me afraid to surrender to deep feelings. She was wrong. I was just an average guy, that's all. There were plenty of men like me.

I wasn't the horse.

While I spied on the family huddle, Comet saw me standing there, and he came bounding over, calling attention to my presence. Several heads turned my way, including Priscilla's. She said something to everyone and then she started walking toward me. Stephen called Comet to return to him and the dog happily obeyed.

Priscilla's expression turned pensive as she neared me, and I felt an apology from her coming on. I didn't really want one. Apologies nearly always felt a bit awkward and unnecessary. And she didn't owe me one. She didn't owe me anything.

"*Guder Mariye,* Jake."

I nodded, eager to take control of the conversation. "Morning. All set, then?"

"*Ya*. My train leaves Lancaster at eleven."

"Is she a nice person, your Great-Aunt Cora?"

Priscilla smiled at my concern. "She's quite the character, but in a good way. She's actually fun to be around and full of stories. I'm sad to hear her health is failing, but I am glad I can help her stay in her own house."

"I'm sure it'll go well."

She inhaled, drawing strength from the morning air. "Look, Jake. About yesterday—"

"You don't have to apologize, Priscilla. Really."

Her eyes widened a bit. "I wasn't going to. I just wanted to ask you to please, please think about what I said."

After some initial surprise, I opened my mouth to protest, but she placed her hand on my arm, gently, the way a mother might. "I know you don't want to think about what I told you. So I am *asking* you to. For me. This whole time I've been back in Lancaster County, you've been the only person I felt connected with at all. That's why I thought I'd finally figured out why God wanted me to come back here, because you…it just makes me sad to think that you'll forget everything I said. I don't want you to. Will you promise me you won't?"

"Priscilla, I don't—"

Her hand on my arm increased its grip. "Please. Just promise me you will think about it. Pray about it. Ask God to help you see what I see. If you want, ask Him to prove me wrong. Will you do that?"

From behind us a car pulled onto the gravel driveway.

"Priscilla!" Amos called.

"Your car is here," I murmured, stating the obvious.

"Promise me."

The car stopped in front of the milling family members. The driver got out and popped open the trunk.

"Promise me!" she said, urgency cloaking her request. The driver placed both her suitcases and a third bag into the trunk and closed it.

I was a man of my word. I always had been. I would not tell her yes if I did not mean it. And a niggling, itching, piercing sensation within me was prodding me to say yes.

I thought back to the night of the volleyball party at Chupps' field when Priscilla promised she would make an effort to get to know people. She did so even when nothing within her wanted to, simply because I asked her. How could I not extend the same courtesy back to her now?

"All right."

The desperation in her countenance lifted immediately. She raised the hand that she had placed on my arm and now pressed it gently to my right cheek in farewell. "Thank you," she whispered.

She spun away from me and walked back to her family. She hugged Amos and Roseanna one last time and then got into the car. The driver shut her door and walked around to the other side.

"Write to us!" Roseanna called out, and from behind the window on the passenger side, Priscilla nodded.

Stephen held onto Comet as the dog barked a cheerful goodbye. The driver eased the car into a wide circle to turn it around, and then it crunched on the gravel back down to the road.

Priscilla shifted in her seat to look at me as the car eased onto the street. She pressed her hand to the glass and then she was gone.

PART THREE

THIRTY

In the days and nights following Priscilla's departure, I did nothing intentional to fulfill my promise to her, yet quite often I found myself pondering her words just the same. Mostly, I couldn't stop wondering if there really had been, as she claimed, something in my past—some incident—that had rendered me incapable of deep emotion. Whenever I considered the possibility, I vacillated between two uncertainties. First, that there *had* been such an incident, and second, that there had *not*.

The way I saw it, if there really had been an incident, then I was going to have to learn what it was. Not only would that mean I was in for an odd and arduous journey to a place far outside my comfort zone, but once I found out the truth, it might be more than I would want to know.

If, on the other hand, there hadn't been any incident after all, then that meant this was just who I was, a guy whose feelings only ran so deep. My life would be one of emptiness and mediocrity, and I would die never having truly felt alive at all—at least, according to Priscilla Kinsinger.

I didn't discuss these things with Amanda. Not the challenge Priscilla had given me or my thoughts and feelings about it since. A couple of times I almost broached the topic with her, but then I would remember what Priscilla had said to me in the birch grove, that I didn't truly love Amanda and, in fact, wasn't even capable of such love in my present state. I finally decided that until I got my head on straight about this one way or the other, I wouldn't bring it up with her at all. And though I half expected Amanda to catch on to the fact that there was something I was holding back from her, she never seemed to notice or care. Amanda had been moody since Priscilla left, and in a way I didn't blame her. It had to be disappointing that despite her massive efforts—including her brilliant plan to match up Priscilla with Matthew—in the end it had all been for nothing.

Amanda wasn't the only one who had grown out of sorts in the days following Priscilla's departure. At the shop, Owen barely said a word to me as we worked. Granted, shoeing was noisy business and conversations were usually short, but even between hammer blows he seemed caught up in a myriad of thoughts he didn't want to share. Amos too. If I hadn't known better, I would have said Priscilla had cornered the two of them the way she had me and left parting challenges they weren't eager to face either.

More likely, though, I had a feeling their preoccupied states had something to do with finances. Ever since Priscilla told me money was tight for the Kinsingers and business over at the welding shop was light, I had tried to be more aware of the situation. She had been so right—and I so oblivious. No question, the welding shop was hurting for customers, and all three sets of Kinsinger couples were pulling in their belts.

The wives were doing what they could to help. Treva opened an honor-system produce stand out at the road, Roseanna upped her hours at the quilt shop, and the generator for Beth's sewing machine—she made quilted potholders and placemats for a local craft store—often ran late into the evenings.

I felt bad for all of them. And though I knew Amos would never openly acknowledge the situation to anyone outside his own family, I wanted Owen to know I was here for him if he needed a friend. I said as much one day when the shop was quiet and he and I were in there alone, but he just smiled wanly and said, "Thanks, Jake. Appreciate it."

As tight as the money situation was for them right now, I seemed to be facing the opposite problem. Because of my success with January, Natasha contacted me not long after Priscilla left to offer me a job as her assistant stable master. I thanked her for her interest but explained that I loved my full-time work as a blacksmith far too much to ever give it up.

She was persistent, however, calling me back twice more in the coming weeks, each time upping the amount of the offer. Her final figure was so ridiculously over the top that after I turned her down yet again, I called Eric to ask him if he knew what this was about. It seemed to me that there had to be more going on than the simple matter of a satisfied customer wanting to hire the man who had helped solve a problem with a horse.

As I had hoped, Eric was able to shed a little light on things. Just as he'd predicted the last time we'd talked, thanks to my work with January, other members of the Chester County horse crowd were now lining up around the block to get the contact info for Natasha's "humble Amish blacksmith" who also happened to be a horse whisperer.

"Natasha's a businesswoman to the core," he said, "and she knows the value of in-house talent. I'm sure she'd be willing just to send referrals to you if you wanted, but she's going to try it this way first. I mean, think about how much more lucrative for her—and cushy for you—it would be to make your services part of what Morningstar Stables has to offer."

I understood what he was saying, and while a part of me was flattered by her machinations, another part of me was bothered by them. Why hadn't she been honest with me from the start? Why offer me "assistant stable master" when what she had in mind was so much more specific than that? I liked the woman, and I respected her ability with horses, but I didn't appreciate being bought like a commodity, especially under false pretenses.

Before we hung up, Eric offered to do for me what so far Natasha had not, which was to circulate my contact information so that those who wanted to avail themselves of my services could get in touch with me directly.

"All part of the dream, man. Don't forget about that," he said, and I knew he was right.

But I also knew that once Priscilla left, for some reason my desire to work with troubled horses seemed to ebb a bit. It wasn't as if I didn't want to do it at all, but more that I just didn't want to do it right now.

I told Eric I appreciated his help but wanted to wait on that until my apprenticeship was complete and I could make a more formal arrangement with my employer. Boarding the occasional horse so I could work with it in my off time was one thing, but taking in a steady stream of clients and using the shop phone as my point of contact was quite another.

It was my conversations with Natasha that finally drove me to write a letter to Priscilla. I'd been wanting to do so for a while, but I could never decide how to start it off or what to say. Would she even want to hear from me? Or was she hoping to cut all nonfamilial ties with Lancaster County completely, just as she'd done once before? Those were the questions that held me back, but once I had a horse-related topic to tell her about, I figured I might as well give it a shot.

I penned my first note to her on a Thursday evening in July, just after the sun dipped below the horizon and a deep violet hue rose up in a broad swath across the orange sky. I saw it as I was walking to the cottage after a long and tiring day, and it made me think of Priscilla's eyes, those same eyes that could see things to which others were so often blind. That's when I knew I had to write.

> Dear Priscilla,
>
> I hope your return to Indiana went well. I know Amos and Roseanna appreciated your call to tell them you arrived safely.
>
> I thought you might like to hear that January is still doing fine. Natasha called recently to offer me a job and said that the horse has never seemed happier. Remember the golden retriever that was there in the stable that night? His name is Atticus, and he and January have become the best of friends.
>
> Sincerely,
> Jake Miller
>
> P.S. I didn't take the job, but it felt kind of good to be asked.

Of course, I wanted to be open and honest about writing to Priscilla, so before I sealed the envelope, I made sure to tell Amanda about it and offer up the letter for her to read. She didn't even bother, waving off the very thought and saying, "Of course *you* of all people are going to write to her. I don't care. I assumed you already had."

Amanda's words startled me a bit. Why me of all people? Trying not to sound unsettled, I asked her what she meant.

She gave a grunt. "Don't you remember, Jake? You were the one who fussed at me for not writing to her myself the last time she went away. You were like, 'Didn't you ever contact her? Didn't any of your friends?' You and I kind of argued about it."

"Oh, yeah," I said, tucking the letter back in my pocket.

Later that night, on my way home, I sealed the already stamped-and-addressed envelope and detoured over to Lincoln Highway, dropping it into a roadside mailbox there.

In the days that followed, I forced myself not to ask if any mail had come to the house for me. I knew Roseanna would tell me if it had—though just to be safe, I sometimes paused at her little desk area beside the kitchen to glance at the current stack of mail.

Near the end of July, about three weeks after Priscilla left, I started the process of refinishing the wood floors in the second bedroom of the guest cottage. The first step was the sanding, which I did in the evening hours. It took longer than expected, but I found I enjoyed the work, especially the way I could lose myself in the repetitiveness of it all. Sometimes I could go an hour or two without thinking—not even about Priscilla or her challenge or the fact that she hadn't written me back.

I wrote a second time.

Dear Priscilla,

I thought you would like to know that Owen and I gave Voyager a new set of shoes today. He continues to seem happy here. He fits in nicely with the other horses, and Stephen takes very good care of him.

Write back when you get a chance. I know you are probably real busy settling in there. How is your Aunt Cora? How are the apples? Is it picking time yet?

Sincerely,
Jake Miller

Once the floors were sanded, it was time to put down the first coat of varnish. It went on smooth and looked great, but the fumes were so potent I ended up having to sleep over in the big house that night.

The next morning I came downstairs in the pearly gray light of dawn to start my chores. I stopped in the kitchen to get the coffee going, partly because the rest of the Kinsingers would appreciate it and partly because I hadn't slept very well. I was pretty sure Roseanna had put me up in Priscilla's old room, and the fact that I'd made zero progress on my promise to her—to somehow figure out why I always kept my feelings at bay—weighed on me heavily.

Thinking of her now, I decided to take a peek at yesterday's mail. While I waited for the coffee to brew, I crossed over to Roseanna's desk and, mug in hand, was startled to see, right on top of the pile, the very thing I'd been watching for—a letter from Priscilla.

Except it wasn't to me.

Instead, this envelope had been addressed to Amos and Roseanna. Though I was disappointed for myself, I was pleased for their sake. As far as I knew, this was the first communication from her to anyone here other than the one phone call she'd made upon first arriving in Indiana.

As the coffeepot began to sputter and fill across the room, I found myself gazing down at the envelope, thinking how pretty Priscilla's handwriting was—much more legible than mine, and more graceful than Amanda's or my mother's. My eyes moved to the postmark: *Elkhart, Indiana*. A place I'd never been. I couldn't even imagine it.

How very far away she was.

"Go ahead," Roseanna said from behind me, making me jump. That, in turn, caused her to laugh. "Good thing there wasn't coffee in that cup, or it'd be all over the floor by now."

I was embarrassed for having been caught poking into their business, but Roseanna didn't seem to see it that way. Before I could apologize, she again told me to read it.

"Go ahead, Jake. It's okay," she said as she moved to the cabinet to retrieve a cup of her own. "Sounds like she's doing real well."

I wanted to play nonchalant, maybe even offer a glib, "Nah, that's okay." But the next thing I knew, Priscilla's letter was in my hands and I was drinking in every word.

Dear Onkel Amos and Aendi Roseanna:

Please forgive me for waiting so long to write back to you. It has taken some time to get into a good routine with my great-aunt. She fell in the bathtub the day after I arrived and fractured her hip. We were all very busy seeing to her needs and rearranging things at the house so that she could come home to recover. She is doing much better now, back to her usual jokes and banter, and she has told all of us to stop babying her or she will run away and never come back.

I've also been busy learning how to manage the orchard. Aunt Cora has ten acres of apple trees, a mix of Red Delicious and Goldens. Her father planted the oldest trees when she was little, and there are about five hundred of them, give or take, so there is much to do. My grandparents own the property next door, and their son—my mother's brother—and daughter-in-law help run the orchard, along with a hired man who works a few hours a week. But you might remember that my grandparents also keep bees and sell and manufacture honey, so they are quite glad that I am here and can take some of the work load off of them, especially during picking season, which has just started for the Reds.

I haven't had much time to socialize. I know I promised you I would make a point of doing that, and I will, eventually. Right now the days are full with

caring for Aunt Cora and learning everything I need
to know about the trees. She sold her horse a long time
ago, so my grandfather is letting me use one of his
for transportation until I can buy my own. I miss
Voyager. My grandfather's borrowed horse is forever in
a bad mood. Daadi says he's just old and doesn't like
change. Jake might find that funny. Once my time
frees up a little more, I will have to write and ask him
for pointers.

I'd better sign off here as Aunt Cora will be
wanting her supper soon.

Thank you again for all you have done for me. I
am sorry if I disappointed you by staying such a short
while. I know you said not to worry about that, but I
so very much want you to know that I did not leave
because I was unhappy there. As I told you from the
beginning, I was fairly certain that my stay would
only be temporary. I am glad I felt God's leading
to come back to Lancaster County, for many reasons,
including the chance to visit my parents' graves and
renew the hope that I will see them again in glory.

I am sorry for all the trouble I caused you when
my mother died. I want you to know that I was not in
the barn when she fell, as everyone assumed (and I
never contradicted). Instead, I had been out on my
father's horse and away from the house without her
permission. Mamm and I had argued earlier that day
and I was angry with her, so I snuck out of my room

when she wasn't looking. This is why I was so racked
with guilt after that, because only I knew the truth,
that had I been where I was supposed to be when the
accident happened, my mother would never have died.

Now that I am older, I have a better understanding
of God's sovereignty and His plan for our lives. He
numbers our days, and for us to think otherwise is
arrogance. But I am sorry I didn't tell you this before.
Please forgive me for letting you believe something that
wasn't true all these years.

I don't know if I will see Lancaster County again,
but I hope it comforts you to hear that I am not the
broken girl who left there the first time. I still miss
my parents very much, but God walks with me in my
loss. He did then and does still.

Much love,
Priscilla

I reread the part of the letter where she mentioned my name, glad and
surprised that I had been in her thoughts when she wrote it. I also reread the
line about not seeing Lancaster County again. And I read it a third time. It
made me strangely sad to think I wouldn't see her again, ever.

I wrote to her again that same night.

Dear Priscilla,

This morning, Roseanna let me read the letter you
sent her, and I thought you should know how pleased
she was to get it. That was nice of you to take the time
to do that, especially because you seem pretty busy.

As for pointers on that cranky horse, have you considered pfeffernusse cookies? Oh, right. That only works on cranky blacksmiths.

If I think of anything else, I'll let you know.

Sincerely,

Jake

The next day Owen was again quiet in the shop and distracted by his thoughts, but this time it didn't bother me. That's because I was distracted enough by my own. The truth was, I wanted to honor my promise to Priscilla, but I couldn't decide how to start. The obvious place to begin was with my mother, but I honestly didn't know how to ask her if something terrible happened to me when I was little that I either didn't remember or had put out of my mind. It seemed such an odd question to ask. She'd want to know what in the world brought it up, and I'd have to have some kind of answer that didn't take a week to explain. I also couldn't help but think a question like that would hurt her somehow, almost as if I was accusing her of not watching out for me or something. Perhaps over the weekend I could sit down with one of my older siblings, maybe Thom, to see if he could help me sort this out.

When Owen and I were finishing up the last shoeing job, I got out the broom to sweep up all the shavings while he tamped down the nails. I wanted to ask him if he'd ever been told he buried his feelings, but it seemed like such a ridiculous question. And he'd certainly want to know why I was asking. What would I say then? *Oh, your cousin Priscilla, remember her? She told me I dash away from any emotion that runs deeper than a rain puddle.*

As it was, Owen hurried to hang up his tools when he was done, saying he needed to cut out a little early and would I mind waiting around for the last of the newly shod horses to be picked up.

"Sure. Everything okay?"

"Treva's *daed* wants us over for dinner," he said, looking as if he'd rather do anything else in the world than that.

"And that's a problem why?" I asked with a smile. "You love going over there."

But he didn't answer me. It didn't even seem that he was listening. Instead, he simply said, "*Ya*. Thanks, Jake. See you tomorrow."

Before I could say another word, he'd turned and was striding out of the shop.

I was set to go to Amanda's that evening after supper, so as soon as the owner of the horse came back and got him, I started in on the evening chores. I sent Stephen a bit early to get Big Sam, Willow, and Mahlon's and Owen's horses from the back paddock where they had spent the latter part of the afternoon getting air and exercise. After cleaning out the stalls and feeding and watering the animals, I went back to my cottage, showered, and changed into clean clothes. Then I heated a can of soup and ate that with a ham sandwich, wishing all the while that Amanda's mom had invited me to dinner.

It was a few minutes after seven when I arrived at the Shetlers' place. I thought we would go for a buggy ride as usual, but instead Amanda invited me inside. Her mother was visiting a friend and had taken the twins with her. Her dad, a shy man whom I was still trying to get to know, gave me a nice enough hello but immediately went outside, saying he had a broken generator to fix.

"Wow, pretty quiet around here," I said, giving Amanda a smile.

She smiled in return, looking awkward—nervous even—as we stood in the kitchen. "*Ya*. Um, want some cobbler? *Mamm* made it yesterday. Apricot, I think."

"No. No, *danke*," I said warily, trying to get a read on her mood. I had never seen her like this. She seemed extremely uncomfortable.

She glanced around the big room as though she didn't know what to do next.

"Is everything okay?" I asked, knowing full well it was not. Was she mad at me because I had been so distracted lately? Had she learned about the promise I'd made to Priscilla and was angry I hadn't told her?

She turned back to face me, her bottom lip tucked up underneath the top one in thoughtful consternation.

"We need to talk," she blurted, the words falling out of her mouth as though they had been poised to be spoken from the second I walked into her house. Maybe even before.

She pointed to the sofa along the back wall. A colorful quilt was folded across its back. "Maybe we should sit down."

We walked over to the couch and took our seats. I couldn't imagine what she had done or not done that necessitated us to be sitting down. Or what I had done or not done. I waited.

She inhaled heavily and then resettled herself next to me. "I don't know how to tell you this, so I'm just going to say it. Jake, I don't want to court anymore."

"You don't *what*?" I echoed, unable to fully grasp her announcement.

"I…I don't want to court anymore."

Was she suggesting we marry? Now? I was still formulating how to say I thought it was much too soon when she continued.

"I've…I'm in love with someone else."

For a moment everything around me and in me and on the very planet seemed to freeze in place. I couldn't believe I had heard her correctly. "What did you say?"

Tears sprang to her eyes. "I'm so sorry, Jake. We didn't mean for it to be like this. It just…happened."

"We?" I said, numbly.

"Matthew Zook and me."

Was this real? Was she really saying this to me?

"Matthew Zook," I echoed.

"I don't even know how to explain it. I just…he…I was trying to help him get connected with Priscilla, you know. I was trying to figure out what he liked and what he didn't like, and the more time I spent with him, the more I found myself drawn to him. And he to me. We didn't…we didn't plan it, Jake. I never meant to mislead you. And Matthew, he's feeling so bad about it, he can't believe he's fallen in love with a woman who's being courted by some-one else. But he can't help it. He loves me. And I love him."

Of all the reactions roiling around inside me, the one that rose to the sur-face first surprised me. "Love?" I said sarcastically, almost derisively. The word sounded ugly on my tongue, and I knew instantly that that word should never sound that way. Ever.

Not only that, but I could see the hurt in Amanda's eyes. I deserved a jab of equal callousness, but she just blinked and two tears slid down her cheeks. "Yes," she said, gently. "I love Matthew. And he loves me."

Her words stung. I looked away.

"I'm sorry, Jake. Truly I am, but I know this is for the best for both of us. I don't love you the way I love him. I'm fond of you. Very fond. And I like you.

You're a good friend. And you're fun to be with and clever and easy-going. But I don't love you, not like this. You should be with someone who loves you, Jake. And who *you* love."

She paused then to let that thought slide over me, surely knowing I would realize— just as Priscilla said—that I didn't love her either. Not the way a man should love the woman he wants to marry.

As I left the house a few minutes later—because really, what was the purpose of staying?—I couldn't keep the rest of what Priscilla had said to me from tumbling around in my head. As Willow clopped down the road toward home, for the first time in I don't know how long I was fully aware of how empty I was inside.

The girl I thought I was going to marry had just rejected me.

And I felt nothing.

Thirty-One

When I returned to the Kinsinger homestead, twilight was just giving way to evening star shine. The air around me buzzed with the sounds of insects, matching the steady hum of the grinding thoughts in my head. Nothing was making any sense. I had spent the last few months imagining myself married to Amanda, raising children with her, growing old with her. The future had seemed so comfortable and steady, like a well-fitting horseshoe. And now that future had been whisked away. Amanda didn't love me. She loved someone else.

I should have felt hurt and anger, and instead I sensed only hollowness.

My thoughts flew to God, and I found myself muttering a prayer for understanding. I didn't know what to make of the emptiness I was feeling.

As I put Willow away for the night, I knew I could no longer ignore outright my promise to Priscilla. Amanda's rejection of me as her suitor should not have had such a numbing effect on me. I felt only a detached disappointment, and even that seemed as thin as gauze, as if I might wake in the morning and forget I had ever courted Amanda Shetler with an eye to marrying her. And somehow I knew that the person who would be the saddest for me if that were to happen would be Priscilla. Surprisingly, that thought pricked me more than anything.

I stepped out of the barn and into the yard, noticing that all of the Kinsingers seemed to be gathered at the big house. I could see them through the main room windows as they sat around the dining table. Though the adults were quiet and seemed intent on something, the laughter and happy voices of Mahlon and Beth's children and Owen and Treva's little Josef floated out to meet me. I found myself jealous of what the Kinsingers were sharing at that moment because it reminded me of how much *Daed* and *Mamm* strove to make a caring home for me and how much they loved each other.

I had always assumed I would end up with a home and family like theirs. I would have a wife and kids, and I would love them the way my parents loved me. But now I realized what a joke that was. How could I ever begin to match what I had been given as a child? I was nothing like my parents. They loved each other deeply, as deeply as I have ever seen two people love each other. And they loved their children that way too. Fully and to the core of their being. They loved with their whole selves.

Priscilla was like that.

Tyler and Rachel were like that.

And apparently now even Amanda—Amanda!—was like that.

As it turned out, *I* was the weird one.

I was locked up inside, just as Priscilla had said. And I didn't know why.

Back at the cottage, smelling only faintly now of the varnish, I made a cup of decaf and took it out on the front step, where I sat and sipped as I gazed into the night sky.

All I could think was how much I wished Priscilla were here so I could talk to her and ask her what to do. Not about the breakup but about this problem of mine, this emptiness that permeated my being.

Even as I had that thought, I realized I already knew what she would say—had already said, in fact, among the birch trees beside Blue Rock Creek.

Something must have happened to you that made you afraid to give your heart fully. You have to figure out what that was.

She was right. I wasn't just a guy whose feelings only ran so deep because that was the way God had made him. I was a guy who had been taught—somehow, somewhere, by someone or something—that the only way I would be safe in this life would be to build a wall around my heart.

It was time for that wall to come down.

Sitting on the porch, a mug cradled in my hands, my elbows on my knees, I looked out across the edge of the property to the dirt path that would take me to the birch trees if I just kept following it. It was time to learn the truth. It was time to go on a search of my past. But what if I really couldn't handle what I found? The answer came to me like the rustle of leaves on a black gum tree.

I can do all things through Christ which strengtheneth me.

With a deep sigh, I bowed my head and closed my eyes, and then I began to pray.

A good while later, once I was done praying, I went back inside the cottage. It was a bit earlier than usual, but I got ready for bed anyway, hoping sleep would come quickly. I had no idea feeling so little could be so exhausting.

I slept in spurts and fits. In the morning, though, I awoke acutely aware that God had heard my prayer from the previous evening. It was a strange feeling, new to me perhaps because I had never before been so conscious of my need. I dressed for my chores, expectant and a little apprehensive. I prayed for God's favor and grace because I knew that when He begins a work of transformation, sometimes the process can be daunting.

I started my day with pen and paper.

Dear Priscilla,

I hope you don't mind that I'm writing so often. I know you will write back once you have a chance. It's early morning, and I can already tell it's going to be a warm day.

Not for the first time, I was thinking how much we learn from horses. Race with the wind. Make peace with your herd. Give all you have and then give some more.

But some of us learn the wrong lessons too. Cover your flank. Watch for danger. Always run away when you can.

I just thought you would want to know I'm not running anymore.

Sincerely,
Jake

I started in on my chores and was just about finished with Big Sam when Amos came into the barn. The sun was peeking through a layer of morning clouds. It was going to be hot today. I was already perspiring.

"*Guder Mariye*, Amos."

He nodded and returned my greeting, but his expression was pensive.

"Something up?"

"*Ya*. I guess you could say that. Why don't you come over to the house for breakfast when you're done so we can talk."

Something was very wrong. My thoughts flew immediately to Priscilla. "Is everything okay? Is anyone hurt?"

He shook his head. "No. No, nothing like that."

"Did I make a mistake?" I asked, though I was sure I hadn't.

Again he shook his head. "You've done nothing wrong, son. Just come up to the house when you're done."

He turned from me, and I could tell his heart was heavy.

I quickened my pace, curious and yet hesitant regarding what Amos had to say. I gave Big Sam his breakfast and then headed for the main house.

Roseanna had made baked blueberry French toast, and the kitchen was rich with the scents of vanilla, cinnamon, and berries when I stepped inside. She greeted me warmly, but her eyes, like Amos's, were sad. She slid a large portion of French toast onto my plate, with a side of melon slices and sausage patties.

"This looks really good," I said to her as she sat down with us with a smaller serving for herself. She smiled and said thank you.

Amos led us in silent prayer, and then we began to eat, the clink of forks on plates the only sound. Why were they being so quiet?

"Anyone else joining us?" I asked nervously, looking from one to the other.

Amos wiped his mouth with his napkin and then took a gulp from his coffee cup. "Not yet. I wanted to tell you this alone. I think you deserve that."

A knob of cold dread immediately formed in my stomach. I put my fork down. "Are you letting me go?" I said, a half laugh making my voice crack a bit.

Amos rubbed his beard with his hand and sighed heavily. "It's not because I want to."

The knob grew into a thudding boulder. I was losing my job. I waited for him to tell me why.

"Like I told you in the barn, you've done nothing wrong, Jake. You're a good blacksmith and I've been very pleased with your work. It has nothing to do with that."

"What is it then?" I said, still in shock.

"As you know, it was always my intention that your apprenticeship would lead to your replacing Owen when he and Treva moved over to her father's place so that he could take on the dairy operation there."

"*Ya.* That's been the plan."

"Except I'm sorry to say it's not going to happen now. Treva's father decided to sell his herd and machinery. The dairy's been losing money for the past few years, and he won't have Owen taking on a business that can't support a family. It's a tough time to be a dairy farmer."

"But Owen might be able to—"

"It's done. He's sold it. It doesn't matter what Owen might have been able to do. Owen's not leaving here, Jake."

I had to think for a minute. "Okay, so he's not leaving. You still have more than enough shoeing for two people."

As soon as the words were out of my mouth, I realized what Amos was going to say. He shook his head, explaining that the welding business wasn't bringing in enough income to justify two workers.

"We've been operating with a deficit since May, and it's not getting any better. So now that we know Owen will be sticking around, we've decided to move Mahlon back over to the farrier side of things. The two of them will handle shoeing the horses, and I'll take care of the welding—what there is of it, anyway."

I nodded. I understood. But I didn't have to like it.

"I wish I had another job for you here, but I don't," Amos added. "And I hate to make things worse, but we've decided that Treva and Roseanna are going to start the guest cottage back up again too. It was a good source of income when Sharon had it. If we make these changes, we should be able to keep everybody in the family earning a livable income and Treva's *daed*'s decision to sell won't affect us too badly."

"The guest cottage," I said numbly.

"We're so sorry, Jake," Roseanna murmured. "I know you were doing a fine job of fixing it up too."

"But…but I'm not even close to finished," I stammered.

"You've worked hard while you lived here," Amos said, "and you've certainly paid off any rent I would have charged with what you've done. But I can't pay you to continue with it, son. Mahlon and I will take up where you've left off. "

I looked down at my plate, my breakfast half eaten. The sweetness in my mouth tasted like cardboard now.

"Your position here always hinged on Owen taking over for his father-in-law," Amos continued. "We had no idea he would suddenly decide to sell. And I never expected the welding business to slow down like it has. I'm really sorry about this. About all of it."

I nodded, wordless.

"I meant what I said. You're a fine blacksmith. And I'd be happy to recommend you to any blacksmith you want to work for. As far as I'm concerned, your apprenticeship is complete. You know what you're doing, and you're good at it."

Your apprenticeship is complete. I had longed to hear those words, but not this way. Not like this.

"*Danke.* I appreciate that."

"Owen and Mahlon feel bad about this. Especially Owen."

No wonder Owen had been quiet lately. His planned-for future had been falling apart just as mine now was.

The three of us were quiet for a few moments.

"When do you want me gone?" I asked.

Roseanna reached across the table and squeezed my hand. "We don't *want* this at all."

I nodded.

"We've been putting it off as long as we could, trying to think of another way," Amos answered.

"So the sooner, the better." I rose from the table, and Amos and Roseanna looked up at me. I could see how hard this had been for them.

"We're so sorry," Roseanna said.

"Don't you worry. I'll be all right. God provides."

I pushed in my chair and thanked them for breakfast. Amos stood and shook my hand.

"You're a good man, Jake."

As I turned to leave them, I wondered what made me good. I didn't feel good. I had nothing now.

I was as empty outside as I felt inside.

I stepped back out into the warm, humid air of the early August morning. "God, what are You doing?" I whispered.

As I headed for the cottage to pack my few things, I sensed Him whispering back to me.

Answering your prayer, Jake.

I stopped dead in my tracks.

Last night I'd asked God to show me what I needed to do to free my heart from the fortress I'd built around it. With no job and no place to live and no girl to court, I had nowhere else to go but back home to *Daed* and *Mamm*.

Back where the answers likely waited.

Back where I began.

THIRTY-TWO

My parents welcomed me home with open arms, as I knew they would. They understood my disappointment, but they could also sympathize with Amos and Roseanna. My room upstairs in their home was as I had left it before I went to Missouri for farrier school, and it was mine again now for as long as I wanted or needed it.

Daed also offered me a position back in the buggy shop, even though I knew he had given my spot to one of my cousins and I'd just be in the way. I told him thanks but that I wanted to keep doing what I was doing. I'd never been more satisfied with my day-to-day work than I had been as a full-time blacksmith.

Dear Priscilla,

I wanted to let you know, when you get a chance to write back, that you shouldn't use the address at Amos and Roseanna's. They may have already told you, but I'm no longer working or living there. Use my new address (well, my old address too) that's on this envelope.

I'm not thrilled about it, but, like a horse, I must be willing to go wherever my Master takes me.

Sincerely,
Jake

P.S. Willow seems a lot happier to be back home than I am.

I told my parents the news about Amanda and me that first night, at supper. Neither seemed surprised. In fact, their reaction came across as relief.

"You didn't like her?" I said, laughing a bit to ease the tension.

"Oh, we liked her very much," *Mamm* replied. "But you and she…I don't know. It wasn't the right match. I was worried—and your *daed* too—that you would want to propose too soon. And that in the end you'd both be unhappy."

"But why?" I pressed. "I thought we were just right for each other."

"Tyler said it best after the family picnic," *Daed* interjected. "He said the two of you were like oil and oil."

I frowned. "As opposed to what? Oil and water? Oil and vinegar?"

Daed shook his head. "He was talking about lamp oil. To burn a lamp, you need oil and you need a wick. Two different things that combine to make a flame. You and Amanda weren't oil and a wick. You were just oil and oil. No wick. No flame."

Mamm took it from there. "He was saying that similarities are good in a couple, but only if they allow you to bring out the best in each other. When it goes the other direction, when they reinforce the worst of who you are, then that person isn't good for you the way they should be—even if they are a good person. Do you see what we mean?"

"I think I do. But I have to ask…" I looked from one to the other. "What do you see as the worst of who I am? Was there something bad Amanda was bringing out in me?"

"Not bad, not at all," *Mamm* said. "Just…" Her voice faded as she gestured helplessly for the right words.

"Well?"

She looked to my father, who reached across the table and covered her hand with his. Then his eyes met mine.

"The marriage vows aren't to be taken lightly, Jake. Life is not to be taken lightly."

"I have to ask you both a question," I said, my voice nearly snagging in my throat. It had been almost four weeks now since Priscilla went away, leaving her challenge behind. And though I had spent much of the time since then ruminating on her words and wondering how I might ever get to the truth, it wasn't until this moment that I had finally summoned the nerve to say what needed to be said. If something had happened in my past that taught me to bury my emotions, I really wanted to know what it was. I really wanted to find the answer.

"Have I always been this way?"

"What way?"

"Unemotional. Shallow. So...cavalier about everything."

They didn't answer right off, and suddenly the room felt very quiet, so quiet I could hear not just the ticking of the kitchen clock, but the very movement of its hands. As I waited for whatever it was they were going to tell me, I felt myself growing acutely aware of this moment, this place where God had plunked me down, back at my childhood home, with nothing to my name but a duffel bag, my horse, a courting buggy, and my farrier tools.

"You're none of those things," *Mamm* said at last, but there was an odd avoidance in her eyes. "A shallow man wouldn't even think to ask such a question. And you were never cavalier with Amanda's affections, were you?"

I shook my head.

"As for unemotional, you're one of the kindest souls I've ever known. So there you go. You are none of those things."

Daed nodded in agreement, his bushy beard bobbing against his collar.

They didn't get it.

"That's not what I'm saying." I looked from one to the other, searching for the right words. "I don't feel anything deeply. It's as though everything with me is always somewhere up near the surface. What I want to know is if I have always been like this, or if something happened to make me this way."

Again, an odd silence descended over the table before my father finally spoke.

"You're a man, son. God designed men for action, for protection. For strength. Feelings—or the lack of them—are beside the point."

I looked over at my mother, but her eyes were cast toward her plate. I returned my attention to him.

"You have feelings, *Daed*, deep feelings. For *Mamm*. For me. For God. You can't tell me you don't."

He pursed his lips and just stared at me for a long moment. "You've grown up fine," he said with finality. "So that's enough of that."

My heart sank. My parents had been my best hope for answers, but now it was clear they could give me none. I returned my attention to the food in front of me, no longer hungry but needing somewhere to direct my eyes. I finished what was on my plate and then stood to carry it to the sink.

I would have thought this was the end of it had I not seen a look that passed between my parents. My mother's face was hopeful. Almost pleading. My father's face held a warning—a raising of the eyebrows, a tightening of the mouth—that told her the subject was closed.

In this home there had been three bedrooms to be divided among the children. Which kid went in which room depended on their age and the total number living here. As the youngest of the bunch, I wasn't even born until the two oldest—Sarah and Sadie—were married and out of the house. At that time, Thom was eighteen and in his *rumspringa*, so he had a room to himself. That left the remaining two rooms to be divided between Eli, who was fifteen, Peter, who was six, and me, the infant of the bunch. Reportedly, Eli and Peter shared and I got my own room—but only until Eli turned sixteen, at which point *Mamm* shifted Peter in with me. I was three when Thom married, so that's when Peter moved back out again. Three kids still at home, three bedrooms, so finally we each had our own.

Until I was six, that is, when I got a new and unexpected roommate.

How he came to me was a long and complex story, but it started with my sister Sadie. She was twenty years older than I, and I'd never had the chance to meet her because she left the Amish faith two years before I was born. Though my parents longed and prayed for her return, Sadie ended up marrying an *Englischer* and moving far, far away. When I was just a few months old, Sadie and her husband had a son they named Tyler, but I never got to meet him either, at least not at first. I grew up knowing of their existence—that my sister Sadie and her husband and child were out there among the

Englisch somewhere—but I also knew it was one of those things we just didn't talk about.

Then, when I was six years old, our family received the terrible news that Sadie had died, suddenly and unexpectedly, of a brain aneurism. My parents were heartbroken, of course, but especially because of the estrangement that had preceded her death. Though it wasn't easy for my parents, Sarah came and stayed with us boys while *Mamm* and *Daed* made the trip to Sadie's funeral. A few days later, they returned—with Sadie's son in tow. Tyler's father was in the military, and he had asked my parents to take in their grandson just for a while, until he finished his next tour of duty. It ended up being a lot longer than that, but that's a story for another day.

Technically, the scared little boy with the Phillies baseball cap and the wrinkled *Englischer* clothes was my nephew. But considering that he and I were the same age, I saw him more as a brother right from the start. *Mamm* moved him in with me, and he and I soon became not just roommates and relatives but friends. Best friends.

We stayed together in that room until Eli moved out and got married a few years later. Once again, we were down to three kids, three rooms, so I shifted into one of my own. That was the one I'd remained in, from the time I was nine until I moved out at twenty-three, first for farrier school and then to live with the Kinsingers.

That was also the room I was returning to now, and I entered it with an odd, unsettled feeling. I had been part of a good family and grown up in a happy home, but I wasn't glad to be here. How could I have ended up in this place after all I had managed to accomplish? Two days ago, my life was on track for work and marriage. Now I was tossing my duffel onto my childhood bed and hanging my hat on the same peg that had held my hats as a boy.

Standing here, resentment and frustration began to swell within my chest, so I closed my eyes and asked God to take those feelings away, to help me be patient with all that was happening in my life—no matter what.

The same words I'd told myself earlier came springing into my mind once again. I was back where the answers likely awaited.

Back where I began.

Except that I wasn't, I realized now, not exactly. I'd begun in the room across the hall, the one I'd first had to myself and then shared with Peter and then had to myself again before sharing it with Tyler. If I really wanted to be back where I began, that was the room for me now, not this one.

The very idea seemed a little silly, but the more I stood there contemplating it, the more I felt God prodding me to move to the other room. I picked up my bag, crossed the hall, and opened the door. In the months Tyler had been gone following his marriage to Rachel, *Mamm* had done nothing to this room other than strip the bed and place a few extra chairs inside along with her old sewing machine. I set my bag down and backed out to get some linens from the closet in the hall. As I was reaching for a set of sheets, *Mamm* came up the stairs with fresh towels off the line for me.

"The linens on your bed are clean," she said, nodding to the room I had first walked into.

"*Ya*. I know. I'm taking Tyler's room."

Her eyes widened in surprise. "What? Why? That room is just for storage now."

"I don't care if you don't care. A few chairs and the sewing machine won't bother me."

Mamm stared at me. I could tell there was something she wanted to say, but she held her tongue.

Forcing myself to respect her silence, at least until I found a way to get around it, I took the pile of clean sheets into the room. *Mamm* followed me in, placing the towels onto one of the extra chairs. "I'll help you with the bed."

We made it in silence. *Mamm* smoothed down the thin quilt that I likely would not need as August was traditionally the hottest month of the year, but it helped the bed seem complete.

"It's been a long time since you've slept in this room."

"*Ya*, it sure has."

She went to the door, and then she turned back to face me. When she spoke, her voice seemed faraway, as though she had just walked down a long corridor in her mind.

"Everything changed for you when Tyler came, didn't it?"

"I don't know. I was only six. I don't remember much from before, if that's what you mean. And we've always gotten along great. Tyler's like a brother to me, *Mamm*. You know that."

She nodded absently. "I just…I wonder…" Her voice trailed away.

"What? What do you wonder?"

For a second she seemed to have disappeared altogether. It was as if her body was still in the room with me, but her heart and soul were whisked back to that dark and painful time when her daughter died.

"*Mamm?*"

She returned her gaze to me, the faraway look still in her eyes. Then, with a slight shake of her head and a squaring of her shoulders, the look was gone, and she was just her usual self again, as if nothing was going unsaid at all.

Even her voice was now clear and matter-of-fact. "I know you've had a rough couple of days, Jake, but it's good to have you home. You can put those chairs into your old…into the other spare room if you want." *Mamm* turned and left, pulling the door softly closed behind her.

My mind swirling, I set about unpacking my things, a task that shouldn't take long. As I worked, I kept returning to my mother's odd demeanor and her question.

Everything changed for you when Tyler came, didn't it?

I thought of Priscilla, in the grove, pleading with me to see the truth, telling me something must have happened to me, some incident that made me the way that I am. Now God had brought me all the way here, to this room, the room I'd shared with Tyler as a child.

Could my "incident" tie in with him somehow? Did it have anything to do with him? If so, I couldn't see how. Lowering myself to the edge of the bed, I tried to think.

I'd never resented having to share my life or my room or my childhood with Tyler. Quite the opposite. My world was so much richer because of him—then and now.

Sure, *Mamm*, everything changed for me when he came, but in a good way, not bad.

He was the one who had lost a mother, who had essentially lost his father, who had to come here not knowing the people or the language or the lifestyle or anything.

He was the one who had lost it all.

I was the one who gained.

THIRTY-THREE

I spent the next week looking for a position as a blacksmith—either apprentice or full-fledged—but there were simply no openings anywhere. It seemed my only choices were to go ahead and open up my own shop or head down some other career path entirely. Neither option appealed to me. The ultimate plan to have my own blacksmith shop someday was far down the road from here, when I had more experience, more savings, and a better idea of where I might want to live.

As for committing to a different kind of work, I saw that as nonnegotiable. After a lifetime of wanting to be a blacksmith, I had finally achieved my goal. No way could I turn my back on it now, not after striving so hard to get here.

I knew I could always take the job Natasha had offered me, as at least it involved working with horses, but that wasn't a long-term solution. Her world was *Englisch* and money and fanciness, mine was Plain and Amish and apart. Her stables had been a great place to visit, and I wouldn't mind doing the occasional consult there, but spending my day, every day, in that environment was about as appealing to me as spending time in a ladies' boutique would be to a horse.

Besides, something about our last few conversations had rubbed me the wrong way. I still thought of Duchess often and would have loved the chance to work with her, and I liked Natasha as well. But I hadn't appreciated her attempts to bring me on board for some exorbitant salary without telling me why I'd be worth it to her. It seemed disingenuous, and I didn't think I wanted any part of it.

As for my own internal state, neither *Daed* nor *Mamm* had been any more forthcoming about whatever it was they had seemed to be withholding that first night I came home. I still had hopes they would open up eventually. Sometimes a person just needed a little space to think things through first.

In the meantime, at least, I had a distraction. Searching for a job was completely filling my days, leaving only the nights for extra thought and prayer.

On the morning of August eleventh, the first day of my second week of joblessness, *Daed* said he had something to show me. As soon as we finished our breakfast, we put on our hats and headed outside into a muggy Monday sunrise.

We started for the buggy shop, a long and wide Morton building that housed *Daed*'s entire manufacturing operation. Six buggies at once could be built inside it, and several more could be in the repair bay. There were sections for welding, fabrication, upholstery, painting, and assembly. I had worked every phase of the buggy operation, as had my three brothers, Tyler, and several cousins.

But *Daed* swung wide of the whole thing. We continued past the building and took a right at its corner by the barn, moving toward an outbuilding in which he stored buggy parts.

We stopped at it.

"I was thinking if you wanted, you could fix this up as your own blacksmith shop. We're far enough away from Amos's place that I don't think he could complain too much."

I appreciated the offer, but I knew he was wrong about Amos. "Our agreement was ten miles at a minimum, *Daed*. You know this can't be more than eight."

"So you go and you talk to him first. I think a couple of miles of grace is the least he could do."

"Maybe so," I said, doubting it, "but what about you? You need this building for your own business. All your spare parts are in here."

"*Ya*, but they don't need to be. It makes more sense to keep them at the main building. Tyler's been saying so for a while. He's figured out a way to rearrange the inventory so we can fit everything in one building. And I know some of the materials in here are obsolete anyway, so it needs a good cleaning out. It's big enough, I think, for a small blacksmith shop. I've seen Amos's setup. You could do the same thing here. It would just be a little tighter. One horse at a time instead of three."

I didn't know what to say. Of course I appreciated *Daed*'s offer, but there was still the matter of my needing more experience. I also didn't know if I was ready to admit my only option was to open a little side business at the buggy shop and hope that it would grow.

When I said nothing, he went on. "I know it's probably not your dream location, son, and it might take a while to fix up and get a forge and all that, but I know how much you wanted to focus on farrier work and how hard it must be to have all that disappear on you overnight. Both your *Mamm* and I are feeling bad about it. You don't deserve what happened to you. I can't front you any money to get things started, but I can offer you this building if you want it."

"Thanks, *Daed*," I finally said. "I really appreciate this. I'll think on it."

And I did think on it for the next few days. At first, it was just a remote possibility, but with every blacksmith shop that said they weren't hiring and every classified ad that did me no good, my father's idea began to grow on me more and more. It still wasn't an ideal location, but at least it was worth further consideration.

On Wednesday evening, *Daed* and I sat down together with pen and paper, a calculator, and a stack of farrier supply catalogs. Together, we worked up a figure that realistically represented the investment required to supply and stock a fully functional blacksmith shop. It was higher than either one of us expected.

I could see the defeat settling into my father's shoulders. When we'd crunched the numbers for a third time and still came out too high, he sighed heavily, turned off the calculator, and slipped it into the drawer.

"I'm sorry, son. I've been thinking you could get something temporary, just to earn your seed money. But this much would take way too long. To reach that figure in a reasonable amount of time...well, that's just not going to happen. I don't know anywhere you could work and earn that kind of money."

I stared at the number on the page. I thought about my other prospects. I calculated how long it would take.

Then I met my father's eyes and told him, "I do."

I finally heard from Priscilla a few days later.

> Dear Jake,
>
> Thank you so much for the notes. I have enjoyed them more than you know. I was so sorry to hear about the job situation, but at least it sounds like you're doing okay.
>
> In my Bible reading this morning, I came across a familiar verse I wanted to share. You know in Ecclesiastes, the part about how there's a time to every purpose under heaven? In the list of purposes, it says there's "a time to weep, and a time to laugh; a time to mourn, and a time to dance."
>
> See? Even God is saying you should be fully aware of what your heart is telling you.
>
> Blessings,
> Priscilla

I wrote back to her that very hour, penning the note at the kitchen table and then taking it to the post office in Paradise so that it would be on its way to her the next morning.

> Dear Priscilla,
>
> It was great to hear from you at last. And thanks for invoking the Word of God to prove your point.
>
> After zero success in turning up work as a blacksmith, I finally accepted a job with Natasha

Fremont that starts next week. It's not ideal, but it's only temporary. My goal is to earn enough there so I can open a shop of my own.

For now, the biggest hurdle with this job is going to be the commute, as you can imagine. Using the bus, it'll be about an hour each way, every day, including one transfer and walking a mile at both ends. Other than that, it should be okay. I look forward to seeing January and Duchess again, and at least it will be nice getting to know all of the other horses there too.

Sincerely,
Jake

The next note, short and sweet, arrived from her within the same week.

Dear Jake,

The best thing about long bus rides is that they give you time to think.

And because you have a lot of thinking to do, I figure this is just about perfect.

Blessings,
Priscilla

Tyler and Rachel came over for supper on Friday night, and it was great to see them. After two weeks of just me and *Mamm* and *Daed*, I was a little too overeager. In my mind, I'd been envisioning a long night of popcorn and brownies and a rousing game of Settlers of Catan, our favorite. But Rachel seemed tired, likely due to her condition, and they ended up leaving by eight.

As I stood in the driveway and watched them pull away in their buggy, I felt a pang of loneliness that twisted into a knot in my gut. I realized I was in a wilderness as far as my social life was concerned. I had already been feeling too old to be going to the singings and such with Amanda, and now that I was no longer courting her, I wouldn't have to worry about that anymore. But that was the only social life I'd had for a while. Most of my friends here in this district were already married. I didn't know what I was going to do with myself in my free time. In the past, I could have hung out with Tyler—hunting, hiking, playing board games or tetherball or whatever—but for the most part those days were gone. He had a wife now and a child on the way. I couldn't ask him for more than the occasional pity hike.

Later, I laid awake for quite a while in the bed that had been Tyler's in the room that had been mine. I kept thinking back to earlier in the week, to the morning *Daed* first offered me the spare parts building for my shop. His words to me as we'd stood there and talked began echoing in my head now.

How hard it must be to have all that disappear on you overnight.

How hard it must be to have all that disappear on you overnight.

How hard it must be to have all that disappear on you overnight.

The echoes wouldn't stop. I started to pray to silence them, but they seemed to only grow louder, as if the very walls of my childhood room were shouting them. A breeze from outside began to sing around the eaves, and it sounded like someone crying.

Someone crying.

I bolted straight up in my bed.

This room, that sound. A memory began to creep over me, indistinct and vaporous. I sat still as a stone as I waited for it to settle and materialize. But then, as quickly as it was there, it was gone.

THIRTY-FOUR

By the end of my first week at Natasha's, I had settled into a rhythm. A lot of my job consisted of the same things I'd been doing since I was a little boy—feeding, watering, and grooming horses. But I also worked with Duchess each morning and exercised the horses each afternoon.

Other than that, my biggest task was to be available to the boarders at all times for whatever they might need. When Ted, the stable master, told me that on my first day, I envisioned myself hitching up trailers and advising on equine hoof care and easing horses in and out of stalls. Instead, it ended up being mostly "Amish man on parade" as I answered what seemed to be a never-ending stream of questions from curious *Englisch* whose horses were stabled at Morningstar. Maybe I should just hang a sign: *Yes, the Amish do pay taxes and we do not have arranged marriages and there really is no such thing as an Amish Mafia.*

Natasha was a busy woman, but she checked in with me near the end of my second day, just to see how things were going. I was frank with her, telling her they might want to rethink that part of my job description, considering how much time I was losing to matters that had nothing whatsoever to do with horses.

She just laughed. "Silly boy. Don't you get it? That's exactly how you should be spending your time."

I didn't appreciate it, but there wasn't a lot I could do about it. Every time I wanted to call it quits and head out of there for good, I would remind myself of the size of my paycheck and the dream of owning my own shop. So far, that had been enough to make me stay.

Dear Priscilla,

I've been working at Natasha's for three days now, and so far it's going pretty well. At least I'm surrounded by all kinds of beautiful horses, and she's letting me have half an hour each morning with Duchess to see if I can help solve her issues with crowds and performing. Natasha is still determined to do that show in Devon next month, so I'm seriously hoping I'll be able to figure this out and fix it before then.

Other than that, the job is a strange mix of gruntwork and glad-handing, which I'll tell you more about some other time. Though I was hired primarily for my skills with gentling, so far the only problem horse I've dealt with is Duchess. Otherwise, Natasha seems to be holding me out like a carrot on a stick. Apparently, people want to board at her stables even more if her in-house Amish horse whisperer has no availability at this time and a long waiting list. Hah!

Till then, I just wanted to say hello and that I hope you are doing well.

Sincerely,
Jake

P.S. I think a lot about the night of the fireworks, and not just in relation to nervous horses.

Other than working with Duchess, the only one other task I enjoyed was exercising the horses, and all of them needed to be ridden daily. After seeing what was involved, I'd sought approval from the church. Once the bishop had given me the okay—apparently, horseback riding within the course of a job was fine—I'd been doing it since.

Ted often worked with me, and each time we put the animals through their paces, I thought of Priscilla and the ride she had taken me on the day before she left. It was again exhilarating to be on the back of a running horse, and I found myself amazed anew at God's creation of such a majestic beast.

I was also reminded that there had never been any fallout from that ride, which meant no one had spotted us after all—or, if they had, at least they hadn't said anything. For that, I was incredibly grateful.

Most of all, though, I just found myself missing Priscilla, painfully so, especially when galloping across long stretches of pasture. She would have loved every minute of it.

Dear Jake,

I am glad to hear that the job is okay and you are finally working with Duchess. Please let me know if I can help in some way. Maybe you should tell me a bit more about her.

You might also be bothered to tell me a little about how those long bus rides are going (hint, hint).

The weather here has been perfect for the apples— warm days, cool nights, and about an inch of rain per week—so everyone is optimistic we will have a good harvest this year. I've been surprised to find how much I enjoy working with the orchard, and Aunt Cora and I are getting along beautifully. As she has no children of her own, she has said that ultimately she plans to leave this place to me. I certainly don't deserve it, but I am deeply pleased and humbled at the thought.

Today I read from the book of Joshua and thought of you. In particular, chapter 6, verse 20.

Blessings,
Priscilla

P.S. I think of the fireworks too.

The days continued to roll along, fat with heat and humidity, the very air seeming thick with its own agenda. Each morning I left the house at the crack of dawn, boarded the first bus toward Chester County, changed routes midway, and then walk the last mile, arriving at the Fremonts' already glistening with sweat. My new routine reminded me a little of my time at farrier school, when I was around the *Englisch* for the better part of the day. I had forgotten how foreign that environment was to me.

Working for a fancy stable filled with rich clientele only made it that much more strange. In addition to having electricity at the ready for every function, including air-conditioning for the stables, there was a constant flow of buyers and sellers, boarders, and visitors, children and parents. The place seemed less and less like a farm to me as the days wore on, and more and more like a business.

On top of that, my Amishness remained a constant source of intrigue to just about everyone I met. It wasn't as if I could hide it, as my suspenders, broadfall pants, and straw hat always gave me away. Thank goodness for the refuge of those quiet moments when I was out on the pasture exercising the horses. No one begged to take my picture or peppered me with questions then. It was just me and whatever horse I was riding.

It was at those moments that I missed Priscilla the most. I didn't know what to make of the fact that I missed her, other than she had seen through to the very heart of me. How could I not find that attractive?

I also didn't know what to do about it. I was here, she was in Indiana. We were writing regularly now, but except for her comment about the fireworks, there was no reason to think she saw me as anything more than a friend. Why would she? She'd had a crush on me when she was a child, but that was ages ago. And she would not want to be with someone like me anyway, someone so even-keeled to a fault.

I decided I was a lot like Connor, the boy who had told her he wasn't good enough for her way back when. For him, of course, it had been a line, just something guys will say. But for me it was the truth. I really wasn't good enough for her.

But the strange thing was, the more I said this to myself, the more I *wanted* to be.

I memorized the words of the Bible verse she had sent, Joshua 6:20:

> So the people shouted when the priests blew with the trumpets: and it came to pass, when the people heard the sound of the trumpet, and the people shouted with a great shout, that the wall fell down flat, so that the people went up into the city, every man straight before him, and they took the city.

For some reason, the first time I read that I actually had tears in my eyes. It wasn't as though I was boo-hooing or anything, but still. If my getting a little misty was a sign that I'd made some progress, then I would take it. I couldn't remember the last time I cried.

Please, God, help take down my wall.

I could see now that the process of becoming the kind of man someone like Priscilla deserved wasn't going to be quick or easy. People didn't become who they were in the span of weeks. Nor did they become someone different in likewise fashion. My prayer was that I would seek to truly please God, and that I would strive to live as only He wanted me to live. And that I would be patient.

If I could do that, then there was no limit to what He could do.

Dear Priscilla,

Thanks for the verse, more than you know. You asked about the bus ride. Here is something I realized on the way home today.

This whole time, I've been praying for God to show me the truth about myself. But maybe part of the problem is that my vision needs improving. Maybe He *has been showing me things all along. It's just that there are scales on my eyes and so I could not see.*

Not trying to be profound, just something to think on.

Sincerely,

Jake

When I awoke on the Friday morning of my second week at Natasha's, I knew a few things for sure.

First, I knew I hadn't shoed a single horse in twenty-three days. I hadn't shoed any this week. I wouldn't shoe any next week. Or any week in the foreseeable future. A sense of melancholy fell over me at how my life had changed in so short a time.

Second, I knew I was making no progress with Duchess.

I needed to understand what was causing her problems, but because no one could get her to replicate those problems until she was in an arena, there was nothing more I could do to help. Except for that one particular startle response, she was already the perfect horse and needed no further gentling from me. I was a guy who liked puzzles, but I feared I had finally met my match.

The third thing I knew for sure was that as dark as it was outside, I was starting to feel even darker on the inside. The morning had come with a drenching rain, one that was supposed to continue well into the weekend.

My bus stop was less than a mile from the house, an easy fifteen-minute walk even in bad weather. Thanks to my hat and rain poncho, I managed to make it there while staying relatively dry. The morning slowly grew warmer, though, so after changing over to my second bus, I pulled the poncho off and set it at my feet. Between the grayness of the dawn and the rhythmic slapping of the wipers, the ride nearly lulled me to sleep. That's probably why, when I reached my destination, I wasn't thinking very clearly. As the brakes squealed to a stop and the door swung open, I grabbed my hat and climbed off, not realizing I'd left the poncho behind until the bus was driving away. By the time I finished my one-mile trek from there to the stables, I was every bit as wet as I would have been had I simply jumped in a creek and swum there instead.

My day didn't get much better. The horses were antsy from the rain, and almost everyone I came in contact with was surly and snappish—employees and customers alike. The only bright spot for me in the whole day was that moment just before quitting time when the office manager came through the stable, handing out white, business-sized envelopes to each employee she passed along the way. With all of my taxes and withholdings, I wasn't sure of the exact amount I would be getting. But when I took a peek inside the envelope, I felt a deep surge of relief and satisfaction. Without a doubt, this was the single biggest paycheck I had ever received, and a great first step on the way to my goal.

To my surprise, when I got to the bus stop near home, *Mamm* was waiting for me with the buggy.

"You didn't have to come out in this," I told her as I hopped inside and slammed the door shut against the rain.

"I didn't mind," she said, but she didn't smile as she said it.

"Is everything okay?"

"Yes, of course. Fine." Though clearly she was not fine at all.

And that's when it struck me. Whatever the unspoken thing was that had been bothering her since the day I moved back home, it had now finally come to a head.

I offered to drive, but she just ignored my words and lifted the reins, signaling her horse to go. He was a dapple-gray Belgian named Jasper and at seventeen hands the biggest horse my parents owned.

I settled back against the seat, my mind moving instantly into prayer. This was the moment I'd been waiting for for twenty-two days, ever since my first night back at home. It had to be. Why else would she come out in this kind of weather unless it was so we could have a difficult conversation in the privacy of the buggy, a conversation we couldn't have around others?

Please God, help tear down this wall inside of me.

"I know there's something you've been keeping from me, something about the past."

She glanced at me, surprised.

"Whatever it is, *Mamm*, you can tell me. What do you want to say?"

She peered out at the road. "That I'm sorry."

"*Mamm?*"

"I…I just can't let this rest anymore. I owe you an apology, Jake. Your *daed* would tell you I don't, but I know that I do."

This wasn't at all what I'd expected. "An apology for what?"

She turned toward me, a sad smile on her face. "For looking the other way. For pretending I didn't see what I saw. I guess I thought you'd outgrow it. It happened so long ago."

My pulse surged as I waited for her to continue.

"A few weeks ago, the first night you moved back home, you asked *Daed* and me a question. We pretended to not understand, but we knew exactly what you were saying."

"Yeah, I kind of figured that. And since then, all I've been doing is waiting—and praying you would decide to tell me soon."

She nodded, her face looking far older than its sixty-five years.

"That night, you said you didn't have deep feelings, and then you asked us if you'd always been that way. That's what you said, isn't it?"

I nodded wordlessly.

"The truth is, no, you weren't always this way. Not at all."

For several long seconds neither one of us said anything. The only sound was the clopping of hooves on pavement and the patter of rain on the buggy.

"You were extremely loving, Jake. Quite sensitive." *Mamm* reached up with one hand to brush away a tear that slipped from her left eye. "The kind of child who was always taking everything to heart."

I nodded, though I found it hard to believe. Priscilla was the kind of person *Mamm* was describing, not me. Even Roseanna said so, in those same words, that Priscilla "just takes everything to heart."

Mamm went on.

"When Sadie passed, your *daed* and I—we grieved so. We had not mended what was broken between her and us, and when she was gone, we knew we had lost any chance to do that. You wanted to understand why we were so sad, but you couldn't because you didn't know your sister. She was just a name rarely spoken. It…weighed on you how heartbroken we were. On those first few nights after we got word that Sadie had passed, I would hear you sobbing in your bed, and I would come to you and ask you why you were crying, and you would say that you didn't know. That's how tender your heart was."

She swallowed hard and forced herself to continue.

"And then we brought Tyler home from the funeral, and you were there to witness every terrible moment of his grief. He doesn't remember much of that time. God has been gracious to him on that account. But you? You saw and heard it all. You saw his sorrow. His anger. His tantrums. His fear. And I was glad he had you there with him, that he didn't have to be all alone. I never once stopped to think how hard it would be for someone as compassionate as you to be present for that kind of suffering."

She pulled the buggy to the side of the road and gave way to her own tears.

"I'm so sorry, Jake. I should have known something was wrong a few months later when I realized you'd stopped crying for him, for us. You just…stopped. It was as though you decided then and there that it was all too much and you were never going to allow yourself to feel that deeply for anyone or anything again. I was so engrossed in my own grief and caring for my grandson that I didn't think how dangerous it was for you to do that. I just…I just was glad there was one less sad person in the house. I am so sorry. I should have done something."

I sat there in the cab of the buggy, listening to my mother's sobs as I tried to grasp her words.

"There was nothing you *could* do, *Mamm*," I managed to utter. "Don't be so hard—"

"Of course there was. I could have sent you over to stay with Sarah and Jonas for a while. I could have paid more attention to what was happening inside your little heart instead of focusing so exclusively on Tyler's pain and on ours. At the very least—the *very* least—I should have moved you out of that bedroom and put you in with Peter instead. At least then you wouldn't have had a front row seat, night after night, to the pain of a child who had lost his mother and his father and his home practically all in one day. "

In my numbness, I heard again my father's words from when he first offered me the shed for my shop. *How hard it must be to have all that disappear on you overnight.*

Closing my eyes, I forced myself to focus. I had questions, so many questions.

"If you knew all this," I managed to say, "then why didn't you just tell me? Three weeks ago, when I asked."

She dug a tissue from her apron and dabbed at her face, which was shiny with tears.

"Because your father and I don't see eye to eye on any of this. We never have. I knew that night that he didn't want me to tell you. He didn't want me to dredge all of this up."

I just looked at her, needing to understand.

"But back then, he didn't see what I saw, Jake. Or if he did, he chose not to believe it. When the worst of things with Tyler was over and I realized what it had done to you, I was devastated. Racked with guilt. Tormented at how your sweet, tender little heart had been buried under all that pain. The more I went on about it, the more your father didn't want to hear it. It was one of the few rocky patches in our marriage. We fought a number of times. He insisted back then—as he still does now—that I was exaggerating. That I was 'borrowing trouble.' That the changes I saw in you back then were just a natural part of growing up and not some horrible fallout from the grief that had filled our house for months."

She pulled in a breath, sharply, and tried to calm her tears as she blew it back out.

"Eventually, we had to find a way to put the matter to rest. At first, we just agreed to disagree. But as time passed, I don't know, I suppose it was easier to pretend that your father was right. You seemed happy. And you certainly loved Tyler with all your heart. So I told myself it was all okay, that it was in the past. Then when you showed up here asking us that question, it was as though a very old scar had suddenly been ripped wide open. I knew what was inside—but I couldn't let you see it. Not yet, not right away. I had to work through it first myself, and then with your father. I knew who you were before Tyler showed up, and I saw who you became after. Now, all these years later, about the only thing I can say to you is forgive me. Please forgive me. Please tell me it's not too late to be who you were before I failed you."

I knew I should have reached over to her to comfort her and assure her she had my forgiveness, but I was like a paralyzed man as a flood of buried memories breached the wall inside me. I could do nothing but sit there as it all came back to me, cold and wet and gray, like the world outside the buggy.

And with the flood within me came the tumbling of bricks.

THIRTY-FIVE

In the days that followed *Mamm*'s confession, we both had to deal with the fallout. When we arrived at home, she admitted to *Daed* that she'd picked me up after work and told me everything, and he hadn't been happy with her. They had argued all evening, mostly in whispers behind closed doors, but I'm sure they both knew there was no taking it back now.

I wrote to Priscilla that night, though it took me a long time to figure out what to say.

Dear Priscilla,

The day you left, you told me something I didn't want to hear. I didn't believe you, so you told me to ask God to prove you wrong.

I asked. He finally answered.

You weren't wrong.

Sincerely,
Jake

The next morning, I spoke to *Daed* on *Mamm*'s behalf, trying to help him understand I'd needed this truth so I could begin to heal. He disagreed, refusing to believe there was any healing to be done. As for *Mamm*, he said he wasn't angry with her exactly, just disappointed that she'd gone to me behind his back and against his word. Mostly, he said, he was upset that she'd dredged up woes that had long been covered by God's grace and ought not to have been exhumed.

Our times around the supper table—the only meal the three of us had together these days, thanks to my job—were subdued, to say the least. We found things to talk about, but they were superficial and brief, and then we would retreat back into our silences.

The truth was, I felt as though I had been stripped of my skin and was now walking around in the flesh of a newborn. Every pore of my being seemed freshly awakened. And even though the depths of my heart were now open to the sun, recalling what had mentally sent me scrambling for mortar and bricks eighteen years ago was not painful in the fearful sense. I felt an ache, crushing at times, but it wasn't the throbbing sting of despair. It was more a tearing away of pretense and calluses.

I was not becoming a six-year-old boy again; that child had grown up. But I did sense that God was handing something back to me, something He had been keeping safe for me during my years in the wilderness of my detachment. He was reawakening my passion for things *He* was passionate about, namely people. I found myself beginning my prayers in the morning and quickly wiping away tears as I prayed for each person close to me. God was regenerating within me a deep and pervasive compassion for those He had placed in my life. My parents. My siblings. Tyler and Rachel. Amanda and Matthew. Natasha and her family. Owen and Treva. Amos and Roseanna.

Priscilla.

Dear Jake,

You may not believe this, but I think I already knew. Somehow, during my prayer times this week, I've almost felt I was hearing the shouts and trumpets as Jericho's walls came tumbling down. When your

letter arrived today, I could only bow my head in awe
and thanks. God is good.

I am praying for you, because I know this has to be
tough. To feel deeply after so many years of barely
feeling at all must be kind of like leaping from a
puddle into an ocean. I can't imagine the pain, the
fear—maybe even the regret—that you're going
through now.

But don't regret it. And remember the good that's
in store for you! Consider John 16:20, where it says,
"Ye shall be sorrowful, but your sorrow shall be turned
into joy." You are now a person who can feel both of
those things, sorrow <u>and</u> joy, and for that I rejoice.

I promise, this will get better.

Blessings,
Priscilla

Reconnecting with that part of me that God had created as a basic element of my personality and which I had pushed aside for nearly two decades
made me quiet, reflective, and more tuned into the workings of God's Spirit
inside me.

Sometimes, it also hurt like the dickens.

Dear Priscilla,

Every day at my job, when I exercise the horses,
I put them through a series of moves and activities
that will not just improve their cardio systems but also
promote muscle growth. At farrier school, we spent a lot

of time studying horse anatomy, and it's been coming in handy during these sessions. Do you know how muscles are built in horses—and people too, for that matter—anatomically speaking?

You never want to pull or rip a muscle, but you do want to work it hard enough that it develops numerous microscopic tears. (That's where the soreness comes after a hard day.) But then, as those tears heal, the body does the most amazing thing: It builds them back stronger than they were before. Thus, the way to grow a muscle is to tear it up so that in the end it will grow back stronger.

This is what I remind myself every single day, that the tearing up is the first, necessary part of the process. But it isn't always easy.

Sincerely,
Jake

Though I still wasn't crazy about my job, I was glad for the ten-hour workdays I had to myself during this time. Almost every day, I would spend the entire commute thinking, praying, and pondering what it meant to no longer be locked up inside. Once I arrived at the Fremonts', there was little there to remind me of my Amish life except for every horse I was growing fond of and every horse that looked to my approach with interest and affection. It wasn't hard to see, now that my eyes had been opened, what Priscilla saw. Horses were not like any other farm animal. They were created with the ability to display trust and affection, as well as the capacity to fear and avoid what they did not understand. Priscilla had told me once that I only cared about *what* troubled horses feared, but not *why* they feared it.

And she had been right. The why of it I had wanted to avoid, because that is what I did—and had been doing every day of my life for many years.

Tyler had said I was even-keeled, and he'd meant it as a compliment. Priscilla had also used that word when she said I was "just one long, even keel, sailing through life down the middle." But I now knew better. A keel on a boat keeps it on a steady course. Without a keel, a boat would soon be adrift. But the direction you choose to travel matters as much as the keel that helps to get you there. As I settled into my new skin and allowed God to have His way in me, I began to sense that the direction of my life was changing.

Dear Jake,

Since I last wrote, I've been thinking more on this topic of sorrow and joy, and I decided I have a suggestion for you: Look for joy.

Even if you are still struggling with the more painful elements of this transition, I challenge you to seek out joy in others. Perhaps doing so will help to awaken joy inside yourself as well.

Blessings,
Priscilla

The second week in September, I was beginning to feel less pain in the day to day, though I certainly hadn't felt anything remotely approaching joy. At first, I took Priscilla's words in a theoretical sense, simply as an encouragement. But upon several rereadings of her letter, I decided she was serious. She really was challenging me.

And so I began to look for joy.

Amazingly, it didn't take long before I began to spot it everywhere...

I saw it in the bus driver who handled the second leg of my daily journey, in the way he smiled and greeted the passengers—especially the regulars like me—as if we were precious cargo. I knew he was a Christian because God's love radiated through every part of him, from the sparkle in his eyes to the peppy hymns he would whistle as he drove to the way he'd call out with every disembarkation, "Have a blessed day!"

I witnessed joy walking home from the bus stop one evening when I came upon a pair of tourists, a young couple out for a stroll. They were holding hands, and an infant was strapped to the father's chest by some sort of cloth sling. Partway down the street, they paused so the wife could adjust the baby's pacifier. Then she kissed him on his fuzzy little head and looked up at her husband, the joy in her eyes striking me so deeply that I had to turn away.

I observed it during Sunday dinners, in how my *mamm* and *daed* looked at Rachel, whose own precious cargo was growing bigger by the week, and Tyler, who was constantly at her side. Even though there was still a bit of a rift between my parents, I could see the joy in their faces whenever they gazed upon their beloved grandson and granddaughter-in-law and the new life— a great-grandbaby—that was growing within.

I felt it in the serene expressions of many of my fellow worshipers during Sunday services.

I recognized it in the eyes of my brother Thom when he bit into a slice of his wife's incredible *schnitz* pie.

I heard it in the squeals and laughter of Natasha's two little girls as they played in their backyard pool.

Mostly, I found it one day when I least expected, out in the pasture with January and Atticus. Like all of the horses, January needed exercise, but she wasn't too crazy about wearing a saddle or carrying a rider. Eventually, I found that I could give her just as good of a workout simply by taking her and the dog into the field and playing a vigorous game of fetch. Atticus's favorite chew toy was a bright orange rope-and-ball sort of thing, and I would start us off by throwing it as far as I could out into the grass. He would take off running, with January close behind, then he'd retrieve it, spin around, and run just as fast to bring it back to me. We would do this over and over until both dog and horse were panting heavily and my shoulder was beginning to ache. At that point, I would usually just plop myself down on the grass for a break, allowing ten minutes or so for them to cool down.

Usually, they just sniffed around a bit after that, Atticus searching the pasture for rabbit holes and January contentedly munching on grass. But once in a while, if they were in a playful mood, they would interact with each other in various ways. Atticus would get January's attention by running circles around her, or January would trot toward the dog and then fake him out by stopping short or making a sudden zigzag. Sometimes the horse would simply lie down on the ground and roll over, feet in the air and belly to the sky. Grunting with pleasure, she would wriggle in a way that told me she was scratching her back. As she did, Atticus would run over to lick her face or sniff her body or press himself against her broad side, as if to share in her joy.

And it was joy. Whether in animals or people, I decided, joy was all over the place. You just had to stop and look for it.

Joy was also the key that finally unlocked the problem with Natasha's horse.

It happened on a Monday in mid-September, on a gray and overcast day with just a hint of coolness in the air. I had already reduced my daily sessions with Duchess down to just twice a week, but now I was ready to throw in the towel. Despite all of my efforts, I was no closer to solving the mystery of her performance anxiety than I had been the day we met.

As I led the magnificent animal from the workout ring back up the hill toward her private stable, I felt my heart growing heavy, knowing I had let both horse and owner down. The Dressage at the Devon horse show was only ten days away, and it was clear to all that Natasha's dream of a successful meet was only that—a dream. Worse, the horse's inevitable failure at the show was going to be like a domino, toppling forward and taking down all the others after it. As Eric had said a few months before, *If Duchess fails, her value as a show horse or even a breeding horse will plummet so far that Natasha may lose it all.* I felt sick at heart, both for her sake and the sake of this magnificent, troubled animal.

Unlike the horses in the big stable, Duchess was housed in her own private building, one equipped with indulgences that boggled the mind. Air-conditioning for hot days, of course, but also heated floors for cooler ones. A horse treadmill. An equine whirlpool. All sorts of state-of-the-art equipment. Apparently, these were luxuries befitting a champion. Sadly, once Duchess failed at Devon, she would be a champion no more.

The only people allowed in Duchess's stable were Natasha, the stable master, and me, and as I opened the door to lead the horse inside now, I saw that the other two were already there, over in the main sitting area. They both looked up as we came in, their expressions hopeful, but I shook my head and continued on toward the stall.

Once Duchess was settled in with fresh water and hay, I came back out ready to tell Natasha that this was about it for me and Duchess. There was nothing more I could do for her, and continuing our sessions would just be a waste of Natasha's money and my time.

Natasha and Ted were both perched on leather swivel chairs, facing a huge flat screen TV and watching, yet again, the video of Duchess's last few competitions, where she'd lost control and reared up, nearly getting hurt or hurting others. I had watched these films myself, several times, to study her behavior and see if I could figure out what might have scared her so and set her off. But it hadn't done me any good, so I'd never felt the need to watch again.

Ted, on the other hand, studied those clips the way a farrier might study diseases of the hoof. All along, he had been of the opinion that there was some specific trigger that kept setting the horse off, and if he could just identify and eliminate that trigger, the problem would be solved.

Natasha wasn't interested in triggers. She was all about obedience training, teaching the animal to resist any aberrant urges—no matter how strong—at the command of her master.

My approach had been to spend time with the horse on a regular basis and run her through various pressure-release exercises in order to build trust.

None of our methods had worked. If anything, the horse seemed to be getting worse, not better. Several times, on busy days when the main stable was bustling with activity, Duchess had caught sight of it and gone into a bit of a frenzy, neighing and shaking her head and stomping her feet until I had to lead her away just to get her back under control.

"Play it again, from the top," Natasha said now, her eyes still glued to the screen.

Ted clicked the remote, and the video started over once more. I watched it as well, but this time something about the clip seemed different to me—or rather, the clip was the same, but I was seeing it in a whole new way. After a few moments, I could feel the hairs begin to rise up on the back of my neck.

"Again," I said when it was over, the urgency and excitement in my voice startling the other two. "Please," I said, gesturing toward the screen. Then I moved even closer so I could see better. "I may have just figured this out."

It took a few more viewings to confirm my suspicions, but by then I was almost certain. I turned to face Natasha and Ted and told them I knew what was wrong.

"All along, we've been focusing on Duchess's fear. But it's not fear that's causing her to rear up and go into a frenzy. It's excitement. It's *joy*."

They were skeptical, so I told them about January and Atticus out in the pasture, about what I'd observed in the exuberant horse's body language. Then I had them run the film of Duchess again as I pointed out the similarities in some of the more subtle elements of her behavior.

The tossing of her head wasn't flight response, I explained, it was glee.

The raising up into the air wasn't defensiveness, I said, it was celebration.

It wasn't the noise or the chaos of the crowd that bothered Duchess at these shows. It was her uncontrollable delight at being surrounded by people and activity and noise and smells and companionship. That all caused her to become so excited that she simply lost control.

Natasha seemed to grow more convinced as she listened to my reasoning. Then, in a flash, she understood the bigger picture. Excitement growing in her eyes, she told us that time-wise it all made sense. According to her, Duchess's uncontrollable behavior had begun not long after earning the title of Prix St. George. Not coincidently, that was about the same time that they had built this magnificent private stable and segregated the horse from the other animals and workers.

"Then that's it," I said, grinning in victory. "She's lonely and isolated. If you want to keep her from losing control at the shows, I think all you need to do is put her back where she belongs, with the others. She needs her community, just like all horses. Just like all people."

As it turned out, my theory was correct. We had to take it slow, but over the course of the next week we were able to successfully integrate Duchess back into the larger stable. She was still off limits to the other employees, but at least now she was surrounded by animals and people most of the time, the perfect antidote to the ailments of loneliness and seclusion.

Once we'd managed to define her prevailing emotion as excitement rather than fear, none of us could believe we hadn't figured it out before. Not every horse loved a crowd, but this one always had, according to Natasha. Only now did the woman realize that pulling Duchess away and setting her apart had nearly destroyed her soul, and she felt terrible about it. Trying to make

Natasha feel better, Ted explained that show horses often suffered such a fate, their value as a commodity outweighing their need for socialization.

The question now was whether or not the solution had come in time to prepare Duchess for competition. Would we be able to satisfy her social needs sufficiently enough that she wouldn't get so worked up at the competition?

In the days leading up to it, I kept thinking about this, mostly with regard to Priscilla. Once again, she had been pivotal in helping me solve an issue with a horse. But there was also a reverse element here. Like Duchess, Priscilla was often isolated and alone. And though she drew no joy from crowds, the truth was she needed them just as much as the horse had needed to be with others. Priscilla needed more people in her life. She needed community. I wrote a long letter explaining all that had happened and urging her to seek others in the same way that she had challenged me to seek joy. I didn't hear back right off, the way I usually did, but I was consumed with the horse show, which took place on September twenty-fifth, a day that was sunny and unseasonably warm.

I was invited along as part of the team, and the event as a whole was quite fun and fascinating. But the longer it went on, the more I kept thinking, *This world is not my home.*

What was I doing here?

Duchess was spectacular, earning up not one level but two. That meant she was now just one step away from the top—and the only thing standing in her way was another year or so of training to go all the way. Natasha was so thrilled that as we loaded up the truck to head back, she told me I was in for a "big bonus." Eric was there too, and he teased her, saying, "Better not make it too big, or Jake just might take a walk."

"Take a walk?" Natasha asked, turning to me. "Why? Are you unhappy with your job?"

I felt a little uncomfortable having this conversation in the middle of the loading area with dozens of people around, but I knew I had to be honest with her.

Bonus or not, big paychecks or not, my time in this world was done.

Natasha asked for a week's notice, which made my last day October first. On October second, a Thursday, I spent the morning at the kitchen table, going over the lists I'd made with my *daed* back in August, when he and I were exploring the possibility of opening up my own blacksmith shop. Between the pay I'd earned and the five-thousand-dollar bonus Natasha insisted on giving me for my success with Duchess, I had now accrued almost half of my goal for seed money. I had no idea what God had in mind for providing the rest, but before I took things any further, there was an important conversation I needed to have.

I still hadn't spoken to Amos about the noncompetition issue. When first becoming his apprentice, I had promised him I would never open up a shop within ten miles of his, but if I were to take advantage of the space my father was offering me, then it would be more like eight miles. As a man of my word, I wasn't about to move forward without first getting that two-mile difference approved by my former boss.

On my way out, I checked the mailbox, but nothing was yet there from Priscilla. I hadn't heard from her even once since sending my challenge for her to seek others, and that concerned me. She and I had gotten into a regular rhythm of writing, and the only reason I could imagine for her breaking that rhythm had to do with her reaction to my challenge. Was she upset with me? Hiding from me? Turning to another man, one who was close by and wanted her as his wife and wouldn't challenge her as I had?

These were the thoughts that rolled around my head as I covered the distance to the Kinsingers. I hadn't been back there once since being laid off, but when I pulled into their driveway, it felt as though it were just yesterday.

I came to a stop out front, spotting Roseanna in the yard putting clothes on the line. She left the basket of laundry and walked quickly toward me, wearing a huge smile. Amos came out of the blacksmith shop, a surprised look on his face, but he greeted me warmly as well.

Rosanna announced it was a great time for a coffee break and insisted that Amos and I come inside. They wanted to hear what I'd been up to and how things were going, so over coffee and a cinnamon roll, I told them all about my job with Natasha. I also explained how God had been doing some great things for me and in me, and that I wanted them to know they had been an important part of it all. It took a little convincing, but they needed to understand that I was even grateful for having been let go, because God had been using that experience to begin a much-needed transformation in my life. I added that Priscilla had been a huge help to me too, and that she and I had been corresponding regularly.

From there, I was about to launch into the main reason I'd come here today when Roseanna said, "Oh, well, if you and Priscilla have been writing, then you must know about this weekend."

"This weekend?"

"Being published and all that?"

I nearly choked on my coffee. For an Amish couple, "being published" meant having their engagement announced in church. It was usually done about a month prior to the wedding. And because weddings were held starting in late October, this was prime time for such announcements to begin.

"She…is she…with Noah? The widower?"

Roseanna and Amos shared a glance. Then Roseanna stood and went to the desk and retrieved her latest letter from their niece. Back at the table, she pulled it from the envelope, skimmed through it, and then thrust it toward me, with her finger pointing at a specific paragraph. Taking the letter from her, I began to read.

You asked about the situation with my special friend, but this is all I can tell you for now. I promised to give him a yes or no by the first weekend in October so that, if it is to be, he can speak to the bishop and get the ball rolling for a November wedding. I will let you know how things turn out after then.

Silently, I handed the paper back to Roseanna. Without a word, she stood and returned the envelope to her desk, where she rooted through a pile and came up with something else. As she brought it over, I expected to see another letter.

"This is from July, when Priscilla was leaving, so it might be a little out of date. But at least it's a start." She gave me a broad smile as she handed me the piece of paper.

I looked down to the page in my hand and saw that it wasn't a letter at all. It was the train schedule from Lancaster to Elkhart.

THIRTY-SIX

I left the next day, and it took me thirteen hours to get from where I was to where I wanted to be. I used the same route Priscilla had, going from Lancaster to Elkhart with just one change of trains, in Pittsburgh. For most of those hours, except for when I was sleeping, I was praying that God would be with me and favor me, and that He would prepare Priscilla for my impromptu arrival.

I also prayed I wasn't too late.

I knew I could have called—should have called—instead. But if there was even the slightest chance that she planned to tell this guy yes, then I had to do this in person. I had to force her to look me in the eye and tell me she didn't love me as much as I loved her.

And I did love her, I knew that now. I was no longer the person who hadn't been able to feel for so many years, who never loved before, who wasn't even sure true love existed. Instead, I was now hands down, head-over-heels in love with Priscilla Kinsinger, and I wanted her for my wife.

My biggest concern was what it might take to talk her into coming back with me. She sounded so happy in Indiana, so pleased with her work and her life there. Even if she loved me in return, how was I going to convince her that she belonged with me in Lancaster County, a place that for her had mostly been one of pain and loss?

I had asked this of my parents the night before, when I sat down and told them what I was going to do.

"When two people love each other, Jake," my mother had replied, "and I mean, really love each other, they cease to think of only themselves. Their natural inclination, if true love exists between them, is to make the other person happy."

"Love gives, not pulls," my father had added, "which is why it sometimes aches. But that doesn't mean it is not the grandest of all virtues, son."

I repeated their words of wisdom back to myself now as the train rumbled along. One thing I did know was that I was not to pull Priscilla back to Lancaster County, I was to woo her back. And maybe that wouldn't be so hard after all. With every passing hour I was increasingly more and more in love with her. She was my soul mate, I was sure of it. I had never felt for anyone else the way I did about her.

I thought of her words that day at Blue Rock Creek when she pleaded with me to open my heart.

Christ loved the church with ardor and an aching longing to see her redeemed. You are to have that same love for your beloved.

Now, these many weeks later, I finally understood what she'd meant, and I agreed with every word.

Priscilla's great-aunt, Cora Kurtz, lived about halfway between Elkhart and Goshen, so when I arrived at the train station, I switched to a local bus that would take me within a two-mile walk of my destination. Seated on that bus for the last leg of my journey, I couldn't help but compare the terrain of Indiana to that of Lancaster County. It was much flatter here, and there were fewer trees, but for some reason the sky seemed bigger. I began to see Amish buggies as soon as the bus eased out of the city center, and my eyes were wide as I took in the differences between those here and the buggies back home. Having been a buggy-maker myself prior to farrier school, I saw things others might miss or not even care about. I kept wishing my *daed* or Tyler were here so we could point out to each other the various differences—in color, shape, accessories, and more—between these vehicles and the ones I'd grown up making in my family's buggy shop back home.

The bus dropped me off at a gas station, and a man working inside told me where I could find the road I was looking for. I hiked my small traveling bag over my shoulder and set out. Despite having had only four hours of sleep on the train, I was nervously energized at the thought that I was now less than a half hour's walk from Priscilla.

I came upon the driveway for her grandparents' house first, recognizing it by the handmade sign for the fresh, organic honey I could buy there. I knew the next place up the road, which I could see through the tops of the rows and rows of apple trees, was where I would find Priscilla.

Lord, this is it. Please be with me now. Please don't let this be for nothing. Please help me convince her to come back to Lancaster County where she belongs.

The Kurtz home was a white two-story house with gabled upper-floor windows and red shutters. A tidy lawn bore two apple trees on either side of a paved walkway. The two trees stood like sentinels, calling attention to the orchard of their brethren all around them. The leaves on the trees were just starting to turn, and nearly every branch was heavy with fruit. Cast iron pots of summer geraniums were situated on the wooden porch, still vibrant but not quite as full as perhaps they had been a few months earlier. Clematis vines twirled about the porch posts, and forsythia bushes lined one side of the house, while a colorful squash garden sprawled across the other side. I could also see a sizeable vegetable garden, recently harvested of most of its wares. Dresses hung on a line between the house and a big barn, some of them large and matronly looking, and others dainty and trim in shades of lavender, rose, cornflower, and celery-green. A gray-striped cat sunning himself on the porch studied me as I approached, flicking his tail in apparent greeting.

The entire aspect was welcoming, the home worn but pleasant looking, the orchard vast and sweet smelling. For a second I wondered what I was even doing. This was a beautiful place, and Priscilla was surely content here, but I shook off the momentary troublesome thought. Love could make a home anywhere. What mattered was who a person spent her life with, not where she lived. If she loved me, Priscilla would come back to Lancaster County with me.

I walked up the pathway to the porch. The front door was open halfway, and a screen door allowed for the aroma of something sweet and creamy to reach me. As I stepped onto the porch and breathed in the tantalizing fragrance of baked apples, the cat stood, stretched, and meowed.

"Hey, fella," I whispered back. Then I knocked on the screen door, waited, and prayed.

"Come on in, Eunice," a voice called from within.

"Um, I'm not Eunice," I replied. There was a slight pause and then an older, heavy-set woman with a cane appeared at the doorway. She smiled at me. "Well, hello, Not-Eunice. What can I do for you?"

"I…I was hoping I might speak with Priscilla if she's home." I answered, a bit nervously.

The woman, surely Cora, cocked her head in curiosity. "Is she expecting you?"

I couldn't help but laugh. "No, she's not."

Cora's smiled deepened. "Are you a friend of hers?"

"*Ya*. She's…Yes. A good friend."

"Well, she's not here right now. Would you want to wait for her or come back later?"

"Do you know where she went? Maybe I could find her."

"Is it that important?" Cora said with a laugh.

"*Ya*. It's pretty important. I've come from out of town."

"Oh?" she asked, moving a step closer.

"I'm from Lancaster County." As if to prove it, I held up my bag to show her.

Her eyes widened, and her smile seemed to take on a different curve. "Ah. So you're him, Mr. Jake Miller from Lancaster County. The man of letters, so to speak. Come on in. I'm Priscilla's great-aunt, Cora Kurtz."

"*Danke.*"

She opened the door for me, and as I stepped inside, I felt a ridiculously deep surge of joy, not only that this woman knew of me but that she knew my name. That meant Priscilla had talked with her about me, had told her I was a part of her life.

I set my bag on the floor near the door. Cora gestured toward the kitchen table, and we moved there together. I held her elbow as she sat, and then I took the chair across from her.

When I met her eyes, I realized she wore an expression of concern. "You are here to tell her something she will want to hear?"

"I sure hope so."

"You came a long way to say it."

"It didn't seem long."

We shared a smile.

"Okay, well, I hope you came in time."

"I do too," I managed. "Do you know…"

She peered at me for a long moment, as if she were trying to see inside me to my very soul. Then she said, "I've been single my whole life, Jake, which was God's will for me. And though I wouldn't have chosen this for myself, I know that a life alone is still better than a life with the wrong man."

I swallowed hard. "She's with him now? With her suitor, Noah?"

Cora shook her head. "She did that earlier. They went off in his buggy right after breakfast and then showed back up here an hour later. She never said a word as to how it went or what she ended up telling him. I've been itching to hear, but she's stayed out in the orchard all day."

"So where is she now? If you don't mind my asking."

"Like I just said. She's out in the orchard."

My breath caught in my throat. "Here? She's in the orchard here?"

Seeing my eagerness, her mouth spread into a slow smile. "Yes, sir. She is. Last time I spotted her, she was in the Reds. Behind the house."

"Do you mind if I—"

"I think maybe you'd better."

"*Danke*," I whispered.

And she beamed.

Once outside, I set off for the trees directly behind the house. As I passed the large barn to my left, I could see a coffee-brown Morgan munching on hay just inside it—no doubt the loaner from Priscilla's grandparents, and I noted that the building needed some repairs. A hinge on the door was half on and half off, and the entire structure could use a fresh coat of paint. I wished I were staying longer so I could fix a few things.

I began my search for Priscilla by looking up every row directly behind the house, searching for a flash of pastel amid the rusty greens, brown, and red. Then I heard a voice, the sound of someone humming. It was a tune I didn't know, but it sounded happy. My heart began to thud in my chest as I scanned the rows. And then I saw her, about halfway up the last row. She was bent over with a shovel in her hands, her back to me.

I prayed a silent prayer and started up the path between the rows. I hoped that when I drew closer, she would hear my approaching footsteps and turn around. I didn't want to frighten her. But her humming and the scrape of the shovel masked the sounds of my steps. When I was just a few feet away, I could see that she was working in between two mature trees that were laden with fruit, and she was digging up a volunteer tree that would not be able to continue where its life had started. Near her feet was a five-gallon container partially filled with soil. Priscilla was not cutting down the little tree that didn't belong there. She was carefully removing it so that she could transplant it to a place where it could grow.

In that same instant, I was nearly knocked over by an echo of an earlier bit of advice that now seemed to slam into my chest.

When two people love each other, Jake—and I mean, really love each other— they cease to think of only themselves. Their natural inclination, if true love exists between them, is to make the other one happy. My mother's gentle words to me just last night now shouted their truth. It didn't matter where I lived my life; it mattered whom I lived it with.

Here was an Amish community that was not so very different than my own back in Lancaster County.

Here was a house and land and orchards that needed tending.

Here was a barn that needed a man's muscle, and which was plenty big enough for a blacksmith shop.

Here was where Priscilla was.

I knew in an instant I could be at home here. I could be a blacksmith here. I could be who I already was here. I could be anywhere with the person I loved most beside me. If she wanted to stay, we could stay.

"Priscilla," I said gently, almost in a whisper.

She bolted upright and spun around. The shovel slipped out of her hands and landed on the little mound of dirt she had made.

"Jake!" she exclaimed, her hand going to her heart.

I took a step closer to steady her. My hands on her waist seemed the most natural feeling in the world.

For a second neither one of us said anything. I could not trust myself to speak, and yet I had so much to tell her. I pulled her close to me because no words seemed adequate in that moment.

"Jake." She said my name again, this time not in amazement, but in the most tender of tones, seeing in person that what she had wanted most for me, I had been given. Just as she was not the broken girl who had left Lancaster County all those years ago, I was no longer the broken man I'd been the last time she saw me.

"Am I too late?"

"Too late?"

I inhaled the sweet scent of her skin, her hair. "The guy. Noah. Did you—"

"I told him no."

"You did?"

"*Ya.*"

"Why?"

A slow smile crept across her lips. "You know why. How could I marry one man when I'm in love with another?"

And then, because no words would suffice, I cupped her chin in my hand, tipped it toward me, and kissed her, her lips on mine like the soft petals of the freshest rose.

When we parted, her eyes were rimmed with tears. As were mine. My kiss had not surprised her as much as it had overjoyed her. I knew she had dreamed of that kiss, just as I had.

"But wait…How…how did you get here?" she asked, her hand now on my cheek.

I tipped my head into her palm. "Don't you know?" I whispered, smiling as I gazed into her beautiful violet eyes. "I followed my heart."

EPILOGUE

Despite the cold outside, I opened the barn window and turned on the fan to air out the space after a morning spent hot-shoeing three horses in a row. The acrid smoke slowly but steadily escaped through the opening, rather like my burgeoning business was progressing. Slowly but steadily.

In January I'd hung out my sign—the word "Blacksmith" welded together from actual horseshoes, a wedding gift from Owen and Treva—and now, after being open for just two months, I was already booking ten to fifteen customers per week, plus a handful of walk-ins as well. That wouldn't have been enough to support a full-fledged blacksmith shop back in Lancaster County, but here in Elkhart, where costs were cheaper and our housing was provided by Aunt Cora in exchange for Priscilla's caregiving, it was enough to get by on for now. It also left me with plenty of free time to assist with the orchard and to handle the various fix-it projects around the farm.

And goodness knows there were plenty. Pretty much since the day after our November wedding, I'd been tackling loose doors and rotting boards and rusted hinges from one end of this place to the other. It was hard work but incredibly satisfying, especially when Cora would notice some new repair and beam from ear to ear. She and I had hit it off from the start, and once I had married Priscilla and moved in with the two of them, the older woman somehow managed to share her home and life as easily as if I had always been here. Last month she'd even made official her promise to Priscilla and drawn up a will leaving the house and property to the two of us, though it wouldn't be needed for a good long while, God willing. For now, we three had settled into a comfortable rhythm of day-to-day life together in the charming old house.

My biggest debt to Cora, of course, was that she'd been willing to let me turn part of her barn into a blacksmith shop. She'd agreed to that back before I even moved in, when Priscilla and I were still in those first heady days of working out logistics and making plans for the wedding and my move. As I hadn't yet earned enough money to cover all of the needed equipment and supplies, I'd thought it would be a while before I could actually make it happen. But then Amos and Roseanna gave us their wedding gift, a brand-new forge just perfect for a one-man blacksmith shop. That had allowed me to get rolling much sooner than expected. Needless to say, both Priscilla and I had been thrilled.

I smiled now as I remembered how she'd been even happier when she got my wedding gift to her. Thanks to my buddy Eric and his family business, I had been able to transport both Willow and Voyager from Pennsylvania to Indiana. The truck and trailer showed up one Thursday afternoon just a week or so after the wedding, when Priscilla was coming in from the clothesline. I'd managed to keep it a secret, but as soon as the vehicle turned into the driveway, it was as if she knew exactly what was going on and who was riding in the back. The fact that in the midst of her excitement a whole basket of just-cleaned laundry ended up upside down on the dirt was a small price to pay for the pleasure of her joy.

And joy was definitely in abundance with us these days, I thought as I adjusted the fan to clear the last lingering wisps of smoke from the room. That remarkable afternoon last September when I showed up here and kissed Priscilla among the trees had been the start of an amazing journey. Not only were we engaged within the hour, we'd also made the decision to get married during the current wedding season rather than wait an entire year. We'd been afraid some family members might think we were rushing things, but as it turned out, those on both sides seemed quite pleased and couldn't have been more helpful. By bunking next door at Priscilla's grandparents' house, I'd been able to stick around for a few days on that first visit. And though it had been hard to leave, I managed to come back twice more before the wedding to help with the planning. Still, two months had never felt so long as I counted the days to our becoming husband and wife .

And what a wife Priscilla had turned out to be! The young woman who had once seemed so difficult to get to know, so complex, so deeply emotional, was a veritable bedrock of determination and patience and loving-kindness. Oh, how she loved, especially once we were wed, with her whole heart and body and soul. I'd never known I could feel this way about anyone—and then I'd wake up each new morning realizing I loved her even more than I had the day before.

I was thinking about that, about the heart's seemingly infinite capacity for love, when I shut down the fan and went over to close the window. As I hooked the latch, I saw my beautiful wife emerge from the house bundled up from head to toe, ready for an afternoon's work at my side in the orchard. Yesterday, her grandfather had taught us how to do the early spring pruning, and today we would be on our own, beginning a process he said could take as long as a month. With more than five hundred trees to care for, the job would not be easy, but it might be kind of fun. And at least she and I worked really well together, no matter what the task.

The plan was for me to do the high pruning, taking off all the limbs that were damaged or diseased, as well as any new "watersprouts" as he'd called them, which were errant limbs shooting up at the center. Meanwhile, Priscilla would handle the lower branches and the suckers at the base of the trunks. This morning between customers, I had taken time to sharpen our clippers, which were now waiting for us on the front table, their blades sparkling in a sunbeam that slanted across the shop.

When I heard Priscilla stomping snow from her boots just outside the door, I swung it open and gave her a broad smile.

"Good timing," I said, enjoying the way her cheeks always turned pink in the cold.

"*Hallo*, Jake," she replied with a smile, gesturing toward the clippers as she stepped inside. "Think we're ready to fly solo?"

"Fly solo?" I echoed, laughing. "Where did you learn a term like that?"

She rolled her eyes at herself. "Where else? *Englischers* at the Haven."

The Haven—short for Galloping Meadows Horse Haven—was a local nonprofit, a horse rescue and sanctuary where Priscilla and I volunteered for a couple of hours each week. To our delight, one of their biggest needs was for horse-gentling—or horse-*befriending*, as Priscilla preferred to call it—a service the two of us provided as a team. We also taught our techniques to others, who could then continue our work even when we weren't there. Though the job didn't pay, it was totally worth it, for the horses' sake and for ours too. Not only did we enjoy it immensely, but it was providing a great way to get to know non-Amish horse lovers in the region. Ephrata was no Chester County show horse circuit, but the people here were kind and friendly toward me, and they had been helping to spread the word that this part of the county finally had a blacksmith of its own.

"Did you want a snack before we go out?" Priscilla asked now, interrupting my thoughts.

I shook my head, still full from the meal she'd made for me just a few hours before. Moving to the coat hooks beside the door, I began to suit up for the cold myself, pulling on gloves and scarf and trading out my straw hat for a thick wool cap. It was a beautiful but brilliantly cold day, and I knew before long we'd be feeling it in every inch of skin left uncovered.

"You ready, Mrs. Miller?" I said as I pulled the cap down even farther over my ears.

"Sure am, Mr. Miller," she replied with a wink.

Stepping outside, I closed the door and flipped over the sign that advised customers to clang the bell if they needed help. The sound of the old school bell I'd mounted there on the beam could be heard throughout the orchard and kept me from missing walk-ins.

Finally, with Priscilla carrying the clippers and I the ladder, we trooped out into the snow and headed for the trees. We started at the northwest corner with a Red Delicious, awkward and clumsy at first but slowly growing a little defter with our efforts as the hours passed. By the time we finished for the day, we were mighty cold—and hungry too—but pleased with the progress we'd made. Our steps fell in sync as we walked back toward the house side by side, and again I thought of what a great team the two of us made. The little tomboy and the clueless object of her affection from all those years ago had come a long, long way to get to where we were now. I had a feeling our shared sense of teamwork would be a big factor in where we continued to go from here, especially in how we raised our family, should God be so gracious as to grant us children.

God had certainly been good to Tyler and Rachel, I thought as we paused at the mailbox, took out the contents, and saw that the mail included a letter from them, as it often did these days. Their absence from our wedding had been the only dark spot on that otherwise-wonderful morning, but with Rachel so far along in her pregnancy, they hadn't been able to risk the trip to Indiana. Good thing too, because their healthy, eight-pound-two-ounce son was born just a week later, on Thanksgiving afternoon.

Priscilla opened the envelope now and read the letter aloud as we continued on toward the house. We both enjoyed hearing from them, and somehow Rachel's gift of description brought alive their new life with baby Joel better than any photos ever could. Big Joel—my father and Tyler's grandfather—was smitten with his little namesake, a fact made even more obvious with today's note, which recounted how Rachel had caught him cooing baby talk to his great-grandson when he thought no one was listening.

"I always knew *Daed* had it in him," I said with a laugh when Priscilla finished reading.

"So cute," she replied, tucking the letter back into the envelope and then sliding it into her coat pocket. "I guess your father will be twice as thrilled when he learns that baby Joel is getting a new cousin."

"A new cousin?" I said as we moved up the driveway toward the porch. "Who's that?"

She didn't respond, so I glanced over at her—and something made me do a double take.

Maybe it was the smile on her lips.

Maybe it was the way she was resting one hand on her stomach.

Maybe it was the glow that seemed to radiate from her entire being.

Whatever it was, I came to a stop, frozen in place, my eyes wide, my heart pounding.

"Priscilla?" I rasped, swallowing hard. "Are you— Are we—"

She grinned and then whispered, "*Ya*. And *ya*."

With a loud whoop, I scooped my beautiful wife into my arms, turning in circles right there in the driveway as she laughed and scolded me to put her down. Finally, I came to a stop and lowered her to the ground, though I didn't let her go.

"Easy, boy," she teased, patting me as if I were a horse even as she settled contentedly into my embrace.

As I held her close, all I could do was gaze at her, at this woman who loved me so completely, who had taught me to feel again, who allowed me to love her in return. Why God had chosen to bless me so thoroughly—first with a wife beyond my wildest dreams and now with a child on the way—I did not know. All I knew, I thought as I closed my eyes and slowly brought my lips to hers, was that we were a perfect fit.

Priscilla and I were oil and wick.

DISCUSSION QUESTIONS

1. Jake considers himself to be an "unemotional" type of guy, but that notion is later challenged. Do you believe there are people who "just don't feel things deeply," as he claims? Or do you think such claims always indicate that the person is masking/hiding from deeper feelings hidden away below the surface?

2. Priscilla suffered a terrible tragedy in Lancaster County before going away to Indiana at fourteen. Now she has returned, even though she didn't want to, because she feels it is God's will for her. What does this say about her as a person? Have you ever felt God leading you to do something you didn't want to do?

3. Jake describes Amanda as "laid-back and understanding and uncomplicated." Do you think this makes her a good match for him? In what ways is she a better match for him than Priscilla? In what ways is she worse?

4. When Priscilla returns to Lancaster County, Amos and Roseanna open their home to her, hoping she'll stay and make a new life for herself there. Do you think Amos is right to ask for

Jake and Amanda's help in getting his niece reconnected with other young people in their district?

5. Jake and Priscilla sparred over whose technique was the most effective in helping troubled horses. What were their differences in approach, in your opinion? How were they alike? Do you think one approach was better than the other, or did the two approaches work best when combined together?

6. Jake describes the various ways that people view horses, including as animals, friends, companions, loved ones, moneymakers, symbols of wealth and prestige, entertainment, employees, and more. Which of the above terms, if any, would best describe how you view horses? Do you agree with Jake's assertion that farmers tend to think of horses differently than nonfarmers?

7. Do you think God uses elements of His Creation to teach us? What did Jake learn about himself through his relationship with the horses in this story? What have you learned via something that God created?

8. Natasha has staked much of her reputation and livelihood on the upcoming performance of a single horse. What motivates a person to get involved with a sport that has such huge costs and high stakes? In terms of time, money, or something else, what's the costliest commitment you've ever made for a sport?

9. When Jake realizes Tyler and Rachel are expecting, his emotions are mixed. Have you ever had a similar reaction to what is essentially good news? Does it surprise you that many Amish don't openly discuss certain topics such as pregnancy?

10. Jake's parents are reluctant to tell him about what happened when he was a child. Do you think it's wise for parents to keep silent on such matters? Or is it always better to bring past traumas out in the open, even if they happened decades ago?

About the Authors

The Amish Blacksmith is **Mindy Starns Clark**'s twenty-third book with Harvest House Publishers. Previous novels include the first book in this series, *The Amish Groom* (cowritten with Susan Meissner), the number one bestseller *The Amish Midwife* (cowritten with Leslie Gould), and popular mysteries such as *Whispers of the Bayou, Shadows of Lancaster County, Under the Cajun Moon,* and *Secrets of Harmony Grove.* Mindy has earned numerous honors, including a Christy Award (for *The Amish Midwife*), a Career Achievement Award from *RT Book Reviews* magazine, and an Inspirational Reader's Choice Award from the Romance Writers of America. She lives with her husband, John, and two adult daughters near Valley Forge, Pennsylvania. You can connect with Mindy at her website: www.mindystarnsclark.com.

Susan Meissner is a multipublished author, speaker, and writing workshop leader with a background in community journalism. Her novels include *The Shape of Mercy,* named by *Publishers Weekly* as one of the 100 Best Novels of 2008 and a Carol Award winner. She is a pastor's wife and the mother of four young adults. When she's not writing, Susan writes small group curriculum for her San Diego church. Visit Susan at her website: www.susanmeissner.com, on Twitter at @SusanMeissner, or at www.facebook.com/susan.meissner.

An E-Short Story
Coming January 2015!

The Tender Prequel to The Men of Lancaster County Series

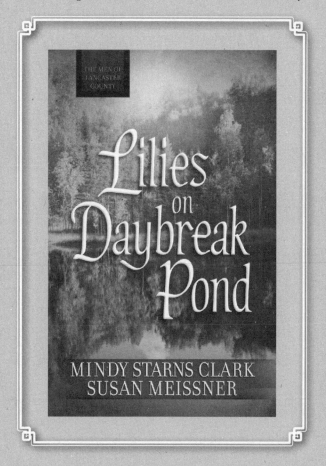

A delightful short story of discovery and hope
available only from your favorite ebook retailer.

HARVEST HOUSE PUBLISHERS
EUGENE, OREGON

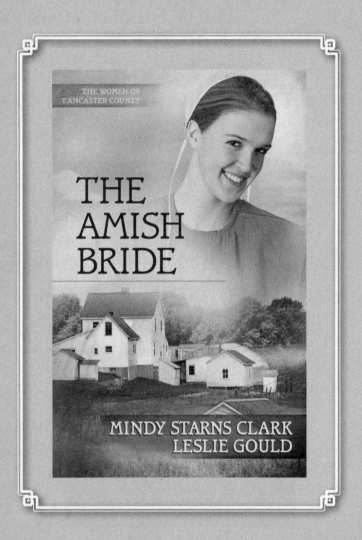

THE WOMEN OF
LANCASTER COUNTY

THE
AMISH
BRIDE

MINDY STARNS CLARK
LESLIE GOULD

**A long-lost painting…
a journal with a secret code…
a father's mysterious return…**

Mennonite-raised Ella Bayer has two big dreams: to operate her own bakery and to marry her Amish boyfriend, Ezra Gundy. Ezra adores Ella as well, but his family wants him to marry within the faith.

Hoping some distance will cool the romance, Ezra's parents send him to work on an Amish dairy farm in Indiana. But when Ella's estranged father returns to Lancaster, she heads to Indiana as well—and ends up at a farm linked to her great-grandmother's coded journal. There, her attempts to break that code are aided by Luke Kline, a handsome Amish farmhand.

As Ella makes her way in this new place, she's forced to grapple with the past and question the future. Will she become Ezra's Amish bride? Or does God have something else in mind for the proud and feisty young woman who is used to doing things her way?

A captivating journey of hidden secrets, old love and new love, and discovery of how a life guided by God can be a life of incredible hope and adventure.

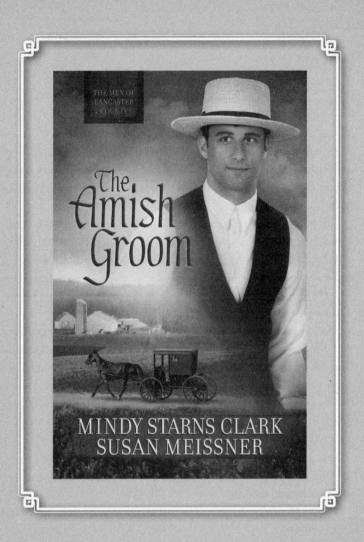

THE MEN OF
LANCASTER
COUNTY

The Amish Groom

MINDY STARNS CLARK
SUSAN MEISSNER

**The time for wondering is over.
The time for commitment is now.
And yet...**

Tyler Anderson is torn between two worlds—Amish and *Englisch*. Born to an ex-Amish mother and an *Englisch* father, he is raised as a military kid until his mom passes away and his dad places him in the care of his Amish grandparents. Now 23, Tyler knows it's time to commit to the Amish church for good. Still he hesitates, unsure if he'll ever truly belong.

Rachel Hoeck has been patient as she waits for Tyler to make up his mind and become her husband. But as much as Tyler adores Rachel, he can't be certain this is God's plan for his life. Conflicted, he prays for direction and peace—only to find himself being pulled to the outside world yet again. During a stay with his father's second family in Southern California, Tyler meets a free-spirited young woman named Lark, putting his future with Rachel even more in question.

As pressure mounts on both sides, will Tyler choose to stay with Lark and remain an *Englischer*? Or will he find his way back to Rachel and become her Amish groom at last?

A poignant novel of the search for identity and lifetime love, nestled between a beloved Amish community and an exciting modern world.

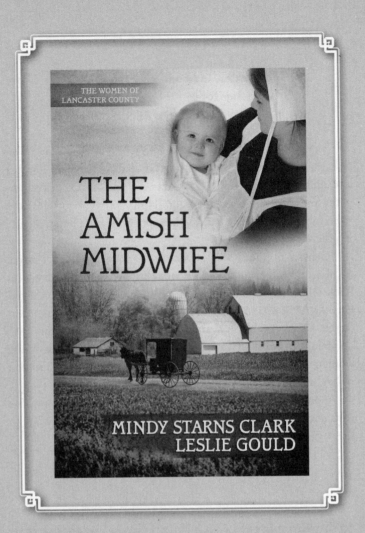

THE WOMEN OF
LANCASTER COUNTY

THE
AMISH
MIDWIFE

MINDY STARNS CLARK
LESLIE GOULD

**A deathbed confession…
a dusty carved box containing two locks of hair…
a century-old letter about property in Switzerland…**

Nurse-midwife Lexie Jaeger's encounter with all three rekindles a burning desire to meet her biological family. Propelled on a personal journey of discovery, Lexie's search for the truth takes her from her home in Oregon to the heart of Pennsylvania's Amish country.

There she finds Marta Bayer, a mysterious lay-midwife who may hold the key to Lexie's past. But Marta isn't talking, especially now that she has troubles of her own following the death of an Amish patient during childbirth. As Lexie steps in to assume Marta's patient load and continues the search for her birth family, a handsome local doctor proves to be a welcome distraction. But will he also distract her from James, the man back home who lovingly awaits her return?

From her Amish patients, Lexie learns the true meaning of the Pennsylvania Dutch word *demut*, which means "to let be." Will this woman who wants to control everything ever learn to let be herself and depend totally on God? Or will her stubborn determination to unearth the secrets of the past at all costs only serve to tear her newfound family apart?

A compelling story about a search for identity and the ability to trust that God securely holds our whole life—past, present, and future—in His hands.

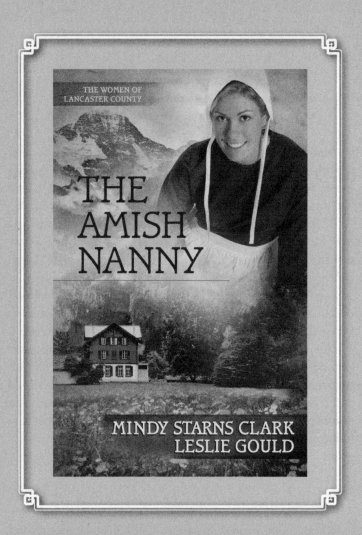

THE WOMEN OF
LANCASTER COUNTY

THE
AMISH
NANNY

MINDY STARNS CLARK
LESLIE GOULD

A cave behind a waterfall…
a dying confession…
a secret agreement hidden for a century…

Amish-raised Ada Rupp knows nothing of these elements of her family's past. Instead, her eyes are fixed firmly on the future—for the first time in her life. Now that a serious medical issue is behind her, Ada is eager to pursue her God-given gifts of teaching at the local Amish school and her dream of marrying Will Gundy, a handsome widower she's loved since she was a child. But when both desires meet with unexpected obstacles, Ada's fragile heart grows heavy with sorrow.

Then she meets Daniel, an attractive Mennonite scholar with a surprising request. He needs her help—along with the help of Will's family—to save an important historic site from being destroyed. Now Ada and several others, including the young child in her care, must head to Switzerland to mend an old family rift and help preserve her religious heritage.

In order to succeed in saving the site, Ada and Daniel must unlock secrets from the past. But do they also have a future together—or will Ada's heart forever belong to Will, the only man she's ever really wanted?

A fascinating tale of a young woman's journey—to Switzerland, to faith, and ultimately to love.

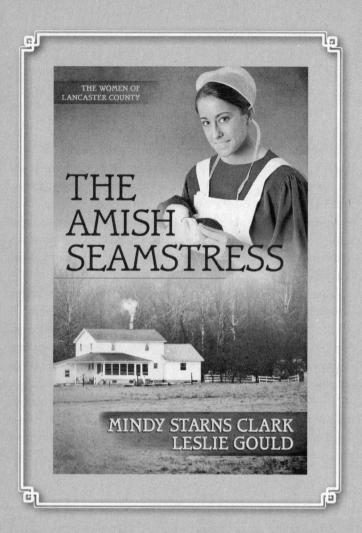

THE WOMEN OF
LANCASTER COUNTY

THE
AMISH
SEAMSTRESS

MINDY STARNS CLARK
LESLIE GOULD

A beautiful misfit…
A handsome young filmmaker…
A shocking family secret, hidden for 200 years…

A loner and a daydreamer, Amish-raised Izzy Mueller doesn't fit in with her family or her community. About the only person who really gets Izzy is her best friend, Mennonite-raised Zed Bayer, but soon he'll be leaving for college, hundreds of miles away. Worse, he's completely unaware she's in love with him.

Izzy works as a caregiver, a job which suits her gentle ways and kind spirit. She's also a talented seamstress and often sits with her patients, quietly sewing, as they talk and reminisce about the past. Izzy has always enjoyed hearing what they have to say—until the day one of them shares some unsavory news about her own ancestors.

When Izzy searches for the truth behind that lore, she begins to question her life—her creative longings, her relationships, and her heritage. Caught in the swirling dynamics of Zed's family once she becomes the caregiver for his grandmother, can Izzy learn from the past and from others' mistakes? Or must she step out in faith and forge a future all her own?

A moving account of one young woman's search for direction and acceptance as she takes her first brave steps on a path leading to a brand-new future—and to love.